THE EASTLING

Also By James Collins

Into the Fire
You Wish!
Jason and the Sargonauts
The Judas Inheritance
Lonely House
Remotely
Honestly
The Saddling
The Witchling

Symi 85600
Carry on up the Kali Strata
Village View
Symi, Stuff & Nonsense

JamesCollinsAuthor.com
www.facebook.com/Jamescollinsauthor

RC Publishing

First published in Great Britain in 2018
Copyright © James Collins 2018

The right of James Collins to be identified as the Author of the Work has been asserted by him in accordance with the Copyright, Designs and Patents Act 1988.

All rights reserved. No part of this publication may be reproduced, stored in a retrieval system, or transmitted, in any form or by any means without the prior written permission of the publisher, nor be otherwise circulated in any form of binding or cover other than that in which it is published and without a similar condition being imposed on the subsequent purchaser.

All characters in this publication are fictitious and any resemblance to real persons, living or dead, is purely coincidental.

Cover: Andjela K
Cover author photograph: Neil Gosling
Proofing, Ann Attwood
(https://www.facebook.com/AnnieA2017/)

Printed by CreateSpace, an Amazon.com company.

Paperback ISBN: 9781728852003

Available from Amazon.com, CreateSpace.com, and other retail outlets.
Available on Kindle and other devices.

For Pete

Acknowledgements

I am indebted to Ann Attwood for her proofreading, Andjela K for the cover design, Forgotten Books for their advice on the use of A Dictionary of the Kentish Dialect and Provincialisms, and W. D. Parish for compiling it in 1888.

James Collins
Symi, Greece, October 2018

Dialect

The dialect used by some of the characters is based on A Dictionary of the Kentish Dialect and Provincialisms in use in the County of Kent, by W. D. Parish, 1888. The reprint copy I have is from Forgotten Books (www.forgottenbooks.com). These are words that were in use across the whole county in the 19th century and may not necessarily be in use on the Romney Marshes. I have also used dialect I remember from growing up on the marsh and have invented some of my own. The meaning of most dialect words should be evident to the reader, but I have provided, below, a glossary of some of the more unusual ones. There are so many that I could have used; the language is rich with unusual words that bring a wry smile, but I didn't want the reader to wrongtake me nor be stounded nor put in a mizmaze. Below are some words used in the story which were not so easy to make obvious in the text. Some of these are my own invention.

Glossary

Aepelling	A pre-wedding celebration
Backstays	Wood attached to shoes like snow-shoes
Bads	Regrets
Bannocking	A thrashing
Blackwing	A rook
Blarring	Bellowing, bleating
Bobbery	A squabble, a fuss, a row
Boblight	Twilight
Bolter	Rabbit
Boneless	Ice-cold
Bootshoes	Thick boots, half-boots
Brungeon	A brat
Cailes	Skittles, ninepins
Carvet	Thick hedge, a lope-side copse
Ceremony	A fuss, bother

Chiese a-worrying	Cease
Clackety	Scaremongering
Conygarthe	A rabbit warren
Cooch-grass	A weed
Cope	To muzzle, or sew up a mouth
Cucked	Cuckolded
Dang	Damn
Dead-alive	Dull, stupid
Drean	A drain
Fessed	Puzzled
Five-bar	Five bar gate
Furbrat	Insects found near fires; lazy children
Furrage	Hunting, to forage
Furriner	Someone from outside of the parish (foreigner)
Garreted	'Not rightly garreted,' not right in the head
Hoogoo	A bad smell
Inned	Irrigated
Jawsy	Talkative
Lomp	thick, clumsy, fat
Lyste	A path on the edge of a field (lyste-way)
Maden	Maiden. Virginity.
Misthelm	Covering of mist (Anglo Saxon)
Mizmaze	Confusion
Prehaps	Perhaps
Quilly	A prank
Readying Week	The week before a wedding
Red-crown	A cockerel
Shuck it	Damn it
Skarmish	A fight, row, horse-play
Spoketales	Unwritten folktales
Stulpe	A post
Thick-thumbed	Clumsy, uncoordinated
Treddles	Sheep dung
Worrit	Worry
Worriting	Worrying
Yawnup	Lazy, uncouth

Note

The village of Saddling exists only in my imagination. The church that inspired the location is real and is there on the Romney Marshes, although I have taken some liberties with its description. You can visit it at Fairfield and, if you do, I am sure a donation towards its upkeep would be appreciated.

One

September 23rd, 1293

The night mist crawled in from the east smothering everything in its path. The dykes glimmered restlessly as the shifting cloud approached, the water trickling like black blood along the winding channels. On the surface, the speckles of moon-reflected brilliance lived short lives as the mist, low and deliberate, poured over the deek banks and spread to the far sides. There it climbed silently, rolling and churning to the lyste before sinking to cover the dowels and inch towards the next field. Weaving among the tufts of coarse-grass and emmet-castes, it snaked its way to the village of Saddling in rivulets of malevolent vapour. Independently, they twisted this way and that before finding themselves and joining to become one mass, deepening their shade, furthering their cause. The brume embraced the marker stone on Saddling's eastern border, enveloping the monolith as it twisted and rose, pouring over itself on the other side, a waterfall of smoke, tumbling to the damp ground before journeying on.

The Romney Marshes knew the misty grey-hang. It rose from the reclaimed land on warm nights, hung above the frosty ground in winter and when there was a change in the atmosphere, appeared, disturbed, at dawn, woken from its ethereal slumber by the inevitability of daylight. It scattered when the wind blew from the west, and reluctantly vanished when the spring breeze lifted the sunrise and the promise of warmth.

On the night of the autumn equinox the grey-hang had always rested untroubled among the wattle and daub dwellings. It lay at the feet of the small, stone church, protecting it, and guarded the villagers as they celebrated their harvest. But in twelve-ninety-three, the year after the great Saddling storm, the mist came late, and the shepherd with the black locks understood its reticence.

It had been waiting.

The man, almost as thin as the crook on which he leant, let his woollen cloak dampen where it fell among the grass, and narrowed his eyes to the silvery glow as it neared his paddock. It brought the unmistakable smell of death as it crept stealthily closer, and he bowed his head.

'The boy's come 'ome,' he whispered. 'Come a-seek them as did 'im wrong.'

Blacklocks' voice carried through the stillness of the night, and the woman at his feet looked up from her wooden cross.

'It were all a us.' His wife stood and swept her flame red hair from her face before she pulled aside his cloak and linked her arm through his. 'But it were you what said we should a-done it sooner.'

He pulled his arm to his body, trapping hers, and his thin fingers sought her hand. He gripped tightly, entwining their bones and raised her chilled flesh to his cold lips. The kiss did nothing to warm his heart, and the feel of her skin gave him no comfort. He could no more bear the touch of her barren body as she could no more bear him an heir. Their only son had died ten months previously, his throat slashed by the sweep of a knife in the hand of the village cleric, Di-Kari. The boy had fallen into the flood waters, his lifeblood draining towards the church door carrying the Blacklocks line with it. As his son was dead to him, so might his wife be. She was too old; she was redundant.

The mist gathered at the base of the small coterell on which they stood, waiting for its arms to encircle the mound before beginning a steady climb.

'Be 'e really a-come 'ome?' the wife asked as her hand was lowered.

''E be a-come fur sure,' Blacklocks replied. 'I see 'im in this eastern misthelm. I feel him near me. Raise your 'ead, Mistus, and breath 'im. Our boy John be riding in that mist. You believe me?'

'Our John be taken from us last storming.'

She didn't need to remind her husband. The boy had died in his arms. 'Died a-save the village from the flooding,' he said. 'Taken by nature, and here she be returning 'im a us.'

The eastling-breath reached their feet and the wife shuffled uneasily.

'Be still, Mistus,' the shepherd admonished, crushing her hand again. 'Believe in the lore a nature.'

'We 'ave a-believe in the law a God, Will,' she dared to reply.

'You 'eard what I told Di-Kari the night John died? That god 'e prays to don't live in our village no more. It's our earth, our deeks, our sheep and planting what keeps us on the right side a death's fog. Stay silent and be wi' your son one last time.'

'One last time?'

The misthelm rose to their waists as a sheet of grey, enveloping them in its clammy depths, and although the shepherd didn't feel it, he heard its whispers. It brought possibilities and hope as it seeped into his chest and fuelled his heart with anger and courage.

His free hand shifted towards his belt.

'Do you sense him?' His words were hushed and fell from his mouth to sink into the layer of vapour at his chin.

The moon found a path between the clouds and threw a lustrous glow on the waxy surface of the eastling-breath just as it passed Blacklocks' eyes. He was submerged. The world beneath the fog was lost to grey as the fields vanished, and the moonlight soaked into the ether that dulled the sound of the man's quickening breath. An impenetrable sea of damp air stifled his lungs but strengthened his resolve.

Disguised, his fingers gripped the wooden handle of his new slitting-knife. He had made it for one purpose.

'Our John be near wi' us, Mistus,' he said, his voice calming and gentle as he turned his wife to face him. 'You'll be knowing 'im soon.'

'You're talking aginst Di-Kari's teaching, Will,' she warned. 'We should be a the church-house wi' the village. It be the time fur thanking God fur the 'arvest.'

'Oh, Rose,' he said, drawing her close and tenderly. 'We got time fur that when we've met our boy agin.'

'Our John be dead, Will. We 'ave a let 'im be. It were God's wanting, 'is wish.'

'We may not see our John agin, but we can be wi' 'im. Can't you sense 'im in the grey-hang? Our boy be near us now.'

'I'd be knowing if 'e were, Will,' she said. 'I felt 'im when 'e were growing inside me. I felt 'im as I brought 'im into the world and held 'im when I offered 'im a you them sixteen year past. I know there ain't no other life after this except fur what God gives us if we do 'is work and live 'is way. You 'ave a-see that an' all.'

'I see only what I 'ave a-do.' His lips were a breath away from hers. He let go of her hand and gripped her shoulder. The action and his intent disturbed the grey-hang and it backed away nervously to give the couple room.

His wife smiled, and her green eyes caught the dull shafts of moonlight that filtered like the sun through a cloudy ocean. 'You 'ave a-kiss me, 'usband,' she said.

He did, but only to stifle her scream as the blade slipped effortlessly through her tunic and twisted into her belly. As she died, he held her in the same way as he had held his son, watching her fall lifeless into his arms before lifting her, offering her to the unseen marsh and the enveloping fog.

Blacklocks dropped her body and it rolled into the gloom to fall with a muffled splash into the deek. The water would carry her away. A poacher would be blamed.

'Fader?'

Blacklocks spun, scattering the grey with his cloak and lifting his crook in readiness.

'Who be there?' he demanded, his pulse racing.

A ghostly silhouette formed from the ether and approached until Blacklocks could see its shape. The eastling-breath revealed a wiry youth with strands of black hair trickling from beneath a cowl. His face was death-white, and the blood from his throat blackened his skin.

'Fader,' the boy repeated.

'What eldritch horror...? John?'

It was his son, dead these last ten months, slain at the height of the storm that his sacrifice appeased. His sorrowful eyes didn't see his father, they looked beyond, yearning for his mother.

'What 'ave you done?' The apparition passed Blacklocks and glided to a halt at the coterell's ridge.

It stood with its back to a father who fought to find words. Remorse, regret, neither were enough.

'I see you,' the boy said. Was he talking to Blacklocks or to the marsh? 'I see 'ow things be. I see what's been done a me.'

'John, your death were an accident.' The shepherd's mind raced as fast as his heartbeat. Too panicked to think logically, it dodged and dived like a whiteback chased by a herding hound. 'You saved the village.'

The boy twisted to him, and the mist regrouped around his harrowed body. 'The village what killed me?' he scoffed, his mouth warped in bitterness, his lifeless eyes narrow. 'The people what took me life away after only fourteen year?'

He stepped closer, and Blacklocks was unable to move. The stench of death invaded him, sickening his stomach with its nauseous sweetness.

The shepherd tried to speak but breathed in only blood-blackened air. It seeped into his veins, darkened his soul and made its home.

'What you done you ain't only done a me and mother,' the boy hissed.

His voice and his threat cut through the night and the mist thickened. 'This place'll never be free a me. Your village 'as damned me a-walk these marshes 'alf living, 'alf dying, never doing neither.'

Blacklocks fell to his knees, sobbing like a child. The slitting-knife fell from his hand, its curved blade stabbing the earth.

'I'll take that wi' me,' John snarled. 'Fur every time I come back.'

The harvest moon broke through the clouds, bathing the marsh in pure, silver light and the mist dropped as though made of lead. It rolled back, slipped from the dowels to the salterns and vanished leaving no trace of the dead boy or the knife.

Two

September, 2015

Dan Vye unscrewed the lid from the brown glass bottle and put it to one side. He lifted the inch-high vessel to his nose and sniffed the scent of crushed camomile mingled with the mildly earthy smell of ground witch hazel diffused in rainwater. Satisfied, he placed the bottle carefully on the table beside a bowl of oranges and opened the medicine chest to remove a piece of clean linen. With everything prepared, he turned to the room.

It had changed over the years. The bed had gone, the old school desk had been burned on the fire-pile last Witchling Day along with the broken chair, and the wardrobe had been converted into a cupboard for books and jars. Tom had slept in this room when he first came to Saddling, but he was the only out-marsher in living memory to seek shelter in the village, and it was unlikely any others would come. Dan needed the space, it made sense to convert the spare room into his…

What was it? What should he call the collection of shelves, cabinets and tables? It wasn't exactly an apothecary, and it wasn't a surgery. It was, perhaps, a treatment room, cleaned daily, dust-free and well-lit now the Payne brothers had installed a larger window. It smelt of lemon and vinegar, but when the breeze disturbed the drying garlic and rust-weed grasses, the basil and bottle-drop, their scents mixed, laying a pleasing aroma over his medicines.

The treatment room was a sight that made Dan proud. He had found his vocation and, although he still helped his mother with the inn, this was the work he was born for.

'You going a-do something with your poisons, or what?'

Becki Tidy's voice drew Dan from his self-satisfaction, and he dropped his eyes to the young woman waiting nervously in the examination chair.

'They're not poisons, Becki,' he said, pulling over a low stool and sitting. 'Though some can be if mixed right.'

'Whatever they be I don't care, long as they stop this bloody aggravation.'

'Don't rub them.' Dan pulled Becki's hand away from her face. Her puffy eyes were ringed with red, and the lids were swollen. 'Worst thing to do.'

He reached for the bottle. 'Tip your head back.'

His patient did as she was told, her eyes screwed tight against their itching. She gripped the chair arms and gritted her teeth.

'It's not going to hurt, you great lomp,' Dan laughed as he drew himself into position. 'It's going to make it better. I'll do it this once, then you take the drops and put them in every four hours. No more, understand?'

'What's in it?' Becki asked as Dan gave the ingredients one final mix.

'Never you mind. Just don't use it too often.'

'As you say, Doc.'

'I ain't a doctor. Now, hold still.'

He opened one of Becki's eyes with his thumb and index finger. He was always entranced by her washed-blue irises, but today they were dulled by a film of pink. He leant in closer, his face a fraction away from hers, their breath mingling, and counted as he applied three drops of the potion before moving to the next eye and repeating the process.

'Three every four hours,' he said. 'If you can't manage it on your own...'

'I'll come back.'

'You'll ask your mother to do it.'

'Rather ask you.'

'Aye, well, you've done that, and that's what I'm telling you to do.' Dan sat back, the treatment partly completed. 'Don't rub it away, just let it rest there and run off natural.'

He screwed on the top and pushed the bottle between the young woman's fingers. 'Keep them shut a bit longer.' Dan took the linen from the table and dampened it with a mixture of mint and water. Folding it in half, he said, 'Just going to lay this over here a moment,' and placed the cloth across Becki's nose.

She gasped. 'Some'd say that be witching, Daniel Vye.' She was smiling more broadly, impressed. 'It be like the whole mess 'as gone away sudden.'

'Aye, well it won't last. Not as long as you insist on being in the fields.'

'I must,' Becki protested. 'Me fader's not managing as well as he did, and now Edward has the forge, and Lucy's after 'aving a child, there's only me.'

'Maybe, but threshing and baling clearly aren't the things you're cut out to do. Stay away from the corn dust, the barns, the ersh, and find something else 'til harvest's done, else you'll be as toad-eyed as a green speckled deekhopper 'til festival day.' He removed the cloth. 'Right, you can open them now, but you keep your fingers away.'

Becki had already raised her hand. She lowered it.

'Sorry,' she said. 'I'll leave them be if that's what you says.'

Dan nodded and held up a finger as a sign for her to wait. He picked up the bowl of oranges and took another small bottle from one of the cabinets. This ointment was difficult to make, but he had managed to create it by following his late aunt's guidelines. He knew Becki wouldn't waste it.

'What you can do,' he said, handing her the bottle, 'is put a little of this under your nose from time to time. It'll help keep out the dust.'

'Is that what causes it?' she asked as she applied some.

'Dust, aye. And other things. And these…' He gave her an orange. 'These are what you eat. Two a day. There, that's you done.'

'You're a right throwback to Miss Eliza,' Becki said, lifting her slender figure from the chair. She brushed down her cotton shift even though it was perfectly clean and offered her hand.

Dan shook it briefly, nodding once. 'Is what I like doing,' he said. 'So, you can go now.'

'Thanks, Daniel.'

'No need.'

The woman was not going to leave and her stare fixed Dan as if she was expecting something more. Eliza's cure had begun its work, and the pink was receding, allowing back the dazzling blue, intensified by the sparkle of the eyedrops.

Becki was just another person who trusted Dan and his skills, and as such, she occupied a place in his heart. Not as much space as he allocated for Barry or Tom, but almost as much as he kept free for his intended, Jenny Rolfe. Becki was just a friend. A year younger than Dan, they had attended school together but never been overly-close companions. There were times, however, when her keenness to spend time with Dan caused him uncertainty, and he had to take a step away.

'Who's that from?' he asked, turning Becki's hand to admire a ring, hoping to break her grip. 'Is it silver?'

'Aye, it be,' Becki said, smiling and refusing to let him go. 'Twenty-third birthday gifting from me parents. Look close and you can see where Mackett carved me name on it.'

She lifted their hands to his face, causing Dan to shift uncomfortably as he pretended to admire the engraving.

'Not bad.' He noticed the rough way Jack had scratched the lettering.

He'd seen better. 'Did Jack make it an' all?' He pulled his hand free from her grip.

Becki's smile waned, but her swollen eyes remained hopeful. 'No, Edward makes them at the forge, our uncle afore him. I'll get him a-make you one, as a payment fur me treatment if you want,' she said. 'Unless you can think of another way I can thank you.'

'You don't have to pay me.' Flustered and blushing, Dan turned to the window and set about tidying his table. 'Looks like my next patient's here.' Tom was crossing the green towards the inn. 'I should get ready.'

'I'll leave you be.' Becki sighed. 'But I'll say me thanks once more. You're a good man, Daniel Vye, despite what Sally Rolfe says.'

Dan laughed and looked over his shoulder. 'She's not had a good word to say about me since I chose Jenny over her.'

Becki wasn't pleased to be reminded that Dan was betrothed. 'Aye, well...' She snatched up her purse from the chair. 'The Rolfe women are a prickly lot, as you'll soon be learning.'

'I'm a lucky man,' he said. It might have been rubbing salt in the wound, but he added, 'Jenny will be a loyal wife.'

Becki looked as if she could spit, but she mustered her dignity and adjusted the low neck of her summer dress as if she was redressing after embarrassing herself. 'I bet they never thought they'd have a doctor in the family.'

'I'm not a doctor.'

Downstairs, the back door closed with a thump followed by the tread of feet on the stairs.

'I'm going then,' Becki said hoping Dan would tell her to wait.

'Aye. I'll see you about the village and at the aepelling if not afore.' He was still facing the window, half of him wishing Becki would leave, the other half wanting her to stay. She was attractive and usually something of a tomboy, working the fields like many of the girls, but also taking ale at the inn and cracking jokes with the men. It was her mix of femininity and boyishness that intrigued him. She was gentler than Jenny, better spoken and more...

A knock at the door gave him an excuse to kick the thought from his mind, and he turned to greet Tom. 'Morning, Mr Clerk,' he said, beaming and wiping his hands on a clean towel.

'Oh please.' Tom flung himself into the chair. 'I had a French teacher at school called Mr Clarke. I don't want to be reminded. Are you alright, Miss Tidy?'

'I am now,' Becki said, still showing no signs of her promised departure. 'Thanks to the miracle-man.'

'For pity's sake, Becki!' Dan protested. His tone was playful, but she took the hint.

'You're a gentleman, Dan Vye,' she said. 'I'll gift you for the poison.' She backed towards the corridor trying to think of another way to prolong her visit but couldn't. She touched her forelock to the men as a polite farewell, spun on her heels to make a memorable exit and banged into the open door.

'Damn and blast it,' she mumbled as she finally left.

Dan waited until she was out of the building before setting free a stifled laugh.

'Poor girl.' Tom rolled his eyes. 'You've become popular.'

'Aye.' Dan nodded. 'And it ain't just because of the wedding or this here herbaling. Not in her case.' He regarded the doorway for a second and sat on his stool before pulling his thoughts together. 'Something I can do for you, Tom?'

'I hope so.' Tom undid his shirt, picked up an exercise book and fanned himself. 'It's so close out there, I'm sweating like a wether at ramming time.'

'That'll be sweating like a ram at wethering,' Dan corrected, grinning.

'Whatever. I'm sure it wasn't as stuffy as this at last year's harvest.'

'The boneless will soon blow from the north, Tom, and then we'll be crowded 'round the hearth telling stories of summer and even missing autumn. What's up?'

Tom sighed. 'Have you got anything that'll help me sleep? It's not just the heat, I'm having trouble settling my mind.'

'Devil's Choke?'

'I've tried that,' Tom said. 'But these days it only makes me...' He cut himself off and glanced at Dan. 'Never mind. What else might get me to sleep?'

Dan knew the effects of the choke plant. He had considered smoking a large pipe full before his wedding night to help him through his expected duties. 'Is it the pressures of being Minister Cole's right-hand man?' he asked.

'No. It's not council work that keep me awake. It's something else, and I don't know what. Barry says I should work on the farm more, says that'll knock me out, and he's probably right. He's been sleeping like an ancestor since harvest started. Drives me mad, snoring as loud as the threshing machine come nine o'clock. I have helped at the farm of course, but even when my body's aching and it's all I can do to climb the stairs, as soon as we blow out the lamps, my mind wakes up.'

'With what, if it ain't council troubles?'

'It's hard to explain. Strange thoughts I didn't know were in my subconscious. They eventually turn to dreams, but even then I see faces dancing before me, and the thoughts become other men's voices, telling me stories of people I don't know.'

'Sounds as if you're overdoing the Devil's Choke if you ask me.' Dan opened a medicine cabinet.

'Do you get nights like that?' Tom asked. 'When you can't sleep even though you're so knackered you can hardly breathe?'

'I'm sure we all do, Tom.'

Dan dropped his head, his hand resting inside an open drawer. Yes, he did, was the honest answer, but the reasons for his recent troubled sleeplessness had nothing to do with his work or Devil's Choke, or even the fractious council and the tensions in the village. He couldn't tell Tom what his troubles were, they were too closely connected to Tom's life.

He found what he was looking for.

'Take a couple of sips of this before you turn in. See if it helps.'

'What is it?'

'Why does everyone keep asking me what's in things?' Dan threw up his arms. 'Don't no-one trust me?'

Tom leant forwards and gripped Dan's knee. 'I was only interested. Are you okay?'

'Aye,' Dan sighed. 'Sorry 'bout that. Like you say, stuffy day. It's just a few herbs.' He pointed to the bottle, and Tom withdrew his hand. Dan didn't mind if he left it there or took it away; Tom was his best friend, and he knew where he stood.

'Thanks, I'll try it.'

'Oi! Carey! Where you be at?' A thickly accented voice bellowed from the green. 'I got a bolter fur the stove.'

'The master's home from the fields.' Dan winked. He rose to the window and waved.

Tom slapped his hands on his thighs as he stood. 'And it's my turn to cook.'

'I'll come with you.'

Dan signalled to Barry and, having made sure his table was tidy and nothing had been left open, turned to follow Tom.

He was standing in the doorway, one arm across his chest, the other bent up to chew on a nail. His face was pale, and his tired eyes fixed on the far wall where there was nothing to see but white plaster.

'What is it, Tom?' Dan sensed that whatever was troubling his friend's sleep was also troubling his waking mind. 'Tom?' he prompted. 'Barry's waiting.'

Tom blinked. 'What? Oh, sorry.'

Dan approached and gave his shoulder a squeeze. Sometimes that was all Tom needed to lift his mood. Today, it didn't work. 'What's wrong?'

'Something's coming,' he answered, his voice a hoarse whisper. 'I feel it in my dreams. I sense it when I can't sleep. It's coming for me, and I don't know what it is.'

Three

Barry was waiting on the green when Tom joined him. His brown curls were haphazardly decorated with corn stalks, and his trousers were floured with dust. Despite the clammy afternoon heat, he wore his sheepskin jerkin, also corn-riddled. Barry's sunburnt face rounded into a broad smile and Tom fought the urge to kiss him right there despite the skinned rabbit he held in one hand, its fur in the other. He made a quick scan of the green, but Mrs Rolfe was pretending to fuss at the shop window, a cover for her spying.

'Afternoon,' Tom said, greeting his partner discreetly but with the same enthusiasm. 'Good day at the farm?'

'Nearly atop the baling on North Feld against Mackett's fence, and the beets over west side are in thanks a Uncle Ben and 'is boys. What you been about?'

'The usual.' Tom took the rabbit from him. 'And preparing for this evening.'

'Aye, well good luck wi' that, I be 'ome drekly-minute.' Barry wiped his hand on his trousers as he set off towards the shop.

'Where you going?'

Barry waved the fur. 'Get us carrots and greens,' he called. 'Not long. Af'noon, Dan.'

'Come see me about your hands.'

Tom turned to the voice behind him. He'd not heard Dan arrive. 'What's wrong with his hands?'

'Didn't you see those blisters? He needs a poultice on them else they'll burst, and we'll never hear the end of it. I'll drop it round later.'

'Cheers, mate.'

Dan draped one arm around Tom's neck. 'I'm guessing your troubles don't have anything to do with Barry.'

'Hell, no,' Tom laughed.

'So what is this… thing that's keeping your mind so alive? What's coming?'

'I can't explain it.' Tom allowed himself to be led across the green towards home. 'It's a weird feeling inside that something's not right. Just strange stuff that I can't get out of my head. I think it started when I was going through the papers we found at Eliza's shack.'

When Dan's mother had decided to tear down Eliza's disused outpost home, Tom and Dan had spent two days clearing out what they thought should be kept. Dan inherited his aunt's still useable supplies of herbs and remedies and took her books of recipes and cures. As the newly appointed village clerk, Tom claimed a collection of leather-bound journals, papers and record books dating back several centuries. Not even Matt Cole, who had been the previous clerk for years, remembered seeing them, and Tom was surprised that William Blacklocks when he was minister, had not gathered them and guarded them with the other Saddling records.

'She used to call them her history library, or some such,' Dan said. 'Mainly songs, stories and blindly scribbled rubbish ain't they?' They arrived at Tom's front door. 'There'll be nothing to disturb you in those old books,'

'Not in what I've seen so far,' Tom agreed. 'But there's a load more to go through. I've found interesting accounts of village happenings, and am transcribing them into a new book so that I can store the originals safely. Did you know, for example, that in eighteen-fifty...'

'Aye, aye, Tom Carey,' Dan interrupted, not in the mood for a long talk on village history. 'No doubt we'll hear it over a pint later. Right now, I have to go see Jenny. Tell your man I'll be in later with a poppy and cornflour rub for his palms.'

'How is Jenny? We've not seen her a while.'

Dan's face clouded momentarily, and he glanced towards the shop where Barry was haggling with Mrs Rolfe. When he looked back, he was smiling, but it was forced.

'She's in her readying week now,' he said. 'Got to spend time with her ma working on dresses and garlands, cakes and other treddles needed for the day. She gets the busy time now, and I get it after the ceremony.'

Dan nudged Tom and winked, but there was anxiety in his expression, and his smile wasn't sincere.

Tom had been attracted to Dan from the moment he first saw him, and the seeds of possibility had been sown early. The attraction had grown, promising and tempting, but was cut down when Barry entered his heart. Dan was a marker, a best friend.

'Nervous?' Tom asked.

'I suppose I am, but mainly about the ceremony and Minister Cole taking it. He'll give me a right ear bannocking if I get my words wrong.'

'And so will Jenny if you're late.' Tom nodded towards the shop where Dan's intended stood watching from an upstairs window. Barry had negotiated his barter and was walking back to them. 'And I'll be getting one from Barry if I don't get this rabbit in the oven. See you later.'

Inside the house, Tom took the rabbit to the kitchen and cleaned it at the stone sink, gazing from the window at the line of distant mother trees. They dripped red and orange leaves into the deek, revealing the twisted fingers of their branches. The afternoon sunlight threw warm shadows across the fields where the whitebacks grazed, and a tiding of magpies croaked just beyond his back-out, the section of field behind the house. The sound reminded him of dice being rattled in a plastic shaker before being thrown.

'Sack of veg.' Barry arrived, triumphantly dropping a bag on the table with a thump. He wrapped his arms around Tom from behind and hugged him, planting a kiss on the back of his neck. 'Missed you all day out in them felds,' he said.

'Missed you leaning over my shoulder at the desk.'

'Aye, like you ever miss that,' Barry joked.

'I miss you every time you're out of the room.' Tom twisted to repay the kiss with one on Barry's forehead. 'But I did get a lot of transcribing done today.'

'That be nice. What time'll she be ready?' Barry withdrew and sat at the table where he unknotted his bootlaces.

'Couple of hours.' Tom laid the rabbit on the draining board while he cleaned the sink. 'While it's doing, I've got things to prepare for the meeting. You coming?'

'Do I 'ave to?'

Barry was never particularly interested in the council meetings unless they were discussing crop rotation, or who was to have use of the automated threshing machine that season. Saddling only had one, kept in reasonable working order by Nate Rolfe. Dating back at least one hundred years, he had adapted it to run on gas. Each harvest, the council passed the use of the machine to another farm, it was easier to share it that way than to allot hours or days per business; it was a heavy thing to move. This meant that for most years Barry and his family were left to reap and thresh by hand, but next year they would be allowed the machine.

'You don't have to come,' Tom said, turning his attention to potatoes. 'Your dad called it to give the factions a dressing down. They don't know it yet so don't say anything.'

'I won't, mate,' Barry replied, pulling off a boot and throwing it vaguely towards the pantry. 'Mainly as I don't know what factions be, and 'cos I ain't meaning a-go out a'night 'til we're at skittles.'

'It's your old mate Aaron Fetcher and his acolytes versus Bill Taylor and his cronies, with the likes of me and Dan in the middle. I'm only there to take minutes. You won't miss anything interesting.'

'I'll miss you.'

Barry said it so often that Tom worried he would grow tired of hearing it, but he hadn't so far, and they'd been living together for nearly three years. A loving couple inside the house, a duo of best friends outside, and no-one asked questions. Even the likes of Aaron Fetcher and Billy Farrow no longer cast suspicious looks or let go snide comments.

'Well, it won't go on for long.' Tom began washing the potatoes.

'Right.' Barry kicked off his second boot and pushed himself to his feet. 'We got hot water?' Tom nodded. 'Then I'm taking me bath.' He started to strip.

'Dan's bringing over something for your hands,' Tom told him. 'And there's some of his herbal bath gunk upstairs.'

'Turning into a right witch, 'e be.' Barry shed his jerkin and unbuttoned his shirt.

'We don't mention that word in this house.'

'A right doctor then. Same thing. What time's 'e coming?'

'Didn't say.'

'Better get a me bath afore 'e lets 'imself in.' Barry dropped his trousers and kicked them away.

'I'll deal with this then, shall I?' Tutting playfully, Tom left the vegetables and gathered the scattered clothes. 'And I suppose you want me to rinse your shirt?'

'I can soak it a me bath wi' me if you like,' Barry suggested.

'It'll come out worse than it went in. I'll do it.'

'Kegs an' all?'

'Aye.'

This kind of domestic scene played out daily in the house, and Tom was in no way offended that Barry appeared to take him for granted. The fact that Barry could, proved to Tom the strength of their bond. When he was busy with council business, Barry took care of the cooking and the house, leaving Tom ample time to write up minutes and keep the village records in order. The partnership worked smoothly, and the domestic chores were shared evenly.

Tom had been appointed the clerk by Matt Cole not long after Cole was officially voted minister two years previously. It had been a close call between Tom and Bill Taylor the clothes maker. Tom had not been in Saddling long enough to be trusted by every villager. A few still refused to see him as a Saddlinger because he had been born out-marsh, but enough of the council elders took Cole's side and saw his reason. Tom was the most educated man in the village, his ancestors had founded Saddling, and Tom had paid for the church-house restoration. The clincher was Jack Mackett's vote and, as Tom had paid for the rebuilding of his farmhouse, there was no doubt where Jack's loyalty lay.

What had been more surprising was Cole's attitude. Tom had expected him to take a long time to accept that his only son was living with an out-marsher, even a Carey, but Matt Cole had seen what the pair meant to each other, and his silent disapproval soon gave way to mumbled acceptance.

Or so Tom thought.

With the rabbit roasting in the oven, the laundry steeping in the tub and his partner wallowing in the bath, Tom sat at his study desk and arranged his papers. He had an hour before the meeting, not enough time to work on his transcription, but enough time to ensure he was up to date on the previous meetings. He was acutely aware that he needed to give Cole's opposition no cause to criticise him. Being elevated to the role of village clerk gave him purpose, but it was an honour that could easily be taken away.

With six o'clock approaching, he changed into a formal shirt, shaved, and combed his straw-coloured hair in the bathroom mirror.

'You look like you be done up for a feasting,' Barry said. He lay in the cold bathwater smoking his pipe, his head and knees above a film of dust and wheat stalks. The smoke from the Devil's Choke hung in the air a few feet from the floor.

'Got to play my part.' Tom spoke to Barry's reflection. 'You know, you're going to have to hose down again when you get out. Looks like you're lying in a deek.'

'Aye. Meet you at The Crow?'

'As soon as I can. Don't fall asleep in there.'

'As you want.' Barry pulled the plug and dragged himself wearily upright.

'Tell you what, Dan's bath gunk ain't 'alf bad. Not a lot aches now excepting me 'eart.'

'Oh, give over, you old softie.' Tom grinned into the mirror as Barry turned on the shower. The water washed away the scum, and his stocky frame became a mass of dripping strands of dark hair.

'Have to go,' Tom said, standing back from the sink. 'Turn the oven off in half an hour. See you after.'

'Enough a let you run,' Barry said.

Tom completed the phrase with, 'Too much to see you fall.'

It was their safe way of saying goodbye. The phrase started with 'I love you…' but they never said those words when parting in case they accidentally said them in public. There was no need. They knew.

Tom collected his papers and hurried to the church-house. He was the first to arrive as always and set about arranging the table-stone ahead of the meeting.

The stone, it was said, was the only surviving part of the original church built by Robert Di-Kari in the thirteenth century. It had served as an altar for a while, but when Saddling turned its back on Christianity and instead followed its own Lore and beliefs in nature, the stone became a table. Three feet high, six long, it was one solid block of limestone resting on blocks at each corner like a raised tomb. It was the source of many myths. It had been dropped there by an eagle, it had been left behind when the seas receded after the marsh was inned, it had been carved from a cliff on the other side of the distant hills and dragged to Saddling in antiquity. Tom would never know the truth.

He laid a white tablecloth over the table and pulled up the seven stools, placing them in a semicircle facing the nave.

No matter how the stone came to be there, it had remained unchanged through time while the building that housed it had been rebuilt. Once because it was destroyed in a saddling storm in 1412, and another time because the foundations rotted and the walls buckled, weakened by rising damp. Its rebuilding in the eighteenth century gave the Blacklocks and Vye families an excuse to dig a smugglers tunnel from the church to the inn, something that Matt Cole had filled in and covered over when he recently improved the crypt. Tom had also been involved in the church-house's history. He'd paid for the new east window which replaced the one destroyed in the solstice storm three years ago.

Villagers began to arrive as Tom laid out the papers the councilmen needed and, by six o'clock, several front box pews had filled, and the council was assembled. Matt Cole, a large man with rough skin from a life of farming, stood and ceremoniously opened the minutes ledger, laying it in front of Tom seated at the end of the table. That was the sign for the congregation to end their gossiping and pay attention.

As the villagers settled, Tom noticed that Cole's hand was trembling. He was not a man given to nervousness and it was unusual to see. He was distracted, and his knitted brow suggested he had something serious on his mind.

'Are you alright, Minister Cole?' Tom whispered, concerned.

Cole looked at him sternly and gave one quick nod before returning to his place. 'First off, this is a courtesy calling,' he said. His assured deep voice reached every part of the whitewashed walls, the furthest pews and the arch-beamed ceiling. 'You're invited 'ere a'night a-listen a what me council and me 'ave a-say on the matter of your complaining…'

'I object at you calling us complainers.'

'Well what else you be doing, you hoogoo?' Cole shot the heckler down in a flash. No-one interrupted when the minister was talking, no-one except the petulant Aaron Fetcher.

Tom noted the word Cole had used, he had a rough idea what it meant but would check the spelling with Barry later. Whatever its meaning, it caused the older men to laugh and Aaron's face to redden.

'You get your time a-talk after,' Cole continued. 'What you got a-'ear first be a reminding that us up 'ere was chosen by all a you a-do the work the village needs doing. This, as you know, be the Teaching.' He lifted one of the volumes Tom had placed on the table. 'And that be what we follow in Saddling.' The book was too heavy for his trembling hand, and he hurriedly replaced it.

'That's the thing though, ain't it, Matthew?' Mick Farrow, the white-haired farmer who kept sheep out at West Ditch, spoke quietly but with authority. 'We be suffering as we ain't got no teacher right now.'

Mick was part of the council and Cole wasn't happy that he had spoken out of turn. His face paled, and the corner of his eye twitched with annoyance. 'We can discuss that later, Mick,' he said. 'If you don't mind holding your talk awhile.'

'Aye, as you wish.' Farrow shrugged and placed his pipe in his mouth, sitting back and folding his arms. Smoking was forbidden in the church-house and the pipe remained unlit.

'So, all we're 'ere fur is a-listen a you old folks 'bout what you think's best fur us. Be that it, Minister Cole?' A high-pitched voice sounded from the pews. Billy Farrow sat beside Aaron Fetcher, his marker, also with his arms folded and an unlit pipe in his mouth mimicking his grandfather.

'If you'd only 'old your voices…'

'Mick's right. We ain't got no decent teacher,' someone from further back shouted. 'We need a-sort the eastern sewers and Mother Seeming's cesspit's overflowing. The fetching truck ain't going a last the winter, and there's been nothing discussed about the rituals.'

'We shouldn't be suffering no cesspits,' Aaron said. 'And Nate Rolfe's never going a-be able a-fix that truck…'

'Should never 'ave done away wi' the saddling,' another voice chipped in, and the older men agreed.

'Easy fur you a-say,' A teenager behind Aaron turned to reply as other men stood to shout their complaints.

The meeting was easily and unusually disrupted, and Tom gave up trying to note the comments. Cole's face turned from pale to crimson as the voices crescendoed, the older men calling for a return to the old ways and the younger shouting them down. Aaron Fetcher was on his feet hurling insults across the aisle to Nate Rolfe about the state of the truck, Billy Farrow struck up a conversation with the youths behind him, and even the council six were arguing amongst themselves.

Cole was caught between the voices, his head turning from one man to another. His mouth opened but no words came. Tom had never known a meeting like it, and it pained him to see how quickly Cole lost the room. He'd had his run-ins with Barry's father in the past, but Cole was the only other level-headed man in the church and Tom's anger simmered to see him disrespected. Somebody had to act.

'I blame that out-marsher.' Aaron Fetcher pointed an accusing finger at Tom, his face taut with anger and his voice slicing through the melee.

'Enough!' Tom slammed his ledger on top of another and the thump, combined with his hollered word, echoed through the church-house, staying for as long as it took for the surprise to be wiped from Aaron's face and the other men to fall silent.

'It's clear what the problem be,' Tom said when thirty shocked eyes found him. The clerk usually only spoke if called upon to do so by the council. He slipped into the Saddling dialect. 'We got the young'uns on the right as wants things new and changed, and now they be past age and able a-vote, they want a-see things done different. They've only been living twenty or so year, mind, and doubtless they won't remember the first five a them. Then over 'ere on the left, we got them as 'as lived in-marsh for seventy-five year or more and they can't remember seventy of those.'

Mick Farrow laughed and said, 'You be right there, Carey.' The congregation's reaction was mixed.

'You're just the scribbler,' Aaron growled across the space between them. 'And you ain't from our village.'

'And you're a waste a space, you loudmouth yawnup. If you were mine you'd be bannocked regular and set a-work cleaning out Mother Seeming's cess wi' your paws, you jawsy coot.'

Heads turned to the back of the church where the broad and dark figure of Jack Mackett dominated the centre aisle. His fisted hands dug into his hips, and his piercing eyes flashed from his weathered face. The two Feld brothers flanked him, equally as tall. Their presence brought a worried silence.

'Me apologies, Minister,' Jack said, advancing. 'I didn't intend a-disturb your meet, but Simon 'ere's got a tale a-relate what's going a-send all your other paltry matters straight a Seeming's cesspit and put your truck business aside fur another lifetime. You should 'ear what 'e's got a-say, and you keep your filthy trap locked while 'e says it, Aaron Fetcher.'

Tom caught a smile of admiration on Cole's face, but it was hurriedly replaced by a more authoritative expression when the villagers turned to gauge his reaction.

'If it's urgent enough that it 'as a-disturb this rabble,' he said, 'then you can come up and tell us, Simon Feld.'

The looker hesitated, throwing a nervous glance to Jack.

Aaron Fetcher used his hesitation to his own advantage. 'I call fur a people's imposition,' he shouted, bringing gasps from the older men and a growl from Matt Cole.

Simon Feld's massive shoulders slumped, and he hung back, knowing he had to wait.

The minister glared at Aaron, but the lad's defiance was unwavering.

'You sure, Master Fetcher?' Cole asked.

Aaron cleared his throat, glanced at Billy for support, found it and said, 'Aye.'

'Clerk?' Cole turned to Tom. 'Be there process fur that?'

A people's imposition was an ancient and little-used right to challenge the village council by vote. It could be called at any time and by anyone over the age of eighteen if the caller felt there was just cause to challenge the leadership. Tom knew of it from one entry in the Saddling Diary. It had been used only once, sometime in the fifteenth century, but that was precedent. Aaron had every right to call it.

'From what I read,' Tom said, thinking fast, 'it ain't a thing much used out a politeness and respect fur our appointed minister.' His words brought agreement from a third of the gathering. 'But, aye, if someone wants a-throw the status quo into turmoil fur their own...' He tried hard to sound impartial, but it was difficult. '... their own self-satisfaction, then aye. It can be called.' Aaron's followers raised a cheer. 'But...' Tom cut them off. 'It 'as a-be seconded by another.'

Cole sighed and raised his hands in defeat. 'Get on wi' it.'

Tom stood. It was the clerk's job to make a formal announcement, but there was nothing written in the Lore or Teaching to tell him what to say. As he scanned the room, searching for words, he realised that in fact, he couldn't remember reading anything about a people's imposition in either book. Aaron Fetcher must know his Lore intimately to know of such a thing.

'Well?'

Tom opened his mouth hoping appropriate words would flow. 'Be there another here what thinks 'e as grievance wi' our village appointed minister and council? Be there more than one what reckons 'e can make a better job a what 'as a-be done fur us all by our properly elected elders? If there be such a one, 'e is a-speak now.'

He waited, hoping there was no-one else headstrong, brave or pig-headed enough to challenge Cole's position.

'I be doing that.' Bill Taylor stood, swiping his grey hair from his narrow face.

Tom's heart fell. This was not how the meeting was meant to turn out. Cole hadn't had time to put forward what he intended to say. In fact, he had let the meeting run off its rails and had given up any hope of restoring order or quelling the divisions in the village.

The men were waiting. Cole's head hung in defeat, and there was nothing Tom could do.

'In that case,' he said, 'we have no choice but to accept your imposition.' He placed one hand on the records ledger and another on the original Book of Lore and adopted his official voice. 'The people's imposition called by Aaron Fetcher and Bill Taylor, both of age to call… will be held and heard when such time has passed for all sides to be diligently and accurately… honestly and without prejudice, informed of the effects of a council change, a… replacement of leadership and a new direction for the village of Saddling founded here before time and lived according to the Lore.'

It was a formal speech intended to bamboozle, and he was more impressed with the fact that he had thought of it than the way he had delivered it; breathless and stuttering with nerves.

'We don't need time a-explain a folk what they already know,' Aaron called.

Annoyed, Tom repeated and emphasised, 'Will be held and heard when such time has passed for all sides to be diligently and accurately…'

'I call it now,' Aaron persisted.

'Well you can't you wet-weening teg.' Mick Farrow stood, knocking over his stool. His weathered face glowed beneath his messy shock of white hair. 'And if you knew your Teaching you'd know that interrupting a council member, the clerk or a meeting is cause for church-house banishing.'

The older men on Bill Taylor's side applauded, and Aaron sat, his face twitching with anger.

'Thank you, Mick,' Cole whispered as Farrow righted his stool.

Tom continued. 'The imposition shall be heard two weeks from today after…'

'No.' This time it was Cole who interrupted. 'There be no point delaying, Clerk Carey. Saddling knows what'll 'appen should the likes a Master Fetcher get a-stand 'ere in my shoes, and they know what we'll be a-going back to should Bill Taylor wear the minister's robes. The imposition will be 'eard, and the vote taken come Eastling Day, after the festival when the whole village'll be a'gether, 'ere at the council table. That be it.'

Stunned by how easily Cole had given in, Tom lifted the Book of Lore. 'Unless,' he said, facing the congregation, 'there be found a part a-the

Teaching or Lore that forbids such a vote or renders your request invalid.' It wasn't a declaration written in any book, but he doubted anyone in the church-house knew that. 'Are we agreed?'

He paid special attention to Aaron who, with his friends, called 'Aye' and raised a hand. Bill Taylor's supporters did the same.

'It's going a-take all your learning a-get us out a this mess, Carey,' Cole hissed as Tom sat. He spoke louder to call forward Simon Feld. 'Come 'ere then Simon. Tell us your news and stop your fretting. What's so bad as you 'ave a-cut short a council?'

The looker, over six-feet tall and built for pulling ploughs, twisted a handkerchief in his hands and kept his bulldog eyes on the floor as he approached. He shuffled his feet, glanced over his shoulder to his brother who nodded encouragement, and turned to face Cole.

Tom took up his pen, ready to minute whatever the shepherd had to say.

He stopped writing after one sentence as the meeting once more descended into chaos. This time it was caused by panic, and it took all of Matt Cole's strength and Tom's tact to call the villagers to order.

'You want a-say that agin, Simon?' Cole asked when silence had been restored.

'Aye, Minister,' the tall man nodded and turned to the villagers. 'I be afeared that the eastling be coming. I saw it out a East Sewer last night.'

Four

Later that evening, Tom and Barry sat with Dan in The Crow and Whiteback at their usual table apart from the other men. The inn was busy following the meeting, and the room vibrated with heated conversation.

Tom was relating the events of earlier, as were others in the inn that night, each one putting their own spin on what had been said.

'Who put forward that stupid idea?' Dan asked.

'Aaron Fetcher,' Tom replied. He lent in to talk without raising his voice. 'He was mouthing off all evening, and he's got a fair few supporters behind him. Sounded like a right Neo-Nazi.'

'A what?' Dan queried.

'Never mind.'

'They can't get 'im out,' Barry said. 'Fader's been in place two year and fairly chosen. 'Besides, we never challenge our minister.'

'Times change, mate,' said Dan. 'But not to worry, your fader won't let it happen.'

'That's the thing.' Tom lifted his ale. 'Minister Cole had to agree.'

'Now I know you're pulling me off.'

Tom spluttered on his drink. 'Barry, it's either having me on or pulling my leg. Best not to mix the two.'

Dan whispered in Barry's ear, and Barry's smile faded. It returned with a vengeance when Dan explained his mistake.

'Well, I can do that an' all,' he leered, winking. 'But why would me fader agree a them idiots and their demands? Bain't like 'im.'

'To keep the peace, I imagine,' Tom said. 'But he didn't have a choice. It's called for festival day unless I can find a way around it. Have you ever known anything like this before?'

'Not as I remember 'earing,' Barry said. 'The Teaching says the minister be there fur life.'

'Then they'll be some way out. I'll see what I can turn up in the books.'

'You do that, Tom,' Barry squeezed his hand. 'Besides, wi' Feld's story running 'round the village faster than a frightened rat, folks'll 'ave more on their minds.'

'All sounded perfectly explainable to me.' After Simon Feld described what he had seen, Tom easily found rational explanations for the sighting. 'What do you reckon, Dan?'

Dan was staring into the distance, both hands holding his ale jug as though he was warming his fingers.

'Dan?'

'What's that?' He focused on Tom. 'Sorry, I was further away than Far Field.'

'You wi' us, mate?' Barry knocked him on the shoulder with his fist. 'Or you got your mind on your wedding night?'

'Er, aye, both.' Dan put on a more cheerful face, but it was underpinned by apprehension.

'Want to talk about it?' Tom asked.

'What, me wedding night? With you two?' Dan laughed briefly. 'I reckon I know how it works. I've read me aunt's books.'

Tom was unconvinced. 'I mean talk about what's really on your mind.'

'You know me, Tom. Always something going on up here.' Dan ran his fingers through his auburn hair and lifted it, pulling a stupid expression and crossing his eyes. When his companions didn't react, he let go and swiped his hand through it, flattening the copper back into place. 'I'm fine, but thanks for your concern.'

'Only if you're…'

'I be sure an' all,' Dan insisted. He sat up straight. 'So then, we got this stupid vote coming up, but there's no cause to worry, things'll stay as they are and just as we want them, but what of what Simon Feld saw? What d'you make of that?'

It had taken Tom a long time to accept the Saddling Lore as more than superstition. There were many stories in the village history which he once dismissed as fairy-tales and myths, but he had witnessed both natural and supernatural forces in Saddling and trained himself to be open-minded. It was still in his nature, however, to look for the logical first and the illogical later.

'Seasonal weather,' he said. 'The humidity we've been having clouded his view of one of the western lookers. Maybe even an out-marsher come close to West Ditch. It happens.'

'I can accept that,' Dan said. 'But it's what came with the sighting. That's a foretold sign of the eastling.'

'We ain't 'ad no eastling 'ere fur long as no-one can remember,' Barry mumbled. 'I'd throw clackety Feld in a cold deek, tell 'im a-grow up and act his years, then take no notice. Like Tom says, autumn grey-hang, be all.'

Tom tried to gauge Dan's reaction, but he gave nothing away as he looked back with eyes that were almost lifeless.

'What do you say, mate?' Tom prompted.

Dan moved his head from side to side weighing up the possibilities. 'Could be either.'

'That be so you, Daniel Vye,' Barry teased. 'You never know what side of the five-bar you be on not even when we tells you where you be.' He straightened his accent as best he could and attempted to mimic his best friend's softer voice. 'Should I wear my 'air longer, or 'ave it shorn side and back? Think I'll learn 'ow to make shadow-wert soother today, or prehaps I might check on me 'ops and chase up the brewing.'

'Give over, you lomp,' Dan grinned.

'Should it be Jenny, or should it be Sally? How about the other…'

'I said give over.' Dan's voice was firmer, and any humour left him in an instant. 'It's Jenny. I've not be courting the girl these past two years to change my mind now.'

'We know that.' Tom squeezed Dan's hand. 'It's okay. He was joking.'

'Which is all he ever does.'

Barry thumped his glass on the table and turned his chair to face the redhead beside him.

'We'll be stopping this right 'ere,' he said. 'We're not falling out over your blasted wedding, Daniel Vye. I'm going a-be there as your marker and your best mate, which what I always been wi' ye. We took our own pact you and me, and I knows you remember. Spring solstice, out by the bridge, looking south to beyond. Whatever comes along in our lives, it comes a both of us.' When his friend turned away, Barry yanked his arm and forced him to look him in the eye. 'If you got troubles, they be mine.'

'And mine,' Tom added, but the words sounded intrusive.

'I know.' Dan sighed and slid lower in his chair, hunching his shoulders. 'There ain't nothing wrong, honest. I'd tell you if there were, both of you. Everything's right on the track it needs to be on. I know what I'm doing. I know where I'm going. Fact, I'm in a better place now than I've ever been, what with Eliza's knowledge, my treating room, my two best mates living across the green like…' he lowered his voice, '…a married couple.' He continued more clearly. 'And seeing you two shows me what I could have, and that's what I want. So, no, honest, there is nothing wrong. It's just… No, makes no never mind.'

Tom exchanged glances with Barry who rolled his eyes impatiently. 'It be just what?'

Dan shook his head. 'I can't explain it,' he said. 'I'm not unwell, I'm not worried, or unhappy, nothing like that. I just feel…' His eyes travelled the bar as though the answer was among the decoration of drawings and farming gear. 'I just don't feel right.' He clicked his fingers at Tom. 'How did you say it before? So knackered you can hardly breathe? Well, I've been getting some of that, and I can't place why. So, if I am troubled by anything, it's not knowing why my mind doesn't focus so well, and it ain't the choke, Barry Cole, afore you say something.'

'I were only going a-say, is that all?' Barry said feigning a huff. 'Then I were going a-say, now we knows, we'll stop fretting 'bout you.'

'Hardly fretting,' Tom said. 'But we were worried. Thanks for telling us, and yes, it's a weird feeling. Comes and goes, can't shake it off. But it passes.'

'There you go, Doc.' Barry slapped Dan's thigh, making him jump. 'You can put that in your book a treating. And this…' He collected their empty tankards. 'Cole remedy for glumness; three pints a Old Tickle.'

'Sorry, Tom,' Dan said as Barry went to the bar. 'I'll be myself come morning.'

'I would say doctor heal thyself, but I know you don't want to be called a doctor.' Tom could see that Dan appreciated that. He knew he didn't consider himself skilled or learned enough to be thought of as a man of medicine. He was, though, the closest thing the village had to one. 'What I will say, however, is what do you reckon to Simon Feld's story?'

Dan shook his head. 'We got many stories in Saddling,' he said. 'But that's not one no-one needs to worry about. Like you say, autumn mist, wandering out-marsher.'

'I don't remember reading about the eastling,' Tom confessed. 'There's nothing in the Teaching, and the Lore is strangely sketchy on this piece of folklore.'

'See? Not worth the bother. At least Feld's dramatics put a stop to Aaron's blarring, by the sound of it.'

'That it did, and we were thankful.' Tom was going to say that the meeting had left him with the feeling that most of the village were turning against him, but he didn't want to add to Dan's unease. He changed the subject to ask about the wedding arrangements.

Dan and Jenny were to be married on the day after the Eastling Festival, what had been called Harvest Festival in Tom's childhood. He associated it with church, gathering donations for the poor and long, boring services with the same old hymns year after year. Eastling Festival in Saddling was a wilder celebration.

Tom had witnessed two since he had lived in the village. Trestle tables were arranged on the green, with the households that circled it putting seating on their front grass. Anyone could sit anywhere apart from the top table. The wives of the wheat, corn and root farmers sat there, treated as the guests of honour. The reasoning behind their singling-out was that they were the ones who had sustained the men through the planting and harvest, and it was they who provided the village with future generations to grow the crops that kept Saddling fed. A spring festival was held to celebrate successful lambing, and the two were depicted in the new east window of the church-house along with the saddling and witchling festivals. Eastling Day was for sharing produce and feasting, at least during the afternoon.

In the evening, as long as the Vye beer kegs kept flowing (and they always did), fires were lit, and the party spilt over onto the near field where the farmer's sons competed in bale-tossing until there was a winner. The victor had the honour of addressing the crop-wives once everyone had gathered back on the green to mark the end of the festivities. The strongest youth formally thanked the women for their work and asked their permission to enter the church-house. There, with the villagers watching, he took pride of place beside the minister at the table-stone. He swore an oath on behalf of the men to maintain the good work of the farms and feed the community for another year. Both times Tom had been present, Barry had won the bale-toss, although he suspected that Jack Mackett had let him win by pretending to be drunk. When it came to the final, Jack was unable to lift the pitchfork, let alone the weight of hay. Later, he'd been completely sober, unlike most of the men, some of whom had to be helped into and out of the church-house.

'It's going to be a busy two days for you,' Tom said. 'Catering the festival with your wedding the next day. If you need a hand, let me know.'

'With what?' Dan's head jerked back. 'My wedding night?'

'Hell no!' Tom chuckled. 'I meant with getting the ale ready and moving the tables. The festival.' He became serious. 'Why? Are you worried about it?'

Dan shifted in his seat and looked away.

Barry returned, slopping beer onto the floor. 'Ma says she'll have a word wi' ye later, Mr Town Clerk,' he said as Tom took one of the tankards before it was empty. 'And you can wipe that grin off a your face, Daniel. Your mother-in-lore ain't going a-be no better. Aunt Rebecca taught my ma everything she knows 'bout herding young'uns. If you're going a-be me cousin, you better get used a-doing what you're told.'

'We'll see,' Dan said. 'I'm not worried about Rebecca Rolfe. Besides, we won't be living there.' He changed the conversation with a cheery but forced smile. 'Here's to the end of your harvest, farmer Cole.'

They clinked their glasses, and Dan's mood lifted. 'Game of cailes?' he suggested. The skittle alley had been free all evening; the men were more interested in their speculation and debates.

'Promised me fader we'd team up,' Barry said, searching the room. 'But 'e ain't been in. Bain't like 'im after a meet.'

'Told me he had work to do,' Tom said, rising. 'If you ask me, he's someone else with something on his mind.'

Once again, Dan fell into a faraway gaze. His mouth narrowed, and he licked his bottom lip with his tongue, thinking.

'You coming, cousin-a-be?'

Barry woke him from his reverie, and he adopted good humour. 'Course I am,' he said, standing and stretching his long arms. 'Not going to miss the chance to give you two a bannocking.'

'Like that's going to happen,' Tom grinned confidently.

Dan called over to Jason Rolfe to make a four-a-cailes and Barry's blond cousin joined them on the way to the alley. His presence immediately lifted Dan's mood although Jason himself appeared nervous in Dan's company.

Dan joked and laughed throughout the game, but Tom was still unable to shake off the worrying suspicion that he was keeping something from them. He didn't know what it was, but he had an uneasy feeling that it wasn't just to do with his forthcoming wedding.

Five

As The Crow and Whiteback emptied, Irene Cole put away the last of the dried glasses and told Susan she was done for the night. She had only helped because it was a council night and the inn was busier than usual. Susan was grateful for the help she had given and offered her a small keg of ale in payment.

'Not tonight, thank you,' Irene said, politely declining the offer. 'Keep it back for when Matthew comes in and spend it on 'im.'

She lifted the hatch and squeezed through to the bar, hurrying to catch Tom before he left.

'Barry,' she said, reaching the closing door and holding it. 'You get yourself home, I want a quick word with Tom.'

'As you like, Ma.' Barry gave Tom a quick nod and continued on his way, leaving Tom alone in the doorway to fend for himself.

'I'm so sorry,' he said. 'Dan did tell me, and I completely forgot.'

She didn't reply, but instead, took his elbow and led him across the green to the bench where the streetlight threw its yellow glow. She sat with her back to it, making her little more than a round silhouette as Tom sat side-saddle facing her. He couldn't think of a reason for this late-night conference. As far as he knew, Irene was still of the opinion that he and Barry were friends sharing a house. She had never hinted at anything else and had even made a quilt for their second bedroom. However, her regular and often unannounced visits to the house to check on it meant that Tom and Barry had to keep the spare room permanently 'in use', pretending it was Tom's, neat and orderly. Had it been Barry's, they would have had to litter it daily with different dusty clothes, pile the laundry rather than fold it, and make sure the bed was constantly unmade. They slept in the main bedroom, pretending that it was Barry's. Tom often longed to tidy it, but it was a pointless task with Barry in the house, and the mess gave believability to the pretence.

He waited while Irene straightened her dress and made sure there was no-one else on the green. Tom heard his front door close, and the lights in the Rolfe house dimmed before Irene turned to him.

'Barry seems in good form,' she said, glancing to where her son was drawing the downstairs curtains.

'He is.' Tom thought it best to keep his answers succinct. Irene opening with a mention of Barry could mean that the conversation was heading towards their living arrangements.

'Been working muchly over at the farm,' she added, making small talk.

'That's true.' The short answer was not enough; she was waiting for him to say more. 'But then it's a busy time of the year.'

'Aye. It's done him good.'

A stilted pause unnerved Tom. It suggested she was trying to think of a way to broach an awkward subject.

'What has, Mistus Cole?'

She slapped his arm playfully with the back of her hand. 'You got a-stop calling me Mistus Cole,' she said, chuckling. 'I think of you as part of me family now.'

Tom's heart skipped a beat.

'What with you and Barry being homed a'gether. How you put up with the runagate in your first bedroom I got no clue, but living with you has done him good, and I be grateful he's your lodger.'

Tom's heart calmed. Matt Cole had still not let her in on the secret, and that was for the best. 'He's a good man to have around,' he said. 'Shares the chores, looks after the repairs, brings home the occasional bolter for the cooker…'

'You're doing a better job bringing him along than I ever did,' Irene said. Tom wasn't sure if she was joking, until she added, 'Should have set the two a you up sooner. Would have saved me a load a bobbery. Still, that ain't why I wanted a-talk with you.' She cleared her throat. 'I'm worried,' she admitted. 'And I don't want a-talk with Barry about it.'

'Worried about what?'

'I got a-trust you, Tom, but after what you done fur him that witchling time and what you done fur Susan's Daniel afore that, I knows I can. All the same, I want you a-promise me you keeps this between us.'

Another pause left no doubt it was Tom's turn to talk next. 'Of course,' he said. It wasn't exactly a promise, and it wasn't quite not, but he hoped it would satisfy her. He had no secrets from Barry, but then again, he didn't want to step on the wrong side of Irene.

'Got a-promise me,' she insisted, and Tom was trapped.

'Then, yes. I promise.' He wondered if crossing two fingers behind his back might absolve him. This was Saddling; the village of superstitions.

'Then make sure you keep that promise, and I only make you 'cos it won't do no good fur your mate Barry if he knows what I suspect.'

'I'm all ears.' Tom smiled, but in the weak light of the lamp and with the moon clouded, he doubted she could see him.

'That you ain't,' Irene said. 'You're all heart, and that'll be your undoing one day.' It was a compliment delivered as a warning. 'But never mind your failings, it's Matthew's what concerns me.'

'Mr Cole?' Tom would never call him Matthew or Matt. It would be like a pupil using a headmaster's Christian name. 'What's up?'

'Well...' She straightened her dress again and shifted the weight of her ample rump. 'Maybe there's nothing, but... Oh!' She slapped her leg and shook her head. 'I'm just a worrier. Pay me no never mind.'

She was standing when Tom stopped her. 'No, wait.' His interest was aroused. 'Honestly, what is it?'

His tone must have reassured her because she settled and, although she didn't look directly at Tom, she spoke plainly.

'One of the reasons Barry's been so much at the farm,' she began, 'is 'cos my Matthew's not been himself of late. His brother, Ben... The one as runs the farm with Matthew... but you knows that seeing as how you've worked there... well... Ben tells me that Matthew's not been pulling his weight as he did afore. Now, I reminded him that my husband holds a high position in Saddling, but Ben says it's only been of late that Matthew's passed his work to Barry. So, I say to him that it's harvest and we got a wedding coming up, and Matthew's more busy with council things, and why not? I mean, there's Barry at the farm with the strength of two horses... well, a pony prehaps, but still a strong lad, and there's you a-call on when needed an' all, so he shouldn't be worrying over me husband taking a step back to concentrate on the council matters.'

Tom waited, but she appeared to have finished. He unpicked her babbled conversation, looking for its meaning.

'That makes sense to me,' he said, once had had found the thread of what she was trying to say. 'But you think there's something else? To do with Mr Cole?'

'Barry says his fader's just getting old.' Irene still spoke to the darkness. 'But like me, he's only a few years into fifty, always been fit as a plough, strong as any other, and though he can blow up noisy and sudden as a cask a bad ale, he's never much of a one fur worry or being tetchy.'

Another pause, as if she was still trying to find the right words.

Tom waited, wondering where this was going. Cole had not been his usual commanding self at the meeting that evening, but he'd attributed it to the pressures of harvest, the upcoming festival, the wedding and the fact that the minister had been working long hours in the crypt on the estate books and accounts. The meeting had been a long time coming. Aaron Fetcher, the Taylor family and others had been wanting a row for weeks, and Cole had put it off for as long as possible. It had been bound to go badly.

A heavy hand on his knee made him turn to look at Irene and, as he did so, the moon, a few days away from full, appeared from behind the cloud and lit her worried face. Her hair, gradually changing from dark brown to grey at the sides, appeared silver.

'What d'you know of the eastling?' she asked, holding Tom with her dark eyes.

'I know it's the festival we have at harvest,' he said. 'Why?'

'What else d'you know?'

'Not much. It's got something to do with celebrating?'

She shook her head.

'Then no, I don't know what you're alluding to,' he said.

'You ain't to blame this on me age, Tom,' she said. 'But I want a-show you something. Fetch that lantern off Bill Taylor's house...' She indicated a hurricane lamp hanging in a nearby porch. 'Go on, he won't mind nor miss it. I'll wait here.'

More intrigued than ever, Tom did as he was instructed. He was still adjusting to many of the village ways and borrowing from a neighbour what you needed when they weren't using it was one of them. Borrowed items were always looked after and returned, but Tom was still uneasy when helping himself without permission. The moon threw enough light for him to see his way back to Irene who stood to face the church-house.

She said nothing but moved off towards the knoll as soon as Tom was beside her. He kept pace, assuming they were going to find Matt Cole in the crypt. There were no lights burning inside the building, which was not unusual for that time of night, and he was sure that Cole must have gone home by now. They climbed the mound, but Irene led him to the west end of the building and into the graveyard.

The moon carpeted the grass with a dull glow and washed the uneven headstones with a luminescence that glittered on the broken granite. The gravestones sloped downward to the ancient wall that bordered the near field, with shadows of darker night patchworking the uneven ground. He had always found it strange that the stones faced north and not the traditional east, but then Saddling was traditional only within its own way of life. Some customs matched those of the wider world, but many were the invention of a timeless village that worshipped only nature and its own lore.

Irene stopped at a particular stone. It, like many others, was lopsided but well-tended and, as he crouched to join her where she knelt, his lantern cast its light onto dying summer flowers.

'This sleeper-stone be one a me husband's ancestors.' She whispered as if she didn't want to disturb the body beneath. 'Long back, mind, but I still keeps the grave.'

Tom lit the headstone and read the inscription. 'Jane Rolfe, eighteen-ten to eighteen-thirty-one.'

'Aye,' Irene said, nodding sadly. 'You'll know I'm from the White family 'cos you know everything about the Saddling lines now.'

'Not everything,' Tom corrected. 'I'm still learning. But yes, I know you married into the Rolfes but I don't recognise this person. She died young.'

'Twenty-one as you can see.' Irene touched the stone tenderly. 'Always thought she and me had much in common though I don't know nothing of her, course. Don't know what *it* is, but lately, I been more drawn to young Jane here. Come here many nights when Matthew's working and Susan don't need me. It's good to have someone a-talk to.'

'I should tell Barry to visit you more often.' Tom tried to lighten her reflective mood.

'Barry's alright when you're looking for someone a-make you laugh,' Irene said, her attention remaining on the inscription. 'But I've not been feeling much like laughing these past days.'

'Understandable. You're worried about your husband.'

'I'm worried fur more than that, Tom.'

Irene stood, and Tom followed suit. He held the headstone for support as the blood rushed to his head. The stone was cold beneath his palm, but it was solid, and through it, he felt a connection between himself and the body in the grave.

He had experienced the feeling before. His body filled with a sudden flash of understanding when a Saddling custom, or part of its lore, preposterous in the outer world, unexpectedly made sense. The villagers kept the memories of their ancestors alive in their hearts and in the tended graves. During one of the many nights they had sat on the ancient wall listening for foxes and watching the stars, Dan told him that he kept his connection to his late Aunt Eliza by touching her grave. When he was unsure of a cure or hadn't understood the scrambled, blind-woman notes in her books, he had come to her sleeper-stone to hold it. It linked him to her, and her writings became easier to comprehend. Tom remembered how, on the night before his saddling, Dan had stood at his father's grave, holding it, connecting.

He had just experienced the same thing with a woman who had died one-hundred-and-eighty-four years previously. There was no way to explain how or why, but he accepted, that in Saddling, explanations were not always necessary. What the sudden jolt of closeness to a once-living person did tell him, however, was that he was one step nearer to losing his innate scepticism and becoming a Lore-accepting villager.

'I can see you sense it.' Irene had been studying him in the gloom.

'I sense… something, but I can't say what.'

'It be the eastling,' she said.

'The festival?' That didn't make sense.

'No, not that.' Irene stood opposite him, the gravestone between them. 'I heard you found Eliza Seeming's books.'

'Aye. Daniel and I discovered them when we dismantled her shack and pulled out the cupboards for last year's fire-pile. She'd kept the books inside the wall behind them.'

'That'd be Eliza.' Irene looked towards where Eliza's grave stood, whiter and newer than most.

Tom followed her gaze, but his fell on the smaller stone nearby. The one that commemorated the unknown man found drowned after the Saddling storm. He knew who it had been. His then one and only friend, Dylan, a young man whose death was still a mystery.

Irene turned her head and collected Tom's attention on the way.

'You won't find the eastling story in the Lore or the Teaching,' she said. 'But there's more behind the festival than just palming us farmer-wives off with special attention once a year. Look in them books a hers, Tom, as that's what you be good at. No doubt Blacklocks had thoughts on the legend, maybe you'll find other talk in his.'

'What would I be looking for?'

'I don't know. Some of that talk be beyond me, Tom,' Irene confessed with a sigh. 'Us women don't get a-talk on such things as well as the menfolk, not being so educated...'

'Irene,' he interrupted. 'You're one of the cleverest people I know. Who else could train Barry to cook?'

His attempt at humour fell as flat as the marshland that surrounded them, and Irene ignored it. 'But I was told, by me Grandmother-White, of a strange tale that had us girls afeared through the nights. Used to think it were just a way to frighten our bedtime gossiping into silence, but now... well, now her words come back a me, and I can't help but wonder if what she told us weren't more than that.'

Tom was trying hard to follow her train of thought, but she was not making things easy. 'What did she say?' he prompted.

'Stories. A tale from way back afore the time a writing, when villagers sat around one fire and the minister spoke a things past. There be a long tradition a that in Saddling, talking the stories down to the under-generations, and that be why the older ones ain't much written. The eastling were one such. Prehaps even our oldest.'

'Then what do you mean?' Tom asked, trying not to sound annoyed at her ambiguity. 'And what has it to do with your concern for Mr Cole?'

Irene came around the sleeper-stone and, to Tom's surprise, linked her arm through his. She turned him to face the marsh, a wide expanse of darkness that ended with the distant twinkling of lights in the world on the other side of the Saddling boundary, its ceiling a piebald pattern of stars and moonlit clouds.

'They say it comes from out there,' she said. 'As all our troubles do. They say it goes back a the time of the founding a the village, or just after. The great storm that were only stopped by the first saddling, and when it comes back, it blows bad things afore it.'

'Things? Sorry, Mistus... Irene, but I don't follow you.'

'That be 'cos I don't know much about the eastling,' she said. 'No-one does on account it only comes twice each one-hundred year and has done since it started. All we knows is that if it's coming, it comes at the harvest and it drives afore itself all manner of soul-trouble that can't be undone 'til the eastling's done what it came a-do. Be everything I know, Tom.'

'And what does it come to do?'

'Comes a-take someone's life, my Grandmother-White said. That's why nippers got a-be silent in their beds. That's why lads have a-work hard in the felds and madens stay chaste until they be wed. You can throw your bads in the fire-pile at Witchling Day all you want, your confessions won't make no never mind if the eastling be among us.'

'Take someone's life?'

'It ain't just love that can twist in your heart, Tom.' Irene's voice was distant. 'Its ghostly knife can tear living flesh. Its wandering, sad soul can find yourn and smother it with burden and weight it with fear. You can hide fur every day out of the century apart from two, 'cos on the nights the eastling comes a Saddling, there ain't no escape fur one of us, and none knows who that one'll be 'til they be slit.'

Whatever this unseen thing was, the strongest looker in Saddling had reported seeing it the previous night and had been too afraid to tell the council until twenty-four hours later.

'But what is it?'

'That be what you need a-find out, Tom Carey.'

She entwined her stubby fingers with his, and he couldn't work out if it was a sign of her growing affection for him, or because she was frightened.

'From Eliza's books?'

'From wherever you can. From her books, aye, but from out there an' all.' She lifted his hand towards the marsh. 'From the night, from the land, from the felds where we takes our living. The eastling be approaching us. I can see it in Matthew's state these past days, and in me own. I can see it in the way some in the village want him no longer minister. Them as have supported us these past years, them as stood with him against Blacklocks, them as thanked you after the witchling that time. All of them now be turning their backs and looking only to their own selves. The whole village be afeared, Tom, and I fear it's the eastling coming fur one a us.'

'I still don't understand what it is,' Tom insisted.

'None do, Tom. It's only been whispers and bedtime stories in our lifetime and that of me parents. But what I do know is, if it's coming, it's coming this Eastling Day, and one of us here in the village won't be here for Daniel and Jenny's wedding the day after.' She grasped the headstone. 'Just like Jane Rolfe were preparing fur her wedding one day and were found dead and heart-ripped the next.'

'You think she was…' Tom reminded himself not to judge. 'She was taken by the eastling at her wedding?' His mind was more inclined to imagine a murder by a jealous rival.

'Day afore. Prehaps it'll be in your books, her death, I mean. You can check that with your facts.'

'I will, thank you.'

'No, I got a-thank *you*, Tom. There ain't no-one else here would entertain an old woman's ramblings on such a worry.'

'You're not old,' Tom said, giving her hand a squeeze. 'You said so yourself.'

'I feels many a night older than me years right now,' Irene sighed. 'But me thoughts are made lighter knowing you're going a-cure this fear what's creeping on us and grinding me Matthew to straw dust.'

'Okay, Irene.' Tom held his lantern high, so that she could see his sincerity. 'I'll see what I can find out, so I can put your mind at rest. I expect Mr Cole is exhausted from the summer, the harvest, the council work. You're probably feeling that too. I will see what I can do.'

'You're a good man, Tom.' Irene let out a long breath, as if she had been holding it in fear that Tom wouldn't believe her. They began the walk through the graves towards the green.

Tom might have dismissed her words as another Saddling superstition had he not been inexplicably out of sorts himself. He couldn't place exactly when it had started, but over the past few days, he had become increasingly paranoid that villagers had discovered the truth about him and Barry. It was irrational. There was no need to think that way so perhaps there was something in the air. The autumn mists, the marsh gasses seeping into the atmosphere as the deeks evaporated over the summer and released vapours. Rational explanations were the most mollifying, but for once Tom found no comfort in them.

'I'll leave it with you, Tom,' Irene said as they descended to the flat grass outside the inn. 'I knows you'll do what's best fur the village, just as you do what's best for your Barry.'

She slid away from him and, without saying goodnight, made her weary way home. The clouds regrouped across the moon as Tom returned the lantern, and it wasn't until he was closing his front door that he realised what she had said.

'Your Barry?' he mused.

Perhaps she knew more than she was letting on.

Six

Sleep was evasive. Even with the window open, the air in the bedroom refused to move. It hung listless around him, a damp weight that shrouded him with a thin layer of sweat. Just when he thought sleep had lingered long enough and was ready to take him, a trickle of moisture ran from his hairline and across his face while another meandered down his back to disturb him. Tom tried long, deep breaths and strained to free his mind of the unconnected thoughts that leapt and danced there, bringing with them perplexing images of places and people he had never known, but concentrating on sleep made his sleeplessness and his frustration keener.

Beside him, Barry slept well. Unaffected by the humidity and exhausted from his day's labour, he had drifted off in seconds leaving Tom to envy his tranquillity. His gentle snoring, usually a comforting sound, wasn't helping.

Tom gave up and swung his legs from the bed. He pulled on a pair of summer trousers cut off above the knees and groped his way through the dark to the stairs. At the front door, he took a lantern from its hook and let himself out into the night.

He hoped the September air might be cooler outside but walking through it brought no respite from the clamminess, it only hugged him more closely. His lantern and the streetlamp were the only lights on the green as Saddling slept, or tried to. The houses stood with their windows open as if entreating a breeze to come to them, but the only thing that entered was moonlight when the clouds silently uncovered it in random rhythm.

The dewy grass beneath the soles of his feet was the only cool comfort as he skirted the inn walls to reach the near field. The brittle leaves of the marsh thistle gave beneath his tread, their stalks brushing his ankles, and his lamplight showed him a path between the emmet-casts and treddle-piles as he picked his way to the deek bridge.

His mind was no clearer out here. Irene's words and Cole's distraction vied for first place in his concerns. The eastling was coming. She didn't know what it was, but she was convinced its presence could be felt in Saddling again. Twice in every one-hundred years. A legend little written and easily forgotten. Part of the Saddling Lore manifesting infrequently enough as to fall easily from the living memory, but feared enough to warrant Tom's investigation. Something that could frighten the strongest men on the marsh, and something yet to be understood. It was a puzzle to be solved, but what was it?

He reached the bridge where the wood was warm on his skin and stopped when the clouds gave way to the moon. A weightless mist rose from the deek, the channel appearing out of the gloom as a steaming path between the dried reeds and dark fields. The warmer air above met the cooler air of the water leaving dew on the fields and lifting to hang like a fine veil a few feet above the land.

The clouds rested in patches leaving star-filled holes in the sky, as moonbeams picked out clusters of distant trees and the shapes of sleeping whitebacks. There were no fox cries, no owls swooped, and the deek-bank voles kept silent vigil within their burrows. The night waited around him, impossibly still and heavy with silence.

He breathed in the dank air, closing his eyes and imagining a curtain of black falling to cover his fragmented thoughts, but the broken images and restlessness shone through and troubled him. Cole was losing his grip. What effect would that have on the village? What could it do to Tom's standing? There were those who sought to fight against his presence, and others who sought the power to change the village way of life. Tom was a stranger, an out-marsher who had wandered into Saddling and claimed his ancestral right to live there. Not everyone had taken to him, and there were many who wanted to see him gone. They had forgotten how he had ended the saddling ritual and dismissed his banishing of the witchling as meddling. They were jealous of his education and ungrateful.

He knew the reasons for his unease but couldn't understand his increasing paranoia. He had lived peacefully in the village since the saddling and his place there was made more secure by his appointment as council clerk, so why should his worries take root now? The more contented his life became, the more he wanted to share his happiness, and the more he had to keep his true self hidden, for Barry's sake if not for his. Was it this frustration that caused the sleepless nights? Or was it the breathless weather?

Whatever it was, he found no answers in the autumn night.

A gentle creak behind him made him turn as a slender figure stepped onto the bridge.

'I saw your light from my window. You not sleeping neither?' Dan whispered as if he didn't want to disturb the rising mist.

'I took your potion, but it's having a tough job doing its work.'

Like Tom, Dan wore only summer shorts and carried a lantern that spilt buttery light onto the planks and shone beams beneath his chin. His pale body glowed, and his auburn hair was as black as the shadows beneath his cheekbones.

'Is everything okay?' Tom asked as Dan came to stand beside him. He seemed to glide, his feet swirling the grey-hang that crept across the bridge.

'Aye. Mostly worrying about the festival. Have I enough ale? Where will we find the tables? Got a few helping me, but all the same, you'd have thought Mr Cole would have given the job to someone else, seeing as how it's my wedding the next day.'

'I did suggest your mother saw to it, but…'

'It's a time for the men to let the women rest.' Dan sighed. 'No, I don't mind. Be honest, it takes my mind off being wed. I've left Jenny to make the arrangements for that if her ma will let her. Women aren't supposed to do much in the week before the festival, so why they chose the day after for the bloody thing gets away from me.'

'It'll be fine,' Tom said.

They rested side by side on the wooden rail, facing the west where the night was darker.

Tom nudged his friend. 'Your ma will be able to rest up once you have Jenny living at the inn.'

'The last thing my ma's good for is resting up,' Dan replied. 'But, aye. Life will be easier with the work shared. I can look after the hops better and brew more ale.' He nodded ahead. 'Mr Rolfe says I can take part of that field as a dowry. Says it'll be good land for junipers and blackthorn from the sloe. Might use it to see what herbs I can grow.'

'Sounds like you've got it planned.' Attempting to lift Dan's sullen mood with encouragement helped take Tom's mind off his own problems.

'Aye, I have.' Dan didn't sound convinced, but Tom said nothing. 'Why ain't you sleeping, Tom? You ain't got worries over Barry, have you?'

'No, not at all. It's just the weather. And the mosquitoes, the bugs that burn on the lantern glass, the moths flitting in your hair at night. You know.'

Dan took his hand for no other reason than they were friends, and they stepped back from the rail.

'Aye, I know, Tom,' he said. 'And I reckon I know you. There's something else troubling you, and you're not ready to talk to me. Which is fine,' he put in rapidly when Tom took a breath to speak. 'And you know where I am when you need me.'

'Adding psychiatry to your list of talents now?' Tom said through a smile.

'If by that you mean am I open to hear my best mate's worries, then I suppose I am.' He changed the subject. 'You want to walk more?'

'No. It'll be dawn soon, and I need to at least try and sleep. Walk back with me?'

'What's that?'

Dan let go of Tom's hand and pointed towards the east where Tom expected to see the first greying of the dawn. Instead, he saw a monochrome watercolour of mist-washed fields and twisted tree shadows. The view was dissected by the steaming deeks, the rising vapour uplit by the moon's reflection.

'It's the humidity,' Tom said.

The shimmering of the marsh-mist was the only movement until something shifted in the distance.

'No, there,' Dan said more urgently. 'Who is it? It ain't a looker.'

A single upright form glided from a copse two fields distant, moving stealthily to the north. At first, Tom thought it was cloud shadow, but it was too fleeting. It was too tall to be a sheep. Its path was too deliberate to be anything but human.

'Who else is out here at this time of night?' Dan's voice was hushed.

'We're not the only ones who can't sleep,' Tom reasoned. 'Whoever it is, he's heading towards Martin Rolfe's land. It's probably him.'

'Aye. Prehaps one of his all-workers searching for poachers.'

The black shadow of the man merged with that of a mother tree, and, as if woken by the movement, a cloud slid in front of the moon, draping darkness over the scene.

'You know who he makes me think of,' Dan said, his voice barely audible.

Tom knew. He was thinking the same thing. 'Very unlikely,' he whispered.

'We don't know what happened to him. Last anyone saw he was walking into the west, into the flooded fields and swollen dykes.'

Tom remembered the saddling storm and its aftermath as vividly as he remembered the last sight of William Blacklocks. The minister had paid for his treachery with the life of his only son. Exposed by Tom and Matt Cole as the duplicitous evil that he was, Blacklocks had banished himself to the marsh carrying his dead boy with him. He had not returned and, although the deeks had been cleared annually, no bodies or bones had been found.

'Like I say,' Tom said. 'Very unlikely. Come on.' He tugged Dan's hand and yawned. 'I think your potion's starting to work.'

The pair walked silently homewards, saying a quiet goodnight by the inn. They left behind a landscape made uneasy by the presence of the eastling-breath and the dark, thin figure that drifted through it until the haze absorbed him and nothing stalked the marsh but the night.

Seven

Barry had left for work by the time Tom woke the next day. Groggy, he came downstairs to find a note attached to the bread bin. 'Got a new loaf. Butter/cheese on cold shelf, jam in the bucket. Remember to see Rolfe for your books — beets in pantry for exchange. Love.' The note made him smile. The butter and cheese were always on the cold shelf and Barry was always trying to find new ways to keep the ants from the jam. Today's experiment involved standing the cloth-covered jar in water, and, so far, it was working. Tom had remembered that he was running short on exercise books and had already made a mental note to see Sam Rolfe to order more. Barry's message was unnecessary, but the domesticity of it appealed to him.

Smiling, he realised that the uneasy feelings of the previous night had been absorbed by the little sleep he had managed, and he prepared his breakfast in a positive mood.

Barry had been busy before work. Last night's washing up was done, the stove lit, and the kitchen tidied. Tom stretched as he marvelled at Barry's energy. He waited for the kettle to whistle before making tea and using the rest of the hot water in the sink. The stove cooled during the morning, and in the meantime, he opened the back door to let out the unnecessary heat.

Back at the table, he sat with his back to the door to catch any breeze that might wander in and sawed through Andrew White's notorious white loaf, resting once to sip his camomile tea. As he ate, he jotted a plan for the day.

'Put in fetcher-order,' he muttered as he wrote. 'See Cole.' He didn't write it, but he said, 'And say nothing about Irene's concerns,' to remind himself of his promise. He often spoke aloud to himself when he was alone, it helped him clarify his thoughts.

He paused as he breathed in a heady scent of herbs that wafted in from outside. He wasn't sure if it was sage or mint, and then he recognised the musky smell of patchouli. Students had worn it at his university, and he was instantly transported back to his former life. Not liking what he found there, he resumed his task.

'See the Payne brothers about the cellar,' was the final to-do of the day, and he put down the pencil. 'And after that…' He held a piece of bread between his teeth and wrestled it like a dog refusing to give up a stick, finally ripping off a corner with a grunt. 'After that, the eastling legend. Legend? Mystery?' He wrote, 'The history of the eastling.'

'You won't find nothing 'bout that in your old books.'

Tom swivelled on his chair, taken by surprise.

'Sorry, Tom, thought you'd heard me come up.' Jenny Rolfe stood at the back door, the morning sunlight turning her blonde hair white with its glare.

'You're okay,' Tom said. 'I was…' How had Dan put it? 'I was further away than Far Field. Come in.' He stood to welcome her, his boarding school manners coming automatically to the fore, and realised where the scent had originated. 'Nice perfume.'

'Special for me,' she preened. 'Dan mixed. Swore he'd make it for none else.'

'You'll be unique. Want some tea?'

'No, I be fine.'

'Have you cut your hair?'

'I have, Tom. Well, me ma has, ahead of the day. I'm planning joining-wreaths wi' love-in-the-mist, and ma said my hair will sit better if it's shorter.'

There was always something tomboyish about Jenny. She wasn't afraid to stand up for herself and lately she had been helping in the fields. With her hair trimmed, and wearing farm boots, trousers and a jerkin, she looked similar to her older brother. She hung in the doorway, leaning against the doorjamb, one foot on the step.

'That'll look great,' Tom said. 'Did you want something?'

'Aye. Fader asks if you got your list as Peter Fetcher's going out one day soon.'

'I have, and I'm going to drop it at the shop.'

'Then I be getting on. Uncle Michael's waiting on me at the dairy.'

'Before you go,' Tom said, taking a step towards her. 'What did you mean about my books?'

She dug her hands into her pockets and held him with a serious stare. 'You were muttering 'bout the eastling story, right?' Tom nodded. 'I wasn't meaning to listen, but I heard you. I'd heard 'bout this story when I were young and asked Blacklocks to tell me it once. I were only six or so, so can't recall exact, but he said it were one of our oldest and darkest stories and one that not even he had written on paper. Said I were not to mention it agin and he were… adamant on that.' She pulled a face to suggest the late minister had scared her in some way. 'I know you got his old books, and we all knows how long you spend wi' your nose in them, but if you're wanting to learn of the eastling, his books ain't the place to do it.'

'Does anyone else in the village talk about it?' Tom asked. 'You parents perhaps?'

Jenny thought for a moment. 'I only heard my aunt speak of it the once,' she said. 'Aunt Irene told it to get me and Jason asleep when we were playing up, staying over at the Cole house. No-one else has a mind to think on it. Never heard it mentioned 'til I came by your door just now.'

'It's something I'm thinking of looking into, that's all,' Tom said. 'Thanks for the message.'

She gave no indication that she was leaving. She looked at the ground, inspecting her boot.

'Was there something else?'

Jenny looked up, and her pale blue eyes were half-closed, her face distorted until she decided whether to ask a question or not. Her muscles relaxed, and she smiled. 'No, not a-worry,' she said. 'I reckon it'll pass.'

'What?'

'It's only…' She struggled to find the right words and then fixed Tom with her stare, this time displaying concern. 'Is everything alright wi' Dan?' she asked. 'I mean, has he said something to you 'bout our wedding?'

'Only that he's looking forward to it.' Tom had suspicions of his own, but he wasn't prepared to discuss them with Jenny. 'If you want my opinion, he's just nervous. Excited and nervous, you could call it. Men get like that.'

'Do they?' She shrugged. 'No-one tells us nothing 'bout what to expect. Still…' She pulled herself upright. 'Now I know, I won't worry.'

'Why do you ask?' Tom wondered if there was any truth behind Irene Cole's suggestion that unrest was a sign that the eastling was coming. If so, it was that unease that had filtered into Dan. 'What's he been doing?'

'Oh, he ain't been doing nothing in particular. Just quieter than normal, not spending so much time wi' me and me ma. Says it's his new job.' She laughed. 'Job! Mixing herbs and making up bottles of bad tasting stuff what don't do no good. He's turning into a right crank. But that'll end come Thursday.'

Her attitude and implication instantly annoyed Tom. 'He is teaching himself a skill,' he admonished, unable to stop himself sounding like a school teacher. 'As his wife-to-be, you should encourage him.'

'Aye, well, we'll see.' Her words were a threat. 'Me ma knows what she's doing wi' medicines, old Mother White's still got some sense left in her shrivelled brain, and we all know how a-treat a fever. Dan'll have spare time a-work on his ale brewing and keeping us in business when I'm running the inn. He won't have time for mixing potions.'

'I think he intends to do both,' Tom said, and added for emphasis, 'And there's no reason he shouldn't.'

She bristled. 'Excepting he'll be busy changing his bedroom into ours and his treating room into a nursery. Won't keep you, Tom.' She left.

Tom leant out of the door and called after her. 'Have you told him this?'

'Shouldn't need telling,' she yelled back as she walked away. 'You men's supposed a-know your duties.' She rounded the side of the house, heading towards the dairy beyond Robert Seeming's land, and was lost from sight.

Tom breathed deeply to calm his rising anger and noticed that the air was fresher than the previous night. Perhaps it was because she had left, taking her insinuations with her. She was proud to be marrying Dan, but prouder to announce how she planned to change him once they were a couple. Dan would hate that, and Tom doubted he knew what was coming.

He returned to the table to finish his tea, wondering if he should say something, and the creeping restlessness of late returned to his belly.

'She's just trying to assert herself,' he reasoned. 'Dan can cope with her.'

He left his cup and plate in the sink, collected a sack of beets to trade for books and left to find Jenny's father.

The new east window was a blaze of colour as Tom entered the church half an hour later, his business at the shop completed. The sun had fully risen, and until midday, its light would fire the colours of the window's four quadrants. He paused to admire what his inheritance had paid for. A depiction of the old saddling ritual in the top left section, the spring festival beside it. Beneath that, the burning of the bads at Witchling Day in summer, and the autumn equinox portrayed in as much detail as the stained glass allowed leading clockwise back to winter. It had been Dan's design, drawing being another of his talents, and Tom was warmed by pride each time he saw it.

The door to the crypt was open, and as he headed towards it, he thought through what he had to say to Minister Cole. He was nearing the stone stairs when a glint of sun on glass drew his attention, and he backtracked to look once again at the window.

He stepped up to the table-stone and around it into what, in a Christian church, would be called a chancel where he concentrated on the autumn quadrant of the window. He had seen it many times. Along with the council, he had approved the drawings, and he thought he knew it well, but today, something struck him as odd. He took a stool from beside the wall and placed it under the window. Stepping onto it, he was as close to the glass as he could be without a ladder, his head tipped back it an attempt to see more clearly.

The autumn glass was a mix of colour. Warm orange and yellows to depict the harvested fields, with wheatsheaves picked out subtly by black edges. The background showed the marsh running on into a distant horizon where a dark brown curve suggested the far hill. The foreground showed the villagers preparing for the eastling feast. The male figures were bent double carrying heavy bales on their backs while the women in white aprons, set tables on the green. Every one of the figures was standing, dancing or in some way moving, and the scene depicted hard work leading to just rewards. Dan had included one inactive figure. To the bottom left of the window with his back against the church wall was a young man with curly brown hair. The coloured fragments of the figure were no more than a quarter of an inch wide, and in his hand, so small it could only be seen close-to, he held an ale jug. A pipe hung from his mouth.

Dan had depicted Barry, on Eastling Day, and Tom smiled as he remembered how drunk Barry had been last year. The harvest had been abundant, there was plenty stored for the winter months, the whitebacks had bred well, and the whole village came to the festival to celebrate their success. He recalled the singing, how Barry had won the bale-toss and how Jack Mackett, also staggering, had confided that he'd arranged it because he didn't want to have to make the speech. He was, he said, fed up with being nice to everyone's mother when all they'd done was cook and have babies. Tom laughed aloud when he remembered his response to that and the way Jack had sloped off muttering amiably about baven boys. It was the Saddling word for what, in his old life, Tom heard as 'faggots.' There was nothing amiable in the use of the word unless it was used between two friends who knew each other well enough not to cause or take offence. It was Jack's way of thanking Tom for paying for his home to be rebuilt, and his way of letting Tom know he was considered a friend.

'Get down 'ere!' Matt Cole's voice boomed from below, bringing Tom to his senses.

He stepped from the stool and had just picked it up when the autumn quadrant caught his eye again. There was something else he'd not noticed before. He was too close to make it out and took a few steps back to the table-stone. At just the right distance he was able to see more clearly, and he gasped. Not far from where Barry was depicted, a body lay on the ground on its back. At first, he thought it was another drunk farmer, possibly Jack Mackett, but as he squinted, he could tell he was mistaken. Bringing the glass into focus, he saw that the body had a knife sticking out of its chest, and the white tunic it wore was streaked with blood. The mouth was open in a scream of agony, but he was unable to tell if it was a man or a woman. Now that he'd seen it, the rest of the scene took on a different and darker meaning. The villagers weren't celebrating the harvest, they were celebrating because they had not been the victim.

The victim of…?

'You there, Carey?'

'Coming!'

Whatever the meaning of the figure, he didn't have time for it now. He decided to talk to Dan later and, having replaced the stool, hurried to the crypt.

The church-house was cooler than other buildings, but the crypt air was dank and smelt of plaster dust and wet stone. Matt Cole was huddled over his desk, his collar damp with sweat, and he was in the process of wiping his brow with his sleeve.

'Wondered what you was doing,' Cole grumbled, flicking sweat from his cuff.

'I was looking at the window,' Tom said. 'Have you noticed…'

'It were a bloody cart a treddles,' Cole shouted and slammed his fists on the table, shocking Tom. 'The whole bloody lot a them's on no-one's side excepting their own. None want a-'ear our voice a reason, not wi' that furbrat Aaron Fetcher whining 'bout how we should 'ave younger fetchers. 'E be only nineteen and yet screeching on me one side while them old'uns be croaking on the other. Whole village be gone mad, ask me. And what 'bout this imposition?'

He took a breath and veins stood out on his round face like tree roots.

'You couldn't stop them,' Tom said. It was never easy to deal with Matt Cole when he was angry. He was six feet tall, as wide as a door and could crumple a pewter tankard in each fist. 'It's in the Teaching.'

'I know what it's in, Carey,' Cole bellowed. 'What I want a-know is how we get rid of it.' He waved his hand towards the bookshelves. 'Been through every single one a them things. No bloody good. What you come up wi'?'

'Come up with?'

Cole gripped the table, his shoulders hunched, and glared at Tom through menacing eyes. 'You agreed last night. You was going a-go through your books and find a way a-stop them voting.'

Tom hadn't forgotten, but it wasn't safe to admit that he hadn't yet begun. 'I have made a start,' he lied. 'It's going to take time, but we have a few days.'

Cole growled.

'Don't worry, Minister. I'll find something.'

'Aye, well you best had. There ain't no way I'm leaving this village in the 'ands a Aaron Fetcher, bloody runt-squeak, and that Taylor ain't coming nowhere near our ancient ways, nor being left with the Lore in his charge.'

Grumbling, but calming, Cole sat, clearing his throat as he rearranged his ledgers.

'What do you mean, "leaving this village"?' Tom drew a chair away from the desk and lowered himself into it, studying Cole's face.

'I mean I ain't passing on my duties.' Cole's voice was quietly apologetic.

'And I'm right behind you on that.' Tom wanted to add that it was the villagers' democratic right to call an imposition, but he didn't want to inflame Cole's wrath. He hoped the conversation was over. 'So, I've been to see Sam Rolfe…'

'Don't mention that family's name right now, nipper,' Cole interrupted.

Calling Tom a nipper was sign that Cole was mellowing.

'Why's that?'

'It's all I bloody been getting from that family. Wedding stuff, I mean. Irene's niece 'as got a-'ave this and we must bring in some a that. Only the costing stuff, you understand.' He slipped into a higher register, imitating his wife. 'You're the minister, what you says goes and our Rebecca's heard 'bout wine that Peter Fetcher can pick up in Romney, so you get us plenty a that. And I might have one of them dresses with the fancy lace that Mother Seeming used to make, but can't now her fingers be twisted. And you've got a-wear your robes… I'm living in a chicken coop with no cock.'

Tom was laughing but stopped when Cole switched back to his own voice.

'Aye,' he said. 'I'd laugh if it weren't coddling me brain. Sooner that boy's trapped, the sooner they'll all shut their five-bars and give me quiet. I've 'ad enough of the Rolfe in-lores fur the now, so...' He took a breath. 'Start agin.'

Tom poured himself a glass of water from the pottery jug and chose his words carefully. 'I've been to the shop and placed the order.'

'When's Peter fetching in?'

'It was supposed to be today or tomorrow,' Tom explained. 'But Sam Ro... Sam just told me Peter's taken ill and Drew Fetcher's still harvesting, so it'll have to be after the festival. Mistus Cole will have to miss out on her lace.'

'Well, that's a saving, though I'll never 'ear the finish of it. What's up wi' Peter?'

'Nothing serious, I was told. Just not feeling up to it.'

Cole made a noise in his throat; unimpressed acceptance.

'I asked him to bring in new writing books. It's not urgent but it does remind me that we're coming back to school time and we don't have anyone to teach the children.'

'What's Annie Tidy been and done? Why ain't she going a-do it agin?'

'The boys complained that all she taught was sewing, cooking, the names of flowers...'

'Aye, sounds likely. What of...' Cole clicked his fingers, trying to remember.

'Marty Farrow?' Tom prompted.

'Was it? Aye. Wasn't 'e appointed?'

Tom was concerned. Cole knew this information, they had discussed it only a few days ago. He didn't let his apprehension show, however, it would have worsened the man's mood to be told he was becoming forgetful.

'Marty Farrow managed one season,' Tom said. 'But the girls complained that he only taught sheep slaughtering. No-one was learning how to read or write, and Farrow himself resigned because the children were calling him names.'

'Names?'

'Aye, well...' Tom wondered how to say this. 'His name is Marty Farrow and kids have a way with spoonerisms.'

Cole looked at him blankly. 'Don't know what you be blaaring 'bout,' he said. 'But it makes no never mind. Answer's simple. We got the perfect man right 'ere. Knows the Teaching, knows 'bout working the land, reading, writing, history.'

'You mean Daniel Vye?' It was an obvious choice, except Dan wouldn't agree to it. He had his own plans for his future — assuming Jenny allowed them. 'He's teaching himself herbaling right now,' Tom said. 'We need a healer in the village. Widow White's not growing any younger, and she makes the kids scream when she treats them, but Dan's studying everything Eliza…'

Cole raised his hand for silence.

'I were meaning you, Carey.' For a moment, the minister sounded cheerful.

'Me?'

'Aye, and why not? But…' The hand was raised again as Tom began to protest. 'But it ain't a talk fur now. You come a-tell me the next fetching order's been placed, so that be done. That's all I need from you a'day.'

'Oh.' That was Tom's cue to leave, but the conversation had ended too abruptly. He had things he wanted to discuss, the east window being one of them, but that wasn't going to be happening. 'Shall we talk tomorrow?' he asked as he rose.

'Might.' Cole had his head over a ledger and paid little attention. 'You go and get me that answer. We're not letting them 'ave a bloody vote. It'd kill the village.'

Matt Cole watched from under his eyebrows until Tom had left the crypt.

He shouldn't shout at the lad, but it was Cole's way of venting frustration. Carey was a good man, and he felt regret at dismissing him so suddenly, but the pain had grown in his chest, and he needed to be alone. He drank water and took deep breaths until the ache subsided.

Each time he saw Tom, he took the opportunity to look deeply into his brown eyes and contemplate their laughter wrinkles. He studied the dark blond stubble on his chin, his handsome face tanned by field work. He tried to see beyond that and into his mind, wondering what was in there. What knowledge and experiences Tom had, what had made him a man who could throw himself into danger for the sake of a friend one minute and then ask, sincerely and softly, for Cole's understanding the next. Where had that courage come from?

He didn't know, but he knew where it went. Two years ago, Tom had saved Cole from madness, but a sliver of witchling evil had taken root inside. He was sure it was that causing the pain that flared in the centre of his chest.

Not only had the village been saved that day, but so had his only son. It wasn't an easy rescue to accept, but Cole tried every day he saw the two of them together. If Tom had not stayed in Saddling, Barry would have gone with him, leaving Cole and his mistus childless. He hadn't reached the point where he considered Tom part of his family, certainly not a second son, but as the months passed, so his confusion softened towards understanding. He was still unable to accept that Barry could be in love with another man, but he tried for the boy's sake. The dichotomy between what he had been taught was out-marsh and what he knew to be right for his boy, raised questions and he could find no answers. Meanwhile, the stress of trying to understand bore heavily on his health.

He was happy about one thing. Carey would make an excellent schoolteacher, and he intended to make that happen once Eastling Day had passed. He closed his ledger and stood to fetch another from the shelves.

The pain came without warning, rising through his gullet and burning his ribcage from beneath. Pressure was the only thing that relieved it, and he lay flat on his stomach across the desk. The pain increased, forcing him to screw up his eyes where he saw dancing, white flashes. He gripped the desk, groaning until the heat within began to cool and his tense breathing calmed.

He coughed and spat blood.

Eight

As they harvested the fields, the farmers ploughed the earth, fertilising it with livestock silage stored through the summer. The smell drifted across the village from any direction the breeze chose and found a home in Tom's nostrils as he left the church-house and took the few steps home. At first, the smell had been overpowering, it made him nauseous, and he wondered how anyone could put up with the mix of manure and deek-debris, churned and thrown from the back of a cart by the all-workers. Barry came home from the fields reeking of it, and no amount of washing would rid his clothes of the stench. This year was Tom's third harvest, and he now welcomed the smell. It meant that the work was nearly done, not that farm work was ever finished, but Barry would soon have more time at home.

The thought put a spring in his step as he made his way upstairs and even remembering that he'd forgotten to see the Payne brothers to discuss the cellar didn't dampen his mood. He had jobs to do too and, back in his study, he was finally able to move onto the tasks which interested him more than ordering village supplies and dealing with Matt Cole in a rough mood.

He sat at his desk with the window open before him and arranged the books he thought he would need; the Book of Lore, the Teaching and the Saddling Diary. He only had two things to do, but neither task was easy. If there was a legal way to head off the dissenters, the Teaching should advise on it, but it was a heavy book and not indexed. It had grown organically over time and one of his future tasks, if he could bring himself to do it, was to transcribe it in logical order. Reading through it again was a job that could take days. He needed someone who knew the Teaching better than he did because, in there, would lie the answer to Cole's problem.

He placed it to one side and looked out of the window. Dan stood opposite in his treating room, and Tom waved. He received a courteous nod in reply before Dan turned away.

'Must have a patient,' Tom reasoned and reached for his notepad where he made a note to see the Payne brothers.

He had a plan for the recently discovered cellar. It was an airless, damp room with no windows and only the one entrance beneath the staircase, but it had potential. It was cool, and he intended to have it floored and shelved to use for storage. He and Barry might claim part of the space, but the rest would be available to Sam Rolfe for excess shop supplies as long as they could find a way to light it.

He had toyed with the idea of having Nate Rolfe repair the generator he'd once installed at the inn, but Barry vetoed that because of the noise, the cost of fuel and the fact that Saddling had lived nearly nine-hundred years without electricity.

'Besides,' Barry said. 'Dan only 'ad it working fur a few days, none liked the music from the machine it ran, and 'e were spending most 'is time out the back kicking the bloody thing into life.'

Barry was right of course. The introduction of electricity to the inn in twenty-thirteen had not been a success, it had been short-lived but gave the younger villagers a taste of what was possible. No-one had approved its removal, but no-one was sorry to see it go, apart from Aaron Fetcher.

The memory struck a chord with Tom. Once Aaron had seen and heard the jukebox, his traditional village attitude towards the outside world had changed. When, around the same time, he learned that Matt Cole, Barry and Tom had been beyond the Saddling boundary, it worsened. Cole soon realised there was no need to involve the village more closely with those around it, and no-one other than the fetchers had been beyond the border since.

It was too late. Aaron Fetcher's interest had been aroused to the point that he now wanted Saddling open to the world without understanding what that would mean. Worse, he had turned his imagined utopia into facts that were lies and infested the younger villagers with his own misguided ideals.

Perhaps Aaron had a point, and it was time for Saddling to open itself to the wider world. When Tom first came to Saddling he had been shocked that there were no phones, the younger generations had nothing to do and no internet, and the older had no access to modern medicine. Now, he imagined Saddling with those things and found the image appalling.

He regarded the Book of Lore by which the village lived, another weighty work that took days to read.

'No,' he said. 'These things can wait.' Instead, he reached into the bottom drawer of the desk and lifted out Eliza Seeming's pile of papers and journals.

The official Saddling books, ledgers and their copies were always written in hardback, leather-bound tomes, one of the few things that Saddling imported from beyond its borders. Eliza had kept a few such volumes, but her books were mainly the ones used in the schoolhouse, cheap paper, produced en masse somewhere else and bought by the fetchers in exchange for Saddling crops. Whereas the council books were written in imported ink, Eliza's had been written in a concoction of her own making, a mix of resins, dyes and water. What was more startling about her loose papers, pages and jottings, however, was that they were written at all. Eliza had been blinded on the day of her brother-in-lore's saddling. She had lived another twenty years before her death, and during that time, she had transferred her skills and knowledge to paper, sometimes in a scrawl that was hard to read, but at other times in a perfect hand which, Dan had assured him, was her own writing. On one side of the green Dan was using her recipes for his healing, and on the other, Tom was using her history.

The thought that Eliza was in some way still living brought a sense of security as he opened the first page and began to read.

An hour passed before he found the first mention of anything strange. The date caught his eye, September 23rd, Eastling Day. It wasn't, as he had expected, written in Eliza's hand, but the page had been torn from somewhere else, folded and glued into the book in a way that it could be unfolded to its full size. It had come, it appeared, from one of the grander village archives but the paper was brittle with age. He handled it carefully as he laid it flat and studied the account.

A telling of the haunting of Derville Blacklocks in the village of Saddling
Sunday, September 23rd, 1862

Written by Edward Blacklocks (minister)

The account shall be written here fair and true according to the Saddling Teaching.

The following narrative is a reflection of that which was reported to me at the meeting of the Council two days following the climax of the strange events which took place on Sunday, 23rd September in the year of the Lore, 1862:

James Collins

The first suspicion of an unusual event was raised by the deeker, James Payne. He had, for some time, been at work on the east sewer bordering the Farrow land and during that time, reported to the village his sighting of a low mist beyond our reach. Such a sight was not unusual in autumn, but what disturbed him about this particular mist was the fact that it had been there from dawn until dusk for several days, each day appearing closer to the village.

On Sunday last, towards boblight, Payne was engaged in clearing the mud-settle and dead reeds to better flow the sewer seawards. He was assisted by the boy, Sam Cole, and James Payne's cousin by marriage, Derville Blacklocks, my second cousin who had reached the age of twenty. The deek level was low following the harsh summer, and James and his men were at a height below the ridge of the deek having waded to their middles and, in the case of Sam Cole, to his neck.

Having scraped and cleared a portion of waste to the western side, Payne took the boy Cole with him to climb the bank and drag the clearance into the Farrow pasture to use as fertilizer. Derville was left to begin on the next section, a task he set upon with his usual healthy fervour.

It was while dragging the clearings that Payne noticed a change in the eastern landscape. Above the hill, he said, a cloud had risen and was in the motion of teaming down and rolling onto the already misty marshland. It drew his attention because the cloud was moving over the ground and yet the sky above was perfectly clear.

'It were as the world was turned with its upside down,' he reported. 'I never knew such a thing afore, looking down on the sky.'

The cloud, he soon realised, was in fact fog, but a thicker, faster-approaching fog than he had seen at any time in his fifty-five years. Before long, it was at the Saddling markers. His boy had stopped his work and was gaping in awe to the west from which direction the fog was also approaching. As it closed in, so it thinned until it became nothing more than a mist. On the east bank of the sewer, it gathered and piled until it became a wall several feet high.

'I can't say what it were that made me shout a'wards Master Blacklocks still in the deek, but it were like the grey-hang knew what it were about, and I was afeared fur the safety of me man.'

Payne called to Derville but received no reply. The Cole boy was by now whimpering and shaking in his backstays. (His own telling describes him

The Eastling

as certain that evil was coming his way even though he had no reason to fear a simple mist. He was so afeared he made wetting on his legs.) Payne approached the deek to call at a closer distance and, as he advanced on the bank, so the mist progressed toward the other side.

'I swear this a-be true, Sirs. It were like it were mimicking me. One pace fur me, one pace fur it. I were looking straight into it, but course there were nothing there but grey and white... Until I did see something. A shape were growing darker, and the darker it went, the more shape it 'ad until — and I swear on the Lore that this be true, Sirs — until it took the figure of a man, a youth more like.

'Now at this breath in the telling, I were thinking that it were Derville coming a'wards me out a the mist, see, but when I looked into the deek, there 'e were, still up to his waist, waders flooded and the mud-settle 'olding 'im rooted. The poor wretch 'ad seen this youth out the mist and, afearing as we all were, tried to get out a there, but 'e were too firm sucked in.

'As fur the next minute (or maybe it were only seconds), it were like we was all in that grey-hang. There were no Saddling land, there were no marsh, no sun nor sky, only the deek and then only the part where Derville stood and cried, and that ghost of evil were floating down the far bank and coming at its victim, fur I knew that's what Derville were a-be. It were so quick. Somehow Derville were flattened on the deek surface but with his legs held by the mud and then 'is 'ands were caught by the reeds. It were like they reached fur 'im and wrapped 'round 'is wrists.

'Then I saw a knife. Short handle, curving blade like a slitting-knife. Well, maybe that's what it were and it were in the grip of that apparition. It was 'eld in the air one blink and then slashing poor Derville's throat the next and straight through. It was same as we witness at the saddling, same as we'll be a-seeing when the Saddling Festival come round agin.

'And it were at that time I were afeared for the boy's safety, and so made escape wi' 'im tucked under me arm. We'd not gone but ten fast paces when the grey-hang were gone. I mean, just not there, like it 'ad never been there. Thing was, Derville were still as dead as a sleeper, and there were no sign of that murderous ghost, nor its very real knife neither.'

Payne described the apparition as being of medium height and slimly built. A boy of saddling age, he said, in his fourteenth or fifteenth year.

'Though it be 'ard a-tell exact.' He wanted to make that clear. 'I weren't able to make out no features, I just 'ad this feeling that it were a lad. Not one I knew but 'e was black of 'air, and it were long down his front from under his cowl. The thing were wearing an 'ooded tunic, wet, and tied with rope over breeches.'

The Council was impressed at Payne's memory, myself rather sceptically at first because he saw these things at dusk, but he explained that the vision had stained his eyes. He was unable to forget it and was thus able to recall details.

The Cole boy was of little help in his narrative and added nothing apart from to say how frightened he had been. He spoke of a sense of knowing something evil was approaching but, keen that we did not consider the boy to be weak of mind, his mother took great pains to inform us that the lad had not been able to sleep well of late.

The meeting was adjourned for further discussion of the facts, and the funeral of my second cousin, Derville Blacklocks agreed for tomorrow morning.

Tom sat back, remembering the shadowy figure he had seen during the night, a fleeting movement in the humidity witnessed through sleeplessness and by shifting moonlight. The account of the death of Derville Blacklocks painted a sharper picture, but it made no mention of the eastling itself, only something that had happened on what was now the festival day. It could have been a murder committed under the mask of a fog and witnessed by a superstitious man and a younger boy. Or it could have been Payne himself who murdered Blacklocks, threatened the Cole lad and invented the story to cover his tracks.

There was no evidence there, and Tom folded the article back into place before turning the page. On it was written a verse, and the word eastling leapt out at him from the first line.

'Now we're getting somewhere,' he muttered.

Pulling his notepad closer, he read the untitled poem.

Each hundred year that passes here the eastling comes but two,
At harvest tide, no place to hide as eastling passes through.
Stalking time to reap the vine of those who took his life,
Two-eight-hundred seasons come, and fourteen know the knife.
Lament the fact, unless you act, he'll start a second breath.
In chances one there be a son to end his way of death.

The Eastling

None shall know the way to go 'till one man's peace be made,
Go he will when sons shall kill with ancient rock-bound blade.

He pushed his pad away and cracked his knuckles as he stretched. His belly rumbled, and he wondered what the time might be. Dan was at his window again and, having caught Tom's eye, waved him over. Tom stood and, leaning across the desk, shouted, 'What?'

Dan opened his window. 'Want lunch?'

'Is your ma cooking?'

'No, you're safe. I done it.'

Tom laughed and held up a thumb. A pint and a pie at the inn would take his mind of Eliza's old stories. He placed a bookmark in the journal and reread the poem.

'"Each hundred year that passes here the eastling comes but two."' As he read aloud, the sound of his voice brought back the conversation with Irene. '"You can hide all you want fur every day out of the century apart from two,"' she had said. He read the second line. '"At harvest tide no place to hide as eastling passes through."'

Twice every one-hundred years the eastling returns to Saddling at harvest time.

'Which is why we call it the Eastling Festival,' he reasoned and closed the book.

He left the house and was crossing the green when the words of the poem began to seep into his mind. The more he tried to remember it, the more intrigued he became, but his official matter had to be seen to, and more urgently. There was too much to do, and he needed help.

Barry sat on a bale to eat his lunch. His all-workers sat apart sharing a bottle of ale, but Jason Rolfe joined him bringing water, and was welcomed.

'What's that in your tommy?' Jason asked, pointing to Barry's open tin box.

'What Tom calls a sandwich,' Barry said, holding up two stiff pieces of White's brown bread with cheese and salad squashed between them.

'It's just bread and cheese,' Jason sneered. 'Why give it a fancy name?'

'Tom's got many fancy words fur things.' Barry held the sandwich in front of his face and winked at Jason. 'Wish me luck.'

'White's loaf ain't that bad, not now the flour's fresher.' Jason bit into an apple, and the two ate in silence until he asked, 'What's it like, living with Tom?'

'Be like living with any a your mates,' Barry replied. 'Why you asking?'

This wasn't the first time Jason had probed into his private life, and Barry was wary of giving too much away.

'Just got to wondering,' the younger man said. 'You're good mates wi' Tom, ain't you.'

'Aye. We be as close as markers. That be all.' He hated to lie, but his father had advised him not to talk about Tom as anything but a mate, and his father was always right.

'Tom and Dan be close an' all.'

'Aye. And your point is?'

'Just asking.'

Barry put his sandwich back in his box and set it aside. 'What's on your mind, mate?' He sighed as he turned to Jason. 'What d'you really want a-ask?'

Jason blushed and swept his fringe from his forehead, looking into the distance nervously.

'Look, Jason,' Barry said. 'You ask what you want, and I'll not be telling no-one your asks. But I might not tell you the answer likewise.'

'It's… No, I shouldn't pry.'

'We 'ave separate bedrooms, if that's where you be going.'

Jason twisted to him, shocked. 'No, I weren't going a-suggest that, honest, Barry.' He blushed further. 'I were going a-ask you 'bout Daniel.'

Barry relaxed. 'What 'bout 'im?'

'He's good wi' ointments.' Jason showed Barry his hands. 'Blisters have most gone overnight and not come back a'day.'

'True that.' Barry held up his work-worn palms, also healing after using Dan's treatment. 'But your ask ain't 'bout Dan's medicine, right?'

'Aye, sorry.' Jason took a deep breath. 'I only ask this 'cos he'll soon be wed a me sister,' he explained. 'But, d'you think it's what he wants?'

'What d'you mean, is it what 'e wants? You mean do 'e want your ma fussing round the inn all hours, plotting wi' Mistus Vye 'bout flowers and ale, tables and dresses? No, I doubt Dan wants that at all. But if you means, does 'e want a-marry Jenny, then aye, far as I know 'e does. What's more, I'll be there aside 'im as me fader takes the ceremony. I be Dan's marker ain't I?

So, if 'e's got any troubles 'e'll be a-coming a me wi' them, and 'e ain't done that yet. Not 'ad no say-so from 'im on the matter so, aye, 'e's marrying the girl 'e loves.'

Barry wondered why he repeated himself. It was as if the more he said that Dan was happy, the less he believed it and the more he had to convince himself.

It looked like Jason wasn't convinced either. 'I were worried fur him, nothing more,' he said. 'But I'm thanking you fur your honesty.'

'That's all I ever been,' Barry said. 'Well, 'part from that time in the school house when Blacklocks were blaaring on 'bout bads and fire-piles and asked me what I'd done wrong that week. Told 'im nothing, and I would a got away wi' that if Dan 'adn't started laughing.'

'I remember.' Jason smiled. 'You two was always sat the row in front of me.'

'Aye, and you was girl-soft on 'im then just as you be now.'

'I ain't girl-soft on no-one!' Jason raised his voice and stood, drawing the attention of the all-workers.

'You could-a fooled me,' one of the men shouted back as the others laughed.

'Keep your calm, Jason,' Barry tutted. 'Just saying.'

'Aye, well, don't. I be worried fur Daniel not in love wi' 'im. I'll let you get back a your tommy.'

He skulked off, head down, throwing a wary glance at the workers across the yard.

Barry shrugged and returned to his sandwich. He knew perfectly well what Jason was suffering, he'd suffered that way himself. He wouldn't be surprised to learn that every person in their generation had felt the same way about Dan, boys and girls alike, but that was their matter. Barry was settled now, but the pain of being girl-soft on Dan was clearly eating away at Jason. Barry could ease his pain by telling him he was not alone, but that might cause troubles for everyone involved.

'All be a mess a treddles,' he mumbled and gathered himself to have another go at Andrew White's bread.

Nine

The Crow and Whiteback was empty save for Dan waiting for Tom at their table near the bar. At that time of day during harvest, most of the villagers were out in the fields, the men threshing and the children cording hay into small ricks to deliver to their homes and neighbours for their chickens and pigs. The work had to be finished by the night before the Eastling Festival, or else they risked bringing bad luck to next year's harvest.

'You been busy?' Tom asked as he slid into a chair and took the ale Dan offered.

'Not so much. Didn't sleep until a good hour after I saw you. Ma woke me early to start on the harvest lunch.' He thumbed towards a plate and four round pies, still warm. 'Bloody Becki Tidy came back a second day for her eyes, and Jason Rolfe was in to get more ointment for his blisters. What you grinning at?'

Tom was smiling in admiration.

'You and your heart. You're just so good to everyone, no wonder you're attracting a following.'

'Give over, I ain't, but someone has to tend them as is unwell. Not that Becki's hay fever or Jason's blisters is exactly dragging them towards death, but everyone's as important as everyone else, so I do what I can.' Dan sipped his beer.

'You're too modest.'

'Doubt that. So, what you been working on?'

'Actually, there's a favour I wanted to ask you.' Having just been told how hard Dan was working it seemed wrong to ask, but time was limited.

'Anything you want, mate,' Dan said.

Tom bit into a pie. 'Hey, these are good,' he said. 'What's in them?'

'What do you want me to do, Tom?' Dan grinned. 'They're treddles, and you know it.'

'No, honestly. You've used different herbs?'

'Just followed one of Eliza's recipes,' Dan said. 'What favour?'

Tom reluctantly set aside the pie. 'Okay,' he said. 'Do you have time to read the Teaching for me?'

Dan's face was a picture. His square jaw dropped, and his blue-grey eyes widened. 'You having a joke on me, Tom Carey?' he said, dumbfounded. 'Why do you want me to do that?'

'You won't have to read all of it,' Tom explained. 'I need an answer to a question, and you're more likely than me to know where in the book to find it.'

'Aye, that makes sense. What's the question?' Dan drank more beer, looking at Tom over the rim and raising his eyebrows.

'It's to do with this people's imposition.'

'Not a lot you can do about that.'

'Mr Cole seems to think there is. He's told me to find a way out of it, and I reckoned there would be something in the Teaching, but I can't remember everything that's in it.'

'Well, Matt Cole should, seeing as how he's minister an' all.'

'True, but he's got other things on his mind.'

Strangely, Dan didn't query that. 'I think I'd know where to look,' he said. 'What are you hoping it says?'

'What needs to happen for a minister to dismiss a people's imposition. It's not that I... It's not that the council doesn't want to hear what the complainers have to say, they have done. You've been there yourself when the Fetchers and Taylors, and the others, have started up with their grievances. The council's dealing with those issues, but the... rebels are still not happy. Aaron forced the imposition and Cole had to accept it, but he's convinced the village will suffer long-term if either side gets their way.'

Dan nodded. 'Aye, and he's right. What Saddling has always had and still needs is someone to lead us by the Lore and someone to administer the Teaching. It's worked for over seven-hundred years as it is, and nothing's ever changed, apart from you ending the saddling ritual.'

'That's it though, isn't it?' Tom said, just about to eat. 'It's because I interfered with — excuse me saying this — that barbaric custom that Aaron Fetcher thinks anyone can run the village and change things. That's change for the sake of it in his case.'

'But the others are against him,' Dan pointed out. 'Maybe they'll win through. Be better than Fetcher being voted minister. He's too young.'

'And there again it's thanks to me,' Tom said. 'To the old'uns, I'm a meddling out-marsher who's gone and altered Saddling, therefore I shouldn't be village clerk, and I probably shouldn't even be living here. The council and the village are stuck in the middle of it, and either way you look at it, I'm to blame.' He threw the second half of the pie into his mouth and chewed hard to stop himself ranting.

Dan turned his tankard between his hands. 'Of course I'll look through the Teaching, Tom,' he said. 'I reckon I can remember the places where the council ways are written. Might have to ask you for help on the older parts where the spelling gets weird. I'll start this afternoon.'

Tom nodded and held up a finger, his mouth still full. The crisp pastry had turned to mush, smothering the flavour of the carrot and turnip.

Dan waited patiently until Tom swallowed, gasped and took a mouthful of ale.

'Very nice,' he said, banging his chest and swallowing a burp. 'And thanks. I've got the copies, you can use one of them. Meanwhile, what do you know about the eastling story?'

They sat for half an hour, a minute of which was filled by Dan admitting he knew nothing except he'd been told the ghost story when he was a child as a way of keeping him in bed.

The rest of the time was filled with amiable chatter concerning the forthcoming wedding and the festival. It wasn't until Tom stood to return to work that Dan remembered something else.

'Eliza,' he said, collecting the tankards. 'Aunt Eliza did it different.'

'What do you mean? Did what?'

'I remember my ma at the end of my bed telling me that the eastling made off with little boys who did bad things to their friends, told on them, went behind their backs. And boys who strayed from their rooms at night and wandered the fields, which is what I liked to do. By the time she started telling me how the thing worked its evil, I was under the cover and trembling. But Aunt Eliza used to sing it.'

'Sing...?'

'The story, aye. She'd not come in the village after...' He ran one of his long fingers across his eyes. 'But I'd go to her at harvest. Ma was always busy making for the festival, so she left me with Eliza first thing most days. Mistus Cole collected me at night, but in the afternoon, Eliza made me sleep a while. She sang to me as she put me on her straw. It were a song about eastling, or harvest, or... maybe not a song.' He gazed into the near distance, his brow furrowed. 'It were strange words, and she used to explain it to me.' He shook his head, unable to remember. 'I was only a nipper.'

The Eastling

Tom took the tankards from him and put them on the bar. 'Dan,' he said. 'Have you got a minute? I want you to look at something.'

'So, the eastling is a ghost?' Tom asked as they crossed the green.

'I suppose. It's not known exactly what it is, but the children's story calls it a ghost.'

'And it drives evil things before it.'

'There are several versions of the story,' Dan said. 'It's an old one that's not been written, so it's likely changed over time. It's one of our oldest spoketales.'

The word was apt. Tom let them into the house and ushered Dan upstairs. 'Go to my study,' he said. 'I'll bring us some ale.'

When he brought a jug and two glasses a few minutes later, Dan was standing in the middle of the room turning a slow circle, admiring the walls.

'Your room looks like mine,' he said. 'Except mine's drawings and yours is… Is it all of us?'

'Not everyone.' Tom put the glasses on the desk. He filled them and placed the jug on a side table safely away from his research. 'It's only the principal family lines. I did start trying to map the whole village, but there's not enough space. I've identified the oldest Saddling families and started from now, working back. You're over there.' He pointed to the wall beside the desk, and Dan studied it closely.

'There's your entry, January 1st, nineteen-ninety, Daniel Vye.'

'I know my name, Tom.'

'Your mum and dad and grandmother. Oh, sorry.'

Dan's grandmother had died four months previously. She had suffered a stroke while witnessing her son's saddling twenty-two years ago and had never fully recovered.

'It's not a worry, Tom,' Dan said. 'Death is a part of life, and we accept it with no grieving. There's nothing we can do to stop it, so there's no sense in sadness.'

Tom had often wondered if it was purely a Saddling thing, the way no-one grieved when a loved one died. The dead were remembered, and their lives celebrated, but once a last breath had passed, the family continued without suffering. Tom had yet to come across how a sudden and unexpected death was handled.

'You marked ma's side too?' Dan was tracing a line from his name to his mother and her sister, Eliza and above. 'Grandfather John Seeming,' he read. 'Marjory White, both gone, and her sister… Oh. You put their work?'

'Some,' Tom said. 'But not with every name. Around here everyone's a farmer apart from a few. Your family is interesting because of the healing skill being passed through the generations. Grandmother White, Eliza, you. Anyway…' He took a pace across the room. 'You can take this Book of Teaching.' He pulled down a copy from the shelf. 'This is one of the older transcriptions, so be careful with it.'

'I'm not your thick-thumbed Barry,' Dan sniggered, taking the heavy volume and putting it to one side.

That was true. Where Dan was lean and graceful, smooth-shaved and precise, Barry was stocky and dark, his brain too clumsy for his hands. A racehorse against a carthorse, but racehorses could be skittish and unpredictable whereas the carthorse plodded loyally until the end.

'This is what I want you to look at first.' Tom sat, and Dan stood over his shoulder. 'This is one of your aunt's books. Have a read of that.' He opened the journal to the poem, and Dan leant in, one arm around Tom's shoulder, the other resting on the desk.

'Well, who'd a thought it?' Dan breathed. 'Aye, that's it, and I'd say it's probably the most accurate version of the story. Well, song. I don't remember every word Eliza sang, but some of them jump at me. Eastling, of course, harvest… "Stalking time to reap the vine…" I remember that because it didn't rhyme and that annoyed me. I'd forgotten the number, two-eight-hundred… But aye. I'd say that was the song she sang. What of it?'

'Pull up a chair.'

Having Dan's arm on his shoulder gave Tom a feeling of security, but they were both sweating, and their proximity was made less enjoyable because of it. Dan withdrew and sat beside him, just as close, as though he was the one needing security.

Tom explained that he had started looking for lore concerning the eastling, and the only things he'd found so far were in Eliza's books. He also told Dan that Irene had asked him to investigate because she feared the eastling was about to pay another visit to Saddling.

He had promised her that he would keep that a secret, but this was Dan he was talking to. There were no secrets here.

'So,' he concluded. 'This song is the only clue so far as to what it could mean if the... ghost from our spoketale should return.'

Dan nodded thoughtfully. No-one derided such ideas in Saddling; folktales, whether spoken or written were considered truths.

'It makes a bit of sense to me,' Dan said, lowering his voice as he considered the lines. 'The eastling comes twice in every one-hundred years. I reckon most folks remember that and it's a way of saying, not to worry, chances are you'll never see it. Of course, when we're nippers, we don't think that way, we think of the second line. No place to hide when he gets here, and that's where the grownups add on the bit about being naughty.'

As he thought through the rest of the song, Dan's eyelashes flickered, and he sucked in his soft bottom lip. Tom drew his eyes away and read the verse.

'Stalking time,' he said. 'Is that a farming reference? A harvest thing?'

'You're thinking corn stalks,' Dan said. 'I reckon you should be thinking stalking the village. No, it ain't a farming expression that I know.'

'Hell, I'm so thick sometimes.' Tom tutted.

'What?'

'To reap the vine...' He pointed to the family charts covering his walls. He stood and approached one. 'The Rolfes,' he said. 'Irene Cole showed me the grave of Jane...' He found her in the family tree. 'Jane Rolfe who died in eighteen-thirty-one. Irene suggested she had been taken by the eastling.'

'Taken by?'

'Well, to be accurate, she said the girl had been found dead, and it was around harvest time, so it was most likely a coincidence or a murder. The same as the one of...' he moved to the Blacklocks line, '... this chap in the same century. But Eliza had a report from the time of this one, and it described...'

A name beside Derville Blacklocks distracted him because the details were incomplete. He'd either made a mistake on the family tree, or there was a nineteenth-century Blacklocks ancestor with no recorded date of death. It was unlike Tom to have missed such a thing and unlike...

'Well?' Dan was waiting. 'Described what?'

'Never mind.' The missing detail had to wait for another time. 'Irene Cole's thinking is that this... thing is coming back to kill someone as it did her ancestor.'

Dan, rereading the poem, said, 'I still don't understand the rest. Second breath, what's that? The second death in each century? But the end… Looks as if she's saying there's a way to be rid of it, whatever it is.'

'A ghost,' Tom reminded him. In his old life, he would have cringed with embarrassment.

'Still don't get the numbers, though,' Dan muttered. 'Something to do with time?' His head jolted up, and he stared through the window. 'Damn it.' He leapt to his feet. 'Sorry, Tom, I left something in the oven. Must go.'

He was out of his chair and striding to the door in a flash.

Tom laughed. 'They've got you slaving in the kitchen, and you're not even married yet,' he said as Dan hurried past him, snatching up the Book of Teaching on his way.

'Aye, that be true, but I'll soon be the man of the house.' His voice trailed off as he flew down the stairs.

'If she'll let you,' Tom mumbled under his breath.

He had considered telling Dan what Jenny had said that morning, but he was already flaky because of the wedding. It was best not to mention it. As he'd thought before, Jenny was just trying out her authority in a way she'd no doubt seen her mother do at home. Dan wouldn't let her take over the inn or his life as she intended, not in a hundred years.

He returned to the Blacklocks line and the name he had seen. The charted details for the Blacklocks family were complete apart from the death of one man, Nigel Blacklocks. Born in 1844 would have been eighteen in the year his brother was killed, and Tom remembered entering his birth on the tree because it was an unusual name for Saddling. He was the only Nigel in the records then and now which would make his death date easy to locate. He made a note to come back to that later. It wasn't an important error, but if the man had been recorded as born in Saddling, his death should be on the records for completeness.

He returned to his desk in time to see Dan running into the inn through the back door and realised he'd not mentioned the church-house window.

'That can wait.'

The riddle of Eliza's song was more intriguing.

'"Two-eight-hundred seasons",' he read, repeating the number in the hope it meant something. It didn't. '"And fourteen know the knife." What's that about?' He stared at the word "knife" and realised. Flipping back a few pages, he scanned the torn-out record of Derville Blacklocks' death.

Then I saw a knife. Short handle, curving blade like a slitting-knife.

He skipped back to the beginning.

Such a sight is not unusual in autumn...

'Autumn?' One of the four seasons. 'What if...?' He reached for notepaper and scribbled numbers, wishing he had a calculator. It was a complicated calculation for Tom, mathematics had been one of his weaker subjects, and although Sam Rolfe had an abacus in the shop, he had no idea how to use it.

'Two-eight-hundred...' He wrote the numbers. 'Two-thousand eight hundred divided by four seasons per year... Bugger it!' He'd forgotten how to do long division. 'Take off two zeros... Right... Two into twenty-eight equals fourteen... Fourteen know the knife.' He thought he was onto something until he realised his mistake. 'Four seasons not two... four into twenty-eight equals seven... Put back the two zeros. Seven-hundred.'

What did that mean?

'Two-eight-hundred seasons at four seasons per year means seven hundred years. Fourteen shall know the knife...' He almost had it. 'The eastling comes twice every one-hundred years. The rhyme suggests that fourteen will die, and thus it will take seven hundred years for the... manifestation to reap from the family tree of those who caused his death... When?'

He checked his chart for the death of Jane Rolfe, 1831, and subtracted seven-hundred.

'Eleven-thirty-one.'

Why would the legend begin with a death in 1131? The date didn't have any significance as far as he could remember. The Saddling Diary only spoke of events from the great storm onwards, 1292 and the first...

'Jesus Christ! Think, dick-head!'

Jane Rolfe's death could have been a murder, even the one depicted in the church-house window; it had happened at harvesttime. It could equally have been an eastling reaping, to use Eliza's words, but not necessarily the first. Why not 1162? Seven-hundred years before Derville Blacklock's ghostly death, if that was in fact how it had happened. There could be other mysterious deaths, but only a trawl of the records would tell him, and only if they had been properly recorded.

'Too many ifs,' he said, reaching for his beer. 'What if it was seven-hundred years ago from this year?' 1315, another date that meant nothing.

'What if it was seven hundred years before...' He reached to his right and planted his finger on a family tree to choose a date at random. 'Nineteen-ninety-two.' His finger had landed directly on Becki Tidy's entry, and he noted 1292.

That was a date that meant something. The first Saddling, the great storm, the night his ancestor, Robert Di-Kari killed the fourteen-year-old son of the shepherd with the black locks.

Fourteen-year-old.

'If that was the event that started this...' He scribbled another calculation, working it through twice to make sure he was correct. If the myth started at the time of the first saddling, then just over seven-hundred years had passed. The thing had returned fourteen times, one for every year the youth had lived and, more satisfyingly, it would have run its course by now.

'Got it!'

If he considered that to be a correct assumption, he had nothing to worry about. It was, however, only a hunch and he needed proof. After all, if level-headed Irene Cole was concerned that the evil was returning, and if someone as unmovable as Simon Feld had been terrified because he thought he saw the apparition, and if...

'Still too many ifs.' He threw down his pencil.

It rolled across Eliza's poem towards the spine of the book before running back. He made to grab it before it fell to the floor, but it stopped of its own accord, the sharpened lead pointing to one word in the fifth line, 'act.'

A warm breeze nestled at Tom's neck, but no papers moved on his desk. He breathed a whiff of lavender which faded as he exhaled, to be replaced with the usual background smell of muck-spreading.

Eliza's book, her handwriting and now her scent.

Tom smiled wryly. 'I get it, Eliza,' he said and read the complete line.

Lament the fact, unless you act, he'll start a second breath.

As he heard it, he knew what she was telling him. Once the eastling had taken revenge fourteen times, it began again. It didn't matter when the myth started, it was in place for eternity. What he needed to concentrate on was how it could be stopped.

The last few lines of the song began by giving him hope. There was a way to end the eastling's return. The last one, however, caused him only more confusion. *Go he will when sons shall kill with ancient rock-bound blade.*

Ten

Barry came home from work to find the kitchen empty and the smell of yearling mutton roasting in the oven. A pan of prepared vegetables waited to be boiled on the stove, and the back door was open to let the heat escape. He dumped his dusty clothes on the floor and stood naked to listen to the sounds of the house. Water was running upstairs, and the boards of the bathroom creaked overhead.

'You 'ome?' he shouted from the doorway.

'Up here.'

'I ran your bath,' Tom said, passing him on the landing and delivering a quick peck on the cheek. 'Dan's coming over for dinner in half an hour.'

''Ang on!' Barry grabbed his arm, swinging Tom around so they were face to face. They might have needed to be discreet outside, but alone at home was another matter. He pulled Tom to him, and they kissed.

Barry still didn't understand what it was that held them together. Where he was shorter and hairy, Tom was tall and smooth, his brown-blond hair hardly showing on his chest. Where Barry was rough of tongue and uneducated, Tom was better spoken and spent his days reading. Barry left his clothes where they fell, used Tom's towel if his was out of reach and spent his days among fields and sheep, Tom, on the other hand, spent his time at his desk and tidying up after Barry.

'Don't know what you see in me,' Barry said, stroking Tom's head as it rested on his shoulder.

Tom's arms tightened around Barry's back. 'Moments like this,' he said. He planted a kiss on Barry's neck and untangled himself. 'I'll get the dinner on.'

Tom had added Dan's herbal mixture to the bathwater, and whatever it was made of, it helped unknot Barry's muscles and soothed his sore hands. The wheat crop had been harvested a few days ago, leaving only the ersh in the fields. The task now was to thresh the heads from the stalks. As the thresher was in use by another farm this year, and as his father was involved in the council's current crisis, the overseeing had fallen to Barry. His all-workers and their women were making good progress, but there were only two more days in which to complete the task, and only half of the winnowing had been done.

'It'll still be there a'morrow,' he mumbled, sliding lower in the warm water and closing his eyes. 'No point in thinking on it now.'

He was woken a few minutes later when Tom appeared with a mug of ale.

'I've put the table in the back-out,' he said, handing it over. 'Thought we'd eat out there and watch the sun go down.'

It was a perfect evening for it and, clean, relaxed and wearing just a pair of loose fitting, light trousers, Barry could think of no better end to the day. The coral sky was an oil painting of broken cloud pouring towards the west as if drawn by the setting sun. It lit the clouds in warm shades, leaving the blue above to fade to grey. The earth below lay flat all the way to the far hill and gave off a soft haze that hung around the ankles of the whitebacks grazing through it.

Dan's ale was earthy and welcome, and Barry sipped while Tom clattered in the kitchen. The smell of the roast wafted over him to mingle with the now fading smell of the spreading and chaff dust that hung across the village on autumn evenings. He could only have felt happier if he didn't have to think about Jason Rolfe.

The lad was only two years younger than Barry, but as skittishly young acting as a teg and just as confused. He needed shepherding towards an enclosure but hadn't made up his mind which one to investigate first. Barry knew how that felt and was determined to help Jason in some subtle way but subtlety was not his strong point.

His thoughts were interrupted when Dan appeared at the side of the house. His russet hair caught the dying sun and mirrored the colour of the boblight-tinted grey-hang.

Barry rose to greet him, and they hugged before Dan took hold of his hands to examine them.

'Doing well,' he said. 'But I brought you more of this.' He gave Barry another bottle of ointment.

'Thanks, mate. I've got the old bottle a-give back a you, and we could do wi' more a your bath gunk.'

'Gunk? It's pure dandelion and camomile!' Dan feigned outrage. 'And there's a fair bit a ginger in it too, and that ain't easy a-come by.'

'I don't think it be gunk,' Barry stammered. 'It's what 'im indoors calls it.'

'Oi!' Tom shouted from the kitchen.

'Sit down, marker-mate.' Sniggering, Barry pulled out a chair for Dan. 'I got a bag a apples fur you, 'less you be wanting grain or mutton.'

'I don't want anything but your company,' Dan said, and helped himself to the ale.

All through the simple dinner, Barry tried to think of ways to broach the subject of Jason Rolfe. He was distracted and in his own world while Dan and Tom discussed the Teaching and an issue they were dealing with. He vaguely heard them mention names and realised they were talking about the division that has opened up in Saddling over the past couple of weeks, but that was business for the council elders; he had his own concerns. He was unable to put them into words until Dan passed his pouch of Devil's Choke.

The choke had different effects on different people and at varying times. After one smoke, Barry could sleep for a whole day, but another pipe of the same batch and the choke fired his brain, cleared his thoughts and fed his imagination. At other times it made him as rampant as a stud bull, something Tom never complained about, but on most occasions, he mellowed and saw the world in vibrant, raw colours.

Tonight, the choke inspired his thinking. He hung lanterns among the reddening leaves and branches of the hawthorn tree to divert the insects from the table and returned to his chair with his words planned. The lamps threw just enough light to see by, but the sun had set now, and the marsh was bathed in a post-dusk light that silhouetted the trees and fences but left the horizon a band of dulling yellow.

'Want a-talk wi' you two 'bout a matter,' he said. He knocked out his pipe and refilled it. 'I got this thing what's going on wi' one a me all-workers, and I reckon I needs advice.'

'If it's farming, you should speak to your fader,' Dan said.

'Aye, I would but 'e's all worriting 'bout the council and it ain't 'bout the farm as such.'

'What is it?' Tom asked, slicing apples for dessert.

'Well, let me put it like this…' Barry cleared his throat and sat straight. 'There be this worker, right, and 'e's a good worker mind, even though the land ain't 'is usual job and 'e'd rather be a…' He stopped himself in time. He didn't want the others to know who he was talking about and saying that Jason wanted to be a fetcher would have given the game away. He was sure that neither Dan nor Tom would betray Jason's secret, but he wasn't completely sure that Jason had a secret, not yet. 'That makes no never mind,' he said, waving it away. 'Thing is, I reckon this all-worker 'as a problem and 'e can't make up 'is mind what a-do, and ain't got none a-talk wi' neither. So, 'e's been coming a work and working 'ard, but lately 'e started asking me questions. Thing is, when I goes a-answer 'im, or ask something I reckon would be useful fur me a-know, 'e gets clammed up.'

'Is it to do with work?' Dan asked.

'No. Personal.'

'A girl?'

'No, Tom, not exactly.'

'Ah.'

Barry could tell that Tom knew where he was going with this, and Dan also understood because he shifted uncomfortably in his chair and relit his pipe.

'Is it Jason?'

Tom's question took Barry by surprise. 'Why d'you say that?'

'What's 'e been saying about us?'

There was no point trying to be subtle now, and that put Barry at ease. 'I got me doubts 'bout 'im is all,' he said, glancing at Tom. All he could see was a dark shape against the lamp glow from the kitchen door. 'But it ain't 'bout you. Nor me,' he added to make sure Tom understood that Jason was no threat. 'Be about Dan.'

'I know what this is,' Dan said. 'Jason used to be girl-soft on me during schooling. We were good mates, we had a falling out, we sorted that two years back. What's he doing now?'

'He's still girl-soft on you, mate,' Barry said. 'Trouble is, the other all-workers 'ave picked up on it, and I'm afeared someone'll make trouble if Jason don't start behaving different. 'E be 'iding it by saying 'e's worried 'bout 'is sister's wedding, asking if I reckon you're marrying 'er 'cos you want to. I told him, aye, 'course you be, but that's not what 'e be asking, not really.'

'I get where you're coming from,' Tom nodded. 'And you want to help him, right?'

'Aye. Not 'cos I be interested, mind.'

'I didn't think for a minute that you were.'

'But it ain't the kind a thing no-one's ever talked 'bout in Saddling. Well, you know 'ow it be wi' us. It'd be worse fur Jason 'cos 'e don't 'ave your outside knowledge, which is the only way I can think of a-describe it.'

'Shall I talk to him?' Tom didn't sound as if he minded, but it was hard to see his expression in the near-darkness. 'Or ask Jack, his marker?'

'I'll do it.' Dan drew in on his pipe, and the embers in the bowl glowed, lighting his face momentarily. He held the smoke and then let it cloud across the table towards the lanterns where it hung between the hawthorn branches. 'Well, he be in a mizmaze about me, so I should be the one to put him right. To be honest, I thought I'd done that, but if he's still not letting go…'

'Aye, but don't say I said nothing,' Barry said. 'Least, if you do, tell 'im I were worried 'bout 'im, not the work, 'cos 'e's been threshing 'arder than the others, like 'e wants a-prove 'imself the better man.'

'He probably is,' Tom muttered.

'Leave it with me, mate.' Dan reached across the table and gripped Barry's hand. 'He'll be coming to see me about his blisters before long.' He released Barry, leaving a warm imprint of comradeship, and pointed his pipe to Tom. 'He's another one who comes for treatment he doesn't need.'

'The right village darling, aren't you?' Tom laughed. 'It's your fault for looking like a catwalk model, knowing how to draw, knowing how to cure and being such a caring listener.'

'A cat what?' Barry said. 'Dan be more like a wolf than a cat.'

'I meant he's handsome,' Tom explained.

'Aye, there be no denying that,' Barry said, kicking Dan gently under the table. 'But it ain't that. It's 'cos 'e's got a big cock.'

'Oi!' Dan swiped for him but missed in the darkness.

'I were talking 'bout that red-crown you let out fur breeding, you lompy loon.' Even though Barry had meant to make a joke, he still found himself blushing and was grateful for the lack of light.

Tom had started laughing and, by the sound of it, was having trouble controlling it. 'You've got a chicken called a red-crown?' he said between chuckles as he ruffled Dan's hair. 'Suits you.'

'It's me ma's.' Dan brushed him away. 'And it's not a chicken, it's a…' He started laughing with Tom, unable to say the word.

When Tom banged his hand on the table and gasped, 'Red-crown cock,' Barry could no longer hold back the effect of the choke, and they laughed loudly together about nothing.

'Hey! Shut your cackling, Barry Cole,' the neighbour, Jim Fetcher, shouted from behind the hedge. 'Me mistus ain't in the mood fur it.'

'And I ain't surprised, neither,' Barry leered back. 'Look who she 'as a-do it with.'

'Barry!' Tom chided in a fleeting moment of lucidity and a hushed voice.

'Pah, 'e's alright.' Barry dismissed him before raising his voice towards the cottage next door. 'Tell 'er she can 'ave the use of Dan's big…'

'Stop it!' Dan interrupted, chuckling. 'Sorry, Mr Fetcher,' he called before lowering his voice and whispering, 'I don't think even my red-crown could keep Mistus Fetcher happy.'

'Show off.' Trying to suppress the spasms in his chest only made things worse for Barry and it was still simmering five minutes later when the neighbour's daughter appeared holding a lantern.

'Hey,' Judith said, taking them by surprise. 'Dan Vye, you be needed at the inn. Your ma says you been 'ere too long and you got duties.'

'What duties?' Dan objected. He was refilling his pipe. 'Me ma's working the inn tonight.'

'Not that ma,' Judith insisted. 'Your other ma. To be. Rebecca Rolfe's waiting on you in your bedroom.'

That brought a jeer from Tom, and an 'Aye-aye!' from Barry, neither of which amused the messenger.

'She say's you got a-be 'ome dreckly or you ain't going a-be fathering no babies.'

'What the f…?' Tom bit his tongue.

'Don't think you got no worries 'bout that, Judith Fetcher,' Barry leered. 'Dan's got a red-crown…'

'Shut up!'

Amid the laughter, the lantern cast shadows onto the girl's face from below, giving her a menacing, distorted look. Anger showed through it. 'You can take your Lore unserious, Barry Cole, and be that on your own 'ead, but Dan's from better stock and 'e knows what 'is duties be this week.'

'Better stock?' Tom rose to his feet, but Barry held him down.

'Leave 'er be,' he said, suddenly sober. 'Bloody maden.'

Dan had also risen. 'I have to go,' he said, also remarkably level-headed. 'I got something to do.'

'Want us to come with you?'

'No, Tom. This duty's for me and the women only. Bugger it.' He tapped ash into a bowl. 'Clean forgot I was getting wed come Thursday.'

Barry took his pipe from him and cleaned it, as was the tradition between the two markers.

'Tell them I'm coming,' Dan said, and Judith disappeared into the gloom.

'Thanks, mate,' Dan said. 'And you, Tom. I swear I'd go mad 'round here if it weren't for you two. And leave that Jason Rolfe thing with me. If he's going to be my brother-in-lore, we need to get some things straight. See you tomorrow.'

'Straight,' Tom said, and started giggling.

Dan knew something was wrong as soon as he entered the inn. Loud, rhythmic knocking sounds came from above.

'Bollocks.' He groaned.

Say-swears or miswords as they were also called in the village, were heavily frowned upon, but Dan had learnt a few from Tom, and a couple were on his lips as he trudged towards his bedroom.

The knocking sound became a banging and, as the landing came into view, he saw that his door was open, the gas was fully lit, and shadows were moving along bare walls. The sound of female whispering grew louder as he approached but stopped when he reached them.

His heart sank before his anger rose, and he struggled to control the latter. Where that afternoon his drawings had hung from the walls in neat formation, they were now piled badly by the door. Where only a few hours ago he'd had his single bed, his cluster of books beside it and his childhood cover to dress it, there was now the sight of Jimmy Payne's sweaty back. He was crouched beside a bed frame, knocking in slats. On the other side stood his son, supporting a straw mattress, ready to drop it into place. The frame and the mattress were huge, leaving little room for any other furniture.

What was worse, what little room there was, was crowded with village women. Rebecca Rolfe stood among them, taking most of the space for her bulk. Jenny was beside her, and beside herself, it seemed. She clapped her hands excitedly, tapping her fingers on her lips, her eyes wide and in awe of the bed.

As soon as Rebecca saw Dan, she threw her arms wide in hopelessness.

'And so he graces us wi' his presence,' she mocked. 'I hope you're not as slow a-use this thing, and you know what a-do on it.' She laughed — alone. 'Near thirty years of married life, I've had three tegs all of age and none yet bothering to grandmother me. Get in here, boy.'

Dan bristled at being called a boy. It suggested he was an uneducated land-worker, but Jenny had noticed him now, and she wasn't angry, only pleased to see him. He stepped as far into the room as he could, but Jimmy Payne stood, blocking him.

A heavy thump and applause from the women told Dan that the mattress was in place; all he could see was the back of Payne's head.

'Get out his way, Jimmy,' Rebecca ordered, and the carpenter took a step back, crushing Dan's foot.

'Oh, sorry, mate,' he mumbled, turning and squeezing past to the doorway.

His son followed with the tools, giving Dan a sympathetic look, but leaving him vulnerable and at the mercy of the women.

'Who's in the bar?' he asked, seeing his mother crammed into a corner.

'No-one. No need.' Rebecca answered before Susan had a chance to. 'I closed it. Come and stand here. You've got no paper, so you've learnt the song?'

'Song?' Dan had no idea what she was talking about.

Rebecca could tell, and she turned to the window, elbowing women out of the way as she threw it open.

'Oi, Barry Cole!' she bellowed into the night. 'You ain't doing your duties.'

'Hush, Ma.' Jenny tugged at her arm, but it did no good.

'You're a disgrace. And you, Miss Farrow, what's been a-keeping you?' Rebecca slammed the window. By the time she had manoeuvred herself to face the bed, all signs of outrage had gone, and she glowed with sickly benevolence. 'We will start as soon as Miss Farrow arrives,' she declared. Her eyes narrowed when they fell on Dan. 'And you best read from this.' She handed him a sheet of paper.

Dan read the words and the only thing that quelled his rising nervousness was the thought that Barry was probably in hysterics about this right now. As his marker, it was his job to prepare Dan for his wedding, and that included making sure he knew the appropriate Lore, learned his bed-laying words, knew what he had to do at his aepelling and on the wedding day itself. Barry hadn't done any of those things, and Dan hadn't thought to remind him. He wasn't angry, in fact, he found it amusing. Weddings were not high on Barry's list of things to bother about.

The hubbub in the room was silenced by the slamming of the back door as the last of the women arrived.

'Get him over here.' Rebecca clicked her fingers.

Dan was handed from one woman to the next until he was at the foot of the bed where Jenny joined him. Shoulder to shoulder and with the air in the room already stuffy, his unease increased when he heard a bleat, and hooves scuffing the stairs.

'Right. Off you go.' Rebecca stared at Dan.

He was obviously expected to do something, and he looked at Jenny for support.

She took his hand and whispered. 'Sing the song. It's the same tune as "Spring a Marsh".'

Luckily that was a song Dan knew well and, scanning the words, he saw how they fitted. It was only two verses, and the spring folksong was always sung quietly. With any luck, no-one would notice that he couldn't hold a tune.

Suddenly nervous, he self-consciously began to sing. 'Bring a bed and bring my wife...' He was silenced by a sharp nudge from Jenny.

Rebecca Rolfe took an angry breath.

'Louder,' Jenny hissed. 'The louder you sing it, the more fertile you'll be.'

The word made Dan squirm. Blushing, he glanced from the page and caught Becki Tidy watching. Her wink scared away his gaze and, wishing he'd had more to smoke, he began again, loudly and out of tune.

'Bring a bed and bring my wife, bring the child to pass the joy, give us girl and give us...'

He was interrupted by a fracas in the doorway as the tall, silver-haired Miss Farrow was dragged into the room by a sheep. The other women lifted their arms and sucked themselves in to let her pass, but the young ram, seeing nothing but a forest of legs, tried to bolt. Lucy Cole, Barry's unmarried cousin, leapt on the animal, trapping it between her legs and guided it to the bed.

The effects of the choke had lingered after all, and a bubble of laughter stirred in Dan's chest. He suppressed it when Rebecca clicked her fingers and shot daggers.

'Bring a bed...'

Dan sang as best he could and made it through both verses without corpsing, despite the look of anguish on the women's faces, and his own mother biting her lip to keep back a fit of giggles. When he had finished, she smiled at him and nodded. The gesture boosted his confidence, but when she rolled her eyes over Rebecca's shoulder, he had to cover a spontaneous laugh with a cough.

The womenfolk began to sing while throwing clover and pasture plants onto the mattress and Lucy Cole expertly contained the sheep. At a specific point in the song, she heaved the first-year whiteback onto the bed, keeping hold of its tether just in case.

'What the hob-lamb takes the couple makes,' the song continued.

Dan watched the ram snuffle about the bed. It was a teg, probably no more than six months old, but it staggered like a new-born as the mattress dipped beneath it. It turned and looked at him, standing still for long enough for him to think it was asking a question; why?

'May your man be a ram, not lamb.'

Dan's hand was sweaty in Jenny's, and he wasn't sure if it was the heat or nervousness. He was uncomfortable in the presence of so many women, Rebecca Rolfe in particular, and the only comfort came from his mother. It should have come from Jenny, surely? He glanced at her, but she was watching the ram and singing. Dan wished Barry was beside him for moral support, but from Thursday onwards he would see less of his friend. Less of Tom, less of Jason and the others. His duties would lie within the inn, providing for his new wife and however many children the roaming whiteback decreed would come. So far it had eaten twice, a good sign that the marriage was going to be a productive one.

The thought unnerved him further. He was twenty-five but, being a follower of the Lore, had no experience beyond kissing. Jenny's expectations of what he would do in this bed were something else he should have talked to his marker about, but then again, what would Barry know? Dan had no father, no uncles, and his last surviving grandfather was too brain-fuddled to know what day it was. He would have considered talking to Matt Cole, as he was the minister and therefore parent to everyone, but Matt had too many other concerns.

The song finished, and the guests applauded themselves.

'He's eaten three,' Rebecca exclaimed leaning over and patting Jenny's belly. 'You're going a-be busy down there, daughter.'

'Husband's going a-be busy down there an' all,' Becki Tidy said, fixing Dan with a disconcerting grin and making the other women laugh.

'Oh no! Ma?' Jenny's cry brought a swift halt to the merriment, and all heads turned to the bed.

The sheep had filled up at one end and was now emptying at the other.

'Get the bugger off the bed!' Rebecca screeched.

No matter how hard Lucy pulled, the ram was not going to move until it had finished, and no matter how hard he tried, Dan couldn't hold back. The choke, his anxiety, the performance were too much for him. Clasping his hand to his mouth didn't help, and when he saw his mother's shoulders also heaving, he erupted into a loud belly laugh.

Outraged, Rebecca Rolfe knelt on the mattress and pushed the sheep from behind while Lucy tugged from the front. Some of the other guests were sniggering, and Dan let go of Jenny to wipe tears from his eyes.

'No, it's bad luck.' Jenny slapped his arm.

She was unable to keep up the pretence of outrage when Lucy yanked the sheep from the bed, and her mother slipped face-first into its droppings. Jenny roared like everyone else in the room and threw an arm around Dan.

She hung on him the same way Barry did, and Dan was reassured. If she could laugh with him about this, there was hope that their marriage would be bearable.

'You should all be ashamed,' Rebecca shouted as she crawled off the bed, rubbing her face on her apron. 'This be one of the most important parts of the Lore and you be forgetting your Teaching.'

'Ah, hush your blaaring, woman.' The words were out of Dan's mouth before he had a chance to consider them. The resulting silence and, from some, look of horror, only hardened his resolve. 'It's a bloody celebration,' he said, mustering courage as best he could. 'We're supposed a-be having a good time.'

Rebecca drew in enough breath for a dressing-down, but Dan wasn't about to let that happen.

'Keep it closed, woman,' he snapped, bringing a gasp from Jenny and a beaming smile from his mother. 'I thank you for your time, Miss Farrow, Miss Cole, Mistus Rolfe.' He put her name last to let her know her place. If he was going to marry into her family, she would have to know what he was capable of. He wasn't going to be the mild-mannered, subservient inn-keeper's boy she thought he was. 'Now I reckon our fun be over. You should get that teg back to its flock, Lucy, and Jenny, you need to rest up ahead of our big day.' He held her waist and kissed her hard on the mouth. Releasing her, he addressed Mistus Rolfe. 'You can see your daughter home now, thank you. I'll leave the mattress outside for you to clean in the morning, that being a woman's duty. Ma?' He looked at Susan ignoring Rebecca Rolfe's outraged glare. 'Sorry this woman's messed up me room.

I'll put my drawings back up best I can when they've gone, which they will be doing now. Thank you, ladies...' He literally showed them the door. 'I'll see you at our aepelling, but I won't see none of you upstairs in my room again. Not unless you want treatment in which case my treating room is next door, but you call for me from downstairs.' He pushed his way towards the exit, herding a few women in front of him. 'Mind your head on that beam there, Miss Farrow, thanks for bringing the yearling.'

He smiled at each of them as they left, received a hug from his mother and a growl from his future mother-in-lore, the last to leave.

'I'm in hopes you do better on your wedding day.' Her threat came under her breath.

'Don't you worry, Mistus Rolfe,' he said putting on a cheery tone and a wide smile. 'I'm looking forward to wedding your Jenny and everything that comes after. I'll be the son-in-lore you always wanted, and I intend to lamb you down plenty of noisy Dan and Jenny Vyes to brighten your life.'

'I hope you mean that,' she snarled.

'Oh, I do, I do.'

He hadn't meant a word of it.

Eleven

Tom slept well for the first time in a week. He put it down to the previous night's relaxation and the Devil's Choke which had, after a third pipe, cast one of its more amorous effects over the pair of them. Barry was out at work and Tom was at his books by eight, refreshed and thinking clearly. Before he sat to read, he glanced onto the green and wondered why there was a mattress leaning against the inn. He would find out later. His task that morning was to check through the Saddling Diary for any records of mysterious deaths.

The Eastling Festival and the people's imposition were two days away. He was confident Dan would find something in the Teaching to help Matt Cole, but not as sure that he would be able to satisfy Mistus Cole's fears. There had been no more reports of strange mists and wandering figures, and whole families were heading out to the barns and fields to finish the harvest.

A pang of guilt stabbed him because he was not going with them, but Barry had told him he wasn't needed, insisting instead that Tom stayed at home to work. Whatever Tom could do to help relieve the minister's stress was of more use to the village than another pair of blistered hands. The same applied to Dan who Tom could now see at his bedroom window, pacing the room and holding up picture frames, as if deciding where to hang them. Becki Tidy approached the inn, sneezing loudly and Dan ducked out of sight.

Tom smiled. He was never short of entertainment in Saddling, but he was short of time, and he opened the Saddling Diary to begin work.

The book was a transcription of several other tomes now lost to time. It had been started by the Carey ministers who kept it up until the seventeenth century when the Blacklocks family took over the role. The late William Blacklocks had been passionate about preserving every scrap of Saddling history and thus the book, the size and weight of the Teaching, contained copies of records dating back to the founding of the village. Many of the original records survived, but Tom daren't handle them, and they were locked in a cupboard in the corner of his study. There was no need to try and read their faded ink; Blacklocks had transcribed them years ago. Everything Tom needed should either be in the records or the diary.

He found the pages dated around the time of Jane Rolfe's burial but saw no entries concerning her death. Jumping forward, he checked the death of Derville Blacklocks, and, reaching 1862 discovered the diary page missing. Comparing the torn-edge to the report glued into Eliza's book, he found a perfect match. At some point, she must have had access to the Diary, and Tom wondered how and when. He had found it locked in a cabinet in the church crypt and jealously guarded by Blacklocks. She must have taken the page before she was blinded. He admired her courage but couldn't understand her reason.

Putting the diary aside, he took the nineteenth-century death records from the shelf and located both entries.

Jane Rolfe was simply noted as a death with the date of her burial, but Derville Blacklock's was recorded as "Drowning while deek raking. Misadventure." The entry was signed by the minister and witnessed, unusually, by James Payne, not by the village clerk who had signed the other entries on the page.

Tom wrote the dates on his pad before returning the records and choosing the eighteenth-century collection. He intended to look for any further misadventures, or out of place causes of death and then check those dates against entries in the Diary. As he began scanning each page, a thought occurred. If Eliza had managed to take the Diary page for 1862, perhaps she had torn out and kept others.

For what reason?

He chewed a pencil while he thought and, as he put the pieces together, Tom imagined the most likely scenario.

The saddling of Dan's father in 1992. The storm building, the villagers in preparation for the ritual. Eliza battling through the rain to creep unseen into the church-house, taking pages from the book, and running into Blacklocks as she made her escape. To distract him, she screamed about going out-marsh, calling the authorities, telling the outside world that Blacklocks was going to murder Martin Vye — legitimately in Saddling because he had been chosen at random, but a crime to rational people. She fled back to her shack and hid the pages. Blacklocks caught her trying to leave the village and blinded her.

'That's possibly how,' he said. 'But what's that got to do with the eastling?'

If other pages were missing, their dates might throw light on Eliza's reason.

He dropped the pencil into a pot of others and focused on the Diary where he turned pages carefully, checking for anomalies. He soon found one. The last sentence on a left-hand page was dated August 1710 and noted how the village was suffering a drought.

"And it be here noted that the Brazier family tending West Ditch be assisted by the council in the matter of watering…"

The right-hand page began, "… binding of the lad Jacob Seeming on the fifth of October to his marker, Tommy Cole, being of the same age." It was dated October 6th and signed by Henry Carey, the village clerk.

Another page was missing.

Returning to Eliza's journal, he picked up where he'd left off the day before. Two pages after the Derville Blacklocks story, he found what he was looking for, and the date leapt from the page. September 23rd, Eastling Day.

An account of the demise of Paul Cole in the village of Saddling which occurred on Saturday, September 23rd, 1710

Written by Nathan Blacklocks (minister)

Strange occurrences have, of late, plagued some members of our community. With the burial today of one of our men, I hope that the dejection which has recently been present in Saddling shall be lifted.

On Tuesday last, Stan Feld, while looking over the whitebacks at Far Field (south) in the early boblight saw what at first he believed to be an approaching deposition, perhaps from Moremarsh, or possibly Brenzett which lie to our south. He was in the proximity of the deek bridge and ran there to meet the stranger to enquire of his business. He followed the bank of the southern ditch in older to better keep sight of the man but, somewhere between Inner Cut and the bridge, lost sight of him in the mist that was blowing in from all sides (he described it as tumbling). He waited at the bridge until long after dark but waited alone. It was assumed the stranger had changed his path.

Later the same night, the widow Brazier, at the opposite edge of our land, found herself suffering a disturbed sleep. She was wakened, she said, by the press of a cold blade on her throat but found no-one else in her cottage. She witnessed the dawn from her back-out and in it, saw a similar figure to that as described by Stan Feld. The youth (she described him as of saddling eligibility and tall with black hair under a cowl and wearing a tunic-like garment over breeches), passed close by her border hedge where the night-mist was settling. As it evaporated, so it took with it the boy. (Mistus White has seen to the widow Brazier since but, as yet, none of her calming remedies have caused the woman to end the distress with which the sighting left her.)

The council, to whom these matters were reported, have investigated the whereabouts of all saddling-eligible youths at the time and date specified, and each has been found faultless of wandering or pranking.

The same has been held true for the following evening, Wednesday 20th when, again at boblight, as the sun was falling behind the mother tree copse on the western Cole land, master Paul Cole was returning home from threshing. The day had been cloud-covered and hot, and there were none in Saddling not suffering from sweating and breathlessness. My own wife, from that day until Saturday, experienced not only the sweating but also troubled dreams and a feeling of being watched. Paul Cole reported a similar unease to his mistus on his return home. (This was not known to me until after the accident that befell the same young man on Saturday last.)

The last unusual incident concerned Matthew Carey, a man not known for his confusions. Carey is in his sixtieth year and has, for his entire life, been known as reliable and stalwart. He is not a man to suffer cowardice, as was proved at the saddling of his eldest son where he, and his mistus, bore their grief nobly.

Matthew Carey had been tending his whitebacks which the family have now begun keeping on rented Cole farmland in the near fields. The day was again damp but warm, and Carey was not surprised to see the marsh mist rising as boblight neared. His path home was a simple one: from Long Field Meadow, over the inner deek crossing and from there, a direct line to his village property. Yet, after only a minute of walking, the greyhang had grown so dense, he was unable to see his way. He continued on what he thought was a straight path expecting to find the crossing at any moment but after several more minutes of careful walking, he realised his direction was opposite, towards the setting sun. He doesn't recall turning around.

The fog surrounding him grew a deep red colour, he said, lit by the dusk.

The Eastling

He retraced his steps and, after a few paces, came across a 'Shadowy figure of a weeping boy, no older than fourteen whose costume I'd not seen in Saddling afore.' He heard the boy's sobs from a distance and was able to direct himself by the sound. Drawing near, he disturbed the lad who leapt to his feet. Carey described the costume as being of a similar fashion to that seen by the widow Brazier. (At this point in his telling, I ordered a search of barns, outhouses and other possible hiding places, in fear of an intruder. None was found.) Carey, however, added that the boy was holding a wooden-handled blade which he first took to be a harvesting sickle, but when the boy turned and came at him, he saw plain that it was similar, but in fact a double-edged slitting knife, slightly more curved than the ritual saddling knife. When asked to describe the face of the boy, he was unable, saying that no sooner had the lad begun to run towards him than the face and the entire body dissolved into the brume which, following a brush of cold wind that rushed past Carey, dropped from the air and shattered as glass onto the landscape.

To my mind, these occurrences spoke of ill health caused by the unusually warm autumn, the damp air, the recent spread of the summer ague (so well treated by Mistus White) combined with over-work due to the harvesting and the low supply of fresh water. They might have been dismissed easily in this way had not Paul Cole died in such mysterious circumstances.

On Saturday evening, following the Eastling Day celebration — after Thomas Seeming had once again triumphed at the annual bale-toss and led the wives to the church-house — a party of abstinent revellers, myself among them, and with Paul Cole in our company, attended the inn for eastling pie. Paul entered last behind us, and we left him to close the door. Landlord Vye greeted us as we came to his counter and then, with no warning, let out such a scream of shock as I have never heard come from the mouth of a man. Turning on my heels to see why his aghast eyes were wide in horror, I and my companions witnessed a sight which shall haunt me until I leave this place to sleep with my ancestors.

Paul Cole stood with his hand yet on the latch, facing us. It was as if he had posed himself in the act of stepping into the inn and, having just closed the door, had got no further than turning to take his next step. The reason for his motionlessness, however, was horror. His mouth hung open, his eyes flared, and his face was white. This was caused by the fast draining of blood from his throat which, in the instant of our entering and him closing the door, had been deeply sliced through.

Matthew Carey was the first to act, but before he could reach the man, Cole had crumpled to his knees and was quite dead. Carey, assisted by the recovered Vye, was out into the night through the back door (the front being blocked by the unfortunate's corpse) where he raised the alarm.

Once again, the instigated search was thorough. The younger all-workers were dispatched at a run to the crossings, those who could ride took their horses and circled the entire Saddling borders overnight and for the next two days, while the women searched every possible place in the village and fields.

Our search has revealed no-one, and we are left to assume that an out-marsher took his chances in the season's mists, trespassed into our village and took Cole's life away with him. Still unable to reason why or how he made himself appear and vanish so fleetingly, we have lain the story to rest alongside Paul Cole. An endowment of produce has been awarded to his widow to see her safely through winter, or until her eldest boy is able to continue Cole's farm.

Tom rubbed his eyes. Having read the description, he could see where Irene Cole's grandmother found her folklore. The details of the events had been officially recorded, but in a book kept locked away by the ministers and their clerks. The general population wouldn't have had access and so, in their telling of the story, would have related suspicions and interpretations, not the stated facts. Over time, the stories had become folklore, and, no doubt, the facts had become distorted and embellished. Here though, in greying black and yellowing white, the events of 1710 were written by the not uneducated minister and therefore were as factual as Tom was ever going to find.

He spent the rest of the morning searching carefully for further signs of damage to the books, and he found one further loose page that matched what had been removed. Using this, and having trawled several centuries of death records, he had a list of unexplained events, the most tragic of which matched up with the victims' burials, where named. It wasn't a long list but, as he ate cold lamb and bread in his back-out, he browsed through it one more time.

There had been mysterious deaths in every century from fifteen hundred to nineteen thirteen. He could only find one in the sixteenth century, but the records for one decade were badly transcribed in that they stated names and dates only, not the cause of death. He had a possible sighting of the eastling from the fourteenth century, written in the Saddling diary in Latin, and it had taken him an hour to translate it using an ancient Latin dictionary with the name William Blacklocks written inside the cover in a child's hand. It had helped, however, and the dictionary, combined with what he could remember from school, told him a story of betrayal. He checked the account twice and wrote a rough translation.

In the year of our Lore, 1319 upon the day of harvest it was found to be the death of a Saddling woman found to have betrayed her husband for the love of another. The husband was not suspected of the killing, having been engaged in fetching on the evening, the harvest of apples in need of trading at Romney. Nor was he aware, he swore on the Lore, that he knew his wife had taken up with a young and unmarried Master for several months prior. None are suspected, but one has taken a life upon harvest day by the plunging of a knife through the stomach of an unfortunate Mistus now beneath her sleeper stone.

If he took the written facts as certain, Tom could deduce that sightings occurred in the days leading up to Eastling Day. The mysterious deaths happened on September 23rd, the autumn equinox and feast day. (Some were not dated, but it had always been a Saddling custom to bury the dead the day after life ended, and the burials happened on September 24th.) The means of death was always a knife.

He wrote a list of possible connections.

The incidents involved the sighting of a male youth. A few only described 'a figure', but many described him as dripping, or wet, or 'mist-soaked.' The victims were (possibly) chosen because they had, in some way, betrayed someone else, usually a loved one, husband, wife, child. There was a suspicion that the eastling nemesis (as named by one of Tom's own ancestors in 1501) fed off the burning of the bads on Witchling Day. *Our smoking bads mingle with the air, so the eastling makes his choices there*, was a rhyme he found randomly scribbled at the bottom of a page. He had been unable to date it precisely, but it appeared a couple of pages after the *Mysterious and horrific death of Sara Vye found body-slit upon the green*, in 1501. It was possibly just a bored clerk or minister doodling an idea, but he couldn't ignore the connection between the dates, nor the relevance of

Witchling Day at summer solstice and the Eastling Day at the autumn equinox.

It was in the early afternoon, once more at his desk, that he began work on the twentieth century. He followed his hunch, that if there were to be any reports of the kind he was looking for, they occurred in September and, after a few minutes, found one that had a link to the present.

Buried today, 24th September, the year of our Lore, 1950. Rowan Mackett of West Ditch Farm, father of Mark Mackett and Elizabeth (deceased). Keeper of common land. Death by unknown hand.

It was a long shot, but this victim's grandson was still alive, and if anyone knew of a murder in his family, it would be Jack Mackett.

Finally, a breakthrough. Tom grabbed his shirt and made for the stairs.

Twelve

Tom knew the way to Jack Mackett's house well, he had visited often during its rebuilding to make sure the money he paid for outside materials was being put to good use. He'd used the time to strengthen his friendship with Jack.

It had taken them a while to adjust to each other. Jack was known for being volatile, a trait that earned him the nickname Wiffle-Jack, a wiffle-wind in Saddling being one that gusts from every direction. Tom rarely trusted anyone with such mood swings and Jack found Tom's studious nature unsettling, but after several months of working together on the project, they had become friends.

His path took him from the back of his house, along the deek, over the bridge to the inner fields, across the closest pasture and towards the edge of the Cole land. The whitebacks grazed at the bottom of the field towards a copse, and above, the sky was a warm white, the sunlight diffused and casting weak shadows. Crossing the first of the Cole pastures, he could see the store barn off to his left, distant but unmistakable being the largest barn in Saddling. Two horses drew a low cart across the stubble between him and where Barry was delivering bales to storage.

The walk from the village to Jack's house was two miles and took Tom close to the western mark where Saddling's land ended in the wide, uncrossable deek, lined on the far side with tall poplar trees. He crossed the four planks that acted as a bridge from Cole to Mackett land, listening to the rustle of warblers in the bulrushes and the plop of frogs disturbed from the banks. The temperature had cooled, but the air remained damp and heavy. A decent thunderstorm might clear it but there was no likelihood of one, the farmers reported the coming of rain as soon as they saw the signs, and no-one had spoken of it for nearly a month.

His mind wandered as he did until he saw Jack's house looming ahead. Restored to its former two storeys but extended to provide him with a decent kitchen and an inside bathroom. It had been built in the same way as many of the more recent Saddling properties; brick and breezeblock (brought in from off-marsh with council permission), internal ceiling beams, plastered walls and a tiled roof, floorboards and wooden-frame windows.

One of the upstairs windows was open and, nearing the fence that encircled the house and its outbuildings, Tom shouted.

'Jack? You 'ome? Be Tom.' He slipped into his Saddling accent when dealing with Jack. It helped put his friend at ease, even though Tom was still not completely fluent in the use of the time-grown dialect.

There was no reply, and he reasoned that Jack was still working in the fields. Communication had been so much easier before he moved to Saddling; a quick phone call or an email. The downside was that he had been overweight, unfit and lazy. A two-mile walk to ask a man a question was the norm in the village and one of the reasons Tom was now fitter than he had ever been.

He was turning to leave, thinking he'd visit Barry and come back later, when the back door opened, and Jack appeared, red-faced and dressing.

'Tom,' he called, wrestling his arm into a sleeve. 'I were washing. What you doing 'ere?'

'Got an ask fur you.'

'Give me a minute, I'll come out. Just get me bootshoes.'

Two minutes later Jack hopped from the house, pulling on a boot. He strode to the gate with his shirt buttoned on the wrong holes and his laces trailing. He rested a foot on the cleft rail fence to tie them.

'What's your ask?'

'I wanted a-talk to you 'bout your grandfather, and how he died.' It was best to be direct with Jack; he wasn't a man who appreciated niceties.

'Grandfader Rowan?' he said straightening up. 'This got a-do wi' what Simon Feld saw the other night?'

Tom was taken aback. 'You've been thinking 'bout that an' all?'

'Aye, Tom.' Jack opened the gate. 'I got a-go check on 'im over a'wards the common any case. Let's walk.'

There was no arguing with Jack, and another mile wouldn't hurt.

Jack closed the gate and hesitated, glancing up to his open window.

'It'll be safe,' Tom said. There was no crime in Saddling.

'Eh? Oh, aye, it will. Only I 'ad a blackwing fly in the other day. Caused a right ceremony. No, she'll be fine.'

It was unusual for anyone to refer to their house as a 'she', but this was Jack Mackett. He walked ahead towards the deek with Tom following. When they reached the lyste-way, they strode two abreast on the flattened earth.

'What d'you need a-know 'bout me grandfader?' Jack asked as they fell into a steady rhythm.

'I want a-know what happened to 'im,' Tom replied. 'I've seen the entry in the records, but it only says death by unknown hand. D'you know more details?'

'What you mean is, do I think 'e were taken by the eastling, seeing as 'ow 'e died on the same date as them others.'

'Yes… Aye, that's exactly it.'

'Well, simple answer, Tom, mate, is I don't know fur sure on account a not being told a lot else by me own fader. Or, if I were, on account a not remembering it 'cos I were only six years when he joined 'is own fader in death.'

'But you think it was the…' Tom hadn't yet worked out what the eastling was, or how he should refer to it. It had been variously described as a ghost, an apparition, a menacing mist, a shadowy figure and an evil spirit. It had been seen, its presence felt and heard, but never touched. 'You think it was the eastling?'

'Sure a it, Tom,' Jack said and threw a matey arm around Tom's neck.

Tom sagged under its weight but bore it without complaint. A friendly gesture of any sort was a thing to be treasured when it came from Jack.

'Aye, I reckon it were the eastling what killed me grandfader,' Jack said. 'But fur the life a me, I can't remember what me fader said 'bout it, excepting grandfader were same as them other poor souls what was taken fur their disloyalty.'

'Disloyalty?' Tom queried. 'You mean your grandfather had betrayed someone?'

Jack bristled. 'No, not saying that. Only…' He stopped, forcing Tom to a halt. 'I asked old Blacklocks 'bout it once.'

'And what did 'e say?'

Jack laughed for a moment and continued walking. 'Said I weren't a-ask such asks. Said there were no truth in the old looker legend, and no boy a 'is school should talk 'bout it. If grandfader Mackett died a the eastling, 'e said — it were roared more like — then it was 'cos 'e'd gone and done something bad, let down a mate, cheated on a mistus, something like that, and it were 'is own fault. Then he bannocked me. But, Tom,' he continued, hardly drawing a breath, 'I'm a the mind like Simon and 'is brother, Mike, that this year'll see the return a the eastling. It be in the air.'

The only thing Tom could sense in the air at that moment was the smell of Jack's sweat mingled with the scent of patchouli and he imagined that his senses were trying to block out Jack's reek with something more appealing.

'And that be what Simon thinks an' all, is it?' Tom asked. 'I mean, 'e didn't come a the council 'til some time after. Can 'e be sure a what 'e saw?'

'Put it this way, Tom,' Jack said, squeezing him closer. 'Simon Feld were so afeared 'e 'id like a teg 'til Mike and me near dragged 'im from the shack and carried 'im a the meeting. But, seeing as 'ow 'e's stronger than you and me stacked a'gether, you don't want a-ask 'im if 'e be sure, and nor d'you want a-question 'is word.'

'Hell, no.'

The Feld brothers were the two largest, heftiest lookers on the land and although violence was against the Lore they respected and kept, they were both capable of breaking a sheep's neck with one hand. There was a rumour that Simon had once dispatched one of Michael Rolfe's sick dairy cows in the same way. He had been fifteen at the time.

They walked in silence a while longer until the lyste-way brought them to the edge of Jack's field and the deek that separated it from the common grazing land. Although tended by Jack and looked by the Feld brothers, anyone could bring animals here, and no one person owned the pasture.

Tom let Jack cross the planked bridge first, watching how the old wood bowed in the middle. He followed him only when his weight was safely on the other side. The lookers hut stood in the distance, and a black shape lumbered in front of it.

'Simon's awake,' Jack said. 'Must be getting on fur late afternoon. Least we ain't disturbed 'im.'

The lookers worked through the nights more often in lambing season, but also to watch for foxes. They were allowed to kill the creatures if they could catch them, but not allowed to lay traps; killing animals in Saddling had to be humane. Fox furs were good trade at the shop, and several Saddling women had fox fur collars on their best winter coats. Tom was never pleased to see them.

'Oi, Simon Feld!' Jack shouted across the expanse of meadow between them.

As they neared the looker's hut, Tom prepared his questions, keeping at the front of his mind that he was not to upset the giant of a man now striding to greet them.

He was pleased that Simon met him with mild distrust and didn't want to shake hands, it saved his fingers from being crushed as Jack's were when the six-foot-six looker greeted him. Simon wore sturdy bootshoes and roughly made trousers that clung to his bulging thighs with sweat. He wore only a sheepskin jerkin, undone to reveal his smooth, heavily muscled chest, and his brown arms extended from it like the boughs of an oak.

'Our clerk's come ask ye 'bout what you saw, and 'bout the eastling,' Jack explained. 'And I come a-make sure you're fit a work and 'ave enough eating. All well, mate?'

'Aye, Mackett,' Simon replied with a grunt, staring down at Tom with an expression that gave nothing away. 'Didn't you get me story at the meet?' he complained.

'I 'eard it, Mr Feld,' Tom replied, unsure whether he should use the man's first name. 'But I was in 'opes you'd be able a-tell me more 'bout the looker legend, seeing how only one 'as taken time a-write it.'

'Didn't think none 'ad written it ever,' Feld replied, suspicion showing through his mud-brown eyes. They narrowed beneath his hedge of eyebrows.

'I found some a Eliza Seeming's writings,' Tom said, trying not to appear nervous. 'But there are parts missing.'

'We got a-be a 'elp a young Tom,' Jack encouraged. 'On account 'e be a mate a mine, and on account all else 'e's done fur us not long passed.'

Simon's eyes shot to Jack and then back to Tom where they remained, pinning him to the ground. The looker took his pipe from his belt and filled it with choke directly from a pocket. He clenched it between his crooked, yellow teeth and lit it with a match struck on his thumbnail. He studied the clerk as he took two long draws, considering the request. He nodded his head and turned back towards his hut.

'Inside,' he said, and neither Tom nor Jack questioned the order.

The hut was a roughly but solidly constructed shed made of wooden planks and salvaged window frames, not unlike Eliza's shack had been. Inside, the sunlight filtered through cracks and fell onto the furniture in shafts of dusty light. The room was a mismatch of salvaged armchairs and tables, a single bed with a curtain half pulled across it, and a few cupboards supporting a stone shelf on which stood a bucket. Tom didn't want to imagine what was in it.

Simon pointed his pipe towards an armchair, and Tom sat, his knees raised because the springless seat sagged to the floor. Jack sat on a packing crate by one of the shuttered windows, and Simon, Tom was pleased to see, sat his bulk into another wilting chair, lowering himself to Tom's eye level. He splayed his legs, relit his pipe and nodded.

'What d'you want a-'ear, nipper?'

'Well...' Tom cleared his throat. 'Tell me again what you saw the other night, and...'

'Saw what's always seen when the eastling's stalking,' Simon interrupted. 'The ghost grey-hang, the shape a boy not more than fourteen, the knife and 'is aching.'

'His aching?'

'Aye. The lad be aching fur the ones what did 'im wrong, and 'e be aching from the pain done a 'im centuries back when one a yourn sent 'im a where 'e still be now.'

Tom wished he'd brought a notebook. 'Hang on,' he said, forgetting his accent. 'Can I just clarify this? You're referring to the original saddling ritual, right?'

'Aye.'

That the legend stemmed from 1292 was an unprovable assumption. 'Do you really think...?'

Simon's eyes narrowed again reminding Tom not to show disrespect. 'I heard your story at the meeting.' He instantly changed tack and tone. 'And it's the same as I've been reading in the books. I'm a believer in the Lore just as you be, Mr Feld, and the Lore states that...'

'We take Saddling wi' all its unknowns,' Simon completed the sentence.

'Quite. Tell me 'bout the knife.'

'Ghost or real?'

'I'm sorry?'

'Ghost or real?'

Tom looked at Jack for support, but he was puffing on his pipe, lost in a cloud of smoke that billowed through the sun-shafts, worrying the motes.

'I don't get you.' He turned back to Simon.

'Tell you what.' Simon leant forward and tapped his ash into a saucer. 'I'll tell the looker's legend fur you, but I'll only do it once.'

'Bit of an 'onour, Tom,' Jack breathed from behind a cloud.

'I'm flattered.' Tom reprimanded himself four sounding weak and not using his local voice. 'Mr Feld, It'd be a very great 'onour a-'ear such a story from a looker such as ye,' he said and meant it.

Simon dropped a heavy arm over the side of the chair, picked up a bottle and swung across the room.

'Take what you want, Mr Carey. My ale be yourn in my 'ouse.'

'Thank you.' Tom's throat was parched from the walk, but made rustier by the unsettled earth dust that danced around him. He pulled the cork with his teeth and took a long drink.

Simon threw a similar bottle to Jack and, having taken one for himself, relit his pipe before continuing.

'It were the time a the great storm,' he began. 'One a them, leastwise. Exact date lost in time, but plenty a generations back and not long after the village were begun. Saddling started wi' us lookers. It were just coterells then, wi' small flocks on them, watery marsh and dowels all 'round. It were lived on by rough men who knew neither writing nor lore 'til the foreigner from the south came off 'is mount and near died in a fleet-flooding. Were a looker what saved 'im. Were a looker what got cheated by 'is family.'

Tom knew parts of this story from the Saddling Diary, but to hear it the way it had first been told sent a shiver through him. The choke fumes and the faint memory of patchouli, the slices of light and the taste of earthy hops mingled and numbed him as he listened. It took no imagination to think himself two-, five-, seven-hundred years back in time.

Simon continued. 'It were a man sent from out there wi' a message a-stop a murder,' he said, staring directly at Tom. 'Fell in the deek, got 'elped by a looker, saw the place as somewhere what needed guiding. That were one of yourn, Tom Carey, and 'e started the village wi' one a the Blacklocks. Then came the storms. Saddling weathered one in… Can't remember dates.'

Tom could. The first great storm recorded in Saddling was in 1287. Lives were lost, and property swept away. Another storm blew up in 1292, and from it stemmed the ritual of the saddling sacrifice.

'Makes no never mind.' Simon took a swig of beer and put the bottle on the ground. 'You knows 'ow the saddling got started. Their preacher cut through the neck of a looker's lad. Killed 'im. Murdered, they say, but whatever it were, it stopped the storm as dead as the boy.

'It were out on the dowels the year after when the boy come back looking fur the knife what killed 'im and looking fur them as killed 'im an' all. Revenge, like we all want time-a-time. The lad's fader were wi' 'im that night, last 'e saw a 'is only boy. The lad's death meant the end a the

Blacklocks line 'less 'e could wed another mistus, but the one 'e 'ad were still living. Not fur long.

'Every one a us lookers knows 'ow the lad comes back and when. Birthday, see, on the day of the 'arvest dance come…' He looked away, thinking briefly before once more fixing Tom with his dark stare. 'Wednesday. We take special watch every year 'round that time as none know when the boy'll be back wi' us. Two time each 'undred year, they say, but no-one counts, and none remember. None know why, neither, but we know what evil it brings.

'It comes from the east, always starts eastwards, down over the 'ill, through the night, sometimes the last a the day. 'E comes when 'e wants and there ain't nothing we can do. 'E's wi' us come Witchling Day though none can see it. Takes the smoke a the bads we burn and sucks them in. Blackens 'is soul more each time wi' the worst of what's in our minds. Suckles our evils from the fire-pile like a teg at a teat and wonders if any 'round that fire be worth taking that year. Witching Day's when it starts its planning. It's always looking for one who's betrayed, see, 'cos 'e was betrayed by them as killed 'im. Rescued by Kari from the storm one minute and 'is neck sliced open the next. It's confused, see? The eastling. That's why you 'ear it crying in the grey-hang, that's why it wanders, shedding our own bads back among us. It's lonesome, and its sadness gets in your soul if you let it. The weak it makes sick, others it makes fret. There's no explaining it.'

Simon paused to drink more ale, and Tom knew not to interrupt. Once he'd swigged and wiped his mouth with the back of his hand, the looker continued, his voice steady, but his hands shaking.

'Moon-nights when we're out on the marsh 'round 'arvest time, we sees the grey-hang waiting at the eastern mark, watching from way off, sniffing out them who's betrayed. The whitebacks baa their way far from it, take hiding in a carvet or put themselves back a their pen. Strange behaviour from a whiteback is a sure sign the evil's nearing. I've stood in the ersh and on the burnt felds, no stars, no moon, just the grey-hang all 'round me clinging, wrapping me in the eastling's breath. I've 'eard 'is sobs, I 'eard them the other night. "What be ailing you, boy?" I said it loud, so 'e could 'ear me, and the sobbing stopped. "What be wrong?" I were bold. It were strange. The grey-hang were protecting me from 'im, and I knew 'e weren't there fur me. Still, it were… uneasy. No words, no blarring, nothing but the breath a the murdered and the glint off the knife.'

The looker leant forward and lowered his voice. 'It be 'ere, Tom Carey, and it be the year fur it an' all. I only 'ope you've not gone and deceived no-one.'

It was Jack who quietly broke the apprehensive silence that followed. 'Is that any 'elp, Tom?'

'Yes... Aye, but...' Tom pulled himself to the front of the seat to sit as tall as he could. 'Mr Feld, you mentioned the knife, but said ghostly or real? What did you mean?'

Jack scoffed, but Simon silenced him with turn of his head.

'It carries its own slitting knife,' he said. 'That's what it kills wi', same as that's 'ow we slit the whitebacks, but the blades we got 'ere in our world don't do no good against the eastling. There be only the one knife as does that.'

'Aye,' Jack said. 'And that's the bit that's treddles. There ain't no real knife, Tom, and what would we do wi'it if there were?'

'It be out there somewhere, Mackett.' Simon kept his voice level, but annoyance darkened his weather-beaten face. 'Somewhere there be the first knife, the one what took 'is life, and it be the only one can end 'is wandering and returning. It be in the song.'

Tom remembered the last line of Eliza's poem. 'You mean, "An ancient, rock-bound blade"?'

'That be it, lad,' Simon nodded. 'You can't see it, it's buried with stone, under a sleeper most likely and none is going a-dig up the sleepers. When I were young and me fader told me the story... It were a chillery night 'round lambing, I were seven, eight, and 'e were teaching me the whiteback ways and the stories, see? Told me 'bout the knife. Got me a-thinking, and I figured it'd be 'neath the eastern dole stone, so I dug up the rock a-look. Made sense a me, but made a mess a the marking stone and I got me bannocking fur it, but there weren't no blade. None knows its place, but if you follow the Lore...' He glared at Jack and sighed. 'Aye. We takes Saddling wi' all its unknowns. Only thing unknown 'bout the first saddling knife is where it be.'

The cellar came to Tom's mind. The house had been in the Blacklocks' family for generations, and the cellar had stayed hidden for many years. In it, he had found a clue to solving the witchling curse, perhaps the village ministers had kept other secrets there.

'What you thinking?' Simon heaved himself from the armchair and towered overhead.

'Blacklocks' cellar,' Tom admitted. 'My cellar now. It's got stone walls.'

'So 'ave half the 'ouses in Saddling,' Jack laughed. 'You want a-pull them all down, Tom?'

'Good point.'

'You do what you got a-do, Mr Carey,' the looker said, flicking a wool cap from a peg. 'But you ask me, the best way a-go is wi' Miss Seeming's thoughts on it, and the old song. There'll be sense there.'

As far as Simon was concerned, that was the end of their meeting. He put on his cap and threw open the door.

Tom struggled from the chair with Jack's help and brushed the dust from his trousers, causing Feld to sneer.

'My earth's as good as your earth,' he said and ducked his way outside. 'No offence…'

'Forget it, mate.' Jack slapped Tom on the back, sending him staggering from the house. 'I'm going a-see Mike. Send me best a Jason, will ye?'

'Aye, Jack.' Tom regained his breath. He recalled Barry's concerns but decided against mentioning them. 'And thanks fur your 'elp.'

'All in it a'gether, Tom Carey,' Jack called, as he strode after the looker.

Tom followed the deek bank that edged the common land, walking towards the Cole farm. The afternoon was turning to dusk, the time Barry finished work. Hunger was gnawing at Tom's belly, but he ignored it as he tried to remember Eliza's rhyme. Most of it now made sense to him, but the last few lines were a conundrum, and there was something in the final line which intrigued him.

Go he will when sons shall kill with ancient rock-bound blade.

'Sons,' he pondered. 'Plural?'

Thirteen

There was a tense atmosphere at the inn that evening. Dan sensed it as he stood polishing tankards. Aaron Fetcher and his group of mainly young supporters had taken the tables nearest the fireplace and pushed them together. Sally Rolfe was among them, breaking off from her chatter occasionally to glare at Dan, while Aaron kept order in what had grown to be a heated meeting.

On the other side of the room, Bill Taylor and his clique huddled around one table, heads close, throwing looks across to the youths. Both groups kept their voices low, but their expressions told of mistrust and anger.

'It's plain daft is what it be,' Susan said, standing beside her son.

'Aye, Ma, you're right,' Dan agreed. 'But something has to give, and neither side knows what it's doing.'

'Nor what it's promising,' his mother said. She dropped a bottle of bathtub into a canvas shoulder bag. 'I best go and see Irene. Make sure they don't get to fighting.'

'Did you pick up that cordial for Mr Cole?'

'I did, Daniel, but to be honest, whatever he's got ain't going to get cured by one of your mixtures. He needs rest and no strain.'

'No chance of that.' Dan nodded towards the two factions. 'Prehaps we should tell them he ain't well. Let them see what they're doing to our minister.'

'No.' Susan held his arm. 'He's asked us not to say nothing. He'll be fine once this people's imposition is out of the way. Everything'll be right again after Eastling Day.'

Dan doubted it, but where Irene had sworn Susan to secrecy about what she thought was wrong with her husband, so Dan had sworn to Cole that he wouldn't tell anyone what he knew to be wrong. The knowledge weighed heavily on Dan's mind. He wasn't even allowed to tell Barry, and he hadn't kept a secret from his marker in his life.

'If that Aaron Fetcher gets jawsy,' Susan projected as she walked towards the door, 'tell him he won't be welcome back here 'til Needling Time.'

'Shan't be getting jawsy, Mrs Vye,' Aaron said. 'We're not like them old'uns what thinks they know what they're about. We listen a each other's voices over this side.'

'Ah, shut your blaaring, Fetcher-boy, else I'll cope your mouth.'

'Oi!' Dan shouted, surprising everyone in the bar. 'You lot act civil, or I'll close the taps and send you home to your mistuses and brats.'

'Only brats we got be over there,' Samuel Rolfe said, causing the older men to laugh.

Aaron leapt to his feet. 'What you got a-offer the village, Rolfe? 'Part from bringing back the saddling slaughter and only allowing fetching twice a year.'

Bill Taylor stood, his straight, silver hair falling to his shoulders, and his narrow mouth twisted into a sneer. 'And putting the voicing age up eighteen a where it should be, twenty-five year at least,' he snarled. 'Make sure you weasels don't get these ideas 'bout their 'eads 'till they at least got a pair of balls a-play wi'.' His group cheered him on. 'Begging your pardon, Mistus Vye,' he added, nodding to Susan and sitting.

'You be the ones what'll learn 'bout balls come Eastling Day,' Billy Farrow yelled across as he pulled Aaron back into his seat.

Mick Farrow, sitting apart from both groups with the baker, Andrew White and the mechanic, Nate Rolfe, turned to his grandson. 'I don't reckon your fader's going a-be joyous when I tell 'im what side you're taking, Billy,' he threatened.

Aaron stood, knocking over his chair. 'You making menace at me marker, old Farrow?' he challenged, squaring his shoulders.

His reaction brought Nate Rolfe to his feet. Blond, fit and level-headed, Nate was considered the sensible one of the Rolfe families, never ruffled and always fair. 'There don't need a-be no change nowhere,' he said. He didn't speak often, and rarely publicly but when he did, men listened. 'Ask me, everything's running just as it should right now and this people's imposition ain't doing no good, not fur the village, not fur you, Master Fetcher, and there's no way I can see your side, Mr Taylor. You should leave the running a village matters to them as knows how to do it.'

'Another one what's blarring,' Jimmy Payne grumbled, and the older men applauded.

Angered further, Aaron took a step closer to Nate, a man twice his age.

Mick Farrow blocked Aaron's path, and in seconds both sides of the argument were being wildly thrown in voices so loud that it was impossible to make out the words. Nate and Aaron stood nose to nose, and while Billy Farrow tried to pull his friend away, Bill Taylor threatened Ben Cole.

Sally Rolfe started shrilling at her elder brother, and Tim Taylor, who was too young to vote, made rude gestures at his marker, Jacob Seeming. The noise was unbearable, but no-one had come to blows. Yet.

Dan had spent the afternoon reading through the Teaching, searching for a legal way to end this in-fighting, but had found nothing. If he had, he would have thrown it in their faces, all of them. His blood was pumping fast, his anger simmering at the pointlessness of what was happening to the village. He stood firmly with Mick Farrow, Matt Cole and the rest on the middle ground. There was no need to change Saddling, and he couldn't let this argument continue. It could only lead to blows, and that was completely against the Teaching.

His mother was watching from the door. She wouldn't leave until she was satisfied Dan had the men under control.

He took a long, calming breath, winked at his mother, and screamed as though he was being murdered. He let the shriek continue until every other voice in the inn was silenced. Thirty shocked faces had turned to him by the time his frustration was spent. His face was purple, and his throat hurt, but his outburst had been controlled. The inn door closed with a latch-click in the stunned pause that followed, and he knew his mother approved.

'Right,' he said, coming through the hatch. 'Here's how it's going a-be, gentlemen and Sally.' He slammed the hatch into place on his next word. '*No* more a this talk in here. You…' he clicked his fingers at Aaron Fetcher whose mouth hung open, his next word cowering in his throat. 'You may sit a your table and drink my ale only if you talk civil, you all may. You…' He aimed this at Bill Taylor. 'You men should know your Teaching better. We don't fight in Saddling, and them that do are turning their back on the Lore.' He walked confidently through the men, and they backed away, reluctantly sitting and reaching for their tankards. 'Aye, Aaron,' he said, his voice calming. 'I know you wants a-be a fetcher more than anything else, and if these old men have their way, there'll be little fetching for anyone a-do. Send out the truck twice in each year only?' he mocked, staring Peter Fetcher directly in the eye. 'You be voting fur that? You're more dead-alive than a yard dog what's cut off its snout a-spite its sniffing. You *are* a fetcher. What you going a-do for work? You don't know the hob-end of a plough from a cow's tit.' Everyone but Bill Taylor laughed, but it was short-lived. 'How you going a-keep up your unlawful cigarettes if you can't go out-marsh?' Sally Rolfe gasped, and a couple of the men coughed nervously. 'And you, Aaron, you're not rightly garreted neither.' Dan tapped his head, and Aaron's face screwed into hate. 'You think that lot over there would listen a you as our minister? What you be now? Sixteen? Slippery as a grass snake and can't hardly read the Teaching? Bill Taylor were right about the balls an' all.'

More laughter was interrupted by Aaron's shrill voice. 'Nineteen and wi' as much right a bring a people's imposition as anyone.' He closed in on Dan who didn't flinch even when their foreheads touched. 'And at least the girls appreciate my balls.'

Sally Rolfe busied herself with her purse.

'Sit on your arse, you brungeon,' Dan scoffed, walking away and outwardly unmoved by the slight. 'My point be, none of you knows what you're standing fur, except you want something fur yourselves. You know that's aginst the Teaching, and I hope you're feeling bad 'bout it. Besides, now ain't the time for this.' He reached the door where he turned and left his words hanging, keeping them waiting.

He heard the click of the latch behind him, the gas lamps flickered, and a breeze wove through his legs. A few of the men appeared startled.

'The eastling's come,' Dan said. He spoke quietly, but they listened to every word as he retraced his steps. 'It's been heard out at East Sewer where the grey-hang's been thicker than it should be. It's been seen in the mist at boblight. Soon, it'll be stalking our homes while we sleep, choosing, seeking out them as has betrayed us, and that could be any one of you. The evil's going a-have a hard time deciding which one of us a-take come Wednesday.'

At the bar, with his back to them, Dan let out a long sigh to still his nervousness. What he had said was true, and the men had been worried into silence, but he was keeping a secret from Barry and Tom. He was as much a traitor as any man at the inn.

'It be true.'

He turned to see Tom and Barry in the doorway.

'What Dan says? It be true,' Barry repeated. 'Our village clerk's been looking into it. Tom's been speaking wi' Simon Feld who's seen them things Daniel talks of. Them Feld boys don't make nothing up, we know that. We got the eastling wi' us this year, so we ain't got no time fur 'aving a skarmish, and that's an end a that.'

'You only say that 'cos you lot sitting on the five-bar don't want your cradle rattled.'

Barry sucked in air through his teeth. He approached Aaron with intent and the younger man, wary of Barry's powerful, stocky build, backed off.

'No, Mr Fetcher.' Barry's eyes narrowed. 'I says that 'cos it be true. We got a bigger plough a-pull right now. This time on Wednesday, one of us is going a-die.'

Most customers left the inn by ten-thirty, leaving only one occupied table. The Rolfes had shifted from their opposing positions to group in one place. Having taken in Barry's words, their sense of family overrode their anger, but not their differing political views. Tom listened to the huddle as he collected tankards.

Nate Rolfe acted as a mediator while his cousin, Steven, argued with his sister about the pointlessness of opening the village to more outside influence. It was an old argument, discussed many times in Saddling and each time nothing had come of it.

Jason sat between them, trying to keep up with the debate and join in, but his eyes wandered to Dan taking his concentration with them.

'Have you spoken to him yet?' Tom asked, as he brought the last of the tankards to the bar.

'Not yet. Tomorrow. Got other things on my mind.' Dan glanced across to Jason before returning to his chores.

'You spoke well,' Tom said. 'Gave them something to think on.

'Aye. Just wish it weren't true.'

'Ah, you'll be safe from the eastling.' Barry nudged him out of the way as he replaced glasses beneath the counter. 'There ain't no-one as blameless as you.'

'Try telling that to Sally.' Dan nodded towards her. 'She reckons I led her on. That's the same as betraying a loved one, ain't it?'

'No,' Tom said. 'For a start, you didn't love her, but you were honest with her. Can't believe it's taken her two years and she's still not over it.'

'Aye, well them Rolfes are a strange lot.' Dan hung up the tankards.

'Bit of a riotous lot an' all,' Barry put in. 'I mean, not often you get the women in 'ere 'less there be a festival and free ale.'

'All part of the call for change,' Tom said. 'And, being honest, I don't see a problem with it.'

'Women have always been allowed in the inn,' Dan pointed out. 'Just they choose not to come in often. I reckon they have their own smoking and drinking time when their men ain't under their feet.'

Barry, sidling through the hatchway to straighten tables and chairs, stopped and turned. 'I right forgot,' he said. 'How were it yesterday wi' your bed making thing?'

'I know you forgot,' Dan replied, half a smile on his face. 'You were supposed to remind me. And what was with that cooting sheep? Fine wedding second you are.'

'I told you 'bout it,' Barry protested.

'When?'

'I don't know. Couple of months back?'

'Well, that ain't any good. How am I supposed to remember that?'

'You remember what shit goes in what bottle and comes from what tree when you be making me bath gunk. You got a-remember me telling you 'bout the whiteback.'

'You talk a nothing else but bleeding whitebacks, Barry Cole. And then there was that song. Sing? Me?'

They bantered on amiably while Tom put away the last of the glasses until all that was left to do was wait for the Rolfes to leave. Once Barry had straightened the tables, Dan poured them each an ale, and they sat at their usual place near the bar to share a pipe.

Barry talked about the farm and how they had half a day's work left before everything was up to date for the harvest. 'Been a long one this year,' he said. 'Me 'ands ain't never been so chaffed, but we got ahead, and two a the men were able a-leave today and go work on the fruit storage for Tidy at the south orchards.'

'You've done your fader proud,' Dan said, passing the pipe to Barry.

'Aye, as maybe, but we could still do wi' me fader being there. Best go and see 'im a'morrow and let 'im know.'

Tom hadn't seen Matt Cole since their meeting in the crypt, and he had expected him to be working on the people's imposition. He was surprised, too, that Irene hadn't been back to him with her superstitions.

'How is your dad?' he asked.

'I ain't seen fill-nor-fall a 'im the past few days. Expect 'e be up a 'is chin in the mire that lot be stirring up.' Barry thumbed to the Rolfes.

'That's what those kinds of oiks do,' Tom said under his breath. 'The likes of Aaron Fetcher, winding people up with false promises just to grab the limelight. There's, what…?' He looked and counted. 'There's seven members of one family at that table, split into three factions. If Dan hadn't taken their mind off their squabbles, they'd not be talking now. You should be a diplomat.'

'I only told them what they needed to hear to shut them up,' Dan said, waving away the compliment before calling across to the drinkers. 'You want a-shift it along? Getting late and I got reading a-do.'

None of the Rolfes replied, but Jason sent back a smile and waved his glass to show he was nearly finished.

'Don't wear yourself out over things,' Tom said. 'Tell me where you're up to in the Teaching, and I'll take over tomorrow. You've got enough on.'

'Aye,' Barry agreed. 'And you got your doctor's room on the go an' all. I bet Becki Tidy'll be back for 'er daily dose a Dan first thing.' He was smirking. 'Sooner you's wedded off, sooner she'll get the message.'

'I doubt it,' Dan said. 'And I ain't a doctor.'

'I don't see no difference,' Barry tutted. 'You make stuff that 'elps and 'eals, they come a you, they do what you tell them, and none else knows 'ow a-do what you be learning a-do. Sounds same as a doctor a me.'

'He's right.' Tom chinked his glass with Dan's. 'Your health, Doctor.'

'Aye, alright.'

Dan was trying hard to be light-hearted, but Tom could tell something was bugging him. 'What's on your mind?' he asked.

'Everything and nothing,' Dan replied.

'Someone ill?' Barry lowered his tankard, his brow furrowing.

'He can't discuss it.'

'Course 'e can,' Barry scoffed. 'We don't 'old no secrets 'tween us.'

Dan opened his mouth but thought better of it. Instead, he stood. 'Looks like they've had enough. I'll fetch the glasses.'

The Rolfes were finally leaving, and Tom twisted in his chair to say goodnight. Jason reached the door first but didn't leave, he hung back waiting for Sally as the others in his family filed past.

'Can I 'ave a word wi' you, Sal? Private,' he said as they left.

Dan relaxed.

'You ain't never going a-get over 'er,' Barry said, cleaning out the pipe. 'But you can't 'ave it all ways, mate.'

Dan swooped up the glasses with a clatter and a growl.

'Leave him be, Barry,' Tom whispered. 'He's got a lot to think about.'
'Bain't we all?' Barry said. 'You sure 'bout this eastling thing?'
'Aye. If the Feld lot are worried, everyone should be nervous.'
'True. But Dan's got nothing a-fret 'bout. Be pure 'eart that man.'
'Same as you.'

Tom kissed him, and Barry pulled back, shocked. 'You ain't never done that in 'ere afore.' He checked to make sure they hadn't been seen. The curtains were closed, and he grinned. 'Do it agin.'

'Oi!' Dan complained in mock protest. 'You got a perfectly good home a-do that in, take yourselves off so I can finish up and get myself to me reading afore bed. A bed, Barry Cole that smells a whiteback piss.'

Barry laughed. 'One a your medicines gone wrong?'

Dan put the glasses on the counter. 'Get yourselves home. You ain't finished your harvest yet, and you, Mr Village Clerk, have minds to put at rest while I got hundreds of pages still a-look at.'

'I said, leave that now. I shouldn't have asked you.' Tom stood and pushed in his chair. 'I can catch up on the Teaching and see Mr Cole tomorrow. If there's nothing in the book, I'll make something up. No-one will bother checking. I doubt Aaron Fetcher can read.'

'Nice idea,' Barry said. 'And totally against the Lore, but Bill Taylor ain't as thick as you might think, and Aaron's more jawsy than's good fur 'im. It's 'is lying and false promising what got the village in this mizmaze.'

'Calm down. I wasn't being serious.'

'Barry's right,' Dan said, now behind the bar, putting the glasses in the sink. 'Go on. Leave my troubles with me and get your rest. We got a big day come Wednesday, one way or the other.'

'We're here fur you, mate,' Barry said.

'And we got a spare room if your bed's too whiteback-pissed,' Tom added.

'Aye and that'd set the fox wi' the hens.' Dan ran water. 'I ain't saying there's anyone more learned than you, Tom, but even the likes of the idiot Bushnell boy out a Dowel Farm can add up two beds and three men in one house. Thanks, but I'm fine. This village doctor's got a reputation.'

'Aye,' Barry slipped behind the bar. 'And we know what yourn be. Dirty Rolfe fu…'

'Oi!' Tom interrupted, laughing.

'I know what he was going to say,' Dan said, washing glasses. 'And he'd be wrong. Wedding night's the time fur that, something else Sally used to complain on. Jenny's been happily quiet on the subject.'

Happily quiet? Dan was approaching his wedding night with more trepidation than Tom realised. Maybe that was what he wasn't telling them.

'You're an old Lore-keeper you are.' Unable to do it from the front, Barry hugged his friend from behind. 'Always be 'ere fur you, mate,' he said. 'No matter what. And when the time come on Thursday night, if you need a-know what a-do, I'll 'elp you out.'

Dan laughed loudly and twisted in Barry's grip. He cupped his face with wet hands and ruffled his curls, making Barry back off in protest.

'As if you'd have a clue,' Dan said, pushing him back through the hatch. 'Tom, take your man out a me bar, and I'll come see you in the morning with whatever I found in tonight's reading.'

'Okay, but…'

'No, no more of your bleating. Get out of here. Go on, buck off.'

'I've got the message.'

Tom took Barry by the hand, and they left the inn.

Dan waited for the door to close before he crumpled against the bar, his head in his hands and tears escaping from his eyes. They flowed and dripped onto the counter to form a puddle as he sobbed. The pressure of keeping secrets from his closest friends, his brothers almost, was too great. He needed release. His tears were ebbing when he smelt his mother's lavender perfume and felt her arms enfolding him.

She rested her chin on his shoulder, kissed his cheek, and said, 'You've important choices to make, Daniel.'

Fourteen

The last light of the day had long faded, leaving wisps of cloud to the mercy of the waxing moon which bevelled their silhouettes with silver. Its reflected light glinted from the wings of an owl as it landed silently in the bough of a mother tree. It gripped the branch with its feathered claws, soft and deadly, and tilted its head, preparing to swoop at the slightest movement.

There was unease on the marsh, a disquiet that seeped from the standing water of the deeks to saturate the withering grass and cause the feather-topped reeds to hang their heads in shame. The air was thick with treachery, the night alive with dismay. Something in the atmosphere was soon to give way and, as silently as it came, the owl left for safer hunting, disturbing a dying leaf as it took flight.

The leaf fell gently through the moonlight to land on the motionless deek instantly becoming part of the pattern of mirrored duckweed and rushes. It disguised itself among the shades of dark green thickened to black by the darkness.

The night waited as still as a sleeper's grave, but the eastling wasn't at rest. The mist began to ascend, appearing imperceptibly in the cooling air to veil the deek before spilling over its banks and spreading to the fields. It blanketed the eastern rows of rowan and willow, and turned the ochre and dull browns of the sycamore to grey as the ancient landscape succumbed to its monochrome world.

The bulrushes quivered in the unseen breeze, trembling as the grey-hang weaved through stalks and caressed long leaves. The grass dampened in the heavy air, moisture pressing flat the none-so-pretty while blue devil-in-the-bush flowers opened themselves to the night air, feeding on the moisture.

A stream of silvery vapour twisted around the trunk of a hawthorn glowing in the wash of the moon. Spiralling and branching, it grew taller, disturbing the reddened autumn leaves which fell away as if the tree was dripping tears of blood. An outline took shape within the billowing ground-cloud as the shape of fingers budded from arms and clawed the wooden handle of a time-sharpened knife. It hung beside a fragile body where shadows fashioned sad eyes and clouded innocent features with intent. From the dark space of a mouth fixed open in agony came the soft weeping for a youth denied. The figure mourned its stolen chances and its unfulfilled potential. It wailed in frustration at the theft of its choices, a cry of broken hopes that cut through the murk to chill the furthest borders of Saddling land, penetrating the sleep of whitebacks and the troubled dreams of villagers.

Gathering its hate in a withered heart, it glided from the hawthorn leaving the branches dripping with the floodwater of seven-hundred years past. Rescued from the storm, given a chance of life only to have that chance ripped apart in one slash of a blade. His rescuer offered hope only to slice it away in cruel duplicity; a mocking jest.

It gripped its knife with renewed intent. The divided village would know the revenge of the youth whose future it killed.

Distantly, between it and the cluster of houses, two figures moved stealthily across the field. Planting their crooks a pace ahead of their steps, their bodies trudged thoughtfully among a flock of sleeping whitebacks. The eastling had seen this on every return. The scene never changed, only the deceits of those who'd come and gone. They had lived lives, been allowed their chances, lied and betrayed.

The eastling sensed no betrayal with these men and moved on, stalking towards the village.

It emerged from waterways to the south and north, gathered and joined, lying low but circling and closing in until it washed up against the walls of the church-house, like ashen waves silently breaking over a rock. It turned corners, tumbled down the knoll to weave among the cottages until the village was covered by a deep carpet fashioned for ghostly footsteps.

Through an open window, around a chair and onto the stairs it climbed, searching, sensing.

There was no betrayal in this house. It faded.

In the next, the ghostling walked the boards stealthily, its presence casting no shadow from the flickering gaslight. It hovered over the bed of a sleeping boy, considering, absorbing, but swirled away. There was no dishonesty here.

Across the green, dulling the lamplight, filtering through the slats of the bench, streaming onto the lope-way. Under a door, through a crack in the bricks, it threaded itself among the sleeping, the fretting and the dying, searching for those who deserved its blade.

It could choose from many. It could reap a bountiful harvest, but it would kill only the most deserving.

It shrouded the next house and oozed inside to hang above a bed where betrayal weighted the air. Dishonesty clustered foul and thick, exhaled as soft night-breaths from the self-satisfied body curled and vulnerable below. It told the story and exposed the lies behind the sleeper's dreams of pleasure and deception.

The dreamer murmured and turned, revealing its face, and the eastling paused to consider before filtering away to once more become nothing but a spoketale.

Fifteen

Early the next morning, Barry prepared for work in a cheerful mood, confident the Cole farm was to have good luck the next season, because all the tasks apart from a few were completed. It was mainly a day for tidying, but there was still some shifting to do.

'I'll be needing bath gunk and plenty a horsebuckle wine come sunset,' he said, tying his bootshoes on the back step. 'But we done it. We got the land fixed and the storing done.'

'Your dad'll be proud of you,' Tom said, handing him his tommy as if Barry was off for his first day at school.

'Aye, well he could come and bloody see what we've done,' Barry grumbled. 'There be other important work than just council business.'

'I'm sure he'll be over to see it later. You best hurry, there's Jack on his horse heading this way. Looks like he wants you.'

'He's finished 'is land,' Barry said, standing and raising a hand to Jack on the far side of the deek. 'If 'e's offering labour fur the day, I want it. See you later, Tom. Enough to let you run.'

'Too much to see you fall.' Tom winked.

'Ah, bugger it.' Barry leant close and whispered, 'Love you.' With that, he hurried from the back-out to meet Jack at the bridge.

Tom stood in the kitchen enjoying the sudden stillness. There was always something of a whirlwind when Barry was preparing for work and the aftermath lay around him in unwashed plates, discarded clothes and unneeded farming tools. As soon as Barry left, the house breathed a sigh of relief, the boards creaked back into place and Tom let the peace wash over him. Today it wasn't completely silent, the sparrows were in the hedgerow, and crows croaked in the field across the deek, but it was quiet enough to allow his mind to calm and focus on the tasks he had to complete.

The all-workers met on the way to the farms not long after the sun began its daily climb from behind the eastern hill.

The men and women who lived in the village collected in groups to swap stories of their rival farms, inflate their achievements or ask for help from neighbours when needed. The shop opened early in case anyone needed supplies, and, at harvest time, those whose work was in other trades set them aside and offered their manpower when they could.

At twenty-three, Jason Rolfe had yet to find an occupation other than lamp-lighter. Although a respectable position, it wasn't full employment. He hoped, one day, to become a fetcher. His family had kept the shop for many generations, and he would one day inherit its running from his father. It made sense for the shopkeeper to be in the fetching business, but the role had lain with the Fetcher family for longer than anyone could remember. There were only ever two, and one of the current men, old Peter Fetcher was having trouble driving. Drew Fetcher, Aaron's father, however, had many years ahead before he could pass down his business to his son.

If he was to stand a chance of even applying for Peter Fetcher's job, Jason must prove himself to the village. He never missed a lamp-lighting or lamp-offing, and for the past eight years, had worked hard on whatever farm needed him at harvest and planting.

He swung his tommy over his shoulder with the bread, cheese and fruit his mother had packed inside and left through the back door. As he walked to the deek at the bottom of his back-out, he felt a sudden jolt of panic.

He had confided something very personal to his cousin as he walked her home last night, and although she had promised to keep the secret to herself while she pondered her advice, Jason worried that Sally might not be so discreet. He had no reason to distrust her, she was family, and the two were close. However, she was the least level-headed of the Rolfes and the one most inclined to forget herself and let a confidence slip, but Jason had been desperate for someone's advice and, after several pints at the inn, had taken the risk.

She met her party where the lope-way entered the green, and his concern increased when he remembered that Aaron Fetcher came that way with others walking out to the south fields. Jason changed his route. Instead of meeting Barry at the back of Tom's house, he took the path between the shop and Jim Fetcher's cottage to watch how Sally met the men.

The group was huddled on the lope-way. His cousin had her back to him, and Aaron was leaning in, listening intently. Jason's stomach turned, and when Billy Farrow noticed him and nudged Aaron, his heart beat faster. Sally turned, put on a smile and waved, but as she began her walk to work, he saw her snigger and share a joke with the other girls.

No-one was coming at him, no-one had thrown any threats or outrage his way, and Jason calmed himself with the hope that Sally was sharing someone else's gossip. He continued towards Tom's house and up the knoll to the sleeper-yard where he was to meet Barry. Only today, Barry was in the distance. He'd left early and was walking with Jack Mackett leading his horse by its reins. Jason reasoned that Jack must have finished his work and come to offer his more than capable hands to someone else. He'd not had a chance to talk to his marker since harvest began, and he felt guilty, knowing that Jack should have been the first person he went to with his troubles. Although Jack scared him, he set off after him, heading to the inner bridge.

'Where you going so fast?'

Jason turned to see Aaron Fetcher weaving towards him through the graves with Billy Farrow tagging along behind.

'What you doing 'ere?' he said. 'You be going the wrong way.'

'That ain't none a your business,' Aaron replied, reaching him.

'And where I be going ain't none a yourn.' Jason continued on his path. His legs were weak, and his heart was pounding. It was as if he knew what was coming.

Aaron grabbed his shoulder and pulled him around.

'Chasing after Barry Cole, are you?' the youth sneered. "E be the one you're girl-soft on is it?'

'Shut your trap, Fetcher.' Jason yanked himself free. 'And get a your work, you yawnup.'

He turned his back and looked for Jack. He had crossed the bridge but was not yet out of earshot. Jason hurried down the slope towards him, but a boot in the small of his back sent him stumbling. He heard Billy shout Aaron's name in horror before he lost his footing and tumbled headfirst over the wall. The stone scraped his shins as he tried to stop himself falling, but there was nothing to hold, and he fell into the field, landing painfully on his shoulder. Winded, he turned onto his back and pain shot along his left arm to his neck.

'Aaron, what you doing?' Billy's trembling voice alerted Jason to a further attack, and he struggled to stand. Billy was ineffectual at the best of times; there would be no help from him. Whatever Aaron was planning, his marker had no choice but to back him up for fear of being at the blunt end of Aaron's temper.

Jason was on his knees when Aaron's compact bulk landed on him, throwing him onto the hard earth. They struggled, but Jason was disorientated and weakened by the pain in his shoulder. He'd never fought, and didn't know how to retaliate. He flailed his good arm wildly and tried to find his footing, but Aaron was too quick. He spun Jason onto his back and pinned him to the ground, then knelt astride and shuffled to sit on his chest, restricting his breathing. Aaron looked around before planting his knee on Jason's painful arm and clasping a hand over his mouth against the scream of agony.

'You got a-know this, Rolfe,' Aaron whispered harshly in his victim's ear. 'There's plenty of us in Saddling what wants thing a-change. There's plenty on my side what's going a-see an easier life when we win our imposition. And there's plenty what ain't going a-like the changes we got in store. One of the things we be doing in preparation is clearing Saddling a the rats we can't bash, you get me?'

It was hard to breathe against Aaron's weight and the hand over his mouth. Jason could only kick his legs helplessly.

'I don't mind a lad falling girl-soft now and then a time, we all do it,' Aaron growled. 'None a us right-minded folk care 'bout that. Not 'less a boy don't grow out a it after twenty-two year. Then we got a-think a way a put a stop on it, you still getting me? Baven boy.' He slapped Jason's face.

'Aaron, no!' Billy's weak voice found strength.

'And you shut your meddling an' all, Farrow, or you be next.'

Jason struggled frantically, but every movement shot excruciating sparks from his chest to his fingers. The pain increased as Aaron pulled at his hand in deliberate, hard bursts.

'And this is how we put a stop a the likes a you, Rolfe,' he hissed, yanking Jason's finger on every syllable. 'So that you remember a-side wi' us come Wednesday.'

Jason was light-headed. Aaron's flesh pressed against his nose, suffocating him as he pushed harder, forcing Jason's head into the thistle-grass. His vision was dulled by a fast-growing shadow that swamped the sunlight and his consciousness.

'You only get one warning from me,' Aaron threatened. 'And this be it. You keep your snout clean, else when you got me as your minister…'

Jason was suddenly free.

He gasped for air before releasing a yell of agony. He rolled to safety clutching his shoulder, saw a pair of boots, felt a hand on his arm. He flinched, but he was being helped.

'It's alright, mate.' It was Billy, doing his best to right Jason without hurting him.

Jason squeezed confusion from his watery eyes as he groaned onto his knees. Aaron was dangling from Jack Mackett's fist, his feet kicking a foot above the turf.

'Well, that ain't going a-'appen if I gets me way.' Jack roared. 'You as minister?' He laughed and dropped the lad in a crumpled heap.

'You got a-go show Dan your injury.' Barry was on Jason's other side, lifting him to his feet. 'Billy, I can take 'im, you get a your work.'

'No, I'm alright,' Billy insisted. 'I want a-stay wi' you.' Aaron was scrambling upright, his face red, his fists clenched. 'I don't want a-work wi' Fetcher a'day,' he added, looking fearfully at his marker.

'You won't get no trouble from this cooch-grass, not less 'e wants a taste of what 'e be so keen a-give out. You getting *me* there, Fetcher-boy?'

Aaron made no reply. He was sulking and plotting revenge. He'd worried Jason before, but now he had scared him.

Jason didn't have long to think. Barry lifted him to his feet, held his uninjured arm around his shoulder and encouraged him to walk.

'Are you 'earing me, Aaron Fetcher?' Jack took a step closer. Aaron turned on his heels and ran. 'Aye, running be the only thing you be good at!' he hollered after him. 'Get a your work while I sees what Cole 'as a-say 'bout this.'

'Let it be, Jack,' Jason pleaded, his voice feeble.

'There ain't no chance a that, marker-mate.' Jack blocked their path. 'You get on, Billy Farrow and you've me thanks fur your speed. Lore knows what that bugger might 'ave don a your mate if you 'adn't.'

'Billy Farrow ain't my mate,' Jason gasped. ''E's one a Fetcher's.'

'All the same, 'e came and got us,' Barry said. 'Jack's right, Billy. You ain't got no concern. You done the right thing and me fader will know it. Off you go.'

'I didn't know 'e were going a-do that, Jason, 'onest.' Billy was only a year younger than Jason, but he stood like an admonished schoolboy, twisting the corner of his shirt. 'I'd a done something sooner if…'

'Aye, aye,' Jack cut him off. 'Get a your work, lad.'

Billy backed up the slope a pace, watching. He was about to say something else when his words failed him, and he turned and walked away.

'You be alright wi' 'im, Barry?' Jack asked.

'Aye. Dan knows 'ow we put 'is arm back in.'

Jason's left arm was swinging, useless and uncoordinated. The sight of it increased the agony, his head swam, and blackness overcame him.

'Do you mind if I use a misword in front of you?' Dan asked when Barry and Jack laid the unconscious young man on the bed.

'No, mate,' Jack answered. 'Could do wi' using a few a me own right now. The whole cooting village be going a the dogs.'

'Thank you.' Dan looked calmly at Jason and then to Jack. 'What the fuck is going on?'

Jack laughed, but cut it short. Hearing Daniel Vye swear was as weird as hearing a cat bark.

'I better go tell me fader,' Barry said. "E's got a-know what Fetcher's done.'

'No!'

Jack was surprised at how passionately Dan objected, and threw him a quizzical look.

'I need you to help me,' Dan explained. 'I'll report this to Mr Cole once I've fixed the arm. You two have work to finish.'

'You got me respect, Daniel,' Jack said, 'but you wasn't there. We saw the whole thing. From afar a-start wi', grant you, but saw it all the same.'

'Then you go, Jack. I need Barry here a short while.'

'As you want.' Jack knelt beside the bed and put his palm on Jason's forehead. "E will be right, though, won't 'e?' He looked at Dan with worry in his eyes.

Dan reassured him with a smile, but Jack could read through it. Something was not sitting well with him. He looked away and straightened Jason's hair with his calloused hand before pushing himself to his feet.

'Then I'll let you get on wi'it.'

'Before you go… Barry, could you get me a bag from next door?' Dan indicated his treating room. 'It's hanging under a shelf. Canvas bag, got things in it.'

'Aye.'

Once they were alone, Dan drew Jack close. 'Cole's at home,' he said.

'At 'ome? The minister? On the day afore the Eastling…?'

'Aye, that's where 'e be, and when you get there, you're not to say even a hushed word a Barry 'bout what you might see. You get me?'

'What's going on, Vye?'

Dan glanced uneasily at the door. 'Promise me, Jack.' He squeezed Jack's arm before letting him go.

Jack shrugged. 'As you say, Doc. You ask me, that Aaron Fetcher needs a good bannocking. Tom should turn 'is cellar into a prison and chuck 'im in it wi' the shit a me 'orse fur company.'

'Jack, find Mr Cole. Treat 'im gentle. 'E's got a weight on 'is mind.'

Barry returned with the bag. Dan took it and sat on the bed to unbutton Jason's shirt.

Jack noticed the way Barry looked at the lad. The two of them couldn't be more different. Jason with his fine, blond hair, his angled cheekbones and his soft face, lay like a sleeper, content and at peace with himself. Barry, on the other hand, was dark with anger, his thick, curly hair messed and wild. Through his rage, though, Jack detected a softness the same as Jason's. His compassion was obvious.

Dan removed Jason's shirt, and Barry hurried to take it. Drawing up a stool, he began to sponge the blood from the boy's face while Dan lifted his arm to gently feel his bones. There was a kinship in the way the two men worked together that caused a lump in Jack's throat. Barry worked carefully, tending to his friend, Dan worked studiously, diagnosing the problem, and both worked to help Jack's unfortunate marker because they cared.

And so they should, he thought, pulling himself together. That's what the Teaching taught, and yet there was something else between the two of them, something deeper. Not as deep as he'd noticed between… He glanced outside to the upper story of Tom's house. Carey sat with his back to the open window, his head bent over a book. As Jack tried to figure out what that something deeper was, Tom ran his hand through his hair from front to back and grabbed it at the nape of his neck. A click in Jack's head spurred his thoughts in the way he clicked his horse to trot. He had seen Tom do this before when he was concentrating. It was an unusual mannerism he'd only seen in one other person.

He looked back to Barry. He was doing the same thing.

The trot became a canter, and within seconds the horse had bolted taking Jack's imagination with it.

'Well, bugger me!' he exclaimed, unable to hold back a grin.

'Are you still 'ere, Mackett?' Barry barked. 'Go tell me fader. Like as not 'e'll be a the church-house.'

Dan shot Jack a look, and his eyes flashed to the door.

Jack nodded and took a step backwards. 'Afore I go,' he said and cleared his throat. 'Barry?' He jerked his head to the corridor.

'Be quick,' Dan snapped. 'We need to put his arm back in its socket before he comes round.'

Jack dragged Barry into the passage. 'Just want a-say...' He stopped. What was he going to say? The words sounded easy inside his head but stuck behind his lips as stubbornly as a whiteback refusing a gate.

'What?'

His head and his throat might be messed up, but Jack's heart knew what it was doing. 'Just wanted a-say...' He mustered his courage. 'It's fine by me.' It was warming to say it, and he smiled inwardly.

'What be fine?' Barry was outraged. 'Aaron Fetcher using fists on a neighbour?'

'No!' Jack thought he'd been clear enough. 'It's fine by me,' he repeated, nudging Barry's arm.

'What is?'

'It.' Jack nearly shouted, but he controlled it. 'You know... You and...'

'Barry? Get here!'

'Jack, I got a-go. Tell me fader everything, right?'

'Aye... Wait.'

'What now?'

'Barry!'

'I'm good wi' it,' Jack stammered. 'Not 'cos I be like it, 'cos I ain't, and I want a-get that known, no offence. No, it ain't 'cos I... But it's 'cos you're good folk, and that's what Saddling needs these days.'

'Jack, I ain't got a notion what you be...'

'Barry, please, mate.' Dan was at the door.

Jack swore under his breath. 'You and Tom Carey shacked up same as newlyweds,' he blurted. 'It makes no never mind a me long as you be 'appy. That's all I want a-say.'

He hurried down the stairs, stumbling on the last two, and ran to the Cole house.

He was sure he was right about Barry and Tom, and he was sure it was none of his business. He had meant what he said though, and he had said it because if Jason was the same, then they could tell him his marker was behind him.

'No, not behind him,' he gasped as he ran, horrified at the double meaning.

'Ah, forget it, Jack. You only get yourself buffle-headed when you start a-be nice a folk.'

He put the thoughts from his mind as he approached the lope-way. What mattered now was putting a stop to Aaron Fetcher, and if a hard bannocking was called for, Jack wanted to be first in line for the pleasure.

Sixteen

Tom set to work in his study not long after Barry left for work. He had one full day left to put people's minds at rest about the coming of the eastling. The trouble was, if Eliza's mythology was to be believed, all the signs were there, and the eastling's return was inevitable. It seemed logical that if there was a solution, it would be found in her notes. There was no harm in a second reading.

He leant on the windowsill with the morning breeze cooling his back while he turned pages, pausing now and then to smooth his hair and scrunch it at the back. Gripping it in this way helped him concentrate although he was unaware he was doing it.

By the time he had finished reading, he was confident that the only answer to the myth lay within the song. He understood that unless the eastling was stopped permanently, its cycle would begin again in perpetuity. What he was left with were the last three confusing lines.

In chances one there be a son to end his way of death.

On the face of it, Eliza was suggesting that it was possible to end the eastling's random killing, but there was only one chance to do it. How?

The next line suggested he wasn't meant to know. *None shall know the way to go 'till one man's peace be made*, but that made no sense. Which man? What peace? How would he or anyone know what to do when this unnamed man made his peace? Peace with what?

At least the last line offered vague hope. *Go he will when sons shall kill with ancient rock-bound blade*, the knife of the lookers' legend that took the boy's life in 1292. The line offered more questions than answers. Where was it? How could it have survived? And, what the hell did 'rock-bound' mean?

Tom pushed himself from the windowsill and sat at his desk. If he was prepared to believe that the murdering apparition existed, then he had to accept the knife existed too. He needed to find it, or at least other mentions of it, and there were no more references in Eliza's papers. He could recall nothing from the Saddling Diary on the subject, and there was nothing written in the Lore. There was no definite answer in the lookers' spoketale either and nowhere else he could think of to find further clues.

'Ancient rock-bound...' he mumbled.

The desk drawer ran smoothly and quietly on its runners as he opened it; the desk was beautifully made. It was the only piece of Blacklocks' furniture that Tom had kept when he bought the house. Jimmy Payne told him that Blacklocks had commissioned it not long before he vanished, and Jimmy and his son were so proud of their work, Tom had agreed to keep it. It had become his desk now, but each time he opened a drawer or polished the walnut sides or the leather top, he recalled Blacklocks and wondered what had happened to him. According to Feld, the first victim of the saddling ritual was a Blacklocks, slain by the first Carey to settle on the marsh. The two families had been inextricably linked ever since and here they were using a shared desk. The thought reminded him of Nigel Blacklocks, the uncharted descendant from the nineteenth century with no death record, and he glanced to the family trees.

'No,' he said. 'No distractions.' It was an enticing riddle, but one for another day.

He found the map he was looking for, and unrolled it on the table, pushing a pile of books to one side and using them to keep the parchment flat at the corners. The map, three-feet by two, was, like everything else in Saddling, created by hand. It was dated 1939 and signed by a Robert Vye beneath the legend, "True copy of the Vye map of Saddling from 1322." The original was kept in a chest in the crypt and never seen, another document whose condition did not allow it to be handled, but the map Tom studied was an accurate reproduction. The Vye families were known for their skill in art and now, apparently, cartography.

'And don't forget healing,' he said, as he settled into his chair, smiling at the thought of his friend across the green in his makeshift clinic. He intended to visit later that morning to see how Dan had faired with the Teaching. Meanwhile, he had something far more addictively puzzling to consider.

The map showed him the four Saddling markers that stood at the extremes of Saddling, one for each point of the compass. The northern marker was not far from the Feld hut where Tom had been yesterday. The southern one was near where Eliza's shack had once stood in the south. He'd seen the western mark out at West Ditch on Mackett's land too, a weather-rounded piece of limestone no higher than a small child. Like the one at East Sewer that Simon Feld admitted to disturbing when he was young, it was nothing remarkable and, as far as Tom could recall, none of the stones was inscribed, none showed unusual patterns or signs they might reveal a hiding place. If they had, the knife would have been found by now.

The verse might mean that it had been buried beneath one of them, but if that were the case, time would have rotted it to nothing.

'East,' he pondered, scanning the map for other standing stones. 'The harvest mist first appears from that direction... But would it travel over the resting place of its own way of death? And can you believe you are talking like this?' He looked again at his hand-drawn ancestry charts, the other maps, the notes and clippings, the record books and the literature of Saddling Lore. 'Yes,' he said grinning, 'I can,' and returned to the map.

The patterns of the deek-flows were marked, some were hair-thin lines, the outer, bordering deeks, wider moats, their bridges accurately noted. There had been two crossings in Saddling in 1322, but now there was only one, the southern bridge. There were fewer houses too and only a scattering of farms, but they bore the names of centuries ago. Cole's farm to the west, Tidy, spelt Tidie, to the south-west, Farrow and Rolfe to the east. A second Cole farm now existed. Not far from the main settlement to the east, it was begun by Matt Cole's great-grandfather and was the most modern of the Saddling homesteads. There was no sign of it on the map, of course, and the cluster of houses around the green, the semicircle of two-storey cottages Tom could see from his window, were set further apart. There had been five in 1322, now there were seven, and more had been built along the lope-way and behind as the village spread. Tom's house was named 'The Minister's Dwelling', and it had been smaller back then.

The map was a distraction. He needed to concentrate, and poring over the village history was not, in this case, helping. He removed the books from the corners, and the map rolled itself into a scroll.

Tom stared at it, grinding his teeth, until his focus blurred. There was something else to do with rocks... 'Rocks?' he questioned. 'Paving stones?' An answer nagged behind his mind where he couldn't reach. 'A building?' He'd read something... A page? A song? Or had he seen something? In the last few days... It had something do with a rock. The harder he tried to recall it, the deeper the memory hid. 'Think of something else and it'll come back to you,' he said, putting the map away carefully before slamming the drawer in frustration.

The sound was followed by heavy footsteps on the stairs, and he rose, expecting to see Barry come home for something he had forgotten.

'What it is?' Tom called, before he stepped onto the landing.

Jack Mackett gripped the bannister, his bulky frame filling the stairwell. His tanned face was drawn, and he was wiping his forehead with the back of his hand.

'Bloody hell, Tom,' he said, short of breath. 'I just come from the Cole 'ouse. We're in shit.'

Tom had never seen Jack this worried. 'What's up?' he asked, as an uneasy premonition shivered through him. He was in for dire news, but he could never have imagined what Jack said next.

'I don't envy you your task. But you got a-tell your lover-man that 'is fader be soon dying.'

First, Tom was confused by the words "Lover-man" spoken so easily. Then it was the fact that Jack had used them at all, followed in a flash by the realisation that Jack knew the intimacy of Tom's relationship, and equally as rapidly by the shock that he appeared not to care. The confusions scattered like ninepins when the rest of Jack's announcement sank in.

'Matt Cole's dying?' Tom stammered.

'Near death.' Jack turned and headed downstairs.

'What are you talking about?' He caught up with him in the hall. 'What do you mean?'

'It be a coots-bugger of a mess, Tom,' Jack panted. 'What with what's 'appened a Jason, what's wrong with Matt Cole, what's a coming a'morrow. It be beyond me, I got a-get back a me mount.' He let himself out.

'What do you mean dying?' Tom insisted, following.

'Go a 'im, and you'll see.' Jack glanced up to the inn. 'Last I saw, your man were in there wi' Daniel. Tell 'im not a-worry 'bout 'is work. I'll see a that. 'E won't need the worry a finishing 'is 'arvest chores, not a'day.'

Tom was unable to take in the information. 'I saw Mr Cole on Sunday,' he said. 'He was fine.'

'Aye, well 'e ain't fine now, poor sod. Who knows what this is going a-do to that imposition. If Cole can't 'ang on a couple a days, Fetcher and Taylor'll 'ave no trouble riding saddleless over the deputy. I 'ave a-get on, Tom.' Jack walked away, but stopped to look back. 'If it be any 'elp, Carey,' he said, 'I can't think a none other who can sort this mizmaze. Best a luck.'

Seventeen

Tom needed proof that the state of affairs was as dire as Jack had suggested. He crossed the green and took the lope-way to Matt Cole's house a few doors along the path. The upstairs curtains were closed, but the front door was open. As he approached, Irene came from her kitchen and, seeing him, beckoned him inside.

'What's happened?' Tom expected to see her in tears, but she greeted him with a smile. Perhaps Jack had misunderstood.

'Tom, be a love will you and go find Barry. It's time he knew.'

'Jack's just been to see me…'

'Aye, Matthew told him he should.'

'Is he alright?'

'Who, Jack? Aye, he be…'

'No, Minister Cole.' Tom lowered his voice. The house was gloomy, and he was aware of a stillness that hadn't been present on previous visits.

'No, not so good, but he's got some kick left in him yet.'

Tom couldn't believe her calmness. 'What's wrong with him?'

'Tom, just go and find your Barry and bring him here. Tell him his fader's waning, and he'll understand.'

'Should I go for an ambulance?'

She pushed past him to reach the stairs. 'You been here long enough a-know that's not how we do things, Tom. Please, bring Barry. And Daniel if you might.' She began climbing the stairs, pulling herself up by the bannister. 'Quick as you can.'

Tom ran from the house, his mind working as fast as his feet. Cole's illness, whatever it was, must have come on suddenly, and he imagined it was a heart attack. Too much pressure from the warring factions, the approach of the eastling, the wedding… He slowed his pace when he reached the green. If Cole wasn't well enough to officiate the wedding, Mick Farrow would have to take the ceremony. That wasn't a problem, but when it came to the people's imposition, Jack had been right. Mick Farrow was no speaker and without a leader, the village would side with whoever promised them what they wanted to hear. More worrying, however, was how he was going to break the news to Barry.

He found him in Dan's bedroom sitting on the bed beside Jason Rolfe.

Jason's arm was in a sling, and Dan was applying a purple liquid to cuts on his shins.

'Say, mate,' Barry said, as Tom stood breathless in the doorway. 'What you in such a 'urry fur?'

The words were firmly lodged in Tom's throat, and he held up his hand for patience while he regained his breath. He pointed at Jason's arm.

'Shoulder came out,' Dan explained. 'We reset it.'

'Always doing it at the farm,' Barry said. 'Don't know 'ow a-lift a bale, the little oik.' He ruffled Jason's hair.

'Think you'll do now,' Dan said, corking the bottle. 'Don't use that arm a few days if you can help it.'

'I'm sorry, Barry,' Jason said. 'Don't think I'll be up to working a'day.'

Barry waved it away. 'I'll see a the work, you rest up and make yourself ready for tonight's aepelling.'

Dan groaned.

'No point moaning 'bout it now,' Barry snorted. 'You made your bed…' He kicked the new wooden frame. 'You be 'aving a-lay in it afore long.'

'Dan, can I take a word wi' you afore I go?' Jason stood, and blood rushed to his head, causing him to sway.

'Easy there.' Dan steadied him by his undamaged arm. 'Stand a while 'til you're straight again. What are you needing, Tom?'

Hearing his name focused Tom's mind, it had drifted into a stream where words bobbed out of reach.

'Dan, it's urgent.' Jason spoke before Tom had a chance to reply.

'I got a-go a the farm.' Barry pushed himself to his feet. 'I'll stop and see me fader in case Mackett didn't give 'im every detail 'bout what 'appened. That Aaron Fetcher's got a-be punished good, and fader'll want all witnesses.'

'Dan,' Jason implored. 'It's something difficult I got a-tell you and it ain't a thing as can wait.'

'Sorry, it's going to have to,' Dan said. 'Tom, are you unwell? What's up?'

What was the word Irene had used? Waning. It wasn't an expression Tom had heard for what was happening to Cole.

'Barry, mate,' he said, taking a step towards him, his legs weak and his stomach knotted. 'I just come from your fader's house…'

'Had Jack been?' Barry broke in. 'Did he tell fader what 'appened a Jason?'

'What? No…' What had Jason to do with this? 'No, it's not that.' Tom took Barry's hand, not caring what Jason thought. He was ready to hold

Barry as soon as he told him the news. 'It's your fader,' he whispered. 'Your ma says to tell you… Your dad's waning.'

Barry's expression of mild confusion didn't change. He blinked and took in a slow, deep breath before taking Tom's other hand and squeezing it as a thank you.

'Your ma wants to see you,' Tom said. 'And you, Dan.'

Dan had turned away and was resting on the table, his head hanging.

'Aye,' Barry whispered. 'We'll go dreckly-minute. Did she say 'ow long?'

Tom had been young when his parents were killed, but the pain and shock were still with him after twenty years. He had expected Barry to fall apart at the news and couldn't comprehend his coolness.

'How long?'

'Aye,' Barry said. 'Do 'e 'ave days, a week, hours?' As with his mother, there were no tears and no hysterics, in fact, he hardly reacted.

Again, Tom fished for words that didn't come.

'Dan?' Jason, also unaffected by the news, pulled at Dan's sleeve. 'I really got-a tell you…'

'Not now!' Dan swatted him away. He searched through his bottles, his hands trembling and clumsy.

'Did she say?' Barry insisted.

'Say? No. Just said you were to come at once.'

'You can't just say someone's waning and not tell 'ow much time 'e 'as,' Barry tutted. 'Typical a me bloody mother, that is.'

'Did you know?' It was the only reason Tom could think of for Barry's lack of concern.

'No idea, Tom. We'd best go, I reckon.'

'It's days.' Dan said. 'He's only got days.' He turned, sad and frowning. 'I'll cancel the wedding.'

'Aye,' Jason leapt in. 'That's the best thing. I'll tell me sister…'

''Old on.' Barry let go of Tom and turned to Dan, realisation growing. 'You knew?'

'Barry…' Tom warned.

'You knew, and you didn't tell me?'

'He asked me not to.'

''Ow long you been keeping this news inside you, Daniel Vye?'

Barry was angry. Finally showing emotion, he edged around the bed, his fists balling.

'Barry, stay calm.'

Tom was ignored as Barry pulled Jason out of the way. 'Get you 'ome, mate,' he said. 'Do as Daniel says, rest up, and not a word a no-one, 'specially not Jenny.'

Jason objected, but Barry pushed him towards the door.

'Barry, wait...'

'Go, Jason.' It was a threat, and it came from Dan.

'Then I'll tell you, Mr Carey,' Jason blurted, but Tom shook his head, his eyes fixed on Barry. 'I 'ave a-tell someone.'

'After!' Barry yelled, leaving no room for debate.

Tom was hardly aware of Jason's yell of frustration as he left. Barry now stood directly in front of Dan who, though taller, cowered beneath his friend's distress.

"Ow long you known?' Barry growled.

'Couple a weeks.'

Keen to separate them, Tom made his way around the bed. 'I can take the trap. Get Peter Fetcher to drive him to hospital...'

'Couple a weeks?' Barry's outrage increased.

'He told me not to talk of it. Didn't want to put you off the harvest work.'

Dan reached for Barry's shoulder, but his friend knocked his hand aside 'The 'arvest could a gone singing,' Barry said. 'But what you been doing 'olding this from me fur all this time? Why couldn't you tell me?'

Anguish bubbled beneath the surface of Barry's anger, and tension thickened air.

'He's not allowed to discuss patients,' Tom explained, desperate to mediate.

'I'm sorry, Barry.' Dan was now more ashamed than frightened.

'No, Daniel. I'm the one as is sorry.' Barry rolled and unrolled his fingers.

'Barry, don't do it...' Again, Tom was ignored.

'Fader should a let you tell me, Daniel. You been carrying this around in your 'ead and not able a share wi' even me?' Barry raised his hands. 'Daniel Vye...'

Tom tried to hold him back, but he fought free. Tom readied himself for the fight, but...

Barry threw his arms around Dan, and they clung to each other, embracing silently.

Tom stepped back, relief muddied by confusion. Barry was more upset for Dan than for himself? And he was crying. He held Dan's head in his hands and searched his face.

'You be so cooting… stupid-loyal, Daniel bloody Vye.' Barry kissed his forehead before clinging to him again. 'I be so sorry me fader done this a you.'

'It's okay, mate,' Dan whispered. 'But if you forgive me, we should go see him.' He held Barry at arm's length and wiped his cheek with his thumb.

'Aye.' Barry nodded. 'But nothing a-forgive. You alright?' he asked.

'Aye.'

'Never mind Dan,' Tom said. 'What about you?'

Barry turned to him and held the back of Tom's head, drawing him close. 'Thanks fur telling me, Tom,' he said. 'That's a favour I owe you, but it ain't as much as I owe this one. Poor lad, having a-keep that news inside.'

'Yeah, okay, I get that,' Tom said. 'But aren't you upset?'

''Course not, lover. Sleeping comes fur everyone. What we got a-do now is get on wi' what we got-a get on wi'. Go see me fader, wish 'im well, and after…' He gave Tom an impromptu kiss and squeezed past him. 'After, we got Daniel's aepelling, the festival and some bloody wedding or other. Coming, Dan?'

Barry was out of the door and heading to the stairs.

'Is this normal?' Tom asked, incredulous.

Dan nodded as he dropped a bottle into his bag and slung in on his shoulder. 'Saddling, Tom,' he said as if that answered everything. 'Death's only worth a worrit when we don't expect it.' He ushered Tom backwards to the door where he followed Barry to the top of the stairs, his mind tumbling.

'It's in the Teaching,' Dan whispered behind him. 'There are things us friends must do for him and Irene and the rest of the family, and we will, in time. There's nothing we can do for Matthew now except take his burden, which is why…' He leant over the bannister and waited for Barry to leave the inn before continuing. 'We carry on as usual, no matter what. I've upset Barry enough by holding a secret, that's going to worry him more than the natural passing of his fader.'

'But we can get him to a hospital. What's wrong with him?'

'How do I know?' Dan shrugged as he took the stairs. 'His guts are chewed up, and he knows he can't be cured. Same as his fader. Come on, mate, your minister's waiting on you, and you don't have time for fussing.'

Tom was still in shock when they arrived at the Cole house, and his confusion increased when he followed Dan into Cole's bedroom. The curtains were drawn, and the gas lamps turned low. The minister was sitting up in bed talking to Barry, neither displayed grief.

'So, that's 'ow I'm leaving it wi' you, boy,' he said. 'I done the papers a fortnight back. It be yourn now.' He raised a finger to Tom. 'Come in, Carey. You and me got business a-sort.'

'Minister Cole...'

'Aye, I know,' Cole interrupted. 'You're sorry, you wish there were something you could do, and you want a-bung me in Fetcher's clapped out truck and cart me out-marsh. Well, that ain't going a-be 'appening, not least 'cos it would go an prove Aaron Fetcher right 'bout us needing out-marsh ways. Dan reckons I got a couple a days. I want a be 'ere fur 'is wedding, but I doubt I shall.'

'Mr Cole...' Why wasn't he distressed?

'I won't make your aepelling,' Cole said, turning to Dan. 'Sorry a-miss it, but I reckon I needs me strength fur the people's imposition come Wednesday. I'll be 'ere fur that, long as you got more a that medicine a yourn.'

'I have, Mr Cole.' Dan handed him the bottle from his bag. 'It's helping the pain?'

'Middling, but pain's nothing, not when I got me sleeping a-look forward to.' He took a swig. 'Don't know 'ow you work this magic, Daniel Vye,' he said. 'But I be glad you do.' He stoppered the bottle and placed it on the bedside table.

'Is there anything I can do?' Tom asked, not sure whether to sit on the bed or stand to attention. He'd never been at a deathbed, and Barry was being of no help. He was reading sheets of paper and eating an apple.

'Aye, Tom,' Cole said, pushing himself up on his pillows and grimacing. 'You can listen up. I ain't going a-leave Saddling in the 'ands of the likes a Aaron Fetcher and 'is... What d'you call them, Daniel?'

'Neo-nancies.'

Despite everything around him, Tom sniggered.

'Good to see you got 'umour, Carey,' Cole said. 'You're going a-need it. I'm not leaving Saddling in their 'ands, so I'm in 'opes you got me answer from our Teaching or Lore. You found a way out a this yet?'

Tom shot Dan a look, but Dan shook his head.

'Still working on it, Mr Cole,' Tom said and turned to Irene at the window. 'But I might have found a way to end this eastling panic, Mistus.'

'Panic,' Cole laughed. 'Aye, good word fur it. Folks only panic when they don't know the 'our a their sleeping. I can tell you, them as do are the lucky ones, which be why I ain't worried. I can see you don't understand none a this, Carey.'

'You're right, I don't.'

'Aye, well you're in Saddling now, and it looks like you're not going a-bugger off out a it, not come a long while, am I right agin?' He tipped his head towards Barry, still poring over paperwork.

'You are correct, Mr Cole.'

Cole regarded him, thinking for a moment before speaking. 'As I feared. Well, Carey, I can't pretend I understand you two, and I can't say I'm ever going a-find complete approval in me.'

Tom expected there to be a 'but' after that, but no, that was all Cole wanted to say. He was not prepared to give his blessing to Tom and Barry, not even on his deathbed.

'I do 'ave business fur ye, though. Irene?' He waved to his wife, and she passed him a book.

She took no notice of Tom. Either she'd not heard what her husband had said, or she chose to ignore it.

Tom recognised the Book of Authorisations, one of the ledgers from the crypt, in which the minister noted and signed what Tom called executive orders. Cole had rarely used it because his council acted in harmony, but the entries from previous years were numerous, each one signed by William Blacklocks.

'Over 'ere, Carey.' Cole waved Barry out of his way, and Barry, hardly noticing, took his paperwork to a corner.

'Do you need me?' Dan asked. 'I have reading to do.'

'Aye, I do,' Cole said, and that was the end of that. Irene passed Dan a chair.

'Carey.' Cole began in the voice he used to open council meetings. 'We've had a breach of the Lore in the village this morning, completely aginst the Teaching, and it's down a you…' He scrawled Tom's name in the book and offered it. 'Down a you a-see it through. I'm leaving this permission fur you, but I suggest you consider whatever me second, Mick Farrow, 'as a-say. I be asking you a-do this 'stead a 'im on account a you being more level-'eaded than anyone other in Saddling — 'part from Daniel prehaps. So, sign this and you 'ave me power a-punish.'

Tom was honoured by the gesture but not sure he knew what to do about it. He signed, and Cole shoved the book to one side. 'Next thing,' he said. 'I reckon I've got 'bout ten minutes afore Dan's potion brings up 'alf me stomach and a bucket more blood…'

'Oh, the bucket!' Irene left the room hurriedly.

'So, listen up, Carey. I spoke a Mick 'bout the Eastling Day. Outside this room, Jack and Mick's the only others what knows I'm on me way. No point telling the village else Fetcher'll get it into 'is buffle-'ead that 'e can use it fur 'is advantage. So, order is, everything runs as it always does, and I'm in bed wi' a rough case a fever. Only me family and Dan can come see me. Got that?'

Tom nodded.

'After, when whoever wins the bale-toss…' He threw his pen at Barry who glanced up from his reading. 'And I expect that a-be you, nipper, leading the village a the church-house.'

'Aye, Fader.'

'After that, Carey, you and Farrow got a-tread careful and quick-thinking. The people's got a right a the imposition, always 'ave 'ad and always will 'less a future council put a stop on it, but it ain't never been used fur something as twisted as this afore, understand? It ain't 'cos we ain't been listening a what the young'uns want, we 'ave, and none more closely than you.'

That was a veiled compliment, and it boosted Tom's morale.

'But as I said afore, now ain't the time fur the village a-be split. You got a-bring them back a-gether. I ain't got the strength fur it. I know I'm talking good now, but I can't be sure I'll even be 'ere a'morrow. If I ain't sleeping by then, you get me a that church-'ouse if you need me. But only if it ain't going a-give Fetcher more lead fur his shotgun, got me?'

'Aye, Sir.'

'Mind, none of that's going a-be necessary 'cos I got no doubt you'll find something in the Teaching by then and'll put everything right, fur the sake a the village.'

'We're trying,' Tom said, realising that he'd not checked how far Dan was in his research. He should have taken the task himself and left the eastling myth where it belonged; as a bedtime story.

'That be all I can ask,' Cole concluded. 'And everything I can tell you, excepting this.' He beckoned Tom close to whisper. His breath smelled of blood, rancid and warm, and he spoke pointedly. 'I'm leaving me Barry wi' ye, 'cos I ain't got no choice, bloody runagate that 'e be. But I ain't never going a-forgive you fur taking away 'is natural right to 'ave a boy of 'is own a-pass the farm to when 'e be sleeping 'long-side me.' He pushed Tom away.

Much as he wanted to argue and explain, this was not the time or place. Tom knew he would never be accepted as part of Cole's family.

'Lads,' Cole said, 'I be 'bout a-vomit, so I wants you away. Daniel Vye?'

'Yes, Sir?'

'You get your aepelling sorted and be sure a-'ave a good 'un. Barry? Mackett's seeing a the farm a'day, so you can 'elp Dan. Remember your duties as 'is marker and make me proud.'

'Aye, Fader,' Barry said, wandering to the door, turning pages.

'Carey?' Cole studied Tom and shook his head. 'Well, you know what you got a-do.'

He pointed to the door and shouted for his wife.

Tom stood back as Irene, pink-faced but nonplussed, returned with a bucket.

'Try not to worry, Mistus Cole,' he said before following Barry and Dan. 'Is that it?' he hissed. 'We just get on with it as if nothing's happening?'

'Tom, mate,' Barry said waving documents in his face. 'I got me own farm a-think on now. Fader'll be remembered and missed. The only Saddling minister who weren't a Blacklocks nor a Carey? That's going a-be in the 'istory lessons. Come on, you can share me tommy wi' me.'

'How can you eat? How can you not be upset?'

'Oh, Tom,' Barry sighed. 'You're going a-live wi' me in Saddling 'til the day we sleep, and you're never going a-get it, are you? We don't fret 'bout death. We be taught from young that there ain't nothing a-be upset wi' when it be time a-die. It's what you do when you're awake what counts, and me and Fader's 'ad nothing but good... Mainly. You'll get our ways sometime, but fur now, I be 'ere a-see you through.'

'Me too.' Dan opened the door, ushered the others into the sunlight and rubbed his hands together. 'Right! I'd better go and find one hundred hurricane lamps,' he said with false cheer. 'Bloody wedding.'

Eighteen

Tom tried to come to terms with the reaction to Cole's terminal illness, but none of it made sense. People in Saddling didn't see death as something to grieve over. There was no part of the Saddling Lore that promised life after death, no heaven and no hell. There had been no religion in the village since the late thirteen century, since when the Lore had grown as organically as the marshes, inspired by the elements. The village was led by the weather, the flow and ebb of the deeks and the death and regrowth of the land. Contained within it were the basic principles of community living; trust, honesty and sharing.

Matt Cole was going to die. It was expected, and it would be dealt with.

He left Barry and Dan outside the inn where they began preparing Dan's aepelling. Having been assured that he was of more use checking the Teaching, Tom returned home.

The morning had slipped away from him, and by the time he had eaten and sat at his desk, it was early afternoon. The aepelling was due to start half an hour before sunset, giving Tom enough time to scan the second half of the book, he thought. In fact, he was able to reach the end long before then and, to his dismay, found nothing to head off the people's imposition.

'Damn it!' he cursed, shoving the Teaching disrespectfully across the desk. He rested back in his chair, staring at the tomes on the shelves. 'There's got to be something in here…'

He rose and stood at the window, staring across at a group of men who had gathered at the back door of the inn. Barry was among them, and another, young Tim Taylor, held a pony by its reins. The men were stacking a cart with hurricane lanterns, and Samuel Rolfe was bringing more of them from the shop.

On the other side of the green, Jenny Rolfe sat with a group of women weaving small flowers and grasses into wreaths. When enough were completed, Aaron Fetcher took a basketful and delivered them to various houses while Bill Taylor and Jimmy Rolfe set up trestle tables on the green ready for the following day.

Standing alone with his arm and shoulder bandaged, Jason looked on from the end of the lope-way. Forlorn, he watched his sister direct her helpers before turning to the inn, shaking his head and glancing to Tom's window. He waved as Aaron Fetcher approached him holding out a wreath. Apparently the animosity between the two youths had evaporated.

Tom waved back, and a thought struck him.

Both sides of the current people's imposition were working together, seemingly with no hostility, and for the benefit of the soon-to-be-wed couple. Everyone in Saddling worked together, and everyone's point of view was valid. Why should he be searching for a way to block their right to question their minister? Shouldn't he let things run their natural course? Aaron and Taylor had as much right to ask their fellow villagers for their confidence as Matt Cole or anyone else. What if Tom chose not to find a way to stop tomorrow's vote and left things to chance?

He was turning away when laughter drew his attention back to the green. Aaron was forcing a wreath onto Jason's head, causing the girls to scream with delight. Only the women wore the aepelling wreaths. Aaron walked away, lapping up the attention, as Jason ripped the flowers from his head and crushed them beneath his boot.

Tom returned to his desk. Cole was right, they couldn't trust the village with someone as childish as Aaron Fetcher, he doubted the lad even knew the Lore.

'The Lore!' he exclaimed, swivelling in his chair and pulling himself under the desk. He reached for one of the transcriptions and opened it. 'Cole mentioned finding the answer in the Teaching or the Lore. Maybe there is something in there.'

He began skimming from page one but was interrupted a couple of minutes later by a knock on his front door.

Growling, he leant from the window to see Jason standing nervously outside.

'Hi,' Tom called.

'Tom, Sir,' Jason said. 'Can I come up?'

Tom beckoned him into the house and waited at the window. Tim Taylor led the pony and cart behind the church, and the men followed. On the other side, the women were still at their work, now joined by Rebecca Rolfe who brought a large pewter jug. She placed this in front of the group and sat, singing. As the women joined in with the song, they took it in turns to dip a small cup into the jug and drink.

'Sorry.' Jason was in the study. 'Are you busy?'

He was, but he had duties as the village clerk, and if this was village-related, he had to give Jason the time.

'What's up?' he asked, pointing to a chair. 'How's your arm?'

Jason shrugged. 'Happens a lot,' he said. 'Usually 'cos I'm lifting, never done it falling off a wall afore.'

'You were kicked over a wall, weren't you? There's a difference. Is that what you want to discuss? Because I have a punishment for Aaron and will make it known tonight.'

'You going a-do that?' Jason asked, taking the chair and sitting. He fidgeted nervously, his soft eyes darting around the room. 'What 'bout Minister Cole?'

'He's unwell, and I have permission.' Tom took his own chair.

Jason accepted that without question and nodded to the desk. 'You reading the Lore?'

'I am.'

''Cos a the imposition?'

'Aye.'

'Properly worded, if you ask me,' Jason said. 'Bloody imposition to question the minister and the council. That Aaron Fetcher needs putting in 'is place, ask me. Stop 'im, and Mr Taylor'll lose interest an' all.'

'Really?' Tom hadn't considered that possibility.

'Aye. Taylor's only got 'is old folk behind 'im so as a-stop Aaron.'

'So why not back Minister Cole?'

'Things ain't as simple as that 'round 'ere, Tom,' Jason said managing a weak smile. 'Our Lore there, it may say we don't fight nor 'ate each other. It may say we must show respect, but it don't stop folk keeping dark thoughts 'bout the past. Taylors and Coles? A real old fight be going on there. Been rumbling fur generations.'

'Really? I thought this was all about seizing power. I didn't realise it was to do with a feud.'

'There's always two sides to every story, Tom,' Jason said.

That was true and it helped make sense of the way Taylor was behaving.

'Interesting,' he said and waited for Jason to continue.

The youth cradled his arm and scowled. He squeezed his forearm along towards his hand, his gaze averted, thinking of how to phrase whatever he had come to say. Holding his wrist, he finally looked at Tom, his eyes that usually dazzled were dulled with pain, both physical and emotional. He bit his bottom lip.

'You can tell me what you want, Jason,' Tom said. 'But can you do it quickly?'

'Aye, Sir,' Jason sighed. 'Thing is…'

'You don't need to call me Sir.'

'Thanks… Tom.' The lad took a deep breath and massaged his fingers. 'Thing is… Well, this ain't easy. See, like there's problems 'tween the Coles and the Taylors, there's problems 'tween families, and inside families. I got me brother and me sister at 'ome, well, you know that. Thing is, I got this problem and it be 'bout Daniel. Well, Daniel and Jenny.'

Tom knew where this was heading. 'I think you need to talk to Dan,' he said.

'I tried, Tom, but 'e ain't 'ad the time and 'e wouldn't want a-'ear me anyhow. You see…' He cleared his throat and massaged his fingers more vigorously. 'This ain't easy…'

'You're okay, Jason.' Tom spoke kindly, trying to imitate the tone of a particular college tutor, the only compassionate teacher in his life. 'Your words stay in this room.'

'Thanking you, Tom. The thing is…' Jason broke off suddenly and looked at his hand. 'Oh no!' He began frantically searching the chair, the floor, the pockets of his jerkin all the time muttering, 'No.'

'What is it?' Tom asked, mildly amused.

'I gone and lost me bloody ring.'

'Your…?'

'Me family ring. It's got me name in it. We each got one. Fader'll give me a right bannocking if 'e sees I ain't got it.'

'Where were you wearing it?'

'On me finger, 'course.' Jason was on his hands and knees.

'When did you last see it?'

'I don't know!' he snapped.

Tom ignored his tone. 'Take a moment to think calmly.'

'You don't understand,' Jason shot back. He was on his feet, his face red and his eyes watery. 'Me fader be like Blacklocks were when it comes a family things, and that ring be 'is pride an joy. The whole lot a Rolfes wear them and being without it, well, that be almost a worse thing than what Aaron did a-me.' He was trying hard not to cry.

Tom crossed the room and took him by his unbandaged arm. 'Jason,' he said, 'it's okay. Dan probably took it off when he was treating you. Your fingers are still swollen. I expect he didn't want it to cut off your circulation.'

'You think so?' Jason's blue eyes twinkled in hope. 'I'll go ask.'

'He's getting ready for the ceremony,' Tom said. 'And so must I.'

'Aye. I'll 'ave a-go looking fur it after. I gotta find it afore fader notices, else 'e'll drag me on that cracked slab and order I gets a public bannocking or something worse.'

He wiped his face and walked to the door. 'Thanks, Tom, Sir. Oh, 'bout that other thing...'

'Stop.' Tom ordered. 'What did you just say?'

'What 'bout?'

'A cracked slab...' Tom was back at his desk and rifling through papers, leaving Jason wondering in the doorway.

'I still got a-tell you what I wanted a-say.'

'Yeah, sure, later though. Thanks, Jason.'

'Fur what?'

Tom didn't hear him. His concentration switched from ending the imposition to unlocking Eliza's last lines of verse.

His mind raced as he searched. There had been a mention of a cracked slab in one of the reports. Or was it in a book? There was so much research he couldn't remember where he'd read it. He piled the burial records to one side, confident it hadn't been in those. The Saddling Diary was a possibility, and he found it buried under Eliza's collection of traditional songs. Or had it been the Lore? Something to do with a broken stone... a cracked casket, was it? An ancient stone... Possibly. A bed, or a... No, that wasn't it.

'Sir?'

'Ancient rock-bound blade,' he mumbled.

'Sir.' Jason was insistent.

'Later,' Tom nearly snapped, but he remembered himself. He took a breath and faced the younger man. 'Sorry, Jason,' he said. 'I can't talk right now. We'll chat later. Meanwhile, ask Dan about your ring when you see him. You need to go home and dress for the aepelling. You're to be the brother-in-lore, got to show support.'

'Aye,' Jason accepted his words with a sigh. 'I'll go change, but there'll come a time when I got a-say what I got a-say, and I got a-say it afore Thursday or it'll be too late.' He was backing from the study. 'Glad I 'elped you, Sir. Me apologies fur taking up your time.' He spoke in the manner of one who has tried and failed and must admit defeat.

Tom only vaguely heard him, his attention was focussed on his research.

'"Go he will when sons shall kill with ancient rock-bound blade,"' he quoted when he found Eliza's original scrawl of the verse. He thumbed through her other notes, reading out words as he saw them. 'Pain shall go…' A recipe involving poppies and valerian roots that Dan had mastered. 'Reading the bones… Witch-water… On the passing of a Minister? What's that doing here?'

The heading caught his eye not only because of Cole's condition but also because he recognised the colour of the parchment. He flipped it over and back again. It was another torn page, but this one had not come from the Book of Teaching but from the original Book of Lore. He slipped it into his transcription as a reminder to return it to the original tome. 'Not what you were looking for…'

As the day passed him by, he searched his collection until everything on the desk and shelves had been fruitlessly checked. He stood in the centre of the study and scanned the family trees.

'Why was it important?' he whispered. 'A cracked rock… Somewhere to hide a blade… Somewhere in here,' he said, 'is the answer to my bloody riddle.'

A pair of calloused hands covered his eyes, taking him by surprise.

'You talking a yourself agin, Tom Carey?' Barry said, releasing him.

'What time is it?' The room had darkened.

'Time we was getting ready fur Daniel's aepelling.' Barry wore only his under-shorts, tight around his stocky middle, and sweat tricked through the dark hairs on his chest. 'Old Farrow says we're in for a storm come a couple a days, but I reckon not a'night and we're in 'opes not 'til after Thursday. I'll put your clothes out, you go wash.'

'Sure, sure,' Tom held his forehead. He wanted to release his frustration with a yell, but his logical mind fought it and put things in order. He had a duty to perform, and not just overseeing the aepelling. There was Aaron's punishment to administer.

What he had planned could further divide the village, or it could help unite it. He had to think and tread carefully.

He watched Barry trudge into their bedroom, and the sight lifted his spirits. They plummeted again when he recalled Cole's words. The man was going to die hating Tom because he loved his son. Again, a part of him wanted to let the people's imposition go ahead, just to spite Matt Cole, but that was not how life worked in Saddling.

He swallowed his anger and said, 'One thing at a time. Duty, punishment, celebration.' He stacked Eliza's collections to one side of the desk, not realising that everything he needed was in his hands.

Nineteen

Villagers gathered on the green, the women and girls wearing the garlands they had made earlier, the men and boys carrying small, straw dolls. Tom watched from his window with nervousness tingling through his veins. This was to be his first aepelling and, as village clerk, it was his duty to oversee the event as a guest of honour. The village was watching him. Aaron Fetcher's supporters were keen to pick up on any mistakes, Taylor's followers were judging his worthiness to remain the clerk should they win the people's imposition, and the council and those who held true with the status quo were keen to see if he used the ceremony to persuade either side to rethink their position.

'It be meant as a fun night,' Barry said, coming to stand beside him. 'So, stop your worriting.'

'First night nerves.'

'And it be Dan's evening, so 'e won't care if you blunder it.'

'Thanks, another pressure.' Tom huffed a laugh.

'Anyhow...' Barry turned to leave. 'It be me what's got more a-do than you.'

Tom followed him downstairs, stopping in the hall to put on his shoes. He, like Barry, was dressed in white calico from his trousers to a square-necked smock-shirt, the only difference being that Barry's shirt had been embroidered at the collar to single him out as Dan's marker. Jenny Rolfe had sewn the decoration, and Tom admired it while he waited for Barry to tidy his hair in the hall mirror.

'Isn't there a name for that pattern?' he asked looming into Barry's line of vision from the side. '"The Sexy Farmer" or something?'

Barry pushed him aside playfully. 'Aye, but it be called "Farmer's Lad",' Barry explained, straightening his collar. 'The wife-a-be puts a pattern on every marker-man's over-lay and uses whatever pattern suits 'is work. She made this afore she knew me fader was leaving me the farm. Should be more fancy now I'm in charge.'

Since Barry had returned from arranging the evening's celebration, he hadn't mentioned his father nor shown any signs of distress or grief. It was unnerving, but it was expected. Tom kept a careful eye on him, ready to be there if he should fall apart.

'I'll do,' Barry said, stepping back.

'You sure will.' They kissed, and Tom said, 'Wish me luck.'

'Pah!' Barry opened the front door. 'You don't need that, Tom Carey. I be the one 'as a recite bloody lines.'

They crossed the green to where the villagers were waiting in two separate clusters, one around Dan, the other around Jenny. Tom was unable to see either of them in the throng, but he did see an unusual sight trotting in from the lope-way.

'What do you make of that?' he whispered, turning Barry to its direction.

When Barry saw what he was looking at, he burst out laughing, drawing the attention of others.

Mick Farrow, not known for his dress sense, was approaching, wearing the minister's celebration robes of white and green. Being shorter than Matt Cole, he had to hitch up his tunic so as not to trip. On Cole it was a fine cassock and shaped his powerful body, adding to his air of authority. On Farrow, it resembled an over-sized evening dress and one that he apparently didn't want to spoil with mud, not that there was any. He stepped gingerly over dry potholes.

Mirth died to concern whispering at the sight of the deputy minister.

'Minister Cole be unwell,' Mick explained to those nearest him as he greeted Tom warmly. 'Evening, Carey,' he said, shaking his hand as the news spread through the villagers. 'You know what we're doing?'

'Aye, Mr Farrow.'

'It be Mick now, Tom,' Farrow said, releasing his hand and winking. 'Whatever boat we be in, you be in it wi' me.' He beckoned Tom aside as Barry herded the villagers into one group. 'I just come from Mathew's 'ome,' he whispered, their shared secret binding him to Tom as a co-conspirator. 'Told me all. Poor bugger. It'll be his gallbladder most like. Same as 'is fader.' He changed the subject before Tom could ask for more details. 'You got young Fetcher's punishment sorted?'

'Aye.' Inspired by Dan's speech at the inn the night before, Tom had come up with something more than suitable. 'I'll hand it down in front of everyone, then there can be no doubt as to my words. Aaron will twist them or deny them if I see him privately.'

Mick grinned and winked. 'When I first met you, Carey,' he said, his already wrinkled face furrowed further with seriousness. 'I took agin you somewhat. But you've proved yourself over the call of any Saddlinger afore.

Now I can say, and I means it, we're safe in your 'ands. Would be good if we could appoint you in Cole's place, be good to 'ave a Carey as minister agin. Not that I remember one of course, but the reminder a 'istory might please the Taylor lot. Shame 'e didn't see to it afore this imposition; can't do nothing 'bout it now.'

Tom couldn't contemplate the idea of him being made minister. He was honoured enough to be the clerk, but his duties were minor and mainly concerned record keeping. For Tom to be the man in the robe that Mick was now badly wearing didn't seem right. That was a job that should go to someone born in Saddling.

He had no more time to consider the implications. Barry reappeared.

'Everyone be ready, Minister,' he said, bowing to Mick and then to Tom. 'Mister Clerk. Will you both come wi' me a-be joyful in me marker's aepelling?' The words were from the Lore. From now until the end of the ceremony, there was a script for the main players to follow.

'Lead on, marker,' Mick said. 'And we shall learn of future joyous 'appenings.'

Barry coughed. 'Afore we do,' he said, breaking from the script. 'I thought you might be joyous of this, Mick.' He surreptitiously handed the old man a belt.

'Be thanking you,' Mick said, taking it furtively. 'Feel like a bloody mistus in this.' Making sure no-one was watching, tied it around his waist, tucking the cassock into it so it fell only to his ankles. It was an unorthodox improvement.

Tom walked beside the deputy minister as they followed Barry through the gathering of villagers dressed in white, whispering, smiling or frowning at the trio. Tom ignored the looks and blocked out their words. Behind the anticipation of what the evening held in store was a sense of unease at what the following day might bring. Smiles were short-lived, conversations only half listened to as people looked nervously to the east, and children were held close to their parents.

They came to the crest of the knoll beneath the east window of the church-house, now a darkened puzzle of lines and shades as the sun sank in the west. The sight reminded Tom to mention the figure in the autumn section when he was alone with Dan, but the thought fled from his mind when he saw his friend.

He stood facing the marsh a distance apart from Jenny with family and friends behind each one in single file. He turned to Tom, smiling his wide, white-toothed grin framed by his dusty pink lips. His wolf eyes shone beneath his brown brows as he blinked. His deep red hair had been cut short at the sides and neatened on top, and his silver and white shirt hung from his slender frame, the samite catching stray sunbeams and glittering. Jenny's floor-length dress was of the same rare material, simple but rich, and her hair was garlanded with bright blue flowers of the devil-in-the-bush plant. The two made a handsome couple.

Tom and Mick took their places between the two lines, and Barry, being the one to lead the procession, stood beyond them.

'Friends of Daniel and Jenny,' he said, his voice unwavering and strong, 'I invite you a the aepelling of the soon-a-weds. We walk a'gether solemn, but we celebrate 'appy a the Maden copse. Soon in Saddling will be another family a-keep the fleeces, felds and friends living, but there be unweds among us wi' none-found love. Will you come wi' us to find it fur them?'

'Aye!' everyone shouted. Hushed chatter of gossip and opinion was replaced by giggles from younger girls and manly handshakes among the boys.

'Minister,' Barry said. 'Will you come wi'us?'

'I will,' Mick replied.

'Mister Clerk. Will you be wi'us a-see all be done according to the ancient lore a Saddling?'

'I will.'

As soon as he had spoken, Tom was no longer nervous. Barry had been right. There wasn't too much for him to do, it was up to Barry to run the evening. Tom and Mick were just overseers for now, giving Tom time to enjoy the quirky ceremony.

Barry came to stand between Dan and Jenny and took their hands. He winked at Dan, nodded politely to Jenny and set off. Tom and Mick followed, and the rest of the village came behind.

As they rounded the church to the graveyard, the sun was just above the western mother trees, sinking gradually and changing the vast sky to shades of yellow and orange. A few clouds drifted to the north, but otherwise, the sky was a cover of darkening blue. The procession weaved its way among the sleeper stones and passed the grave of Dan's father. He ran his hand over it, and Tom did the same to Eliza's headstone. The words rock-bound blade entered his mind unexpectedly as if the dead woman was reminding him of her verse. Other villagers touched the stones of ancestors, making a brief connection as they passed. Tom couldn't gauge Barry's mood, he had his back to him, but despite everything that was happening in the Cole household, he chatted quietly to Dan, occasionally laughing.

They crossed the ancient wall at its lowest, stepping gently into the near field. Ahead of them, a straight line of hurricane lamps had been set leading them to the bridge. They were alight, but their flames would be of more use later once the boblight faded to darkness. The line led directly north towards the crossing to Inner Field and, when the first of the procession reached it, Barry waited for those behind to catch up. They ambled, talking, distracted no doubt by what was to come.

'I 'eard that it were seen agin last night.'

Tom heard the voice behind him but couldn't place it. A woman, possibly one of the wives from an outlying farm.

'Aye,' her neighbour replied. 'But I ain't got nothing a-fear. I ain't done nothing aginst John, not never.'

'What 'bout the time you made that hole in his squeezebox?' The first woman said. 'Then told 'im it were mice.'

Tom realised he was listening to Ivy Seeming whose husband played the accordion badly. She was talking to her neighbour Martha White.

'That were a bad I threw a the fire-pile years ago,' the second lady protested.

'Aye, but that's where the eastling feeds from, ain't it?'

'Oh, Ivy, why d'you 'ave a-bring that up? I ain't going a-sleep a'night now.'

News of the eastling's presence had spread. Tom was happy with that; the villagers' nervousness might help him gain backing for Aaron Fetcher's punishment.

'You all be 'ere as is coming 'ere?' Barry shouted from the middle of the bridge.

'Aye!'

'Then, Minister, Mr Clerk, I ask you a-wait 'ere while I take the couple a Inner Field and from there a the copse. You unweds,' Barry called. 'You be sure a-'ave your trinkets ready. Mistus Rolfe, mother a the bride, please fetch the water from a pure deek.'

Rebeca Rolfe broke from her line and inched her way cautiously down the deek bank to fill the jug the women had drunk from that afternoon. Tom was worried that she would fall in while also hoping she might, but she collected what was probably stagnant water and, with the help of her husband, managed an awkward clamber up the slope to re-join the precession.

'Mistus Vye,' Barry continued. 'Mother a the groom, did you bring the linen?'

Susan held up a white cloth.

'Then we'll cross to Inner Field.'

Barry turned and walked on. Dan and Jenny followed and, after a suitable time had elapsed, the rest of the village.

The lines passed either side of the minister and his clerk. Married couples held hands, releasing them around Tom and Mick and then joining again as they stepped onto the bridge. The unmarried boys and girls held hands with markers, friends, or those they were sweet on, but let go and nodded their heads as they passed.

Aaron Fetcher approached, shoulder to shoulder with Sally Rolfe. Tom thought nothing of it until he saw the two of them smirking, and their fingers fumbled as if Aaron was passing something across. A love letter perhaps? Tom smiled. Despite being a total pain in the arse, the lad was just a lad and deserved to be treated the same as the others.

He pulled himself up short. He couldn't allow himself any sympathy until after he'd ordered his punishment.

Aaron nodded pleasantly enough, but Tom was sure he'd heard the boy snigger with Sally as they crossed the bridge.

'We got a minute,' Mick said once the last of the party was on the other side. He fished under his skirt and pulled out his pipe.

Tom offered him a match and watched the sunset. Streaks of white had appeared, creating slashes through the blood red horizon, and high above, Venus was a light at the end of an infinite tunnel.

'It be dark soon.' Mick's voice was detached as though he was speaking to himself. 'There'll be a grey-hang rising out the deeks somewhere a-creep over us.'

Air brushed Tom's cheek, a soft caress and warm. The scent of late flowering crescent-daisies wafted over him, and he breathed in a deep breath. It was meant to be comforting, but the marsh was uneasy, and its restlessness was palpable.

'I spoke wi' Jack Mackett,' Mick said. 'Told 'im a set the Feld boys on East Sewer a'night. To keep watch.'

'Aye.' Tom's voice was a whisper.

Mick had been correct, vapour was rising from the near-field deek. A waving line of sunset-soaked mist took shape and hung above the channels in the distance. A swathe of it hovered at the height of the knoll, cutting the church-house from the land, leaving it to float like a lost ship at sea as its walls darkened in the gloaming.

'The eastling'll be about.' The old farmer's words were hushed between wheezing puffs on his pipe. 'Behind us there in the Maden copse, around the trees, in the darkening. 'E won't find no change since when 'e were at an aepelling 'undred year back.'

Tom was hardly listening. He had detected a low, moving shadow between him and the far bridge. It darted from one dark patch, through the milky mist to another as though searching.

'There ain't no-one going a-be sleeping tonight.' Mick's words, spoken like a spell, drifted into the grey-hang.

'There's something out there.' Tom took a step closer to the older man.

'There be a great deal out there, Tom.'

Footsteps on the bridge made them turn. Dan stood with his arms out wide, and the samite smock, catching a theatrical last-throw of the dying sun, reflected a dazzle of rainbow colours.

'Gentlemen,' he said, proud and tall. 'I would very much appreciate you attending my aepelling as my guests in honour.'

He spoke his words confidently, and Tom felt a rush of pride.

'Which indeed be an 'onour fur us who accepts,' Mick replied in a faux upper-crust accent that made Tom smile.

The smile didn't last. Mick, who had taken a step up onto the bridge, stopped dead in his tracks.

'Listen!' he hissed, turning to look back to the village.

Tom stood still, Mick was frozen in concentration, one hand to his good ear, his head cocked.

In the distance, the low shadow ran again, and this time the movement was accompanied by the echo of a far-off scream.

'What is it?' Dan whispered after listening silently for a full minute.

Mick relaxed. 'Just a...' He cut himself off. 'Badger.' He knew it wasn't. He was going to say fox, but to see a fox at an aepelling was considered a sign of trouble to come. 'Trot on, lad,' he said, continuing onto the bridge. 'Let's go and see silly girls find their men-a-be.'

He slapped an arm around Dan's back and led him away.

Tom was halfway across the deek when the sound came again, louder and more insistent. He spun to it but saw nothing, just the murk hanging ghostly and still over the field.

Whatever was out there was waiting.

Inner Field was lit by the flickering lamps, their flames more effective now the sun was below the horizon. They led Tom towards the copse of hazel and rowan interspersed with taller cottonwood and old sycamores that had gathered together over the years to form an island of trees on a coterell. Ahead, Dan moved gracefully, the sheen of his costume dulling as he entered the shadowy woodland. Mick walked silently beside him. Tom came a few paces after, stopping on the lyste where the field met the trees, his eyes straining for any sign of movement. The eerie fog hung stealthily on the far side of the bridge, but within it, nothing stirred.

He entered the copse taking the short path between the trees that inclined to the crest of the mound. He was met by the backs of villagers sitting atop the raised earth, others in disorderly rows before them facing downhill to a small, natural amphitheatre. In the centre, Susan lay a large white linen cloth on which Mistus Rolfe placed her jug. A group of girls stood to one side, adjusting their garlands and sharing secrets. Behind them, the copse provided a cyclorama of blackening greens, autumn russets and dark brown boughs and branches. The lanterns threw light from beneath to illuminate their trunks while overhead the spectrum of daylight colours faded into the waking night. Expectant whispering electrified the air as Tom joined Dan and Mick. They made room for him, and he sat between the two, with Jenny Rolfe joining her fiancé on his other side.

Their presence brought the chatter to silence, and the girls took up their places, sitting in a semi-circle around the water jug, facing the audience. Nudges and giggles were shushed by parents, and a few obvious coughs from younger boys were playfully slapped down by married brothers or cousins.

As Tom waited for the ceremony to begin, he forced his mind to concrete on it rather than his concern for Barry, the imposition, the eastling… Those problems seemed so far away from the glade and its protection of trees, hidden even from the sunset, and for the first time in two days, he was calm.

A voice grew among the rustle of high leaves where the breeze nestled in as if to watch. A man's voice, strong and true, held a steady note that crescendoed as the singer approached the knoll from behind. Beside Tom, Dan and Jenny shifted apart to allow the soloist room to enter. Tom hadn't heard this voice before. It was a high baritone, powerful, swelling, preparing to tumble down the slope and crash into the unwed girls. It waited, holding anticipation that brought smiles to everyone's faces as the singer stepped forward and Tom realised with a mix of admiration and shock that it was Barry.

On that instant, Barry silenced the note, took a deep breath and launched into a lively tune.

'*Marry when the moon is growing, she will set your heart a-glowing.*' He stepped towards the girls, picking his way through villagers who bent and shuffled aside to let him pass. '*Marry when the moon is waning, she will bring you woe and paining.*'

The audience looked to the sky. The moon was not yet visible.

'It's growing.' Dan shouted, referring to the moon.

'I bet it is,' Jack Mackett called back, earning him a filthy look from Mick Farrow.

'*Take her in the spring to wed, and many children bless your bed.*' Barry reached the flat ground, his voice now accompanied by a guitar. Jason Rolfe sat apart from the other boys, picking at the strings, his eyes fixed on Barry for his cues.

'*Take her in the summer heat, and you be blessed with all things sweet.*' Barry faced the slope and opened his arms to Dan and Jenny before moving behind the group of girls. '*Marry in the Autumn mist and know her love…*' He paused, once again holding the note. This line brought with it the suggestion of unfaithfulness, and everyone knew what was coming. '*…and those she's kissed.*'

Jason stopped playing, his eyes fixed on Dan. The audience cheered, and Jenny Rolfe hid her face in her hands. Dan feigned outrage, she looked up laughing and shaking her head, her cheeks red. The men shook fists in mock anger.

'*Marry in the winter fast…*' Barry broke off, the song stumbled, and the laughter ceased. There was no accompaniment.

Jason's mouth hung open, his face clouded with angst.

'Oi!' Barry barked in his usual rough way, bringing Jason back to life. '*Marry in the winter fast and wed a love that's sure to last.*' He knelt among the girls, delivering his last line to them like a teacher finishing a story for a classroom of children. 'But...'

Another pause. Jason held a trembling chord, and each girl lifted a fist and held it over the jug.

'*Marry only for your heart...*'

It was almost too quick to catch, but Tom, watching Barry with intense admiration, saw it. Barry glanced at Dan, his mouth open on the vowel sound, his voice as true as ever, but his expression unsettled and questioning. It was gone in a flash, and he looked back at the girls. Jason, still gawping at Dan, shook his head sadly and angrily struck a leading chord.

The vibration died into the shadowy copse.

'*Else woe will trouble 'til you part.*'

The audience joined in with last line and applauded when the song finished, but Barry didn't move. He waited until he had silence, and then spoke solemnly.

'Unwed girls a Saddling.' His arms opened to encompass the group. 'You be knowing who you desire, and them boys out there know who they be desiring an' all.' It was the script from the Lore, but with Barry's own additions. 'The thing be, we're 'ere at the aepelling a me marker and 'is chosen to show you that it ain't just 'bout desire. Love finds its own path, and all you can do fur now is think on love, not on who you lust fur. They be two different things.' He lifted his head to Mick who stood.

Tom remembered where he was and scrambled to his feet. He was mesmerised by Barry's performance. He had no idea that his lover could speak so clearly, let alone sing so well. His eyes moistened.

'Be they different things, Minister? Love and desire?' Barry asked.

'Aye, Marker,' Mick said, his voice grave. 'Ye lads...' He turned his weathered face to the boys. His hair was a mess of white above his head, and the green of his tunic morphed into the darkness between the trees behind him leaving only curves and twists of white picked out in the lantern light. 'All ye boys remember that no matter what you desire wi' them you fancy, you save your desiring fur your wed-night and not afore.'

His words brought sideways glances from the older boys and chuckles from the younger while the married men nodded stoically.

'And you girls,' Mick continued. 'What you most want, you shall 'ave. But you don't go looking fur it 'til you may, else you be as awe-less of the Lore as the boys.'

The girls bowed their heads to show understanding. Their arms were weakening over the jug, and Sally Rolfe rested her wrist on the lip. As she did so, she looked sideways to Aaron Fetcher, her eyebrows raised.

At first, Tom thought she was just rolling her eyes at Farrow's time-worn speech, but Aaron gave her two quick nods, and she looked away.

'But one thing,' Mick said, drawing Tom's attention. 'The aepelling be just fur fancy. Who you chose a'night may become the one who chooses you later but don't go dreaming on it.'

The other girls were growing restless now, holding one arm with another, their fists still clenched.

Barry sensed it. 'Thank you, Minister,' he said, and addressed Tom. 'Mr Clerk.' He winked, and Tom found it hard to remain serious. 'Tell us, 'as all been said and done according a the Lore and the Teaching of our village?'

'It has.'

'And you shall record it?'

'I shall.'

'Then girls, throw away your trinkets and may they come back a you with the love you seek.'

The girls opened their fists and, one by one, let go a collection of silver rings and pewter broaches or just pieces of copper pipe sawn by the Blacksmith. Each was engraved with the girl's name. They shook the blood back into their hands and sat on their haunches as the audience applauded.

'So,' Barry addressed them, once again taking centre stage. 'Now we get a the fun part.' He pointed a finger, moving it among the villagers, choosing. He stopped, pointing directly at Susan Vye.

Tom smirked. Barry should have chosen the mother of the bride-a-be first, and the expression of outrage on Rebecca Rolfe's face was priceless.

Susan stood, smiling, considered each unmarried lad in the copse, and called out, 'Jacob Seeming.'

The first girl in the semi-circle reached into the jug, fished around, took out one of the rings and examined it. The audience leant forward, drawing breath.

'Lizzy Tidy,' the girl announced and, as everyone else cheered, she passed the ring back to its owner.

'Oh, really?' Lizzy Tidy, at eighteen, was two years older than Jacob Seeming. She acknowledged him politely, but it was obvious they were not each other's sweethearts.

'Miss Tidy?' Barry said, hushing the crowd with the palm of his hand. 'The choice falls a you. Thank you, Mistus Vye.'

Susan sat, Rebecca scowled, and Lizzy reached into the jug. As she did so, she called a boy's name. 'Steven Rolfe.'

'Better not be yourn, Sally!' her brother shouted from the back of the knoll.

Lizzy found a ring and lifted it. 'Lucy Cole.'

This time, as the ring was handed back, it was clear that fate had drawn a winning hand. Steven's friends slapped him on the back while Lucy blushed as scarlet as the light allowed anyone to see.

The audience clapped, Lucy, still blushing, chose a boy's name seemingly at random and drew out another trinket. By the time the sixth girl had been matched with a boy who may or may not be a love, the villagers had begun chatting, only paying attention when something merited it. The ceremony continued, and night completed the sky until only two girls remained un-matched.

Sally Rolfe was paired up with Simon Feld, an announcement that brought laughter and cheering because Simon was far too old. He'd been chosen by the impish Beth Seeming, who, at twenty-one considered herself too mature for this ancient waste of time.

Embarrassed, Sally shuffled her hands in the pockets of her dress and shot a glare at Aaron, who winked. She held her fist over the jug, screwed up her eyes and called, 'Aaron Fetcher.'

She reached into the water and circled her hand while the audience, silent for the first time in a while, looked on intently. Aaron was squaring up to be a potential minister, and any of the un-wed girls could make a good life if he won the title.

Sally lifted a ring from the jug and held it up dramatically.

'Who is it?' Aaron shouted across. 'Who's got the pleasure a being fixed up wi' me a'night?' He leered the words, caused Mick Farrow to twitch with anger.

Sally took her time to read the inscription before glancing first at Dan, then at Barry. Finally, she turned to Mick and held out her hand.

'Well?' he grumbled. 'Why you 'olding us up? Who's the girl as a put up wi' Aaron Fetcher's attentions?'

Sally sighed, her face a badly lit image of shock.

'It be Jason Rolfe.'

Twenty

As soon as Sally called Jason's name, Aaron leapt to his feet, laughing uproariously, pointing at Jason and mocking him.

'Baven boy,' he jeered, looking for approval from his friends. 'Knew it, see? Well 'e ain't coming near me wi' those out-marsh ways, eh, lads?'

No-one else was laughing and his expression changed. Still grinning, he appealed to his marker, but Billy showed him his back. Men grumbled as heads turned from Jason to Aaron, his smile waning as panic set in.

'It were a joke,' he said, appealing to everyone. 'What's a matter wi' you? Can't you tell a quilly when I plays one?'

No-one spoke. No-one moved, but Tom's eyes narrowed.

Jason remained seated, blanched and trembling, his jaw-dropped in surprise. Barry looked between him and Dan who snarled. It took Tom a moment to work through the implications of what had just happened.

'Oh, come on, get on wi' the rest of it so we can drink our ale.' Aaron sat, furious and humiliated. He bent his head to the ground, happy to ignore everyone and, by the looks of it, hoping the misjudged prank would be swiftly forgotten.

The murmuring of displeasure crescendoed into complaint and outrage, people shuffled.

Billy elbowed him. 'Get up,' he hissed. 'Quick.'

Aaron raised his head to see Jason Rolfe wading towards him through the seated villagers. His intent was written across his scowl as he curled his fingers. Aaron scrambled to his feet and braced himself.

Tom knew that if Jason took the first punch, he would receive a punishment along with Aaron, but it was not his place to intervene.

'Hold there!' The power of Mick Farrow's voice silenced the crowd instantly and stopped Jason in mid-stride. 'Hold there,' he said more gently but with just as much authority. When Jason obeyed, he added, 'Sit down, lad. This fight ain't fur you.'

'But 'e set me up a baven boy,' Jason shot back, his face taught, his fist ready.

Jack Mackett, who until then had been leaning against a tree, stepped into the ring of lanterns. 'Marker!' he ordered. 'Over 'ere, mate. C'mon.'

'Aye,' Mick agreed. 'Go a your mate, boy. Keep yourself out of Fetcher's mess, 'e ain't called you no such thing.'

Jack was making his way carefully to Jason, but the youth was teetering on the edge of flying at Aaron and had no thought for the consequences. Aaron was taunting him with his look.

"E's thrown 'is last spite,' Jason fumed. 'I don't care what 'appens, 'e's got this coming.'

'Sit, boy!'

Jason was oblivious to Mick's roar and hurled himself forward. Jack reached him too late, but Billy Farrow stood to block his path. It was the shock of a challenge from Aaron's weedy marker that prevented Jason from lashing out.

'It be alright,' Billy said. Showing no fear, he placed his hands gently over Jason's. 'I know how you feel.'

Jason's eyes flashed. He shoved Billy aside but the boy's hands were back instantly, this time on Jason's chest.

'Please, Jason,' Billy pleaded. 'Don't.'

The pause gave Jack enough time to reach Jason where he lifted him over the heads of the villagers and rooted him to the ground in front of Barry.

'I ain't bothered what 'e thinks a me,' Jason yelled. 'It's what 'e's done a me mate, to Dan, and me sister's aepelling.' Jack gripped Jason's arms, but he craned his head towards Aaron accusingly. 'First 'e knocks me over in the sleeper-yard. Then 'e insults me sister and one of me best mates. If I ain't allowed a see to 'im, then what's a be done?' He yelled at Barry. 'What'd your fader do?'

'Minister Cole be unwell,' Mick said. 'Otherwise, 'e'd do what the Teaching says we do.'

'And what's that?' Bill Taylor stood to put in his money's worth and around him, his supporters also rose.

'Mister Clerk?' Mick called for Tom only two inches away. 'You have a duty. Now might be a good time.'

Tom knew that this was coming, but he had expected it to be after the aepelling had reached a natural conclusion. The interruption had altered the course of the ceremony, and he could recall nothing from the Teaching to guide him. The unexpected twist was unprecedented.

Yes, it was, but it was also an opportunity.

His mind raced as voices dropped, and all eyes fell on him, but it was his heart that was winning the sprint. Far from being nervous, excitement drove him on. If he played this carefully, he could use the disruption his advantage.

'Clerk Carey 'as been given the authorisation of punishments while Minister Cole be ill,' Mick announced.

The news was not well received with either Aaron's or Taylor's crowds, but Tom was prepared to wait for silence. Most of the villagers were decent Lore abiding folks and despite passions running high due to the people's imposition, he was confident that they respected the authority of his position.

As the copse fell quiet, he encouraged everyone to sit, which they did one by one until only Jack and Jason remained standing. Tom beckoned them to higher ground where he whispered an instruction to Jack before taking Jason's arm and turning him to face the trees.

'Calm yourself,' Tom whispered. 'Leave this to me.'

Jason was trembling and breathing fast through his nose. His face, already twisted in anger was further distorted by the uneven light thrown from the lamps, and his eyes, darting to Tom's, offered a mix of suspicion and confusion.

'Trust me, friend,' Tom said. 'I'm 'ere fur you.'

'I ain't a baven boy.' Jason was near tears, anger having turned to shame.

'Bain't what you are or ain't,' Tom reassured him. 'You're better than Aaron fucking Fetcher.'

The misword made Jason gasp a brief laugh.

'Don't forget that.'

'No, Clerk Carey.'

Tom manoeuvred Jason to face the villagers and told him to sit between Dan and Jenny. They, still being uncertain what to do, made room for him and Dan put his arm around his shoulder, possibly to hold him down but more likely to show support.

'Stand up, Aaron Fetcher.' The authority in Tom's voice surprised even him, and he caught a wide-eyed look of surprise from Barry, now sitting with the aepelling girls.

It took a push from Billy before Aaron reluctantly stood. His slouch said it all. He had to take his punishment, but he wasn't going to accept it from an out-marsher.

Tom could handle that.

'I were going a-do this after we'd brought this celebration to its accepted end.' He spoke to individual members of the audience, ignoring Aaron who stood with his hands in his pockets chewing the inside of his cheek. 'But seeing as 'ow the juvenile pranking by one what should know better 'as ruined this couple's joy...' He let the disapproval ripple through the glade until it died a natural death. Aaron shuffled his feet nervously. 'It falls a me, under the authority written in the Book of Authorities by Minister Cole, to decree a punishment as be fitting...'

'It were a joke!' Aaron sneered in the manner of a petulant teenager taunting someone he considered stupid. 'What you out-marshers, you furriners call a prank.'

'You're not making this any easier on yourself,' Tom replied, looking him steadily in the eye. Aaron reminded him of the snivelling Mark Blacklocks, always picking holes, always chipping away at what was good until he got what he wanted. It wasn't so much Aaron that Tom hated but his arrogance.

He couldn't let that influence him. He had a role to play and a sentence to administer. There was no room for the luxury of self-satisfaction.

'Seems a me there now be two crimes committed by this young man aginst the Lore,' he continued. 'This morning, as witnessed by three...' He pointed to Billy, Barry and then Jack who was stealthily circling, lining himself up behind Aaron. 'Aaron Fetcher committed the miss-deed of attacking a fellow villager.' There were gasps from those who had not yet heard the news. 'And this were not only done wi'out provocation, it were done in the sleeper-yard.'

'Never!' Apparently, Rebecca Rolfe had not heard that detail. She glared at her son as if it was his fault.

'Fur that, the Lore states the council will give a punishment.'

'Aye. Bannock 'im,' Jason seconded, but Dan shook him, and he said no more.

'And then...' Tom fell into a confident rhythm. 'Then we 'ave this quilly what's been played upon Master Rolfe at 'is expense, a prank that I believe the lad's own cousin took a part in.'

Sally's head dropped in shame amid tutting from her family.

'I 'ave a-assume that it were she what took Jason's family ring...'

'No!' Sally objected, lifting her head and tucking her hair behind her ears. She pointed to Aaron. 'Were 'im, Minister... Mister Carey. Told me 'imself, and proud 'e were. Pulled it from Jason's finger when 'e...' She offered the ring to Jason. 'It wasn't meant a go this way,' she said. 'But after what you told me, I reckoned this might…' Her voice trailed off.

Tom was intrigued to know what had gone on, but he needed to walk a straight path through this forest of unrest.

'Unimportant,' he said. 'The Lore had been ignored twice today by this young man. An attack on a villager and the disruption of a ceremony. Therefore, there be two punishments.'

'Bannock the little oik,' Bill Taylor said.

'Do it now, so we can 'ave a laugh,' Samuel Rolfe threw in, and others agreed.

'There be two just punishments,' Tom repeated. 'I'm not going to order a bannocking of this soft boy,' he used low Saddling words to further humiliate Aaron but shamed him only as much as was permitted by the Teaching. 'I 'ave things more akin to 'is ambition.'

He let the villagers wonder what he might mean as he came to stand facing Aaron. There he paused a moment, holding the lad's glare of hate until it dissolved into worry, and Aaron swallowed nervously. That was pleasing to see, but Tom had only been pausing to give Jack enough time to position himself within grabbing range of the youth. When Tom was satisfied, he continued, stood behind the white linen cloth and faced the villagers who now hung on his every word. What he did and said next could mean success or failure not only for him in his role, but the entire council he represented.

'Aaron Fetcher be a good man,' he said, enjoying the surprise on the lad's face. 'It be my belief that 'e wants a-do right fur the village…' Bill Taylor began to object, but Tom raised his hand. 'Now ain't the time fur that, Mister Taylor,' he said. 'We'll 'ave our chance a speak after the Eastling Festival. This be 'about what's 'appening now. That alright wi' you?'

'What if it ain't?' Taylor replied, with more of a threat than a question.

'Then we're going a-be out 'ere 'til dawn, and none'll be celebrating a'morrow. 'Sides, none'll get a the inn a'night neither.'

'On your arse, Bill.' Samuel Rolfe tugged at his marker's sleeve. I want a drink.'

Other men agreed.

'My thanks a you, Bill,' Tom said, using his first name for the first time to make Taylor think they were on the same level. Taylor, sitting, appreciated it and nodded acceptance.

'Aye,' Tom continued. 'I do believe that Aaron be a good lad. Look at it this way, 'e's taken time out a 'is life fur village meets since 'e turned eighteen last year. 'E's given time a come and listen, speak up fur what 'e thinks be right, 'e's put 'is points across the church-house floor a the table and 'e's been 'eard. We're 'earing more from 'im a'morrow, and what I say now makes no never mind on what takes place at the people's imposition.'

What Tom was doing had everything to do with tomorrow and, from the corner of his eye, he could see members of Aaron's group whispering to each other. Billy Farrow rested his chin on his knees, studying Tom.

'So, as Aaron is so keen fur 'elping our community, it only be fair and right that 'is punishment fur what 'e did a Jason this morning furthers that desire a 'elp.'

Aaron's face was awash with concern rippling beneath a film of mistrust.

'As appointed a me by our minister, and as the clerk and keeper of the rolls, the book of Lore and Teaching, births and deaths, and as a right passed from our ancestors, this be Saddling's punishment upon Master Fetcher.' Tom huffed a quick breath. He'd remembered the Lore perfectly. The rest would be easy. 'It were brought to fair debate by one a us...' he looked at Jack Mackett, 'that old Mother Seeming 'as a cesspit as is in need a-clearing...'

He needed to say no more. The entire gathering collapsed into fits of laughter, apart from Aaron who blanched as white as Mother Seeming's hair.

'This...!' Tom had to shout to restore order. 'This fulfilling of dues will fall between now and the wedding a Daniel and Jenny.'

'You can do mine an' all,' one of the Tidy family bellowed, and a few more suggestions were offered.

Had the air not been so damp, a spark could have ignited between Aaron to Tom. The youth prickled with hate while Tom bristled with confidence. More of Aaron's friends pointed, sharing jokes and, Tom hoped, saw him for who he was; a nineteen-year-old weakling who couldn't control his actions.

'But!' Again, Tom drew attention back to himself. 'But there is more.' He paced, circling the aepelling cloth and the girls, talking to the villagers as though addressing a jury. 'We saw wi' our own eyes that a-night, the same teg thought it be funny a wreck one a the oldest traditions in Saddling.' He caught Bill Taylor's look of approval. 'Why, the very word aepelling come from further back than even my records stretch. It be a word in use afore me ancestor, Robert Di Kari's 'orse set 'im tumbling a the deek, and Saddling grew.' He paused to gather theatrical outrage. 'And if this be 'ow one of us missuses it now, then me punishment fur that's got a-be severe.'

The villagers listened intently, and several nodded agreement, including most of Bill Taylor's group.

'But still I says…' Tom raised a hand. He was enjoying himself. 'Still I says that Aaron be a good boy at 'eart.' Jenny gave him a weak smile that asked him not to be too harsh. Beside her, Dan still had one arm around Jason, but he rested his other elbow on Jenny's shoulder, his face cupped in his hand, watching Tom's every move with interest.

'We know,' Tom said, dropping his voice, 'that the eastling be wi' us this year.' There was a mixed reaction to that, some scoffing, others gasping, a few asking what the eastling was, or if it was true. 'Aye, sorry if you've not 'eard that afore, Mistus Brazier, Master Seeming.' Tom singled out villagers he knew would appreciate being addressed. It boosted their morale and, hopefully, captured their support. 'It's been seen by Simon Feld, out on the dowels.' He whispered. 'It's been 'eard an' all. The mist's been thickening, our trouble been increasing, our unease… But this…' He opened his arms to the trees and turned a circle. Coming to rest, he brought his hands together and offered the village Aaron Fetcher, as if the eastling was his fault. He waited just long enough for people to become suspicious but, before too much anger could be directed Aaron's way, he finished his sentence. 'This is the lad who can 'elp us rest easy in our bed a-night.'

His ambiguity hushed the crowd.

'As I say, young Aaron want's a-do right by Saddling so, in return for breaking up the aepelling…' He took a deep breath and recited the official introduction, ending with, 'This be Saddling's punishment upon Master Fetcher. That 'e will, a-night, accompany Simon Feld in 'is looking and in 'is guarding aginst the evil a the eastling.'

Aaron could hold back no longer. Terrified, he leapt forward, climbing over the heads of his friends to reach Tom. Jack caught him in an instant and, knocking Billy Farrow out of the way, stumbled forward. He slid on the damp grass, but kept his footing, coming to an ungainly halt at the bottom of the slope. He righted himself and Aaron and, before the younger man could fly at Tom or in any way protest, Jack comforted him.

'It be alright, son,' he said, holding Aaron's arms to his side. 'The Felds'll look our fur you. You'll be safe, and you'll be doing your part.'

'Want me a-'old your 'and?' Jason's anger had easily changed to mockery once he'd seen how Tom had taken control.

'You keep your snout out a this, baven boy!' Aaron screamed and immediately rounded on Tom. 'I'll do the looking 'cos it's better fur the village,' he sneered. 'But what you're doing, trying a-shame me, that's not going a-make no difference come voting a'morrow, is it, lads?' He received little enthusiasm from his pack.

'The punishment is set,' Tom concluded.

It was the line that should have brought proceedings to an end, and Mick Farrow fumbled to his feet to take charge. He was interrupted by Aaron's desperate attempt to raise support.

'Don't you see we got one baven boy sticking up fur another?' he shrieked.

The accusation sent a shiver through Tom, and he couldn't help but flick his eyes to Barry. Barry winked, grinning because Fetcher was making such an ass of himself. His lack of concern gave Tom confidence which he needed when a war of words broke out between the two youths.

'I ain't no baven, you sick-minded drean.' Jason tried to break free, but Dan held him back.

'You even be sitting there snuggled wi' your twisted desire like a teg on a tit.' Aaron, unable to use his arms, jerked his head towards Dan.

'You keep your trap a yourself, Aaron,' Dan spat back. 'Or d'you want a-be insulting me afore the whole village and on me aepelling?'

'That Jason Rolfe be all over you, Daniel Vye, but if that's what you likes…'

'Enough of this!' Mick's voice was harsh enough to cut Aaron off, but not for long.

'Minister,' Aaron pleaded, 'that boy's been girl-soft on Daniel Vye come four year now and if this council can't see that as wrong…'

'I ain't girl-soft on 'im!' Jason broke away from Dan's grip and tried to stand, but his sister held him. He shrugged her off. 'Daniel be me mate. That's it. And I ain't saying that agin.'

'That isn't what you told Sally.' Aaron was back at him in a heartbeat.

'I didn't tell nothing like that a Sally.'

'Not what she said…'

'Enough a this…' Mick Farrow barked.

'You want a know what I said?' Jason took a step towards Aaron and Jenny yanked his sleeve so hard to stop him that it ripped away. He struggled free.

Jack's hold on Aaron tightened as Jason approached.

'You want a-know what I said?' He addressed the crowd, and Mick threw up his hands in despair.

'Jason, don't.' Jenny was on her feet, leaving Dan confused and alone.

'I only told 'er what I been trying a-tell you, Dan…' His face was crushed by heartache. 'I been trying a-tell you, and you…' He faced Barry and then Tom. 'Even you, Sir. Even you didn't 'ave time fur me.'

Jason had tears in his eyes as his anguish morphed into shame.

'I be sorry 'bout what I got a-say, Tom, Sir,' he apologised before returning his desperate gaze to Dan. 'I'm so sorry, Daniel if that's what they made you think a me. I'm sorry if my failure a-tell the truth sooner 'as led them a-thinking you're me mate only 'cos I be in 'opes a somehow be sitting where me sister's sat, but that ain't what this be.'

'Jason,' Jenny pleaded. 'We should go 'ome, it's…'

'No, sister, not 'til I've said what 'as a-be said. And it 'as a-be said, Daniel, especially now wi' the eastling out there on a furrage.' He sniffed, unable to hold back his tears, and staggered.

Tom stepped up to him, catching his arm and supporting him. It was as if Jason wasn't there. His red-rimmed eyes were set on Dan, his lips quivering.

'I ain't girl-soft on you Dan,' he said. 'That weren't what I been trying a-tell you.'

'Then what's got you so upset, mate?' Dan's words drifted into silence among the flickering lamps.

'It's my sister,' Jason said.

'Jason, don't!' Jenny was ashen faced.

He couldn't look at her. He raised his head to Tom and gathered his courage. 'She ain't been faithful to 'er intended, Sir,' he said. 'She ain't kept a the Lore as it be written…'

'Jason!' Rebecca Rolfe was struggling to her feet, not caring who she crushed.

'It be true, Ma,' he howled. 'I seen Jenny wi' another man these past weeks and I been trying so 'ard a-keep it a meself but I can't, not now.'

A flash of memory. The smell of Jenny's patchouli, the same scent on Jack's clothes… Tom's heart sank. Surely Jack wouldn't…?

'That boy 'as sullied me mate's name and stolen me sister's maden.' He pointed to Aaron and crumpled to his knees.

The villagers erupted into outrage. Dan and Jenny stared at each other, his face a mess of confusion, hers red and wet with tears of disgrace.

'Jenny...?'

She scrambled away and fled into the copse.

'Jenny!' Her father ran after her, shouting.

Rebecca Rolfe dragged her son away while others stood and threw questions, incredulous and angry. Tom and Barry pushed their way to Dan as Mick helped him up. His face was white, his mouth open and his eyes dull with shock.

Tom's heart bled for him, and he reached to take his friend's hand. As he touched it, the night was split by a scream.

Twenty-One

The scream came from the darkness beyond the dancing flames. It cut through the undergrowth and mayhem bringing everyone to a standstill, Tom included. He flashed an anxious look at Mick Farrow whose mouth was opening and closing in panic, his head twisting this way and that as he searched for guidance.

'You stay put.' Jack was the first to move. Handing Aaron to Tom, he grabbed a lamp and ran into the trees. Jason and Barry followed.

'Take your lights!' Tom shouted, his voice numbed by the moisture-heavy air and the damp-dripping leaves. The men did as instructed, calling for Jenny. Their voices died into the black, but there was no reply.

'Minister Farrow?' Tom spoke above the worried murmuring of the villagers. 'I suggest you and the men lead everyone back to the village.'

'Aye,' Mick replied, glad that a decision had been made.

'But afore you go…' Tom dragged Aaron by the hand to stand beside Mick. 'Listen. Listen!' He calmed the crowd while listening himself, but heard nothing but Barry's voice faint and faraway calling Jenny's name. He let Aaron go, confident that the lad was too scared to run or cause further trouble. 'We be certain now that the eastling's a Saddling a'night, but it ain't doing nothing but watching.'

Children buried their heads in their mothers' skirts, and brothers moved to stand by sisters, cousins by cousins.

'If you ain't done no wrong, you ain't got nothing a-fear.' Tom's voice was level, his words measured. 'You, young Betty Brazier, ain't it?' He crouched to a child of five who nodded, wide-eyed and trembling. 'You and your innocent kind be safe from the eastling, no matter what bedtime stories your parents tell.' He raised himself to his full height. Every pair of eyes was on him, pupils reflecting the flick of the flames like fireflies in the gloom. 'Only them 'as played trickery with their loved ones need a-fear the eastling's coming a'morrow night. Only them as betrayed a friendship or our village.' He swung his long arm around Aaron's neck pulling him closer. 'But even them as done bad these past days or weeks must 'ave our protection. We live a Saddling, and our Lore tells us we watch fur one another, so no more a this…' He was going to say duplicity but found a simpler word. 'No more a this childness. Get your lanterns. Those who leave last take what lights you can carry, blow out the rest, we don't want a-give the thing a light a-see by. Get a your 'omes, or the inn, or where you 'ave a-be, but don't be afeared.'

'We are afeared, Clerk Carey,' a woman called from far back. 'Afeared a the evil and afeared fur what's 'appening a this village, Minster Cole, this imposition…'

Jenny's plight was forgotten as the villagers once more began to agree or protest, raise their voices and express their concerns. Tom was losing control when the voices around him fell silent one by one.

The moon rose above the treeline, bringing with it the dishevelled silhouette of a giant. The figure carried a load which, when it crested the knoll, it gently lowered to ground.

'Jenny!' Rebecca Rolfe screamed and pushed forwards to cradle her daughter where she tapped her face with slaps of ever-increasing annoyance.

'She be well, Mistus Rolfe,' Simon Feld said. 'Daniel Vye, take your woman.'

'Is she alright, Mr Feld?' Tom asked moving close enough to the hulk to smell his sweat.

'Aye, Carey. I were off taking a…' He coughed. 'She ran fair straight into me, bounced off and walloped a tree. She'll be round dreckly-minute.' He regarded Dan, sitting with his knees drawn to his chest, his head bent sideways to Jenny. 'Daniel Vye?'

Dan made no move, and Tom felt for him. Aaron's meddling had, by superstition, brought bad luck on his forthcoming marriage. Jason's admission and the way Jenny had behaved left little doubt he'd been shamed. Being a cuckold in Saddling was rare and, even before marriage, carried disgrace.

'They're back,' Mick Farrow said.

Somewhere in the dispersing crowd Jack and Jason's voices reported nothing unusual. They were joined by Sam Rolfe and the other Feld brother, both giving news that the mist was up but settled and nothing untoward had been seen.

Tom knelt. 'Dan,' he whispered, holding his head in his palms. 'Jenny needs a doctor.'

Dan lifted his eyes, pink and sagging and shook his head.

Tom signalled for Barry.

'Bain't nothing but a cheating whore trying a-run,' Barry cursed.

Tom took him aside. 'Yeah, alright, mate, hush it down. Take Dan to our house ahead of the others. I'll be back soon as I can.'

'Whatever you want, Tom.'

Susan had arrived behind them and was cradling Dan in her arms, shielding his tears from the passing villagers.

'Bring Mistus Vye an' all,' Tom said. 'If she wants a-come.'

Barry bent to Susan and encouraged her to stand. She brought Dan with her saying, 'Tom'll sort this out, son.'

'It be already sorted.' Dan glared at where Jenny was coming round, her parents fussing over her as if she was the hurt party.

'Dan, mate.' Barry held his chin and directed his face to his own. 'Remember who you be. We'll sort this a'gether, later. Fur now, you're Daniel Vye. Got me? I'm 'Here fur you, friend.'

Dan drew in a long breath, his chest swelling as he lifted his head and flexed his fists. He released the breath, eyes closed, and unwound his long fingers.

'You okay?'

'Aye, Tom,' Dan whispered. 'I will be.' He took an angry step towards Jenny, but after another deep breath, he composed himself. 'Mr Rolfe,' he said, showing no emotion. 'From up here, it looks like Jenny needs a poultice on her temple. She's knocked a tree, is all. No need a-fuss. Mistus Rolfe? You got that balm I made you fur when you scraped your knee. Put that on her, send her to bed.'

He walked on by with Barry at his side, leaving the family grateful and Tom proud. Jason ran to catch up with them, and the last Tom saw, Dan had drawn him under his arm, and they were talking.

'Never known nothing such as this.' Mick had collected the empty water jug and the linen cloth.

'It'll be the work of the eastling,' Tom mused. 'Dragging up bads once thrown a the fire and flinging them back in our faces.'

'You got an answer to that, Mr Carey?' Bill Taylor's voice rang out, causing those within earshot to stop and pay attention. 'You got an answer fur any a this?'

The light in the clearing dimmed as more lamps were taken, but a group of Taylor's supporters hung back. Aaron stood flanked by Jack and the Feld brothers. His friends were heading for home.

'I will have,' Tom replied.

'Will 'ave?' Taylor scoffed. 'What good be that?'

Tom ignored his jibe and raised his voice. 'Listen a me,' he said. 'There be an answer a the vengeance that's coming, and I intend a-find it afore a'morrow night. Meantime, we got our festival day. We got things a-prepare, and we got a-keep our traditions. That be up to all of us, you included, Bill. Don't scare your children with any more tales. We got a watch on East Sewer.' He indicated the Feld brothers and Aaron standing between them, a sapling flanked by two oaks. 'We got Tidy's all-workers watching the south and east, and we got Cole's boys out north. If the ghost be walking in the mist a'night, then so are we. You're safe. Go 'ome, rest, get ready fur the festival and leave village worries to me and Mick.'

Most of the villagers were reassured, they followed the others with their lights until only a few remained.

The ground shook beneath Tom's feet as Simon Feld strode down the bank to him.

'Oi, Carey,' he said. 'What you want me a-do wi' the Fetcher boy?'

'What do you mean?'

'Need's a-be taught a lesson. Do I 'ave your permission a-sort it?'

Tom was tempted to tell Simon he could do whatever he wanted to teach the annoying brat a lesson, but he remembered his position and his Teaching.

'You're right, but no. Take him wi' you, Mr Feld,' he said. 'And look after 'im. Let him go 'ome a-sleep when dawn's up but remind 'im there's a cesspit needing 'is attention afore 'e attends a'morrow's festival.'

Simon released a growl of frustration. 'You're too cooting soft,' he grumbled under his breath. 'But you also be a level-headed clerk, and fair. Aye, we'll 'ave 'im follow on.' He climbed the knoll in easy strides. 'Mick! Bring the lad. We'll show 'im what men's work be.'

Jack left with them, throwing a desultory wave in the general direction of anyone still in the glade. The last of the party followed, and peace moved in. The stars threw little light among the leaves, the moon helped, but all around was a mismatch of shadows and darkness. A few glimmering lanterns weaved between the trees, and the sound of worried voices evaporated with them. The smell of paraffin and wax was replaced by that of damp grass and foggy air. The night was humid, but Tom breathed easily.

'Bit of a bugger's mess,' Mick said. Before Tom could register surprise at his rare use of a misword, he followed it with, 'What d'you want, nipper?'

Billy waited for them by the path.

'Wanted a-walk with Mr Carey,' he said.

'You be twenty year now, Billy,' his grandfather admonished. 'You can walk in the night on your own.'

'Aye, grandfader, but I wanted...'

'It's fine,' Tom said. 'Mick, you go and herd the others ahead, we'll check for stragglers.'

Mick lifted his lantern to his face. 'Aye,' he said. 'Should 'ave brought Gumble wi' me.' Muttering, he set off.

Tom couldn't think what Billy Farrow had to say to him, but he waited until Mick's light was lost in the copse. The wait gave him time to put his mind in order. He mentally arranged his promises to the villagers, his concerns and tasks and agreed with himself that his priority was Dan.

'Who's Gumble?' he asked as they started walking.

'That be his whiteback dog,' Billy said. 'Also be the name 'e calls me grandmother when she's not listening.'

Tom didn't want to imagine, but had to ask, 'What is a gumble?'

Billy cleared his throat and composed himself, giving the impression he was keen to be taken seriously. 'It be a word fur something that fits bad,' he explained. 'Like Minister Cole's robe on me grandfader.'

Tom chuckled and fumbled for his pipe. 'Hold this,' he said, passing Billy his hurricane lamp while he stopped to fill the bowl with Devil's Choke and light it. He took the lamp back, thanked Billy and said, 'So, Billy, what is it you want to say?'

They continued, their feet sinking into the wet grass, the shards of lamplight decorating their bodies and fanning out to offer glimpses of silver trunks and berry bushes. Their footsteps were the only sound until Billy spoke.

'Wanted to ask you, as me clerk, does the Lore say anything 'bout changing a marker?'

After Aaron's behaviour that evening, Tom could understand why Billy was asking. 'Sadly, the answer's no.'

'Is what I reckoned.' Billy sighed. 'Ah well, better do what I can fur 'im.'

'People will understand,' Tom reassured him. 'What he's been doing doesn't reflect badly on you.'

'But it be my job a-keep 'im in line while same time being there fur 'im,' Billy reasoned. 'Bain't an easy task wi' one such as Aaron.'

'He's still your best mate?'

'No, not really.'

'That's a shame, but sorry, I can't help.'

'Ah, you be 'elping more than you know, Mr Carey.'

That was good to hear, although Tom didn't understand what it meant. The wiry young man with the unkempt, curly hair walking beside him, was the same height as Tom, but slighter in build. He was only a few years younger but had always called Tom Mr Carey as if he was the schoolteacher. It made him feel old. 'You should call me Tom,' he said.

'Thanks, Mr Tom.'

'Yeah, whatever.'

They walked in silence until they reached the lyste at the edge of the inner field. Ahead, the meandering line of lights reached a vanishing point at the near-field bridge. It was what Tom expected to see, but what he hadn't anticipated was how the mist had grown. It hung thick and seemingly impenetrable like a layer of frosted ice suspended over black water, circling the copse and reaching far beyond the half-submerged village.

'You know what we didn't do?' Billy asked.

Tom was distracted by the sight and didn't reply.

'We didn't 'ear the girls' aepelling song,' Billy continued undaunted and up-beat. 'Meant a-be done after the rings. A last warning a the bride-a-be.' His good humour left him. 'Me marker put an end a that.'

They stepped onto the grass, the grey-hang a few yards ahead. 'That's a shame,' Tom whispered. 'I've never heard it.'

The brume gave way to their bodies, drawing back and around them at their waists, and they held their lanterns above it as if they feared it would extinguish the flames. The moon behind them cast their shadows over the unbroken grey where their lanterns swallowed parts of the darkness but left patches sliced through by light. The villagers fanned out, going their separate ways around the church-house which stood as a solid, black shape against a firework sky of stars.

'*Monday's groom is a man who feels. Tuesday's groom is a man who heals...*' Billy's voice came tenderly through the dripping air, singing tentatively as if he was afraid to disturb the moonlight. '*Wednesday's man puts food a the table. Thursday's boy be big and able.*' His voice gained strength as his confidence grew. '*Friday's knows where the church-house bides, and Saturday's what its cracked stone hides.*' He projected the last line across the marsh, his

voice high but powerful. *'But don't you wed a Sunday man, else...'*
'Bloody hell!'
Tom set off running, his lamp swinging wildly in his hand, and the mist swirled angrily around him. Another song, another reference to the cracked stone.
'Tom, what be?'
'Sorry, Billy,' he called back. 'You'll be alright.'
He stumbled on an emmet caste, falling forward, but a steadying hand gripped his arm.
'No, I won't,' Billy panted, as he caught up. 'Not staying out 'ere on me lonesome. What's 'appened?'
'You've given me hope, Billy,' Tom said. 'I know where to find the knife.'

The clatter of lanterns and earthly voices faded from the Maden copse, leaving the marsh to the roaming mammals and night-hunting birds. Dying leaves shivered uneasily as the grey-hang shifted in restless waves among the peeling bark, settling above open ground and spreading to the far dole stones and furthest trees. It cloaked the village and its farms, hovered low along the lope-way, rested against the sleeper-stones and undulated curiously along the courses of the duckweed deeks.
The eastling took shape among the sheltering shadows of the sloe bushes, dragging its slitting-knife from earth to air as it evolved into the weeping, half-life body, a spectral form with substance, a boy with no soul. The muggy night was saturated by deception and sodden with new betrayal giving the eastling fresh choices. There were too many this generous harvesttime, and its determined fingers wrapped and unwrapped around the knife-handle as it considered its victim. It moved invisibly through the brume, watching through the clouds of centuries and breathing revenge until it came to the church-house and rolled in through the open door.
Candles flickered, casting creamy light on white walls. A man, tall with straw-coloured hair circled the table-stone while a narrow boy followed, throwing the flame from a close-held lamp. They paused, crouched, peered carefully at the stone, stood, continued, whispered and wondered. Two voices murmuring, one spoke of frustration, the other asked questions. The pacing continued as the half-dead breathed itself from the church-house onto the hushed still of the green and twisted to the nearest home.
At the sound of crying, it sharpened its eyes and quickened its pace,

The Eastling

upwards, around, along. A young man curled on a bed. A flash of red hair, shuddering shoulders, his face buried in his arms. Like the creeping apparition, this man knew the bitter taste of betrayal. Unlike John of the Black Locks, he knew friendship. A darker man, stocky and stoic, soothed his betrayed friend, his hand lay gently on his back, his soft voice reassuring in its empathy.

The invisible swirled away, along, around, above. Out past the dull glow of curtained windows, across, among and in.

There was no betrayal in the next dwelling, only death. A man healthy in look and understanding in finality lay in bed surrounded by his family. A wife, contented words, a happy reminisce and a patted hand. A brother and nephews, tolerant in acceptance, the slow nodding of a head, the hushed agreement of practicalities. No regrets for a life lived, no sadness for days not seen. Instead, thanks for times spent, promises for days to come, kisses and gifts to remember by.

Out, between, through and over, to slip unnoticed around a kitchen table. A family uneasy, plates untouched, but worries palpable. They fed on 'what if' and 'if only', and 'I didn't mean to', until their feast of anxiety filled them with dread for deeds done, bads thrown, lies unintended but told.

There was no betrayal here, only regrets. The eastling smiled at its own work; the pain it washed before itself like a herald trumpeting despair. It drifted away, through, beside, drawn to a room where the gas lamps hissed a taut underscore to weeping and anger. A girl uncrowned wept only for herself, a boy chastised vowed an honest life in bursts of 'I must', 'my teaching', 'my friend.' Words countered by the rage of a mother angrier at herself than her weak target. She seethed her own shame while her husband grasped for the gift of compassion but found only vanity.

The eastling fed well on the treachery here, but there were other courses to follow.

Free, low and creeping it levelled beyond the green, drifted, sought and travelled as candles guttered. The lights of the village gave way to the night-suffocated fields where only darkness was breathed, where tegs nuzzled in the underbellies of ewes seeking dry softness and safe sleep.

The same two men, stealthy and methodical, their pipes glowing, smoke rising to mingle with the fetor of dishonesty that walked behind them. A youth trudging the field, narrow eyes fixed on the lookers, narrow thoughts seeking revenge, blaming the faults of others for his own contempt.

The eastling approached in the silent air, and its fingers tightened on the knife, settling, knowing its choices.

A twitch of a branch in the deek-side coppice and the shrill of a startled mole set a limb of mist fast-twisting towards the sounds and the overpowering stench of its prey. The youth sensed it too. He held back from the men who forged ahead, torches lighting shafts of grey and finding only more beyond. The youth approached the deek-bank, his light held beneath the cloud of ashen moisture, sheltered by it but dampened by the clam and dull of the night.

A shadow among shadows, the tap of wood on wood and the crack of a stick broken by a stranger's tread. The youth's faltering calling gained strength as he approached. The clank of a waved lantern, the brush of leaves as an arm lowered branches, and the careful tread of boots as he came to stand on the bank. His words were spoken to the darkness beyond the water and were answered from a foreign field. Questions and persuasion led to an agreement between strangers and a contract signed with a promise.

Grinning defiantly at the waxing moon, the eastling withdrew, sinking, falling, considering as it skulked away to prepare, gradually thinning until only the knife remained. The blade glinted once in the troubled moonlight before it too was gone.

Twenty-Two

Dan was running across one of Matt Cole's fields towards the schoolhouse. He was late, and his writing book was heavy in his hand. He looked at it and found not a book, but a stone slab on which he had carved words that made no sense. He was going to be in trouble twice over and ran faster. There was no burning in his lungs, no ache in his legs, he was flying across the tufted meadow with ease, but no matter how fast he pounded, the schoolhouse stayed beyond his reach.

Suddenly, Barry was running with him. Young Barry, always late, always unbothered, his hair cut short and his face pimpled. He looked at Dan with his cheeky grin, said something about not needing the book and took it from him. Without the weight of the stone, Dan found himself slowing, and Barry took his arm. They walked, but not towards school. Now they were laughing their way to the broadest stretch of the eastern deek on Farrow's land, the best place for swimming. They walked directly into the water, somehow naked, and dived among the reeds searching out minnows and sticklebacks, gasping when they surfaced, climbing on each other's shoulders, scooping silt and threatening to throw it, ducking beneath the surface as the sunlight rained droplets of happiness, baptising their innocence. They turned to find themselves in the shadow of their teacher, scowling, his eyes slits, his tall body swathed in a robe which opened like the wings of a crow as he flung his arms and roared his wrath.

It was William Blacklocks. Dan was in the schoolhouse with his friends laughing at him; he was still naked.

The first light of the day fell on his eyes as he woke, sweating. He groaned and rolled onto his back. He was dressed, lying on Barry's spare bed where the events of the previous night came back to him, shattering the broken images of the dream and crashing into his chest. His heart leapt as realisation crowded in. There could be no marriage now. How could there be?

'You snore.'

Dan sat up and, resting on one elbow, focused. Barry was sprawled in an armchair on the far side of the room. He still wore his marker's embroidered shirt and was watching Dan over the rim of a mug as he sipped.

'You been there the whole night?' Dan asked, dragging his fingers through his hair and scratching his head.

'Aye. Slept 'ere in case I were needed.'

'You're a guard dog.'

'No, just a mate.' Barry put his mug on the floor and shouted for Tom.

'What time is it?'

'Be gone ten, I reckon.'

'Ten?' Dan swung his long legs from the bed and sat, rubbing his face.

'Aye, but there's no worries fur you. Everyone's too busy wi' the festival a-want a-come fur ointments and such. Even Becki Tidy's at 'ome baking and not pacing your back stairs.'

Tom appeared in the doorway wearing only cut-off trousers and reading a book. He glanced up, said, 'Morning. Want a drink?' and wandered away before Dan could reply.

'Your ma's been working most a the night,' Barry continued, coming to sit on the bed. 'Saw 'er early at me fader's 'ouse. Me ma's working wi' 'er a'day, so you got nothing a-do 'part from sort your business wi' Jenny.'

Dan groaned, and nausea rose to his throat.

'Tom's another what's been up all night,' Barry chatted on. 'Spent most a it in the church-house wi' Billy Farrow knocking their knuckles sore on the stone. Thinks there be something inside. I don't know. Sometimes I wonder if I ain't shacked up wi' a loon, the way 'e's been going on 'bout songs and who knows what else.'

Dan nudged his friend. 'You're a bit more than shacked up.'

'Aye, and a course I don't mean nothing by it. Tom's been up fur 'ours searching fur a way out the eastling's threatening, same time as muttering 'bout tonight's imposition.'

'And?'

'So far there be nothing 'e can do 'bout neither.'

Although he tried, Dan couldn't raise any enthusiasm for village matters, not even the eastling. He didn't believe the myth, no matter what other saw and said. He preferred to see such things for himself than let hearsay and conjecture dictate his worries. 'How's your fader?' He had plenty to worry about, but his friend had a more pressing concern, and it was wrong to think only of himself.

'Fader's no better, no worse,' Barry said. 'Pain comes and goes. Can't eat, but 'e says 'e needs a-lose weight as a-fit in that costume 'e were wedded in.'

Dan smiled. 'Are you okay with it, mate?'

'No, not really. It's got more moth 'oles than threads, but it be what Fader wants a-be sleeping in.'

'I didn't mean the suit.'

'I know you didn't.' Barry sighed. 'Aye, mate, I'm accepting, as is the family.' He took hold of Dan's hand and rested their entwined fingers on his knee. 'Mind you, me uncle's been using a few miswords 'bout me getting me fader's main share a the farm. Wanted it fur himself.'

'Which uncle?'

'All a them 'part from John. 'E be 'appy enough on account a-being a yawnup and unbothered 'bout work. Still, fader spoke wi' them last night, Timmy and the other cousins, and they be accepting now. But that ain't your issue.' He angled himself to face Dan and squeezed his hand. 'What you going a-do?'

Dan knew what he meant and was grateful when Tom interrupted with a mug of camomile.

'That book of Teaching I lent you,' he said, handing over the tea. 'Was it complete?'

The question came out of nowhere. Dan was expecting Tom, like Barry and everyone else, to ask what he intended to do about Jenny.

'Er...' he faltered. 'I never got through the whole book, and I was skimming but... No, hang on. A few parts didn't read right. They jumped from one thing to another, so, maybe. Why?'

'Because both copies I have here, and the one in the crypt have pages missing,' Tom said. 'I've found some, but...' He wandered back to the door. 'Never mind.'

'Missing?' There was too much else in Dan's head to allow room to contemplate the implications.

'Aye. Same pages in each one.' Tom was talking to himself. 'And from the Lore. Can't work out...' He left the room, mumbling to himself.

'What d'you reckon that means?' Dan asked, letting go of Barry's hand so he could cradle his tea.

'I never know the meaning of 'alf a what Tom says,' Barry complained with humour. 'I just nod and say "aye, mate" when 'e gets fessed. But 'e said, earlier, that whatever bits be missing won't 'ave been taught a no-one fur years. Reckons your aunt Eliza took out pages fur whatever reason...' He cut himself off. 'But that's 'is concern a'day, not yourn. You want a-talk 'bout what you be doing next with this wedding thing?'

'Thing?' Dan stood, taking his tea to the window where he gazed over the marsh. 'Be more than just a thing, mate. No-one's been so cheated on, not that I can remember, and I got no idea what's going to happen, or what I'm going to do.'

Barry was at his side, the guard dog now turned loyal puppy. 'Whatever you decide, I'm right 'ere.'

'You're always right here,' Dan said, knocking their heads together gently. 'That's what I need from you.'

'That and me dirty jokes.'

'You don't know any.'

'I'll work on one fur you.'

'I'm not in the mood for jokes, Barry. I just want the whole thing to go away.'

'Aye, I know, but...'

'Why is it,' Dan interrupted, 'that we can be so accepting when someone's dying, but not when someone's been cucked? I'm going to be laughed at, shunned... No-one's going to come to the inn, let alone want me to cure their illnesses.' Anger rose where he had expected self-pity. 'And all because of that fucking Aaron Fetcher.' He slammed his mug on the windowsill, spilling its contents. He waited, expecting Barry to tell him to be calm, expecting a trusty, rough hand to grip his, or a muscle-bound arm to rest on his shoulder, but Barry only drew a deep breath.

'It weren't just Fetcher's wronging,' Barry said. 'Sorry a-be the one what tells you, but word's 'round the village 'bout this, and Jenny's confessed a Mick Farrow. It were 'er what led on Aaron. 'E only took what were offered, same as any man our age might do. If 'e ain't interested in following the Teaching, I mean.'

There was still no self-pity and now, strangely, no anger. 'Not any man,' Dan said, his voice quiet. 'You wouldn't.'

'Aye, but there be a reason fur that.' Barry coughed, embarrassed to say what came next. 'When you think on it, me and Tom's not exactly keeping a the Teaching neither.'

'True, prehaps, but the Teaching doesn't rule either way on... that.'

Dan watched the marsh as he thought, and Barry let him have his silence. Whitebacks wandered the expanse of fields, carefree, and Dan envied their freedom. Poplar trees swayed in the wind that blew in across the outer deeks, and far distant, Barry's farm buildings were just visible in the clouded sunlight.

'Sometimes I wish I were like you and Tom,' Dan whispered.

'Well, you ain't,' Barry replied. 'Excepting your fader's sleeping and mine be settling in fur a long night.'

'Shuck it, Barry…' Dan clutched at his friend's neck, turning, pulling him closer and cradled Barry's head at his chest. 'My mess ain't nothing compared to what you're suffering. I'm sorry, mate. I'm here for you.'

Barry clung to him tightly, but there were no tears.

'To hell with Jenny and fucking Fetcher,' Dan growled. 'Who cares what the gossips are saying. The men'll come to the inn, nothing'll change, the festival will take their minds off it, and I ain't never going to speak with Jenny or Fetcher again. Feels good saying that because I mean it.'

'Well done, mate,' Barry said, pulling away. 'But you ain't got no choice. Sorry a-be blunt.'

To be deceived during a courtship was as bad as being deceived during a marriage. It was not only a breaking of trust but also of the Lore. On top of that, unwed girls weren't meant to sleep with a man until that man was their husband. It was unlikely now that Jenny would wed anyone unless it was Aaron. Dan didn't want to think of it any longer.

'Right,' he said with finality. 'That's it. If you can carry on as normal as your fader lays dying, then I can do the same with my courtship already dead. Jenny never happened, and I'm going to make you a promise, Barry, you ready?'

'Depends.'

Dan opened the window, letting in a gush of warm morning air, and picked up his mug. He checked that there was no-one in the back-out below before holding the mug out of the window.

'Don't do that,' Barry protested, knowing what was coming.

'I am going to do it, mate and I'm going to mean it.'

'Think first, Dan. Whatever you're going a swear wi' me can't be undone if you smash that pottery.'

Dan tipped the contents of his mug onto the grass below.

'Daniel Vye,' Barry warned. 'I be serious. As your marker and your best mate…'

'I know what I'm doing.' Dan raised his voice along with a smile. 'And it feels right. It's lifting from me, Barry, and that's where it's going to stay.

Lifted. I ain't having no more of this Sally, Jenny, Becki nonsense. I ain't having no more of this love-fuddle no more. I…'

'No, Dan, you don't want a-do this.' Barry reached for his arm, but Dan held the mug out further.

'You're my marker, Barry Cole,' he said.

'Which be why I can't let you.'

'Which is why you have to let me.'

'Take a day, a week. Think on it after the bale-toss and the speaching. We'll talk on it…'

'Barry Cole, do you love me as my marker.'

''Course I bloody do, Daniel, and that be why…'

'Then mark this.' Dan squared his shoulders, drawing himself up to his full six feet and spoke solemnly. 'In front of you, I vow that I ain't going to take a Jenny, nor a Sally, nor any other girl in Saddling be she a maden or a maid.'

'You're the last Vye, Dan. There'll be no others.'

Dan ignored him and winked. 'And I ain't going to take a Jason, nor a Barry, though I have to tell you I've considered it.' He enjoyed the flicker of confusion on Barry's face, unfair though it was to have caused it, and spoke directly to the mug hooked by his index finger. 'Hear me vow, and take my vow,' he said. 'Make it irreparable.'

He slammed the mug against the outside wall, watching its pieces fall to the ground before dropping the handle to join the shards below.

Barry groaned. 'You be a bloody nutter, Daniel Vye,' he moaned. 'You know what you gone and done.'

Dan brought his arm in from outside and slapped his hand hard on the nape of Barry's neck. 'I do, Barry, and I ain't felt so unconfused since I was twelve. It's gone now, my mizmaze, my uncertainty…'

'Your chance a-'ave a nipper a-teach your medicine to. Your chance a-work your inn wi' your children…'

'Be happy for me,' Dan said and kissed his friend on his forehead. 'Your friendship will be everything I need.'

'And mine.' Tom lounged against the bedroom door, his arms folded, and a Book of Lore clutched to his chest. 'And although I agree with Barry, if that's your decision, then we'll stick by you.' He opened the book. 'Sadly, this page is intact,' he said, and read. 'A vow made by the breaking of clay before a marker, the minister or clerk shall be bound by Lore.' He slammed the book shut. 'You've just brought an end to the name of Vye in Saddling after eight-hundred years.'

Dan knew it, but at that moment, he couldn't care less. His mother wouldn't be too pleased, but he could cope with that. Nothing could douse the flames of certainty that burned in his chest, and he took four long strides across the room to stand face to face with Tom.

'Thank you, Mr Clerk,' he said and bowed formally. Once he'd righted himself, he tapped Tom on the cheek twice and his face split into a beaming smile. 'You know what I'm going to do now?' he asked, unable to contain his excitement.

'Shag a sheep?' Barry muttered and fell backwards onto the bed. 'Bloody nutter.'

Dan laughed. 'No, mate. I ain't no Aaron Fetcher. Thanking you both for caring for me last night but I'm going to the inn. I'm going to get the rest of the feast ready, lift my head above the looks and gossip, and get on with my life. See you bavens later.'

He walked from the room leaving Barry and Tom to stare hopelessly at each other. Tom was drawing a breath to speak when Dan stuck his head around the door. 'And sorry for the pottery, Tom. I'll get Terry Brazier to make you another.'

It wasn't until Dan was halfway downstairs that Tom remembered the east window. He put the Book of Lore on the armchair.

'Back in a moment,' he said to Barry who folded his hands behind his head and stared at the ceiling.

Tom caught Dan just as he reached the front door. 'Before you go,' he said, 'I need to ask you something.'

'I'm happy with what I've just done, Tom.' Dan was insistent. There was to be no more talk of the matter.

'It's not that.'

'Oh.' He was disappointed.

'It's the east window.'

Dan scanned the hallway searching for a window before he realised what Tom meant. 'What of it?'

'When you drew the plans for the autumn quadrant, did you include a couple of figures, one sitting, one lying on the ground?'

'Have a look at the glass. It's what I drew.' Dan lifted the latch.

'I did. I can see Barry getting drunk.'

Dan grinned. 'All three of us are in the window somewhere.'

'Then who's the person who's been murdered?'

Tom expected Dan to be confused, or to challenge the question, but he was as cheerful and calm after it as he was before.

'That's just an eastling victim,' he said. 'If you look closely at the winter part, you'll find a reference to a saddling victim. Summer's different, but the witchling is still in there, as for Spring…'

'Yeah, okay,' Tom interrupted. 'So you included a victim because it's one of our myths, no other reason?'

'And 'cos the prone body balances Barry's drunk figure.'

'Okay, thanks. The figure in the window is a dead end,' Tom said to himself as Dan opened the front door.

'Well, it's a dead someone,' he joked and left.

When Tom returned to the spare room to collect the book, Barry was still on his back.

'Shouldn't you be doing something useful?' Tom asked.

'Felt wrong,' Barry said.

'What did? Dan?' He regarded his lover. His shirt had darkened in places where his sweat soaked through the material stretched tight over his muscled arms.

'Aye, that too. No, it felt wrong not sleeping aside you last night.'

'Yeah, sorry. We both had other things to attend to.'

'Aye, and look where me attending took Dan.' Black hair sprouted from his embroidered collar, and where the shirt was pulled from the waistband of his trousers, it revealed a strip of tanned muscle.

'At least it led somewhere,' Tom sighed. 'I'm no further forward, and I'm running out of time.'

'Then shouldn't you be doing something useful?' Barry winked. 'Or 'ave you got 'alf an 'our you can take off from killing ghosts and use it a-take me mind off what's going on outside?'

Smiling, Tom knelt beside him while Barry pulled off his shirt. They lay in each other's arms as their scents and sweat mingled. It was the first time Tom had lain on a bed for over twenty-four hours and within a minute, he was asleep.

Twenty-Three

Tom slept for two hours before Barry woke him to tell him he had been called for. Berating himself for wasting time, he rushed to Matt Cole's house where, upstairs in the bedroom, Irene stood at the open window. The hangings were drawn apart, and although the diffused sunlight brightened the room, neither it nor the breeze was able to extinguish the stench of illness. Cole was asleep, and Irene spoke in whispers.

'Daniel came by a while back,' she said as Tom joined her. 'Told me it's better to let the air in.'

'I'm sure he's right.'

'What d'you make of Daniel's business, Tom?' She took his arm and led him to the window where they looked across the lope-way to Mistus Tidy's house. The neighbour's hangings dropped back into place. 'Whole village be talking of it.'

'I think it's between Dan and Jenny,' Tom answered. He wasn't going to tell her what Dan had said and done that morning.

'He was cheery,' she probed. 'Thought he'd have been more upset. D'you think he knew?'

'He's a clever man who has more important things on his mind than gossip,' Tom gently chided.

'Bain't we all? What with the festival, the meeting... I shan't be able to attend either of them, Tom.'

'I know, and to be honest Mistus Cole, it feels wrong to be celebrating harvest with the minister dying.'

'It's what Matthew wants,' she said, glancing back at her husband before leaning closer. 'He asked me to fetch you, but Daniel gave him something to help him sleep. He wanted to know where you were at with the imposition.'

'When he wakes up, tell him I'm doing what I can.'

She studied him with her kind, but intense brown eyes, blinking. 'And what be the real truth?'

'I am doing what I can,' Tom emphasised, 'but I don't think there's any way out of it, except to encourage the debate and hope people make a good decision. It's their right, after all.'

'But Saddling's existence depends on things staying as they are.' She played nervously with her fingers. 'Open us up the Aaron Fetcher way, and we become the same as other places out there. Close us off the Taylor way, and we won't be able a-survive, not only that, he'll bring back the saddling ritual and who knows what else.'

'I know what the stakes are Irene, but the people had a right to ask for this vote, and we must abide by their decision, no matter how misguided, or misunderstood.'

'But what of when a minister lies dying?' Irene dropped her voice further. 'Can't he say who comes after him?'

Tom shook his head. 'Not according to the Lore,' he explained. 'A minister must appoint his successor and have the appointment ratified by the council six months before he resigns or dies. If the onset of death or death itself is sudden, the deputy takes over until the council makes the appointment. There's no other way.'

Irene nodded in understanding. 'Then I shan't keep you, Tom,' she said, resigned. 'Go and get yourself ready fur the festival. I'll tell Matthew not a-worry, though I know he will. Tom?'

Tom was staring blankly at the wall.

'Mr Carey?'

'No other way apart from a people's imposition...' Tom was thinking. 'It's something to do with timing.'

'What you talking of, Tom?'

He shook his head. 'It was a convenient time to call an imposition, don't you think? A rarely used process... The minister dying with his successor unappointed...' He turned his gaze to Cole. The man lay on his back, his face as pale as the grey-hang, his breathing as light. 'When did you know Mr Cole was ill?' he asked.

'Oh, I suspected 'bout a week back.'

'And who else knew? Before now, I mean.'

'Me, Dan, that's it. Susan later. Why?'

A suspicion had let itself into Tom's mind unannounced, but it was cloudy, unfocused and in pieces. Few people knew of the imposition lore, fewer still the protocol surrounding the death of the minister because such things weren't taught.

'No,' he spoke aloud. 'They *were* taught. Once.'

'Tom?'

'Before the pages were removed...'

The touch of Irene's hand on his forearm sent the suspicion scuttling, leaving Tom with the barest thread of an idea. He squeezed her hand, smiled, and said, 'Mistus Cole, thanks for listening,' before hurrying from the room.

Tom was closing the front door as Aaron Fetcher returned home. Unsure whether he should speak to him, wave or ignore him, he faltered, pretending to search for his pipe while watching the approaching teenager.

Aaron had his hands stuffed in the pockets of a pair of deeker's over-trousers. Made of leather and tied tightly, they were tucked into work boots and dripping with slime and muck, much as Aaron was dripping with sweat.

'Finished?' Tom hated the way he sounded like the worst of his old schoolmasters, but he'd issued the punishment, and it was his duty to ensure it had been carried out. Now was as good a time as any.

'All done?' he repeated when Aaron ignored him.

The youth looked up with baggy eyes and, on seeing Tom, his expression twisted into a sneer. 'You should go back a where you come from.' His contempt obvious, he continued towards the neighbouring house.

'Anything seen on the dowels last night? Mother Seeming happy with your work?' Tom pressed him.

Aaron stopped at the gate and examined an upstairs window. 'You ain't in your robes 'ere, Carey. Should never 'ave been given them, ask me. It's only 'cos a that... thing a yourn with Cole's boy that you got what you got.'

Tom forced himself to stay calm. Aaron knew nothing of his relationship with Barry, he was merely trying to antagonise. 'There was a vote,' he said. 'A couple voted against me as you did, but most were in favour.'

'Aye, a vote. Same as what we're 'aving a'night. And I can tell you this, Carey...' He ran his finger across the top of the gate and studied the dust it gathered. 'There ain't nothing you can do 'bout it. There ain't no pages in them books a yourn says you can, and it's them pages what matter in Saddling, not your fancy words and your out-marsh ways.'

'I thought you wanted to adopt more of those out-marsh ways.'

'Not the likes a yorn.' Aaron glared at him, but only briefly, as if he was scared he would lose his confidence if he looked for too long. 'Thing's been changing in Saddling since you got 'ere. Now they're going a-change fur the better.' He clicked open the latch. 'You ain't going-a get anywhere near our

Lore nor our Teaching when I got the minister's place.' Stepping into the garden, he kicked the gate closed. 'So, you better get the most out a your position, 'cos you ain't going a-be in it fur much longer.'

'We shall see.'

The fetching-pony whinnied in the back yard as a frantic gust of wind swirled the dust on the lope-way.

Aaron reached the doorstep. 'And aye,' he said. 'Mother Seeming be 'appy with me work. No, we didn't see nothing last night.' He became even more bitter as if everything was Tom's fault. 'Just the eastling's cloak settling in, ready a-take one of me neighbours in the village where us proper Saddlingers were born.' He threw Tom one last look of hate before stepping inside. 'And I didn't speak a no-one neither.'

The door slam coincided with another rush of the strengthening breeze which frightened the pony. Its complaint drew Tom's attention, and a new idea forming, he headed to the back of the house and the Fetcher's yard.

'You want to bring more stones for that, Lucy,' Dan called across the green to one of Barry's cousins. 'The wind's started to worry itself, and your cloth ain't going to stay on.'

'Aye, Dan,' the woman replied from her table, holding down a piece of hessian that was not doing as she wanted.

Around her, other villagers were setting up their tables. Furniture had been brought from houses and chairs placed on the grass, and where the path met the rise in the knoll, Mick Farrow was overseeing the setting of the wives' table. He had tied its sackcloth covering with twine to keep it in place. The breeze had now become a wind, blowing relentlessly from the east. It wasn't strong enough to knock over the bottles and boxes arranged on plank-covered trestles, or the baskets of vegetables and fruit displayed on others, but the women were grabbing at their dresses, and Mick's hair was dancing like white seaweed in an undertow.

Behind the inn, where more tables had been set with kegs of ale and pottery jugs of wine, Barry oversaw the setting of the bale-toss. Two tall, wooden poles had been screwed into the ground with a bar resting on pegs between them. Hay bales had been arranged as seats in a semi-circle facing the stulpe, the Saddling word for the construction, and several other bales of equal weight had been stocked to one side ready for throwing.

'That looks ready to go,' Dan said, appearing at Barry's shoulder.

'Aye. All ready back 'ere.' Barry shoved his hands in his pockets.

'Are you sure?' Dan asked, scanning the arena.

'Sure as you were when you broke a pot wi' me,' Barry complained, kicking at a tuft of grass.

He was disappointed, upset at the implications of Dan's oath and sulking because Dan hadn't discussed it with him.

'Sorry,' Dan said, pulling a baby pout and snuggling his head into Barry's shoulder.

'So you should be... Get off, you lomp.' Barry pulled away, trying to appear annoyed but failing. 'So, what 'ave I forgot?' he asked, offering his hands to the scene. 'Stulpe's in, bales be weighed, bar's up.' He pulled his curls from his eyes, but the wind whipped them back into place forcing him to press them to his forehead with his palm. 'This bloody wind's a menace.'

'Aye, hot and uncomfortable an' all,' Dan agreed, fingering his collar. 'But I got an ask for you. You remembered the poles and the bales, but what you tossing them with?'

At that moment a pitchfork sailed over Dan's head. Thrown like a javelin, it stabbed the ground between the stulpes, and the handle vibrated.

'Who the...?' Dan ducked and spun to see Jack Mackett, laughing from his belly.

'Toss them wi' that of course,' Barry said as if Dan was stupid, and set off to fetch himself a beer.

'Are we ready a-start, Daniel?' Jack called from a distance. 'Want me a-put the word 'round?'

Dan considered the sky. It was a sheet of white cloud dulling the light except for where the disc of the sun burned intensely beyond. There was no sign of rain, just the aggravating wind. It should have cleared the humidity, but it was adding to it and blowing dust.

'Another half an hour,' Dan replied. 'It's taking us longer than usual to set up.'

'As you say.' Jack joined Barry at the ale.

More villagers were arriving as Dan returned to the green and they brought produce to be shared. It was for those who needed it and given by those who didn't. Small wreaths of dried grasses and bulrushes hung from strings in people's porches jigging like frantic marionettes. The top table looked stable enough, but Mick Farrow was nailing the centrepiece into position just in case. Over at the bench, the musical members of the Seeming family gathered with their instruments, and the only thing that appeared out of place was the shop.

It took Dan a minute to realise why. Whereas the other homes had provided tables and chairs for guests and neighbours, the shop was closed. The curtains were across at every window, including the front door, and there was no festival wreath. Even Tom's house displayed one of those.

'They ain't coming out if that's what you're wondering.'

Dan recognised the scent of blister balm blown from behind him. 'How you doing, Jason?'

Jason huffed. 'Spent 'alf the night wi' me ma screaming at me fur bringing the family into dis… something.'

'Disrepute?'

'Aye. Spent the other 'alf the night wi' me sister screaming at me 'cos I went and told Sally what I knew. And I spent the whole night telling meself that I'd done the right thing.'

Dan could only imagine the scene, just as he could only imagine what Jason had suffered, knowing his sister was cuckolding his friend but not being able to tell anyone or seek advice.

'You should have told me straight away,' he said.

'Aye. But we're still mates, right?'

'As I said last night…' Dan produced his pipe and filled it as he spoke. 'I'm angry because you didn't tell me sooner, but I'm grateful you told me in the end. I been keeping secrets too, so I can't hate you fur doing the same. Aye, we're still mates, Jason. Lore knows you need some, what with the family you've got.'

Jason was not insulted. 'That be true, mate,' he said. 'And you 'ave me thanks.'

The two of them watched the preparations while sharing Dan's choke, until Jason said, 'Does worry me, though.'

'What?'

'That I were keeping a secret, letting you down, what wi' it being eastling night an' all.'

'Look at them,' Dan said, pointing his pipe generally around the green. 'Everyone has secrets. Everyone's let someone down. The mistus there's been a disappointment to the mister over there. This one's told a lie to deceive that one, no doubt. Everyone's in the same barrel when it comes to tonight. But if it makes you happier, others have done worse than you.'

'Aye,' said Jason. 'I'm in 'opes your right. I don't want a-be the one it takes.'

Tom stood at the southern bridge with his back to Saddling. The pony waited behind him, feeding and occasionally snorting at the troubling breeze. If was from here in 1710 that Stan Feld had seen what he thought was an approaching stranger. The description had been written over three-hundreds years ago, but Tom doubted the landscape had altered much since then. No-one was approaching now, but it was still afternoon, and the mist wasn't expected to rise until dusk.

'Nothing's changed over there,' he said. 'But on this side…'

He had been lured through those fields and across the deek into Saddling under false pretences, but despite everything that happened that winter solstice, he had decided to stay. The witchling had been able to create her vengeful magic from the moment Tom stepped onto Saddling land, and he couldn't help but wonder what effect his presence was having on the eastling. Had he brought it? Had he betrayed the village?

'You didn't come here to worry,' he told himself.

He walked the short distance to where Eliza's shack had stood, taking the lyste on the edge of the field as she had once advised him. Then, there had been walls of old timbers, and mismatched window frames, but now there was just a square of blackened earth. The wood had been reused or burned on hearths, the windows recycled, and the furniture given away or destroyed along with any of her possession that her sister and Dan had not wanted. Nothing remained of the blind woman except her sleeper stone and the patch of dead ground where her floor once rested.

Tom expected to sense a connection to her as soon as he stepped over the threshold and put both feet on the dark earth, but he felt nothing, only the sharp sting of dust in his eyes as mischievous squalls whipped it up at his feet.

He moved to the centre of the square, glancing hopefully towards where they had found her papers in case something magical had happened since. Where he needed to see the answers mysteriously appearing, or Eliza herself with her knowledge of the lore beyond the Lore, there was only dried mud.

'There's something under here,' he whispered, scanning the ground for inspiration. 'There's an answer.'

Nothing came. No waft of Eliza's lavender perfume, only the warm air blowing across the marsh, rustling the trees and bringing with it the smell of grass and sheep dung.

There was no connection. Eliza was no longer present in the disfigured place where she had once sat admiring Dan's drawings with her fingers, feeling dead bones, smelling dried plants and speaking sage words.

'There be something unsettled in you, Tom Carey,' she had said, or words to that effect.

She had been right. Before Tom arrived in Saddling, he didn't know who he was. His search for his family history — at first fuelled by his duplicitous aunt and her quest for an answer of her own — had overwhelmed him, and he hadn't realised why, until that night in the church-house. It wasn't until the storm hit, and Dan walked willingly to the stone to be sacrificed, that Tom realised what was unsettled in him and why he had been so obsessed with his past. He hadn't understood his present or his part in it. Not until he stood in the pulpit screaming at the villagers desperate to make them see reason. Not until he saw Barry's calm eyes, his impish smile and realised that where Dan aroused lust, Barry stirred something more permanent. It was in that moment that he knew who he was and gave himself up to the rite, accepting his death in return for the ending of Saddling's ten-yearly slaying. That was what he had been born for, and the cruelty was, as he walked to the table-stone to die in place of Dan, he knew that he had been born to accept Barry's love.

Here he was now, on a patch of land that offered nothing but memories. No clues, no guidance, no help. There was nothing more he could do to protect the village from its past.

'It's a lost cause,' he said and trudged back to the trap.

He clicked the pony into a trot and turned towards the village. Behind him, the creeping mist rose from the deek and hung there, biding its time.

Tom returned the pony to Mistus Fetcher and reached the green where the festival had begun. He made for the inn and found Susan doling out pies and soup through one of the downstairs windows.

'The lads are in the field if you were looking,' she smiled as Tom took a pie.

He thanked her and leant with his back to the whitewashed wall to watch the activities.

Accordion and guitar music accompanied chatter, the clanking of tankards and the scrape of forks on plates. Children played games among the tables and hid beneath cloths, while others rolled potatoes on the knoll in races. Families sat together, talking, while husbands served their wives, and daughters and teenage sons gathered in groups to chew chicken legs and throw bones to their dogs. Distant relatives met and caught up, grandparents saw their under-generations, held them on their knees and gave the babies bread dipped in milk.

It looked the same as last year's Eastling Day, except for the occasional hat that spun across the green, and the angry flicking of cloth corners against table tops.

It looked the same, but the atmosphere was different. A foreboding gloom hung above the muted revelry as the village waited for tragedy. Everyone knew what tonight was to bring. Everyone hoped it wasn't them, but they wouldn't rejoice until each individual knew they were safe. Everyone apart from the one found dead.

'You feel it an' all, nipper?'

Mick Farrow took Tom by surprise, and he spluttered on his pie.

'It be in the wind,' Mick continued without waiting for a reply. 'Come wi' me.'

He led Tom away from the inn and towards the church-house. They skirted the wall as Tom finished eating so that by the time they reached the porch, he had been able to wipe his mouth and brush clean his shirt.

Mick opened the unlocked door, and Tom followed him into the nave. The bare stone floor cooled the building, but the dank air tasted of dust and age. The door closed with a thump of wood and the clang of the latch before Mick's footsteps echoed across the aisle towards the back of the building. He clicked open another door and ducked to pass through. Tom had to crouch and shuffle sideways. On the other side, they stood in a gloomy space no larger than a cupboard while Mick struck a match and lit a candle.

'We got a-be careful a'night,' he said. 'We know why and I ain't just talking 'bout the meeting after supper.'

'The eastling?'

'Aye. I know Matthew set you the task a finding an end a the imposition, and I reckon it be fair a-say you ain't done that.'

'I've not been able to. There's nothing in any book that we can use.'

Mick nodded thoughtfully. 'As we expected, but Matthew did say a me that if anyone could get us out this treddles, it be you.'

'He said that?'

'Thinks highly a you does Cole,' Mick said holding the candle to the wall and moving left to right. 'Don't show it mind, 'cos 'e don't understand the way you and Barry live, but that's just 'im. I were wi' 'im earlier,' he continued hurriedly. ''E said that if 'e weren't going a-be dead in a day or two 'e'd come 'round a you in time. I said 'e ain't got that time and if 'e don't want a-leave 'is boy guilty and angry wi' 'im fur the rest of 'is life, then 'e's got a-come round sooner.'

'You said that?'

'Aye, Tom, and I made 'im think 'ard on me words. I ain't all 'bout wethering, tupping, gimmer and shearings, lad. Ah.' He found what he was looking for; a key in an iron lock. 'I ain't really cut out for much more than that whiteback talk, but I can tell when a man be 'olding back 'is feelings.'

'Thanks, Mick.' Tom was touched but concerned. He wasn't sure if the old man was suggesting he knew about Tom and Barry and had told Cole to accept it, or if he had only been talking about friendship. He decided not to ask.

'Keep your 'ead low and come on up,' Mick said, squeezing through a second doorway.

Tom waited for his bulky figure to climb the ladder on the other side before cramming himself through the gap. The rungs were springy, the wood old and split in places where they oozed a faint smell of creosote and the ladder felt rotten. Cole thought highly of him? He had a strange way of showing it. He thought Tom was the best person for the job? He'd never said so to his face.

The steps ascended to the height of the nave roof and led to the squat, square tower that rose a few more feet above it. Mick was just able to stand with his wild hair dusting the planked ceiling, but Tom was forced to bend his neck.

'What are we doing, Mr Farrow?' he asked raising his voice against the sound of the buffeting gusts and rattling slates. 'There's nothing up here.'

'Ah, but there be much up 'ere.' Mick shuffled to a pair of shutters in the south wall. 'We got a be careful a'night 'cos a the revenge sought. This meeting, this imposition, it's a load a treddles, and aye, Aaron Fetcher might win despite the barn load a bads 'e's known fur. That's 'ow it be. You don't 'ave-be a good person a-win votes, far from it. But we ain't 'ere fur that. Don't know 'ow it's going a-go a'night, but if you can't pull us from the mess, then I'll do what I can a-keep it civil, and we'll pick up the shit from it when the time comes. In the 'ere-and-now, though… We got this.'

Mick unhooked the shutters and fixed them back in their stays before the wind snatched them. Dust swirled up from the floor in clouds and bit Tom's skin as if angry to have been woken. He and Mick crouched at the opening with their heads too close together for comfort and peered through.

Below, the green was peppered with people at the feast. Barry and Dan were collecting pies from the inn and carrying them on trays, offering them as cheerfully as they could, but there was little interest. Behind them, Becki Tidy and Lucy Cole did the same with the wine jugs which were proving more popular. The older men had set up a game of skittles on the path, but the children were playing their own version and kicking them over before the men could bowl. Tom could see little laughter or good humour, and all he heard was the growling wind.

A group of villagers sat apart from the rest in a circle towards the end of the lope-way. Aaron Fetcher was among them, gesticulating and, by the looks of it, pressing points and swaying votes. It was as if his behaviour had been forgiven. Worse, it had increased his popularity. The sight was unnerving.

'Do you sense it?' Mick whispered.

'I feel… something, aye,' Tom admitted. 'But I can't say what. Hopelessness?'

'Been feeling that all week.' Mick pulled back and fought the shutters closed, plunging the space into darkness until he relit the candle. Its flame shadowed every crease of his face. 'Lot a folk been feeling sad, and we know why.' He gripped Tom's elbow with a surprisingly strong hand. 'We can save the village from its wrong choices another day,' he hissed. 'But we can't save one a our own from this.'

He opened the shutters to the east, and a squall killed the candle. Crouching again, Tom saw the marsh below. From this vantage point, the highest in Saddling, he could see across the roof of the church-house and beyond the inner fields to Farrow's buildings and the second Cole farm. They were smudges on the hazy landscape.

The sun was low, casting long shadows of trees and whitebacks as they grazed ignorant of any danger.

'Save one of our own from what, though?'

Mick pointed beyond the eastern reach where the land rolled on until it merged with the distant hill.

'From that.'

Fog poured over its ridge, tumbling towards the marsh, thinning as it descended until it became a semi-transparent film reflecting the sunset colours like oil on water. It stopped at the eastern sewer and hung there unaffected by the wind.

'I reckon we got an hour afore boblight starts a-cloak its coming,' Mick said. 'Bain't no stopping it, and it's going a-be among us 'till one be found slit.'

'It's got a few to choose from.'

'Aye,' Mick nodded. 'But whoever it be, they be one a us. Even if it takes Jenny Rolfe fur what she did, we got a duty a-protect 'er.'

'I understand that, Mr Farrow,' Tom assured him. 'But I can think of no way to stop it. Not unless you know how to break the table-stone in two.'

Mick closed the shutters and relit the candle, tutting. 'Sometimes I worry 'bout you, Carey,' he said.

'It's from the eastling bedtime story.'

'I know what you're on 'bout, nipper. I just thought you was a man a learning, not wife-gossip.'

'To get by in this place,' Tom grumbled, 'you have to be both.'

A muffled cheer rose on a harsh breath of air, followed by applause. Both were soon lost to the shake of the shutters and the rattling of the roof.

'Right then.' Mick prepared to descend. 'Best thing we can do be carry on as they be doing. The bale-toss'll be starting. Let them 'ave their fun, it'll take their minds away a this 'till it be too late. That be, 'less you use your educated brain a-think a something 'afore that slitting knife takes someone.'

Twenty-Four

Before he left the church-house, Tom made sure it was prepared for the meeting. He took the opportunity to examine the table-stone again, but as with last night, he found no sign of a crack or an opening or any way that the mass of rock could be used to conceal a knife.

'Rock bound.' He said it over again as he brought the stools to the table and placed them around the edge before laying a tablecloth.

He took a candle and descended to the crypt where the sound of feet overhead crescendoed and then died as the villagers made their way to the field behind the inn. Lighting the gas lamp from the candle, he stood at the bookcase and ran his fingers across the spines. He found only what he expected; records, ledgers, the detailed working of the village, maps, the landholdings, the rolls… Nothing he hadn't seen and searched before.

The minister's books of Lore and Teaching lay on Cole's table. These were the originals, the books that overrode any of the public copies. Since the introduction of the duplicates by one of the Blacklocks ministers of the past, the teaching had stated that should there be any dispute, the final word lay in these two books. This, it was said, was to ensure that any deliberate changes to the copies could be easily detected.

'Our last hope,' Tom whispered. He touched the Book of Lore knowing that nothing in it could help him.

The desk had been tided as if the person who worked here had been fired and the top cleared for anyone who took his place. The thought sent a shiver through Tom's gut, and he wished Cole was chairing the meeting that night not Mick. Though a solid Saddling man, Farrow was old and couldn't care less who might seize power. Cole stuck up for the status quo in a way Farrow couldn't.

He collected the books and took them up to the table-stone where he put them carefully in their appointed place.

'Candlesticks, lamps, books…' He double checked the arrangements. 'Oh, yes…'

He approached the east window and knelt at a small chest beneath it. Opening the oak and iron lid, he carefully extracted an hourglass. This was a reproduction of the one lost in the last saddling storm. Crafted by Jimmy Rolfe in birch wood to represent the cleansing of the past, and with

James Collins

glass bulbs imported by Drew Fetcher, it stood two feet high, holding enough sand to run for a quarter of an hour. Following the discussion of the imposition, the glass had to be turned, giving the villagers a short break in proceedings where they could discuss among themselves. They would have fifteen minutes to decide Saddling's future.

He placed the hourglass on the cloth beside his minute book and pen and turned it to ensure the sand flowed freely.

'The passing of time,' he said, sitting to watch the yellow grains fall in a steady stream. 'Life draining away…' He thought of Matt Cole. 'Everyone passes…' He leant in, his face an inch from the glass. 'Even our minister.' Each grain was a life inexorably slipping from the upper glass, carried by the weight of those below, until, sucked into the vortex, it had no choice but to accept its passing.

Tom sat back with a jolt.

'Passing?' He reached for the books.

Another vague cheer filtered through the leaded glass as someone threw a hay bale over the bar. He ignored it, turning pages.

'There was something…' Whatever his memory was searching for in its distant reaches, he didn't think it was in the Teaching, so opened the Book of Lore.

Another cheer, another winner in the league had passed the height and could continue to the next round.

'On Witchling Day…' he flipped through the seasonal Lore and celebrations to the more mundane. 'On the celebration of a birth… On the Marking Ceremony of youth… On the aepelling… The Binding of Marriage…' The celebrations came in logical order in this section. 'On the passing of a marker… The passing of a spouse… The Clerk, a member of the Council…' The next page should have mentioned the next person in the hierarchy, the minister, but it was headed, 'The swearing of oaths.' He rubbed the page between finger and thumb hoping that two were stuck together, but no, the text jumped from the Lore concerning the death of a council member to more general matters, oaths and handfasting. He opened the book flat, careful not to crack the binding and brought a candle, cupping it to catch drips. Bending to the spine, he pressed a thumb in the gutter and flicked his nail across the join.

As with the copies, a leaf had been torn from the book.

'No,' he said looking closer. 'Not torn. Cut.'

Why would Eliza cut a page from the original copy of the Lore?

'Are you coming?'

The voice at the other end of the church made him jump. He sat up as more cheering entered the nave behind Dan.

'They're nearly at the final throwing,' Dan said. His leather shoes squeaked on the flagstones, and his loose-fitting shirt flapped as he walked.

'Yeah, I'm nearly there.' Tom closed the book but remained seated. 'Who'd do that?' he asked, more to himself than to Dan, but Dan was opposite him now and contemplating the hourglass. More cheers rang out, this time with less enthusiasm.

'Depends what you mean,' he said. 'If you mean who'd toss a bale, then any farmer's lad or all-worker who thinks he's man enough. If you mean who'd avoid the bale-toss altogether…' He nodded at Tom. 'Then I'd say a man with something more important on his mind. And if you mean who'd run an hourglass for no reason then, on the evidence, I'd have to say you.'

'You're in a cheerful mood,' Tom observed.

'Aye.' Dan threw his eyes across the books. 'But I'm only pretending. Same as everyone else, I don't know I'm safe. I've done nothing to hurt no-one. None of the bads I've ever thrown in the fire-pile have been to do with betrayal or cheating. That's for next Witchling Day when I'll burn the fact I kept a secret from my best mates, but until then, my bad hangs in the air.'

'It won't be coming for you,' Tom said, trying to reassure him. 'There are plenty of others who've done worse.'

'Aye, Jenny included.' He buried his concern beneath false cheeriness. 'Anyway, Barry's going through to the final, and you're going to miss it if you don't hurry.'

'Barry again?'

'And this time Jack's trying to win. You coming? Jack's got to beat Nathan Farrow in the next round first. They're having a beer break.'

Tom came around the table, his mind still on the missing page. 'What's to be gained from it?' he pondered, stepping into the aisle.

Dan joined him and held him in a neck hold for a manly hug before releasing him. 'What you muttering now?'

'Why tear a page from the church-house copy of the Lore?'

Dan thought as two pairs of shoes echoed in unison. At the back of the box pews, he stopped abruptly and said, 'We've got a minute, Tom. Answer me something.'

Tom, holding the door latch, waited for the question.

'What learning you got?'

'Me?' The question transported Tom back to a different life. A different world. 'I have a bachelor's degree in computer science and a master's in video game design. Why?'

Dan's face was a blank.

'You did ask.'

'Aye. But you're a man of learning?'

'I guess so,' Tom admitted. 'But none of it does me any good here.'

'I'd agree if I knew what the coot you were talking about.' Dan came closer. 'But the point is, you got those decrees and…'

'Degrees.'

'Alright, mate, don't get jawsy.' Dan knocked Tom's hand from the latch, and his own took its place. He held the door shut. 'You got that learning, you read your books and study the past and do that kind of clever stuff, yet you can't answer a simple question.'

'I'm not with you,' Tom said. 'And hurry, it's stuffy in here.'

'Ain't no better outside. But answer your own ask first.'

'I would if I could.'

'You can.'

'Dan,' Tom insisted, 'we're missing the fun.'

'Be as little of that as there is fresh air.' Dan glanced at the door. 'Come on Tom, think harder. Who'd cut a page from the Book of Lore?'

'Your aunt did. Or may have done, I should say. She had pages in her possession when she died.'

'Was killed,' Dan corrected.

'Aye.'

'So, what did she want the page for?'

Tom shrugged. 'Good question.'

'Alright then, what page was it?' Dan prompted.

'There are a few.'

'So…?' Dan folded his arms and leant against the door, grinning, satisfied that he knew something Tom didn't. 'Let's say Aunt Eliza did take them. How did she steal them? Why did she want them? And how could she have done it?'

'The pages from the original Lore have been cut out, so anyone with a knife could have done that.'

'Why?'

'Because there's something written there that the thief didn't approve of?' That sounded lame. 'Something they...' Pieces began to shift like the tiles of a Chinees puzzle. 'Something they didn't believe in.'

'Could make sense,' Dan said. 'But not for Eliza. She believed in everything, apart from the saddling ritual. But it's the Book of Lore we're talking on. It's honoured. And then there's how?'

'With a knife, I told you.'

'No, how did she get at the book? The copies, easy prehaps as they're not locked away, but the original? That's only to be touched and read by the minister and his council.'

'Yeah, but Eliza could have got into the crypt.' Sweat trickled along Tom's nose as if it was the last piece of the puzzle preparing to drip into place. It didn't; it just hung there.

'Come on, mate, she wouldn't have done that. And she was blind. Aye, she might have broken in, but someone must have been with her to read the bloody thing. Unless she was randomly scissoring pages out of...' Dan sighed. 'Oh, come on, Tom!' He cupped his hands to Tom's cheeks and directed his head towards the table-stone. 'What's your most vivid memory of *that*. What d'you see?'

It was with Tom in flashed images. The storm. The saddling ritual. Dan in his suit, the material clinging to every inch of his body. The knife. The hourglass. Himself dragged onto the stone. Barry holding him down. The blade on his chest. Barry releasing him. Dan fighting alongside him. The slash and the cut. Mark Blacklock's body weeping blood from its throat. His father carrying his dead son.

His father. The duplicitous minister.

'Blacklocks,' he whispered, and the puzzle was complete.

'Simple if you ask me.' Dan released him and returned to the door.

It was simple. Blacklocks had permanent and unfettered access to the books. He could have cut the pages away as soon as he became minister. In fact, any Blacklocks minister could have done it. Or a Carey.

No, not one of Tom's ancestors. Pages were missing that had been written after the Careys gave up the role.

No, not gave up. Were ousted from — by the Blacklocks.

He was in no doubt who had vandalised the Lore. The question remained, however, why?

'I bet there's something on that page that Blacklocks didn't want anyone to know,' Dan said as he opened the door and let in a rush of warmer but fresher air.

'It makes sense now,' Tom said. 'But it doesn't help if I can't find the page. And I can't.'

They stepped through the porch and into the gathering dusk.

'You know,' Tom said. 'You just came up with means, motive and opportunity. You should be an author.'

Dan laughed once and loudly, a good-natured mock. 'Tom, mate,' he said, holding Tom's neck in the crook of his arm again. 'I'm the village inns-man, healer, cat-model and cuckold. What more d'you want of me?'

By the time they reached the field, the bale-toss was almost over, but there was no sense of an exciting finish or revelry. Jack and Barry stood before the bar, looking at it and conferring while most other villagers talked nervously in groups. Some teetered on the seating bales watching the east where the approaching mist waited, still and untroubled by the gusting wind. The sight was unnerving; the creeping grey cloud remained flat and consistent while the trees above it swayed.

'Is this the last throw?' Dan asked as he sat beside his mother.

'Aye,' she said. 'But none has a mind for it a'night.'

'I thought I heard cheering?' Tom queried, throwing one leg over the straw and hoisting himself across.

'You may have done,' Susan replied, moving to give him room. 'But that was for things Aaron Fetcher was shouting between the throws.'

'What things?'

'Oh, Tom,' Susan complained. 'I ain't going back over them, but they weren't good for you nor Matthew, Mick, nor none of the council.'

She pointed to the other side of the arena where Aaron sat with his supporters. The group had expanded since the aepelling, and any embarrassment the others had shown towards Aaron's behaviour had now gone. Tom had been right; his notoriety had made him popular. He'd become the pop star known and loved for being reckless. Older men had joined him, and his faction no longer represented only the young.

'What's gone on, Ma?'

'Each time someone tossed a bale, he jumped up and made another promise,' she explained. 'Vote fur him, and he'll put an end to cuckolding, he said. Join his imposition, and there'd be no shame in...' She lowered her voice. 'Sex afore marriage.' Raising it again, she added, 'And other things to knock out half our Lore and make Saddling the same as any other place on the marshes.'

False promises and unworkable lies. Tom's stomach knotted with anger. 'How can they be blind enough to believe him? He's got no idea,' he fumed. 'He might rake up a few votes with lies that appeal to individuals, but see them through and the village dies.'

'You can't let him get away with it, Tom,' Susan implored. 'He's leading the ignorant and turning more to his ways. It's going to mean the death of us.'

The chatter that had underscored their conversation died, bringing Susan to a halt with it. Jack Mackett had ripped the pitchfork from the ground and was positioning himself for the toss. Barry stood back to give him room. Last year, Tom remembered, at this point in the proceedings, there had been music with small boys beating on empty beer kegs to provide a drum roll, and Jack and Barry had both been staggering under the influence of alcohol. This year, the field was silent, half the audience were watching the east, distracted by worry and Jack was sober. Barry, shirtless and dripping with sweat stood without lurching.

'Get on with it, bavens,' Aaron yelled.

'Hold your jawing,' Jack threatened him with the pitchfork.

Aaron laughed at his pose. 'Trouble with you, Mackett,' he jeered, 'is you don't know what side of the bar you be on. You with us strong'uns? Or are you with the duffers and their old ways?'

'And the trouble with you, Fetcher...' Barry stepped up to Jack and lowered the pitchfork. 'Is that you don't know what's wrong even when you be it.'

'This ain't the time fur fighting.' Mick Farrow stood to shout, while members of the council complained and heckled.

Tom groaned inwardly. The festival was a washout. Half of the villagers were watching for the fog, while the rest were fighting among themselves with no regard for their neighbours. Mick, as Cole had done, was losing control, and Aaron was taking advantage of it, using his bragging to deflect people's attention from his recent crimes. Tom was preparing to call for order when Barry saved him the trouble.

'Right!' He bellowed, making even the most fearsome of the eastlinglookouts turn to him in shock. When silence had fallen, and before Aaron could leap in, he spoke, loudly, but calmly. 'Jack and I was talking, and we decided that this 'ere final bale-toss be used a-show you what we think 'bout this teg's bloody imposition. Watch closely, Fetcher, so we might learn you something.'

With that, both he and Jack gripped the pitchfork and plunged it into the bale. The held one another's stare, adjusted their grips and nodded when ready. With one almighty heave, they swung the bale from the grass, up and over their heads yelling. Together. Once it was released, they spun to see it sail way above the bar and fall to the ground on the other side where it bounced, still twined and intact, until it came to rest.

The gesture was not lost on Tom, but Aaron couldn't see what they were trying to say. Before he could start up again, Mick Farrow walked into the arena, his arms stretched wide.

'So, that be done, and well done both lads. Working a'gether be the only way.' He raised his hands and encouraged the villagers to clap. Few did. 'Now we can finish the festival, honour the women, get them as wants to vote into the church-house and get this ruddy farce done with. Trott on, all a ye.'

Tom was impressed with his sudden and unusual command of the audience and hope flickered in his chest. People were reacting to Mick's authority, there was still a chance they might listen to his reason once the official meeting began.

He rose to congratulate Barry and Jack, but Mick puffed his way through the shifting crowd.

'This night ain't going a-go well,' he said, dabbing his forehead with a dirty cloth. 'Can you still sense it, Carey? Something's not settling right.'

'Be the uncertainty,' Susan said as she left them. 'None is caring for anyone else other than themselves.'

'Bain't just the eastling,' Mick called after her as he turned to Tom. 'This be beyond me, Carey.' The old man stepped back and waited until they were alone while holding Tom with his questioning look. 'You be the man a learning in Saddling now. You wanted a-stay 'ere. Aye, I were against it at first, but now I see the sense poor Matthew 'ad in 'pointing you as the clerk, trusting you wi' our Lore...'

'Thanks, but...'

'I don't know where Aaron Fetcher and Bill Taylor got their unease wi' the life we got. Who knows why they want a-change what's not needing changing? But I do know I ain't the one as can persuade them a decency. We didn't need you fur the saddling, Tom but you was there, and you started the changes in this village. We need you 'ere fur this night.' He ran his hand through his troubled hair to flatten it, but the easterly didn't allow it. 'One more thing,' he said. 'You weren't 'ere, but Fetcher talked of you.'

'Susan told me part of what he'd said.'

'Well, 'e said plenty, and 'alf the village or more agreed wi' im. We've lost our support, Tom.'

Tom's stomach turned over. 'How come?'

Mick glanced away and rolled his head before his wind-watery eyes once again returned, veined and glassy.

'He said...' Mick sighed. 'Sorry, Carey. He said that the first thing a-be done when 'e gets appointed the people's minister...' He faltered.

'Yes?'

'He'd... Seeing as you ain't from the village... Send you from Saddling fur good.'

'Oh, that's just...'

'That be just what most of them wants, 'e said. And I reckon it be what they'll get. I ain't going a-be able a-stop them.'

Mick walked away, leaving Tom alone in the field as the last stragglers left for the green. The sun was setting behind him and ahead, between the hill and the inner deek, the silvery bank of fog gradually crept closer. To him, it represented the end of his time in Saddling. What more could he do? An ignorant upstart had used a little-known part of the Lore to pull the rug from under his feet, and not only him, the whole village. He'd done it at a time when Saddling was most vulnerable, with a dying leader and the threat of the eastling's retribution weighing on troubled minds. It was as if Aaron Fetcher knew the time to strike.

Tom sat, his gaze fixed on the far trees in the gathering gloaming. Warm draughts of air annoyed his too-long hair and investigated the sleeves of his shirt with the confidence of an arrogant, uninvited visitor.

Aaron wasn't the kind of person to plan. He was headstrong, did things without thinking, acted on impulse as he did that Witchling Day, and in calling his cousins and friends to oppose Matt Cole's ascension to minister. He had been too young to vote then, but now... Now was only two years later. How had he gained this confidence and knowledge in that time?

What had happened for him to turn his back on his upbringing? What had twisted him to this bitterness?

'Tom?'

Barry's familiar and comforting voice landed along with his palm on Tom's head, but Tom didn't move.

'They've called an end a the festival,' Barry said with regret. 'First time in my memory the women ain't been 'onoured.'

It was the first time in Tom's memory that the answer to a riddle had been so close and yet so unreachable.

How did Aaron Fetcher understand the people's imposition? It was not mentioned in the Teaching, only the older villagers knew of it.

'Least it means I don't 'ave a-make no speech.' Barry ruffled Tom's hair. 'You coming, lover?'

How had Aaron known something from the Lore that had never been taught?

'What's causing all this badness, Tom?'

'What...?'

Tom turned to face Barry and knelt on the bale between them. 'Not what,' he said, grinning. 'Who.'

Barry's smile was crooked, and he pulled back his head. 'What you been smoking?'

Tom shuffled across the straw and climbed down. 'He's working with someone,' he said, his mind now wrenched from its despair to the pinnacle of alertness. 'Could be Bill Taylor, could be one of his cronies, or Andrew White... Someone who's been on the council silently plotting to be the puppet master. Could be anyone.' He yanked Barry towards the inn. 'What's happening now?'

'Clearing the green, then into the church-house. Many's already gathered.'

There had to be someone guiding Aaron, he wasn't capable of rallying the village against the council on his own. Someone else had taught him, given him confidence, told him parts of the Lore and Teaching that no-one had seen for years.

The way to prevent the imposition was to challenge whoever was pulling Aaron's strings, and that person was bound to be in the church-house.

'Come on, Tom,' Barry said. 'The imposition's 'bout a-start.'

With renewed hope, and with Barry stumbling after him, Tom hurried from the field.

Twenty-Five

Flames flickered in dying gusts and the few remaining festival decorations spasmed in death throes against front doors. With the green cleared and the sun below the horizon, the remaining villagers made their way towards the church-house. Families stayed together, pulling their young ones close, glancing behind, and holding their lanterns high. The stilling air wrapped them in a sultry warmth, dampening hair and skin, and the atmosphere inside the building gave no respite.

His nervousness troubled him as Tom entered the church. The building throbbed with heated conversation and each breath drew increasing tension into his lungs, feeding his pulse with anxiety. It wasn't just the imposition that clouded his mind, Dan's mention of William Blacklocks had put him on edge. The person behind the current unrest had access to the Book of Lore. It could have been Matt Cole, the clerk for several years. What did he have to gain from it? The man had stood up to Blacklocks and the way he lured Tom into danger. He had been prepared to leave the village rather than see the Lore abused, and he now lay dying. Why would he disrupt Saddling life this way? It didn't add up and, as Tom manoeuvred around some of Aaron fetcher's supporters, ignoring their hissed jibes, he ruled out Minister Cole.

He weaved through the gathering towards the table-stone, his eyes darting from one person to the other. Any one of them could be the man behind Aaron's curiously timed rebellion. He looked for Drew Fetcher, a possible suspect. Aaron's father had much to gain from a new rule of openness with the outside world. More fetching meant more income, and more opportunity to import goods that the younger villagers would barter well for. Tom couldn't imagine an Xbox, a Smartphone, a tablet or a computer in Saddling. He had bought two mobile phones just after the saddling, but they had remained in their boxes. Having seen how things could be during a couple of trips into nearby towns, Cole and the council had retreated behind the safety of the Saddling borders and its way of life. Tom saw the sense in that, and the phones were thrown in the fire-pile one Witchling Day.

He spotted Drew Fetcher sitting with Nate Rolfe and Terry Brazier, two of Cole's staunchest supporters. They were sharing a joke, laughing at

Aaron on the other side of the church. Father belittling son? Unless he was a good actor, it was unlikely Drew Fetcher was involved, and Tom crossed him off his metal list.

'Good luck, Tom, Sir.' Billy Farrow touched Tom's shirt as he passed, his face sincere.

Tom managed a weak smile and a nod of the head. Why did it have to be a man?

Rebecca Rolfe was crowding the already crowded aisle as he squeezed past. There was no reason it couldn't be her, or Jacob Seeming's mother come to that or any of the women, but Aaron's group consisted mainly of male youths and younger women… Which didn't mean his puppet master or mistress had to be among them… There were Mr and Mistus…

Not looking where he was going, he bumped into Dan.

'Your mind isn't with us, is it?'

The collision helped pull Tom's thoughts together. 'Sorry, mate,' he said. 'Was miles away.'

He reached the table while other members of the council fought their way through the throng to take their places. Mick Farrow was the last to arrive, coming from the crypt wearing the minister's gown, open at the front, flowing and jet black with a satin collar. It couldn't be Mick either. He had been on the council for many years, but the councilmen didn't have access to the books unless with the minister in attendance. Mick carried himself with a surprising stateliness. His hair lay flat, he had combed it and washed his face. He could very well pass for a man who knew what he was doing, except he was as much a mess of concern as Tom and the council members.

'We set, Carey?' he asked as he stood centre stage behind the table eyeing the villagers anxiously.

'We are, Sir.' Tom bowed his head.

People were squashed into the box pews, children on laps. The church-house was full on both sides, with the aisle kept as clear as possible.

'How many have turned up?' Mick asked. 'Seems a fair turnout.'

Tom hadn't counted yet, but Bill Taylor was in the pulpit with one of his bony fingers tapping the air as he methodically scanned the room.

'Nearly the whole village,' he called to Mick before descending and taking his place in the pews.

'Then what are we waiting for?'

Mick raised his hand for silence and one by one, the villagers quietened.

'This meet,' he began as the council took their seats, 'will be conducted according to the Teaching and held with respect. There'll be no shouting or defiance. The meet will be run in a civil fashion. Are we agreed?'

A resounding 'Aye' rang out.

'Right then…'

Mick was interrupted by Barry arriving late with Jack Mackett and slamming the door.

'Keep it open!' someone shouted from the other side. 'No air in 'ere.'

'None much out there neither,' Barry replied, ignoring the request and looking for a place to sit.

'Safer wi' the door shut,' a young voice said.

'Nothing's going save you if it be you 'e be after,' Jack pointed out, not helping the child's state of mind.

'Find a place please, Mr Mackett,' Mick ordered before settling himself on his stool.

Tom was impressed with the way he was handling things so far. He didn't seem as nervous as he had been in the tower, and he methodically arranged papers he didn't need, stalling for time and making everyone wait to show who was in charge. The congregation fanned themselves or loosened collars until Mick looked up from the table, stood, and dropped the bombshell Tom dreaded.

'On account a Minister Cole being unwell, and me wi' me bad 'earing,' he said. 'Clerk Carey will be taking this meet. My councilmen are agreeing, ain't we?'

The others nodded, keen not to be associated with either side of the forthcoming imposition. Apart from two, the men were farmers, wily characters who knew how to slip their way out of a problem and leave the responsibility at someone else's gate.

Tom didn't want to be in this position, but there was nothing he could do. With nausea churning in his stomach, he bowed graciously to the councilmen and stood to look over the heads of the congregation. Barry had found himself a seat higher than anyone else, and it took Tom a moment to realise he was sitting on the font. Nervousness made him smile unbidden, but he covered it with a cough. Dan was close to the front with his mother and Jason Rolfe.

The village would continue no matter what happened. Neighbours might fall out over this, but time would heal. He had to be fair.

'Men and women of Saddling,' he began, his heart pounding in his ears. 'We have here a people's imposition called by Aaron Fetcher and seconded by Bill Taylor. As you know, Master Fetcher has exercised the ancient and rarely used right to question this council…' He held up his hands for silence even before the mumbling began. 'Whatever you feel about that, it is an accepted part of our process.' He placed his hand on the Lore. 'We will listen to their propositions in turn, and we will hear from a representative of the established council. Each speaker will have equal time. After that…' He indicated the hourglass. 'There will be fifteen minutes of reflection before I call the vote.'

At the front of the aisle, a child raised her hand.

'The time for questions comes later,' Tom said, smiling. 'But as it's you, Molly. Yes?'

'Be we safe from the eastling, Sir?'

The question was on more minds than just hers judging from the way other children and adults alike mumbled agreement.

'We are safe as a group,' Tom said. 'As individuals…? Well, that depends on how good you've been.' He winked at Molly crossed legged on the flagstones. 'I'm sure you got no worrits.' He addressed the villagers in general, acutely aware of his own words, aware that his breathing was unstable. He maintained an authoritative appearance and buried his nervousness and anger, but his throat was drying by the second. 'We have asked our lookers to be on watch. They are outside the church-house,' he continued. 'Those who saw no sense in these unprecedented proceedings must take care of for their own fate.'

He weighted his words carefully, speaking politely but making it clear that he thought the imposition was wrong. Barry gave him a thumbs up and grinned.

'Now,' Tom said, his heart warmed by Barry's support, 'we will hear from all sides of this argument. First, Master Fetcher as the voice of… your party, please take the pulpit and make your address.'

Aaron inched his way from the box pew amid slaps on the back, jeers and a couple of uncouth whistles from his mates. It was interesting to note that Billy Farrow was not with them. He sat with his father a few rows behind, arms folded, scowling.

When Aaron reached the elevated pulpit, he slicked back his hair, adjusted his shirt and nodded to Mick Farrow who turned the hourglass.

Aaron Fetcher had the floor. He had the ears of the village, and he offered ridiculous ideas that those in his pew applauded and cheered with ever-increasing enthusiasm. Extend the lope-way across the bridge to the southern fields to join a road. Increase the number of fetchers and their trips. His proposal to allow anyone to go with them to barter with other villages was met with derision from all but his supporters. Calls of 'You don't know what you're talking 'bout' from Jack Mackett were reined in. Aaron's suggestion that electricity be brought to Saddling was met with contempt by many until he spoke of how it could make life easier.

Tom couldn't disagree with that, but that was not the point. He knew that what the youth was selling sounded appealing, but his promises were hollow. Aaron was marketing an impossible dream and making it sound feasible and instant.

'Make me minister a'night, and we'll 'ave electric come next week,' he swore.

Months of negotiation with local authorities and power companies were needed, and before that, the world had to accept that Saddling had existed without their knowledge for centuries.

Aaron spoke well but inflected his voice upwards at the end of each sentence as if running things off a list.

The voice grated on Tom, and his mind wandered. There had to be a logic to this mess; he had to put his facts in order.

Parts of the Teaching had not been taught, but Aaron knew of the people's imposition even though there had not been one in the village for centuries. How did Cole and the council know of it if the text was absent from the books?

Tom's mind clicked up a gear when he reached the obvious conclusion. Because someone wanted them to know. Aaron had whispered the possibility like a spoketale. The whisper had become knowledge, and he had used that for his own divisive means. Tom couldn't imagine Aaron planning that alone. He didn't have the temperament or patience to see such a thing through.

He was back where he started; there was someone else behind this dissent.

The boy's voice droned on, and a quick glance at the hourglass showed Tom he had a few minutes yet to speak.

How had the missing pages come into Eliza's possession? If she hadn't taken them, where had she found them? Why didn't she tell anyone? None of it made sense and yet something nagged at the back of Tom's mind. When questioned about his night on the dowels with the Feld brothers, Aaron had pointedly said that he hadn't spoken to anyone. Why say that unless he had? And, if he had, who was it?

William Blacklocks?

Impossible. The man was dead.

Presumed dead.

'No, definitely dead.'

'What was that?' Mick leant closer.

'Sorry,' Tom whispered, waving him away. 'Nothing.'

The person behind this imposition was most likely in the church-house now, wiping sweat from his forehead and listening with a smirk on his face.

Jack Mackett was doing exactly that, his arms folded, leaning against the far wall.

Tom's heart skipped a beat. The scent of patchouli wafted through his memory, prominent among the smells of perspiration and beer-breath. His eyes darted, searching for Jenny Rolfe and he found her among Aaron's supporters. Her gaze was fixed on her lover, now speaking passionately about a future where the village had turned its back on the established way of life. She smiled, blinking coquettish encouragement.

Jack had been wearing the same scent, a scent made especially for Jenny.

'No way,' Tom whispered, looking back to Jack.

He remembered walking with him on the lyste, standing close, talking, patchouli strong on his clothes. The way he had appeared at the door half dressed, fumbling with his boots, looking back to his house and calling it 'She.'

Or had he been talking about a woman inside the house? Would Jack have seduced Jenny knowing that Dan was marrying her? Was Jack the kind of man to betray a friend?

Tom's blood was chilling, and he shuddered. His eyes flashed to the hourglass as the last grains of sand fell through.

'And there's your time,' he said, briefly dragging his mind back to his duties. 'Thank you, Master Fetcher.' He noted Aaron's speech in the minutes' book. 'We will now take a moment while Mr Taylor prepares.'

He called Dan to the dais and took him to one side.

'Quick,' he said, holding Dan close by the elbow. 'Honest and quick answer. That scent you gave Jenny? Did you make it for anyone else?'

Dan was surprised but thought fast and shook his head. 'No,' he said. 'Why?'

'Damn.'

'What is it?'

'Just a hunch.' So, Jack could easily be involved with Jenny, but why? It made no sense. 'You didn't give any to Jack then?'

'No,' Dan said, confused. 'I didn't need to. The Macketts have been making their own for years. He told me how to perfect it.'

'Same smell?'

'Exactly.'

There was Tom's answer. 'Cheers, Dan.'

Satisfied that Jack had played no part, he returned to the table.

Bill Taylor began his speech on the turn of the hourglass, and again, Tom listened to what he'd heard before until his mind drifted.

Time was slipping away. Another fifteen minutes from Taylor, then the council and a further quarter of an hour for the open discussion. Forty-five minutes to save the village traditions and maintain the status quo.

There were too many questions and not enough facts, no proof. But there was a dying man whose last wish it was that Tom healed this division.

Why should he? Why should he care about a village he had only known a few years? A place that had tricked him, tried to kill him and that now, in part, wanted to see the back of him?

Tom owed Saddling nothing. He had arrived as a stranger and still was to most. He was an out-marsher, he was the man who knew the ways of the outside world, and he was the one Taylor's supporters blamed for raising the spectre of modernisation in the minds of others. Tom was the man who ended an ancient ritual and was now leading the meeting that could change a way of life forever.

Taylor spoke of a return to the saddling rite in years to come, the protection of the village from the floods by selfless sacrifice. He was rallying his supporters with well thought out words of how things used to be, how they should be again. He referred to Tom, veiled but obvious. He blamed his influence, subtly accusing him of causing the return of the witchling and the evil stalking the marsh that night. If anyone should fall victim to the vengeful ghost of past crimes, he said, it was such a man.

Tom's head snapped up from his scribbling, his mouth open, ready to object, but he caught sight of Barry shaking his head as a warning, and held his words. Whatever Taylor said, he had to let it pass him by and drift into the rafters. He couldn't show his feelings, he was impartial. He dropped his head to his book. His notes were vague and scrawled.

His mind was as crowded as the church-house with individual threads. Disappearing pages. What was written on them? Why was the phrase "passing minister" screaming to be heard above the other chattering annoyances, injustices, rights and wrongs? Where had he seen it? Questions swirled to the tune of a dishevelled waltz, some ducking under, others rising, bowing and weaving while Tom was caught in the middle, standing as helpless as a lost lamb while the fog of past betrayals fumed around him, centred on him, choked him. Stabbed him through the heart…

He spun on his stool to face the east window. The figure lay on the grass on Eastling Day beside its drunk lover, a knife protruding from the chest of the one who had brought so much trouble and change to the village. The eastling's intended victim.

Tom Carey.

Twenty-Six

While the village debated its fate, revenge took shape among the twisted mother trees at the eastern mark. One gnarled and bark-flaked trunk for every mother who had lost her son to the saddling ritual. Each with a pair of boughs that opened and entreated like arms longing for the return of a lost child. Leaves, turning from the green of innocence to the dull red of heartache, dropped from dying fingers to feed the hungry mist with their sorrow, and were swallowed as the eastling grew in the ether.

The smell of betrayal hung heavy in the foetid air, the odour drifting to the furthest borders where the grey-hang lifted from the low levels and crept ever closer to the village. Clouds scudded the moon, and the wind died, allowing the ghostly half-form of the long-dead youth an untroubled passage across the fields, above the deeks, around the bridges, closing in on the dull, warm light of the highest building; the far-off church-house and the stench of perfidy that bubbled within.

The pain flamed in the memory and throat of John of the Black Locks as he stalked silently with intent. Whitebacks lifted their heads, saw, and turned away. Deek-edge rushes quivered and rustled, whispers in the noiseless air as the shadowy shape slipped by. It knew its victim, it knew its purpose. Its cadaverous fingers played on the slitting-knife.

Tom wiped sweat from his neck and swallowed.

'Thank you, Mr Taylor,' he said, rising as Bill resumed his place in the pews and half the congregation applauded. 'We will now hear from the last speaker.' He turned to Mick, but the old farmer merely shrugged. He was having nothing to do with this. Tom appealed to the other councilmen, but they busied themselves with their notes. 'Is there one here who wishes to speak on behalf of the existing council and ways of our village?' he asked, hoping that the task wouldn't fall to him. It wasn't that he didn't want to tell them what he thought of the proceedings, but he was not the man to do it. They needed someone from Saddling, someone the villagers trusted.

Moisture gathered in his eyebrows and trickled annoyingly into his eyes. He wiped it away leaving his vision focused.

Dan stood in the aisle.

'Aye,' he said. 'If none other has the guts a-say what needs a-be said, then I must.'

'Please.' Tom offered him the floor gratefully and, at the back, Barry cheered.

Others joined in until Dan was accompanied to the pulpit by the sound of half the church-house applauding. Aaron Fetcher's party remained silent and scowling, but it was interesting to see encouragement from several of Bill Taylor's clique.

Was Taylor's support wavering? His speech had been lacklustre and no match for Fetcher's youthful passion. The thought gave Tom hope as he sat to note Dan's speech while he wracked his brains.

Had Aaron spoken to the eastling on the dowels last night? Had he been in communication with the ghost of a murdered boy? Learnt what was no longer in the Teaching, been given secrets and inspiration by the thing that sought vengeance? That was as unfathomable as the existence of William Blacklocks, but as the Lore stated, 'We take Saddling with all its unknowns.'

Tom looked up sharply from his doodling. Dan had said the same words.

'It's what our Lore states,' Dan said. Speaking with authority, he showed no signs of the torment of nervousness Tom suffered. 'So, aye, we do take Saddling with every one of its unknowns, but we don't take any others. The unknowns from out there? What do we need with them? What has out there got that we need? Nothing we don't already trade for. We've survived as a community away from that and untroubled by it. There's no need to open our lope-way, have the influence of what's beyond our borders sully our lives with its pace and its anger, its confusions and its troubles. Why are we even talking of change when there ain't nothing more perfect than what we have now? Besides…' His piercing eyes lasered directly at Aaron. 'Anyone's free a-leave Saddling and not welcome back.'

Tom smiled. The audience was hanging on Dan's words. Some sat, arms folded, their expressions showing they didn't care for his speech, but still they listened. Others, his mother and Barry included, grinned proudly, while Taylor's older allies chewed their unlit pipes and looked on with polite doubt.

Tom's smile faded when he heard his name.

'Tom Carey,' Dan said. 'He's one of the few of us who knows what's out there. He's an asset to Saddling and should be treated as such.'

Tom dipped his head, pretending to make notes.

'We were talking this morning,' Dan continued. 'Discussing what that young man there did to me.'

Tom didn't remember such a conversation but was amused to see Aaron Fetcher shuffle uncomfortably in his seat.

'You see, the thing is...' Dan paused, waiting for the villagers' attention to return. 'That kind of behaviour is common out there. Imagine it. Your daughter is proposed to, ain't she Mistus Brazier?' A woman towards the back nodded, and the girl beside her sat up straight. 'Well, imagine how it'll be with Master Fetcher setting her the example that she can go with whoever she likes afore she's joined, just as he did when he stole Jenny from me.'

That brought whispers in the rows and gained Aaron looks of mistrust.

'Just think on it, Mistus Brazier, and you there, Mr White, what with your boy Harry being so in love with Rose as he is. Imagine how it'd be if a child comes along, and you can't be sure if it belongs to Harry, or Aaron, or any man Rose had taken a fancy to.'

That comment brought louder whispering and a few outraged shouts.

'I'm only giving an example, Rose Brazier and I'm sorry to have used you for it. My apologies to you too, Harry, but you are next in line for a Saddling wedding.' The young people concerned indicated that they didn't mind. 'And there's another thing. How would that wedding be without the Maden copse or an aepelling so well ruined by Master Fetcher? Imagine it without the whole village coming a'gether on the day because some were out drinking and whoring over at Moremarsh...' People gasped. 'Or gone further afield to bring back women of their own from Romney or even beyond the far hill?' Outrage simmered. 'Do you want our land so open that the family you're head of, Mr White, a family seven-hundred-year established, leaves you here alone and scuttles away?'

Mumbling, dissent from the youths, agreement from Taylor's party. Tom grinned, impressed with Dan's manipulations.

'We've always had our arms open a those who live in peace with us.' Dan's voice was unwavering as he projected over the underscore of discord. 'We've had visitors, we welcome them, but aye, we see them on their way, and it don't happen often. I ain't saying what Bill Taylor's been hinting, that we build a wall from the southern mark to the northern dole stone. We don't need that. Our deeks and the wide sewers mark our place in this marsh and in this world, but if anyone wants a-come through, we remember our Teaching, and we welcome them as we must. Nor am I saying that we should encourage it, like Fetcher be saying.' He paused and brushed his fringe from his forehead. 'If you got a problem with Saddling, you come a the council, and they do what they can a-keep you happy. The way it's always been. I'm only asking you one question. What's wrong with the life we have?'

He paused to glance at the hourglass.

'I ain't got long,' he said and gripped the front of the pulpit. He raised his chin, fixed his audience with his piercing wolf-eyes as the lantern light lit him, turning his hair to flame and colouring his pale skin. 'And there's someone else who ain't got long, though only a few knows it.'

Tom sensed what was coming and flicked his eyes to Barry. He sat as enraptured with the man in the pulpit as much as everyone else, his mouth open, pride chiselled on his face.

'It ain't my place to say this,' Dan said, 'but it be the time. Our minister ain't here because he be dying…'

A shockwave rippled through pews until Dan dampened the chatter with his voice.

'Aye, I be sorry a-speak so plain,' he said. 'But what we be believe in… Me, the council, Minister Cole, Mr Farrow, Clerk Carey, all of us who see no sense nor reason in this feud between the Fetchers and the Taylors that's ripping our village in two… What we believe in is honesty. What we have for you is the truth, and that be it.' He pointed accusingly at Aaron. 'And the truth a this imposition be that it were called without knowing why he were calling it.' He used both hands to indicate the minister's seat and Bill Taylor. 'Nor what Bill would with that chair if he were sat in it. And the honest truth tonight is, there ain't no-one worthy a-take Minister Cole's place, and there ain't no lore nor teaching on what we do because someone stole pages from the books we live by.'

Dan had turned up the flame beneath the simmering outrage, and it boiled over. The church-house erupted. Shouts of disbelief, horror and anger punctuated calls for the meeting to be scrapped. Accusations were thrown at the council, Fetcher, Taylor, even Dan.

Tom caught Dan's eye and winked, but his friend displayed no pleasure at what he had caused. He raised his arms, calling for order, and Mick Farrow tipped the hourglass on its side to halt time.

'It be noted,' Tom called, half-rising, 'that Deputy Minister Farrow has paused Mr Vye's speaking time out of fairness.'

'Mr Vye can speak as long as he wants.' The shout silenced the last of the clamour. 'I'm happy a-let him talk for me.'

There were gasps. It was Bill Taylor who had spoken.

'You see?' Aaron turned to address those behind him. 'You can't trust a Taylor. Change their minds faster than...'

Barry interrupted. 'Faster than you bed any lass what's blind enough a 'ave you.' He brought laughter to half the church.

'This ain't the way to stir your family feud, Aaron.' Dan's voice cut through the hilarity, and Mick turned the hourglass.

Dan's speech bubbled beneath Tom's thoughts.

Blind.

He heard Barry's words repeated as their eyes met across the heads of everyone looking up to Dan. The blind woman who collected the missing pages. Eliza who knew of the thefts and was astute enough to find them before Blacklocks slit her face. She spoke out against the saddling ritual. That had been his excuse for taking her sight, but what if it was also a warning? 'Stop meddling with my plan, or I'll do worse.' He imagined the man pressing his blade into her flesh.

He was back to Blacklocks, but it was the eastling that had caused this unrest. Sweeping dissent and dissatisfaction ahead of itself as it approached on the troubled east wind. It had to be stopped.

With ancient rock-bound blade.

The table-stone, the only place he could think the knife to be. He had examined every inch of it. Billy Farrow had lent his sharper eyes and found nothing. Who were the sons of the rhyme?

The hourglass was draining rapidly.

'So...' Dan noticed and brought his speech to its conclusion. 'In the spirit of honesty and fairness, I see no other way for Minister Cole a-be replaced than this divisive imposition. And that's why these men...' he acknowledged the council, 'have allowed it. Not because they approve, or see it as needed, but because they are fair, every one of them, Clerk Carey and Minister Cole in particular. What we do with an imposition and the passing of a minister be a mystery without the Lore a-tell us. So, I be more than happy a-let my council guide us in the way the elders have always done. They be here because we... you... even the Taylors and the Fetchers trusted them. And that's what we got in Saddling. Trust.'

With the congregation's rapt attention unwavering, he lowered his voice. 'We trust the seasons a-come and go, we trust our neighbours when they borrow with no need to ask, and we trust our families a-keep Saddling living. You farmers who grow what we eat, our lookers who guard our flocks, our tailor, our blacksmith, the Paynes who make our tattles, you women who keep us going so the cycle starts agin, we trust each other fur the good a the village. We trust each other because we've always been able a-do that, and I don't see how we could trust that way a life to the hands of a man who cheats on his mates, ruins the chances of marriage for a girl as giving as Jenny, and whoever else he's been with without us knowing. That's all I'm saying. Our minister be passing, the killing be coming to one of us a'night, and we're here, betraying our own selves.'

The hourglass had a few seconds left to run, but Dan let it complete its course in silence as his words sank in.

They echoed in Tom's mind. The passing of a minister. The blind woman. The eastling riddle, the spoketale. The lookers outside the church-house guarding the flock within. The impending certainty of one person's death. Cole dying... The table-stone. Missing pages... Pages... Books and papers... Eliza... Eliza's papers...

His desk.

'Clerk Carey?'

A sharp elbow in his side brought Tom to his senses. 'What? Yes.' He stood to announce, 'Fifteen minutes,' and Mick turned the hourglass for the final time.

The villagers rose to stretch their legs and voice their opinions as arguments developed.

Tom had no time to listen. He knew what he had to do, and he had fifteen minutes to do it in.

'Dan!' he called him to the table while signalling for Barry and Jack. They pushed their way through the crowd while Tom ran through a plan in his head.

'Listen,' he said when the three had gathered. 'My role doesn't allow me to leave the church-house until this matter is concluded. Dan, go to my house. The study, on my desk somewhere there's your aunt's ledgers and notes. In them somewhere there's a page with a title. "On the passing of a minister." Find it and bring it back. Fast.'

'Aye, Tom, but why?'

'No time to explain. You've got less than fourteen minutes. Go.'

Dan shrugged and headed into the crowd.

'What you up to, Carey?' Jack asked. 'What d'you want wi' me.'

'Jack, Barry.' Tom gripped their arms. 'I need you to go to Mr Cole and bring him here.'

'The man be dying, Carey, leave 'im be.'

'If Tom needs me fader,' Barry said, 'then that's what 'e gets. We'll try, Tom.'

'Don't just try, Barry. Bring him and be quick. As soon as that sand's run out, we must allow the vote, and I have a feeling it's still in Aaron's favour.'

'But the Taylor's 'ave our way a thinking now,' Jack began, but Barry cut him off.

'Quit your jawsing, Mackett. Back dreckly-minute, Tom.'

Barry dragged Jack by his wrist until Jack struggled free and the two of them were lost in the throng.

Tom wasn't convinced that what he planned was going to be of any use, but it was the only option he had left. The missing page from the Lore had to be among Eliza's papers, he was sure that was where he had seen it. He could only hope that there was something in the text that he could legitimately use to end the madness.

What he then did about the eastling was another matter.

'What you doing?' Mick Farrow asked as Tom sat.

'Hoping for the best.'

Tom was explaining his actions to Mick when the door swung open and crashed against those crowded near it. Heads turned to Simon Feld, staggering and breathless, his face white and contorted in fear.

'It's out there,' he gasped. 'It's come.'

Twenty-Seven

Dan shuddered at the sight that met his eyes. Three tall figures stood at the bottom of the knoll wrapped in a veil of fog, lit by the eerie yellow of the streetlight with hurricane lamps held high. They turned, their crooks held like swords. The lookers were on guard but anxious. In front of the shop, another was helping Jason Rolfe to his feet.

'He saw it,' Michael Feld called across. 'Stay inside. Oi!'

Barry and Jack piled from the porch.

'Where you going, Mackett?'

'You get closer a the church-house, Mick,' Jack shouted. 'It's them in there what need you.'

Jack took in the scene before running across the green. Barry followed, and they vanished into the mist.

'Jason?'

It was hard to see clearly, but the lad didn't appear to be hurt.

'The boy be shaken is all,' Michael yelled back, his voice numbed by the mist, his body little more than a dark shape in the shifting grey.

'I'm alright, Dan.'

Dan was at Tom's door within seconds, and he turned to check behind before entering. The windows of the church glowed a dull yellow through the humidity. Shapes moved in from the lope-way. More villagers were gathering. Those who had no time for the imposition had changed their minds. Seeing safety in numbers, they advanced cautiously towards the knoll, voices hushed, lamps swinging as the lookers backed to the porch. Michael Feld led Jason closer until they were level with Dan.

'What you doing, Vye?' Feld demanded. 'Get back inside.'

'There dreckly,' Dan said. 'It's Clerk Carey's business.'

'There be no business other than escaping that… thing.' Feld peered into the murk. 'It be closing in.'

'I saw it, Dan,' Jason said, coming to Dan's shoulder. 'Its eyes were sockets, it's mouth…'

'No time.' Dan opened the front door. 'Get with the others.'

'I'm staying wi' you, mate.' Jason followed him into the house. 'What's going on?'

Dan slammed the door to block out Michael Feld's calls for him to return to the church-house and headed for the stairs.

'Got to find papers in the study,' he said.

'Paper?' The younger man was right behind him. 'What paper?'

'Jason, go and be with your family…'

'They don't want me. What papers?'

They were on the landing. 'Eliza's old books and… It doesn't matter.'

'The ones Tom were reading from the other day?'

'Aye.' Dan turned up the gas. Tom had left his study window open, and the grey-hang had risen beyond its level. The room was swathed in damp air. It was like looking through frosted glass, and the gas did little to brighten the scene.

Jason brushed past. 'They were on the desk,' he said and bent to look closer.

When Dan joined him, he was shifting a pile of books, one at a time.

'We're looking for a page from the Lore,' Dan said. 'It'll be old.'

'What's happened at the meet?'

'Nothing yet. Everyone's spoke, now we got only a few minutes before we can't do no more. Careful of your flame.' He moved Jason's arm away from Tom's wall charts.

'Is our village going to change?' Jason asked with hushed concern.

'I hope not, mate.'

The mist deepened, congealed almost, as Dan felt the table top through the gloom, his light fading.

'Where was Tom when you saw him with Eliza's stuff?' he asked.

Jason was a shadow moving gracefully on the far side of the desk. 'Right where I am now,' he said. 'Course, I can't be sure what he were looking at. I was trying a-tell 'im what I knew about Fetcher and your Jenny…'

'She ain't my Jenny.'

'But 'e weren't in the mood fur listening. This it?'

Dan leant across to study a page as best he could. 'No,' he said. 'Keep looking.'

'I be truly sorry 'bout me silence, Daniel.' The words sounded pathetic.

Dan could no longer see his friend. 'Forget it,' he said. 'Just keep… Hold on.'

'You got it?'

'Bring me your light.'

With the two men holding their lanterns side by side, they were able to make out what was written on the yellow paper.

'"On the passing of…" This is it!'

'Good,' Jason said. 'But what's it for?'

'I'm in hopes we're in time to find out.' Dan felt his way to the door banging his shins on a cabinet.

Suddenly there was a hand in his and a second light beside him. 'Come 'ere, you clumsy coot,' Jason said with a smirk.

He led Dan from the room using his more powerful lantern and the invading mist thinned as they approached the stairs.

'Take it careful,' Jason instructed. 'I'll go first case you trip, that way I can break your fall. Keep 'old a me 'and.'

'Is that be the honoured hand of friendship, Jason Rolfe?' Dan asked, his heart warmed by his mate's gesture.

'If you'll allow it back, Mr Vye.'

'I'd be privileged,' Dan said and meant it. 'But I'd be more happy if we got to the table-stone before the hourglass runs dry.'

With more villagers cramming into the church-house, there was hardly room to move. Voices were raised as neighbours argued, bored children played noisily in the narrow strip of flagstones that was all that could be seen of the aisle, and groups gathered in the chancel behind the table-stone. Councilmen tried to keep order and Mick protected the draining hourglass from being knocked over.

Tom mopped his brow with a handkerchief. It was his duty to read back his minutes to anyone who needed clarification on what had been said. Luckily only a few did; his notes were useless, and he relied on his memory.

'We have three minutes,' Mick bellowed after examining the glass. 'I suggest you get a your seats and keep this aisle clear a your tegs.'

Michael Feld and the other lookers arrived, herding the last terrified villagers before them. Talk of who stood for what, the fear of change and the necessity for order were overtaken by talk of the eastling. Fear weaved from the font to the table-stone as news spread that Feld and Jason Rolfe had seen it.

'It appeared behind the Tidy's house,' someone reported third hand. 'Then set off along the lope-way, but a moment later it was at the shop where Jason was trying to keep the lamps alight…'

'Mouth dripping wi' blood where it's been at a teg or two,' someone else falsely claimed. 'Claws like a black-wing crow, and twice as sharp.'

By the time the news washed over the front pews, most people were crammed in, seeking safety with their families and sharing their horror.

There was no sign of Barry or Dan. What if Cole was already dead?

'Two minutes,' Farrow called, and the terrified gossip softened into urgent, heated whispering.

Among the movement and the panic, Aaron Fetcher stood confidently grinning from the back of the church, his face displaying sneering contempt, a youth sure to get his own way.

Tom's heart hardened. He was turning away from Aaron's gloating when a disturbance at the door drew his attention. His heart leapt at the sight of Dan's auburn hair. The door slammed shut.

'Get out me way, you arse!'

If the circumstances hadn't been so dire, Tom would have laughed. The dithering villagers blocking the aisle were shoved to the side as Jason Rolfe burrowed his way through, clearing a path. Dan waved a sheet of paper above his head, and the look of triumph was wiped from Aaron's face in a blink.

Tom met Jason in the aisle, reached beyond him and took the page from Dan. He gripped it tightly. It was from the original Book of Lore, its thick, yellowing paper proved that, and the neat lettering was in the same hand as the pages either side of the one that was missing.

'One minute,' Farrow called. 'Everyone a your seating.'

'What is it, Tom?' Jason looked at him, the twinkle back in his sky blue eyes, his light brows raised to match those on Dan's puzzled face behind him.

Tom held the page, blocking out Jason and read, "On the Passing of a Minister."

Tom had once been severely punished for swearing in church. Once the news reached his great aunt, she had ripped him from the building by the ear, thrown him in the car and slapped at his head repeatedly on the drive home. He had been nine, and the memory came back to him the instant he opened his mouth.

'Fuck!'

He felt the slap of Aunt Maud's hand again. It banished his childhood, but it was not the duplicitous old woman issuing the punishment. It was Dan.

Tom returned to the dais and the table-stone, reading frantically. Only these words mattered now.

Someone was pulling at his sleeve.

Only an edict from the past could help him, but he was almost at the end of the text, and there was still nothing to… The tugging became more urgent.

'What?' He spun angrily and came face to face with Jason.

Jason calmly took the page, turned it around and handed it back. 'Two sides to every story, Tom,' he said, winking, and stepped back.

As soon as Tom read the first line, he knew Jason had found what he was looking for.

'Make way!'

'Shift your arse, Aaron Fetcher.'

The lad was knocked aside by Barry and Jack carrying Matt Cole in a dining chair. His face was deathly white, there were smears of blood on his nightshirt, and where he had once radiated power from his eyes, they now held little more than comprehension that he was still alive.

'What's this?' Aaron shouted as he righted himself.

'Mr Farrow, please hold the sand,' Tom commanded and, confused, Mick did as he was asked.

'None more a your trickery, Carey,' Aaron glowered. 'Turn the glass.'

'Mr Farrow,' Tom insisted. 'If you please.'

Mick's hand hovered over the hourglass, but he rested it by his side when Tom waved the page at him.

Andrew White gave up his councillor's seat for Cole to be placed carefully at the side of the table-stone. With Barry's help, he shifted the chair so he could see the body of the church. The villagers behind him crowded to the sides, and a hush descended in the pews. The candles and lamps flickered, their light playing among the motes and condensation.

Tom waved the paper in the air. 'This,' he said, 'is what Mr Vye spoke of. This is a page that has been missing from the Book of Lore for generations.' He opened the original volume to the torn page. Calling the councilmen to see, he fitted the page against the edge of the cut to show both sides matched.

The council agreed, and Tom handed the page to Cole. The council retook their seats, and the villagers waited in stunned silence.

Tom wasn't sure what he was going to say, but he knew he had to play

The Eastling

the statesman. They had to trust him, and he had to keep one step ahead of Aaron. He coughed, the air was clammier by the second, the oxygen turning to carbon dioxide with every breath of every villager.

'Our history has returned to us,' he said. 'Our history and our Lore.'

It made sense to him now. Why no-one was sure what to do when a minister died suddenly. Why no-one had been taught the lore concerning a people's imposition, and yet some knew. Eliza had known that pages of Saddling history were missing. She found them, threatened Blacklocks with exposure, and was blinded for her insight.

'I will now call on Minister Cole to read the Lore.' He turned to Cole. 'If you are able, Sir.'

'I ain't dead yet, Carey,' Cole grumbled. 'In fact…' He clutched at the table and dragged himself to his feet shrugging off Barry's assistance. He leant against the stone and studied the villagers. 'Sorry 'bout me appearance,' he said. 'But we ain't got time on our side. The eastling's been seen a the marsh and now a the village. If you be worried it be because you got something wrong wi' ye.' His voice rose in anger. 'None in our village should be afeared 'cos none a you should 'ave done nothing against your family, your friends, your neighbours. Bain't that what this book teaches us?' He slammed his fist on the Book of Lore and the dull thud soaked into the atmosphere.

Aaron shuffled his feet and retreated along the aisle, stopping when Tom noticed.

'But you 'ave got cause fur worriting,' Cole continued. 'Near each one a us got cause a-fear the eastling's return 'cos we all be 'ere now fur this meet. I should never a-let this 'appen, and so, aye, I be afeared wi' ye. But I be sleeping soon anyhow, unlike you, William Taylor, and you, Aaron Fetcher.' Spittle shot from his mouth as his accusing finger flew from side to side. 'You, Cousin Cole, and you, Jason Rolfe, Miss Tidy, Master Seeming, Mistus Vye, Mister Feld, all a ye… None a ye stood up and said, "This ain't right." None a you thought to ask what was the good a this, you only though a yourself and what be close a you. That ain't 'ow we live in Saddling and that ain't 'ow you'll be living after I'm gone.'

He sagged, and Barry gripped his arm as he regained his breath. Looking away, he surreptitiously wiped blood from the corner of his mouth, catching Tom's eye. He held the stare as he composed himself. The villagers waited in silence and the air thickened.

'But there be one wi' us,' he said. 'One what's worthy a leading this village.

Only one.' He blinked at Tom and held up the page of Lore, addressing the crowd. '"On the passing of a minister"', he read. 'It be things we already know.' He turned the page. 'But... "On the passing of a minister who knows he soon sleeps", well, that be a different matter and one more suited for now, I reckon.' He took a breath. '"If a serving minister knows the time of his passing into sleep be soon on him, he must appoint his successor immediately with no cause for vote, consultation or disagreement. This is the Lore." And it be signed by the councilmen then and the minister who came up wi' it...' He peered closely. 'Minister Richard Carey, in fourteen-seventy-six. So...' He handed the page back to Tom. 'That be that and there ain't no disagreement, right?'

'Wrong!' Aaron approached, his face tight and reddening. 'We're in the middle of a people's imposition here, and you're right, you ain't dead yet.'

'Sit, lad,' Bill Taylor tried to grab Aaron, but he stormed past.

'We got seconds left a-run, Cole. You can't interrupt the vote.'

'As a matter of lore, he can.' Satisfaction was written across Tom's face, and his features glowed as colourfully as the east window in a summer dawn. 'I'll get straight to the section beneath that which Minister Cole just read.' He raised himself to his full height and swallowed the desire to gloat. '"On the bringing of a people's imposition."' He spoke with such authority that the thickening vapour in the church was unable to muffle his words. '"An imposition shall be nullified should the caller of the imposition be found to be of feeble mind, of an age younger than eighteen years, to be terminally ill..."'

'Well, I ain't none of them things.' Aaron's laugh was threatening, and it morphed into, 'What you getting at, Carey?'

Tom smiled graciously and turned the Lore to Aaron. '"Or anyone who has caused the village to suffer and brought himself punished for his acts." Acts such as interfering with an aepelling, or cuckolding, for example.'

It took Aaron a couple of seconds to realise what that meant, but when he did, his face blanched and screwed into a tightly packed mass of hate. Jack was with him in an instant. Clasping Aaron's arms, he backed him away from the dais and took him to the side.

'Which means,' Cole explained for anyone who hadn't followed, 'that this imposition is over, and you know who you can thank fur that. Playing 'round wi' another man's intended. Should a been bannocked, Carey. Cesspits be too good fur 'im.'

Many in the audience agreed, and Tom found it hard to keep his smile at bay.

'But that still leaves us wi' what I intend a-do,' Cole said. He gripped the table for balance as he came to stand in the centre. He shooed away his fussing wife. 'I got a little life yet, Mistus,' he said before taking several deep breaths, grimacing and propping himself against the stone. 'We now know,' he began, 'I be able a-say who follows me in this job, and I be aware what a job this be. It ain't a thing you take on light nor give away easy. It ain't just 'bout balancing books and ordering fetching, leading the councilmen a-decisions 'bout who gets the thresher and when. It be a place that come wi' more responsibility than any man can manage and any man wants. I be giving this responsibility a someone I trust. Someone we all trust. I know who's coming after me. A man who 'as no choice but a-take the job fur Saddling.'

Whispers, nudges and fascination rustled among the audience. Barry slipped into the chancel, dreading his father might call out his name.

Tom's pulse quickened. Cole wouldn't pass the role to him, surely? He didn't trust Tom, he barely liked him, he knew that he and Barry…

Then again, it could be revenge. If Tom was appointed minister he could expect years of backlash from Fetcher, Taylor and the others who saw him as a threat. His life would be hell, and more than that, he would no longer be able to live with Barry. The minister and a farmer sharing a house?

Cole asked for Tom's minute book and, bending to it and guarding his hand, he wrote a name, signing the book before slamming it shut.

'I've appointed 'im,' he said. 'In there, it be written, and that man be the only one I know as is capable a this job. What's more, I'm in 'opes more a 'is family come after. But you can look to that later. I ain't got a lot a time left wi' ye, and there be something else I got a-say.' His voice cracked, and he coughed into his hand.

Tom saw the blood in his palm. He surreptitiously passed his handkerchief. The dying man's fingers found his, gripped tightly and he turned his head so Tom couldn't read his expression.

'Are you alright, Sir?' he whispered.

Cole gave one determined nod and turned back to the villagers.

'Where's me boy?' he asked, and Barry edged nervously forwards. 'No need a-worry, nipper,' he said taking Barry's hand. 'You got enough a-do with the farm. Carey? Come 'ere.'

Nervousness returned to Tom's throat, and his stomach turned as he came to stand on Cole's other side. When the dying man took his hand, his fears switched from being appointed minister to being outed.

'These men be mates,' Cole said, speaking as clearly as his failing breath allowed. 'And that be what Saddling be 'bout. Friendness. Just as we find wi' Tom Carey and those who've welcomed 'im a Saddling since 'e chose a-stay.' He gripped Tom's hand tighter. 'I ain't always been fair a Clerk Carey,' he said looking straight ahead. 'And fur that I be sorry.' He drew in a deep breath and let it go, fighting back pain Tom could only imagine.

'But I been thinking while I been laying on me dying bed,' he continued. 'Thinking 'bout the value of friendships such as this. And I came a-realise a thing.'

Cole's legs weakened, and he sagged. Tom and Barry cradled the minister to keep him from falling.

'I be saying me a'night a ye, Mistus Cole,' he said to Irene in the front row. She gravely tipped her head in a gesture of acceptance.

Tom shook. Tears fought for release, but the serene look on Barry's face held him together.

'And I be saying me a'night a ye, Son.' He kissed Barry on the forehead before addressing Tom.

Tom had no words, but none were needed.

Cole smiled. 'And I be saying…' He sniffed a trickle of blood from his nose. 'Be saying me a'night a ye…' He planted his lips on Tom's forehead and nodded once. 'Son.' The old man's eyes glinted in the lamplight, and his smile remained firm. 'Look after me boy, Tom,' he whispered, his last words barely audible. 'Please… Love the runagate as much as 'e needs.' His eyes closed, and his body slumped onto the table-stone.

'Fader!'

Barry clung to his father's body as Irene and other relatives pushed forward.

Tom couldn't move. His legs were quivering. In fact, his whole body was shaking unnaturally. People stood, confused, clutching the pews as the wall lanterns danced, played by unseen hands. A vibration grew in the cloudy air, tingling Tom's skin and restricting his breathing. Dust was shaken from the rafters, falling through a deep rumble that grew in volume. Children cried.

The pressure increased. The table-stone shook beneath Tom's hand, and he stepped away, tripping on the step. The ground trembled and the roof beams creaked.

The table cloth rippled. Cole's lifeless body shook, the head jerking, the hands twitching as if in the throes of a fit.

With an ear-splitting crack, the stone broke in two. The pieces collapsed in on each other, sucking Cole's body into the valley. Mick rescued the hourglass just in time, but the council's books and papers slid in, dragging the cloth and piling on the dead man until Cole was covered.

None shall know the way to go 'till one man's peace be made.

Tom stared at the mess. 'But what way?'

The vibration ended and the heavy air resonated with children's whimpers. They accompanied the settling dust until comforted away by their parents, rooted in shocked silence. One by one they raised a finger to their forehead in a gesture of farewell to their minister.

And tendrils of vengeful mist seeped through cracks and keyhole. They tumbled and slipped to the floor where they gathered and grew into one seething, unforgiving mass.

Twenty-Eight

A child at the back of the church-house was the first to scream. The eastling swirled up from the foggy floor, twisting into a half-human, half-spectral being dragging the blade of its knife against the flagstones as it grew. Stormwater dripped from the figure, and blood pumped endlessly from the gaping slash across its throat. The face was a contorted mass of shifting grey. Its mouth gaped as if its jaw was unattached, caught in an eternal wail of frustration.

More villagers screamed when they realised what was among them. Two men struggled to open the door, but it refused to give. Others tried but it was useless and, while they hammered and kicked, people backed to the walls in panic, crushing each other in the madness.

'Stay where you are!' Jack Mackett bellowed until the noise subsided. 'It's only after one a us. No point killing each other. If it's you, it's you.'

There was too much to compute, but Tom had to act. With Cole dead, there was no-one to lead and, when he turned to Mick Farrow, he found him cowering with the councilmen behind the broken table-stone.

The eastling stood at the far end of the aisle, its head turning deliberately from side to side, searching.

'It knows who it's looking for.' Dan whispered, his cool eyes fixed firmly on the apparition. 'What do we do?'

'Everyone in here is safe bar one,' Tom said. 'And I reckon that's me.'

'Could be any one a us.' Barry was at Tom's other side. 'At least it's not going a-be me fader.'

'Barry, I'm so sorry...'

'Now ain't the time,' Barry cut him off. 'You been looking for a way a-kill this thing. Now be the time a-tell us how.'

The eastling took a step forward, and a growl emanated from its slit throat. Fathers held their children closer, and those at the end of the pews shuffled back, some turning away, some stifling screams.

'Go he will when sons shall kill,' Tom said.

'Sons? What does that mean?'

'No idea, Barry, but you've got to forgive me for this...'

Tom fell to his knees and, turning his back on the approaching spectre, knelt to clear the clutter from Cole's body. He called for the Feld brothers, and together they wrapped Cole in the tablecloth and dragged him from the debris, sweeping books and papers to the floor.

The eastling paused, its head snapped to the south wall where it scanned the blanched, fearful faces. The growl grew louder, and blood bubbled at the gash, spitting into the air where it vanished.

'Why ain't you lot doing something?' Aaron Fetcher shouted across the church.

'I ain't the minister,' Mick babbled back. 'I ain't the one a-say what we do.' He appealed to Tom. 'Carey! What name?'

Tom clambered into the valley of the broken stone, one foot on each slope facing the aisle. The creature glared at him, its eyes crying glittering tears of blood. It took another pace closer, lifting its knife.

'What name did Cole write?' Bill Taylor yelled from among the crush. 'Who be our minister?'

'What we looking for?' Barry was behind him, his worried eyes darting from the creature to Tom.

'The knife.' There was no sign of one. 'Rock-bound blade.'

A scream of horror turned Tom's head. The shifting menace towered over Jenny Rolfe, its mouth moving, its groaning crescendoing at its throat. The knife glinted.

'Get away from her!' Dan jumped from the dais and hurled himself at the being. He crashed to the floor on the other side. The thing swung its head growling before swirling to the opposite pews, sending villagers fleeing over the backs and each other.

'Rock bound blade,' Tom repeated as he ran his fingers through the valley, scrambled to the other side, searched. There was no knife. He had been wrong.

'I got the book.' Mick Farrow pushed his way to the pulpit, his progress followed by the ghostly eyes of the half-alive creature. 'I got the minister's last decree.' He held the ledger aloft, and the eastling roared.

The sound shook the walls, panicked the lamplight, and silenced the villagers. It took another step towards Tom. Two more and it would be at the table.

Tom knew he had no more time. 'Each hundred years... At harvest tide... Stalking...' The first letter of each line of the song spelt out the word 'Eastling' in an acrostic, but did that mean anything? *In chances one...* Who? Him? The next minister? *When sons shall kill.* Sons, plural. Whose sons? Coles last words had been to his son, Barry and then he'd called Tom the same thing. Did he mean to imply he finally accepted Tom and considered him a…

Another roar of anger increased the sense of despair in his chest. There was no way out. The knife pointed at Jason Rolfe, and Tom's world fell into a kaleidoscope of images and sounds.

Jason cowering, his father lashing out to protect him. The creature screaming. Through the noise, Mick Farrow's voice, incomprehensible words. Dan was back on his feet and pulling women away from the swing of the knife. The word 'sons' in Tom's ear. Barry beside him. A massive bellow of fury as the eastling took its final step. He was about to die. Barry's hand in his. Farrow shouting for Dan. Susan Vye screaming at the Felds to do something. A tug on his arm.

He was standing on one side of the broken stone looking directly in the warped face inches away. The cloud of its eyes closed and opened, its shrieking stopped. The silence that followed was as sharp as the blade that hung between them.

A voice in Tom's mind, 'It ain't you, Di Kari.'

The apparition turned to Aaron Fetcher, and Tom knew who was to die.

'Tom!' Barry yanked on his hand. 'Look!'

Cracks were appearing in the stone like crazy paving.

'Get away from 'im!' Jack pulled Aaron to safety and shielded him. He stood between his marker and the blade, his fists raised, his face set and determined. His hair was blown back by a gush of bloody breath as he was blasted by ghostly scorn.

'Daniel Vye be appointed our new minister!' Mick Farrow yelled.

The two halves of the table-stone shattered. Tom and Barry landed in the rubble, the sharp edges slicing Tom's leg.

'Look a your feet, Tom!'

It was there among the broken stone; a wooden handled slitting knife, curved and gleaming as though new.

The yelling, the confusion, the fear, Jason holding back Aaron's father, Jack shouting, Barry pushing the rough wooden handle into Tom's hand.

In chances one there be a son to end his way of death.

'Aim fur the bastard's 'eart.'

'I'll kill Jack.'

The ghostly arm was ready. The blade caught the lantern-flicker. He saw white faces, Aaron sobbing, Jenny screaming, the beast preparing to kill.

'You know what you got a-do, Tom,' Barry shouted and leapt from the dais.

Why was he climbing into the front pew? Why wasn't Jack moving aside? Why didn't the screaming stop?

It would stop when Tom acted.

He scrambled from the rubble gripping the saddling knife. It was going to rip through the mist and into Jack, but the eastling would die first.

Jack saw him coming, swallowed and closed his eyes.

The knife held before him, Tom screamed and ran at the writhing shape. It turned and slashed.

Tom lurched into the mist, and Saddling ceased to exist.

The last thing he heard was Barry's voice. 'Enough to let you run…'

The putrid smell of death. Frozen air in his lungs.

He was falling through rain, buffeted by wind, his face soaked by cloud and his arms flaying. The scene exploded with a blinding flash of light. Thunder vibrated through him, and the cloud cleared. He fell with the rain, as one drop of it, the fuming sea churning beneath him, coming closer, the wind an agonising whistle in his ears. The marsh below, the black night illuminated by the constant strobe of lightning. The seawall collapsed, houses were washed away by a tidal wave that spat white fume and felled trees. Ever closer, falling faster.

A small boat, a man rowing frantically as a youth baled water. A coffin knocked the boat, but the man didn't stop. He pulled towards the church, dim light emanating from within. Around it, the water bubbled, bringing up the dead, carrying away sheep. Broken furniture spun and drowned in the swelling sea. The church roof coming at him him, fast, unstoppable and vanishing.

He was inside, looking from the rafters, the storm raging outside. The man burst in, helping the youth to stagger to the shepherd with the black locks who spouted panicked hatred from the altar. They fought. The youth tried to separate them, windows blew in, water invaded the church. They fought on the altar stone as their people cried and wailed. The knife against the shepherd's neck, Di Kary pressing it closer, the boy pulling it back. A kick. The cleric staggering. The grip was lost. The knife swung in a great arc and sliced the boy's throat. He fell to his knees, his life draining from him, dulling his innocent, green eyes and, in his last moment, he looked at Tom.

They were both consumed by the sadness of knowing there were to be no more opportunities, no more chances to live. The boy would never know love.

'But too much to see you fall.' Barry's voice.

A heavy thump on Tom's chest winded him, lamplight flashed past, white faces in a blood red fog, fragments. A crushing blow to the side of his head sent him reeling into darkness.

Twenty-Nine

Birdsong on a cooling breeze woke Tom from the black void of sleep. The next thing he became aware of was Barry's arm around his chest as he spooned in from behind accompanied by familiar, gentle snoring. It was comforting, and for a moment the day was any other day, and there was nothing in his life that demanded concern. He was in his bed, safe and comfortable, with the sounds of the marsh filtering through the open window.

Then the headache kicked in. Pain shot from his temple to his jaw, the side of his face ached with the epicentre just above his eye causing him to squint against it as he gasped. He remembered the scene in the churchhouse, the fall through fog and time. Had he dreamt that? Had he seen the village in flood seven hundred years ago?

Another thought invaded, pushing that one aside; had he killed Jack?

Carefully so as not to wake his lover, he turned to face him and kissed him on the forehead before rolling onto his back. A throbbing in his ankle matched the thumping in his head and, rubbing it with his foot he felt bandages. What had happened? He dropped an arm across his eyes and sighed. Beside him, Barry mumbled in his sleep and shifted closer.

'He's 'ardly left your side all night.'

The voice cut through Tom's pain and panicked him. He sat up, extracting himself from Barry's embrace and pulling the cover to his chest.

'Mistus Cole?'

Irene sat in the armchair facing the bed, knitting. She looked up from her work with no discernible expression other than that of someone counting stitches, and then returned to studying her fingers.

'Expect you've got a headache,' she said. 'You hit the floor with quite a weight on you.'

Tom shifted away from his sleeping partner, his face flushing. The sight of Irene Cole added to his confusion.

'I don't normally sleep here,' he stammered. 'I don't know how this happened...'

'Oh, chiese a-worrying,' Irene said, a faint smile appearing on her lips. 'I know that other room ain't yourn.' She glanced up. 'And that's where we'll leave it.'

Tom's embarrassment deepened when he realised he was naked beneath the sheets. He didn't know what to say. Luckily, another voice changed the subject.

'How are you feeling?' Dan lounged in the doorway.

'Like someone punched me in the face. What's the time?'

'Well past nine,' Dan replied coming into the room and sitting on the edge of the bed. 'You can go now if you want, Mistus Cole.'

'Aye, I'll do that.' She gathered her knitting and shoved it into a bag at her feet. 'Got a few things a-do a'day, so I'll leave you boys a-talk about what needs a-be talked.' She stood and straightened her pinafore dress. 'I don't expect you to be at Matthew's lowering,' she said, fixing Tom with a sympathetic gaze. 'What with your banged head an' all, but I'd appreciate it if you made sure your Barry was up and ready a-lend a hand with it.'

'Lowering?'

The memory of Matt Cole's death flooded Tom's mind. His words, his acceptance, his making peace on the table-stone that cracked and parted…

'Aye. Be this afternoon. Minister Vye will tell you the details.' Irene crossed the room.

'It's just Dan.'

'Not no more, Daniel.' She smiled warmly at him as she passed. 'At least Matthew made one good decision before he went.' She paused in the doorway, turned to the bed and barked, 'Barry!'

Barry woke with a start. 'Doing it, Ma.' He was halfway out of bed on autopilot before he realised where he was and who was with him. 'Oh, aye,' he said as Irene left. 'Very funny.'

'Was she here the whole night?' Tom touched the side of his head and found it swollen.

'Most of,' Dan answered. He crawled onto the bed and sat cross-legged at the foot facing the couple.

'What happened?' Tom couldn't fit the pieces together. 'I remember trying to stab that thing. Where's the knife? Where's Jack? Did I…?'

'Pull in your reins, boy,' Barry laughed, manoeuvring himself to lean into Tom and snuggle under his arm 'Everything be fine. Kind of.'

'Kind of?'

'You ell 'im, Dan.' Barry yawned. 'I need a couple more minutes.'

'It was madness,' Dan began. 'And it happened so fast it's hard to get it in the right order. I didn't have time to think of Mr Cole or what he'd decreed.

I could only think of saving people from the sweep of that knife.'

'Farrow were screaming fur you, Dan,' Barry said from behind closed eyes.

'Farrow was as brave as a buck running for its conygarthe,' Dan scoffed. 'But don't tell him I said so.'

'Right old ceremony it were.' Barry burrowed closer.

'Yes, but, Jack?' Tom was piecing the scene together. 'I was running at the... whatever it was, with Jack only a foot away on the other side.' He tapped Barry's arm. 'You were climbing over the pews, Aaron Fetcher was crying, everyone was screaming, the mist... The table disintegrated... The knife...'

'Slowly, Tom.' Dan stretched his legs and leant against the footboard. 'Aye, the table fell apart after Cole made his peace with you and his runagate.' He kicked Barry gently. 'Then this one saw what the stone revealed and, unlike him though it was, he used his brain, and fast too.'

'Very kind a ye,' Barry mumbled.

'He gave you the knife. We both saw what you were going to do. I tried to pull Jack out of the way, not because I wanted Aaron to get the blade in his chest, but in case what Barry was going to do didn't work. You lunged at the thing, and the knife cut straight through its heart, right through the body and out the other side.'

'Into...?'

'Into nothing but air,' Dan said. 'That lump beside you...'

'Oi.' Barry kicked out but couldn't find Dan's legs.

'As you dived, he threw himself off the front pew just and brought the two of you crashing into the wall before the knife could do any damage to anyone. You hit the floor hard. It's a wonder nothing's broken. You were unconscious for hours.'

'Did you see it?' Tom tapped Barry again.

'Didn't have eyes for nothing but that knife,' Barry yawned. 'Knew I had to stop you stabbing old Jack. Wasn't bothered about Fetcher. Wouldn't a minded if you'd sliced 'im up, of course, but it's no doubt best you didn't.'

'Right, yeah,' Tom agreed. 'But I mean, did you see anything when you passed through the eastling?'

'Just... grey-ang and you. Why?'

'I saw... At least, I thought I saw...'

'What?' Dan leant forward.

'I was falling through a storm, the storm of twelve-ninety-two. Then I was in the church, over it, looking in from above. I saw the boy killed, the first saddling.'

'The bang on your head,' Dan said.

It was more than that. The wind was cold on his face, the rain stabbed at his flesh and the turbulent water roared in his ears. The smell of death still hung in his nostrils. He saw the boy's throat, gashed and pumping. It was a sharp memory, not a fading dream.

'Your connection,' Barry offered.

'Connection?'

'Aye, the way we connect with the dead. You travelled clean through that noisy bastard. So you connected wi' it as you killed its misery. It wanted you a-see what it suffered. Leastwise, that's 'ow it sounds a me.'

Barry was right, and Tom could see the sense in his words, however inexplicable the experience had been. He instantly recalled the sadness in the eastling's eyes, the realisation that he was dying, the fear, and the anger that his life had been ended so early. His body chilled, and he was grateful for Barry's heat beside him.

'Did it work?'

'It was very quick,' Dan said. 'You two flew through the eastling, you from the back, Barry from the side. You collided, the knife ripped the heart, the thing let out a scream which, to me, sounded like joy but I can't swear to that, and then...' He took a moment to remember and find the right words. 'Then the grey-hang that had been floating around us hit the ground. Same as when you drop a beer glass on the flagstones and it shatters. I know it was only air, but as soon as you stabbed the thing, the fog just hit the floor like it was made of stone. Bang.' He splayed his fingers. 'Gone. It just...' He struggled for the word.

'Exploded,' Barry suggested.

'Aye. It exploded into thousands of pieces which swirled a minute...' Dan's slender fingers made patterns in the air. 'Sparkling ice crystals... Dancing and falling... The church-house was freezing... The thing was there and then...' He snapped his fingers. 'Nothing. Can't describe it any better.'

'But it's gone?'

'As far as anyone can tell,' Dan replied. 'Everything was suddenly normal. Well, folk were shocked and screaming a bit, but Mick told them to shut up, and the Feld boys had to stop Billy Farrow shouting some pretty rough miswords at Aaron and calm him down.'

"E were blaming Fetcher fur bringing the eastling on us,' Barry explained, mumbling.

'Me and Mister Farrow got order in the end,' Dan continued. 'And everything looked the same as ever. Apart from the table-stone. We're not sure what to do with that. Can't be fixed. But, there's no more talk of the imposition, there can't be. It never happened. Well, it did, of course, and there are plenty this morning who are embarrassed for what they did to the village.'

'And the saddling knife?'

'Locked in a cabinet in the crypt along with the Book of Lore and the missing page.'

'There are more pages in my study,' Tom waved his hand towards the door.

'Aye, and we'll get to work on that in a day or so, Mr Clerk.' Dan winked, but there was doubt behind his expression as if he was nervous of his new responsibility.

'And is Jack okay? And Aaron?' Tom queried. 'You're sure I didn't stab anyone?'

'They are, and I am,' Dan reassured him. 'Folk are shocked and confused, but you know how things are around here. We take Saddling with all its unknowns. Anyway, Jack and the Feld boys brought you here straight after. I patched you up best I could, and Barry put you to bed.'

'That's where it gets tricky,' Barry said. "Cos me ma came in just as I were doing it and she caught me giving you a goodnight kiss. 'Course, I said it were nothing but…'

'Ha!' Dan slapped his leg. 'She caught you weeping over him, telling him you loved him, didn't ever want to lose him.'

'Aye, alright, Vye, no need to be over-dramatic. Oh, bugger this.' Barry moved away from Tom, opened his eyes and gave up trying to get back to sleep. 'Aye, I did that that, course I did, and she did catch me, but you know what? I didn't give a dang. Turns out, neither did she. She insisted on staying wi' ye a-look after us, not a-make sure nothing were going on.'

'It was a bit late for that,' Dan chuckled.

'Aye, and this one stayed wi' us an 'all.'

'Doing my duty,' Dan said. 'Cleaned up the scrapes on your leg. It'll be fine in a day, and your face has stopped swelling. I put one of Eliza's remedies on it.'

'Thanks.'

'Aye. So, that's where we be, and now you're awake, it's time your runagate got up and attended to his fader's burying.'

Of all the emotions Tom was suffering, grief suddenly demanded the most attention. 'Barry, I don't know what to say.'

'You don't say nothing.' Barry stretched, and his back cracked. 'It be done. He be gone and me all-workers are digging a bed for me fader right now.' He looked at Dan for confirmation, and Dan nodded. 'So there be nothing fur me a-do right now except eat.'

'This is so...' Tom fought to find the word. The ache in his head blocked his thoughts and questions were piling up behind. 'Strange.' It wasn't the best word, and the others didn't know what he meant. 'Okay,' he tried to clarify. 'I get the way of death and burial, and I'll get used to it, but when either of you go, if I'm still here, you can't expect me to be so calm, so accepting.'

'You will be', Barry said. 'Fur one thing, that's a load a years away from now and fur another, it be 'ow it be and you being the clerk a this village, you be expected a-live the Saddling way.'

'You're hardly doing that,' Dan mused, nodding at them with mock outrage. 'And I'm not sure it's appropriate for the village minister to be sitting on the end of your bed.'

'You being serious?' Barry eyed him suspiciously.

'I suppose I got a-be serious,' Dan replied. 'Now I'm...' His head dropped, and he clasped his cheeks in his hands before looking at Tom. 'Do I have a way out of this?'

Of the stack of things on Tom's mind, the Teaching and the Lore were the furthest from the forefront. 'I doubt it,' he said. 'But I don't know. From what I remember, what the dying minister orders, stands, and with "no cause for a vote, consultation or disagreement."'

Dan sighed. 'Right, well, that's something we'll attend to later. For now, I'm going to make you tea. You stay in bed and rest. Barry, you can help me.'

'What? You can't make a mug a tea on your own? Good village minister you be.'

'Barry Cole...' Dan adopted a schoolmasterly tone. 'You will not speak to your council leader in that way.'

'Ah, go boil your 'ead, Rednuts.'

The young minister sucked air between his teeth and his eyes widened.

He glared furiously at Barry, and Tom was saddened. Dan's choosing had already forced a rift between them.

It was an act. Dan's lips twitched, his stony eyes twinkled, and the pair fell about laughing.

'Not so loud!' Tom complained.

Dan slid from the bed. 'Come on, Barry,' he said. 'Let your man get his rest.'

'Why? I be the one as been up most a the night. This one's been sleeping the sleep a the dead near on twelve hours.'

'I'm fine, Doctor.' Tom wasn't, but equally, he didn't want to spend the day in bed. 'I'll come down.' He swung his legs to the side.

Dan frowned but agreed and waited while Tom pulled on a pair of trousers. He stood, wavering, but Barry was behind him, and, holding his arm, led him to the door.

'Do you want to put your clothes on, Runagate?' Dan tutted.

'No, Mister Minister, I don't.' Barry said. 'The grey-hang might a gone from the marsh this morning but the days ain't cold yet.'

'All the same,' Dan said, turning away and shaking his head, 'I reckon you'll have family visitors soon, and naked ain't the right way to greet them.'

Barry mumbled an obscenity and dressed while Dan helped Tom limp downstairs.

The kitchen was spotless, so tidy that at first, Tom wondered if he was in the right house.

Dan saw his surprise. 'Barry couldn't sleep through worry,' he explained, lowering Tom into a chair. 'Spent half the night cleaning.'

'Blimey. And what's that?'

A single mug took pride of place as the centrepiece on the table. It was cracked like a badly made jigsaw, and the random lines reminded Tom of the table-stone just before it imploded.

'That's my oath pottery,' Dan said as he attended to the kettle and checked the stove. 'Your man spent hours searching outside for the pieces and glueing them together. He reckons that if it's completed, my oath won't have to stand. Not that I'm bothered.'

'You mean that, don't you?'

'I do, Tom.' Dan put the kettle on the stove and leant against the counter. 'You remember I made that comment yesterday? Asked what more you wanted me to do? You said I should have been a writer.'

Tom was examining the mug. 'You made me think means, motive, opportunity,' he said. 'Made me think straight, helped me see through the puzzles.' He cautiously returned the mug to the table, and the handle fell off. 'You're better at putting the pieces together than Barry.'

'Aye, well, that's as may be, but you know…? I can't be an inns-man, a doctor, a minister and a husband at the same time.'

Something was wrong. Tom studied Dan's face as his friend looked back at him, the concentric circles of his eyes misting over, his lips quivering.

'What's up?'

'Nothing.' Dan fiddled with cutlery on the worktop.

Tom realised. 'Today was meant to be your wedding day.' He pulled himself to his feet and, clutching the table for support, hobbled to Dan whose shoulders were now shaking.

Dan spun to him, his face screwed up as he tried to keep tears at bay. 'It ain't that,' he said. 'I made my decision on that, and I made my peace with it.'

'What is it then?' Tom held him, and Dan looked away, embarrassed that he was unable to contain his crying. 'Hey, come on,' Tom encouraged gently.

Dan sniffed and looked him directly in the eye. 'I don't know if I can do it,' he said. 'I'm twenty-five, Tom, and suddenly the village expects everything of me. The healing, the ministering… It ain't possible.'

Tom hugged him. 'One day at a time,' he whispered.

'Aye. One day at a time.'

Tom was still calming him and stroking the back of his head, when Barry entered, dressed and muttering.

'Can't leave you two alone for five minutes. What's up wi'' him now?'

'Nothing,' Dan pulled away. 'I'm tired. Sorry, this isn't a way for a minister to behave.'

'Ah, get over yourself.' It was a playful remark, thrown away in Barry's usual fashion and it made Dan smile.

He wiped his face, took a deep breath.

'Thanks, Tom.' He turned to Barry who was investigating the bread bin. 'And you, Runagate.'

'You're welcome, Rednuts.'

'Oi!'

Barry laughed. 'You might be me minster out there,' he said. 'When I be in the church-house fur meets or whatever I'll be sure and treat you as one, but in me own 'ouse, you're just Daniel Rednuts Vye, me oldest mate, so get over it and eat something.'

They sat at the table, sipping tea and sharing one of Andrew White's more acceptable loaves.

'Did you know,' Dan said, 'you've got ants in your butter?'

Thirty

Matthew Cole's burying took place in the afternoon. Dan led the simple ceremony, reading from the appropriate book as those villagers who could attend stood among the other sleepers in the graveyard. Most of the village was there watching Dan to see how he coped.

Tom stood at a respectful distance with his head bowed, leaning on a cane lent to him by Jack standing on his other side. Barry, his mother and uncles, were closest to the gaping pit. Behind them, the other councilmen stood with their wool caps in their hands, sharing whispered memories and approving of Dan's well-spoken words.

Four women stood apart from everyone else. Barry's cousin, Lucy, dressed in a flowing white gown waited in the near field to the north, facing the church and holding a cloth bag. To the west by the bridge, Becki Tidy carried a flaming torch while against the church to the south, Susan Vye looked on, the water-filled aepelling jug in her hand. The eastern watch was taken by Sarah White, the baker's wife who cradled a bag of flour. She shielded her eyes from the glare of the sun, white and dazzling in an unblemished sky.

Crows pecked at the grass and whitebacks grazed distantly, while the mother trees on the edge of the Maden copse sighed in the breeze. The air was scented by marsh grass with a faint and dying whiff of the spreading silage behind it and a marsh harrier hovered high above the church-house, riding the thermals in sweeping circles.

Dan turned a page and adjusted the heavy book resting on his arm. He spoke with clarity and a confidence that Tom wasn't sure he owned, but he didn't choke or falter as the Feld brothers and two other lookers lowered the roughly made coffin into the ground. There were no tears, only whispered words of respect and farewell as, one by one, the villagers filed past the grave to pay their respects.

Jack held Tom's elbow as they took their place in the line.

'Just wanted a-say me thanks,' he said. 'Fur not running me through wi' that blade a yourn.'

'Why were you trying to protect Aaron?' Tom asked.

The question had been on his mind since breakfast. There were many others, but plenty of time to ask them.

"Cos fur all 'is faults, 'e be a Saddlinger same as you and me."

Aaron was slouching against the church-house wall, arms folded and chewing the inside of his cheek. He noticed Tom watching and turned to face the other way. During the day, villagers had called at the house bringing gifts of thanks for Tom and their condolences for Barry. Aaron was the one the eastling had chosen, the one Tom had saved, but the only person so far not to have shown gratitude. Not that Tom wanted any. He'd acted on impulse and simply did what had to be done.

'Still think you need to keep an eye on the coot,' Jack said, lowering his voice further. 'I followed 'im last night. After we carted you a your bed, Simon and me were taking a pipe at the side a your 'ome when Fetcher sneaked out a the church-house. They was clearing up the mess, you see. Mick Farrow arranged it. Bout all 'e be good fur, ask me.'

'What do you mean, sneaked?' Tom's first thought was for the Book of Lore and its missing page. His second was for the saddling knife. 'Was he carrying anything?'

'Only 'is 'ead in shame,' Jack answered. 'No. I don't know what 'e were doing, but 'e came right past us wi'out noticing. Reckon 'e were thinking on something, and I'm in 'opes it were what 'e'd done a the village, but I doubt it were. Simon takes me elbow and says 'ow the lad were seen talking wi' an out-marsher over by the eastern sewer, that night you sent 'im guarding. Simon's got a good feel fur the marsh, fur the whitebacks of course, and fur the ways a people. And when 'e says a-watch someone close, there always be a reason.'

'What did Aaron do?'

'Just went walking,' Jack said, approaching the grave. 'I kept behind 'im across the bridge, over a'wards the east where 'e followed the deek right the way a the south. Ended up by the lope-way bridge just standing there staring a the far trees. I reckon 'e was waiting. Got fed up in the end and 'e went 'ome.'

They had reached the open grave, and Tom looked in. The coffin was variously covered with clods of earth, wool pulled from fences, flowers and straw dropped by those in attendance.

'Sleep on, Matthew,' Jack said. 'Give me regards a me Fader.' He took a bag from his pocket and held it over the drop. 'They dug 'im in low so Irene can go atop when she's ready,' he explained. 'But I don't know how they're going a-get on wi' this.' He let go of the bag, and it landed on the coffin scattering seeds.

'What's that?' Tom crouched gingerly to scoop up earth.

'Rowan fur planting,' Jack said.

Tom released his earth and spoke to Cole in his mind. He thanked him for Barry. To Jack, he said, 'What are they for?'

'Matthew Cole and me fader were good mates,' Jack said as they moved on. 'Me fader were called Rowan, as you know, so I thought a tree wi' that name growing there might be…' He coughed, embarrassed. 'Well, you know.'

'It's a touching thought.'

When those who wanted to had passed the grave, Dan again took up his book and recited a poem. At the same time, Jason Rolfe played his guitar, and his cousin, Sally, sang. Spoken words, music and melody weaved together through the air and among the dead and, by the time it had finished, the four compass markers had joined the group. Their gifts in hand, they processed to guard the corners of the grave.

The rest of the villagers came closer to form a human wall protecting Cole from the outside world.

Becki Tidy was the first to speak. 'From the west,' she said, her voice unwavering. 'The fire of the Witchling to burn your bads to ashes.' She let the torch fall, sparking and smoking as it landed on the coffin.

Susan Vye held the jug at arm's length. 'From the south, the Saddling water to purify your spirit.' She poured it, extinguishing the flaming torch.

'From the eastern crops…' Sarah White opened her bag. 'Blowing on the Eastling air, the dust of our lives.' The flour clouded as the breeze played with it before it cascaded into the grave.

'And from the northern fields…' Lucy Cole came last, tipping her bag of earth. 'The soil of the Needling to nourish your memory and bring life anew.'

The four women stepped away, the ceremony over.

'And from us all…'

Heads turned. Dan stood at the foot of the grave holding the saddling knife. He glanced at Tom as if asking permission and Tom, realising his intent, nodded.

'From every one of us,' Dan's voice rose to attract the attention of those furthest away. 'The saddling knife. Take it with you, Minister, to ensure we never again suffer the worst of our unknowns.'

He threw the knife so that it landed flat on the coffin lid, bowed to the grave and walked away.

Aaron Fetcher watched Tom with his arms folded, and Tom stared back, expressionless. He didn't want thanks, in fact, he wanted as little to do with the pockmarked lad as possible. Judging from Aaron's acidic glare, he wanted nothing to do with the out-marsher either. Still fixing Tom with contempt, he spat, kicked himself from the wall and slunk off to the green.

'Well, that be it,' Jack said. 'Nice touch that.'

The symbolic gesture of burying the knife was not lost on Tom, but he suffered a pang of regret that such an important artefact was to be buried forever.

'Going for a pint,' Jack said.

'Aye, I'll be there dreckly-minute,' Tom replied as Jack joined other men heading to the inn.

He watched Dan move through the villagers towards the green. Some dipped their heads in respect while others took his hand and offered words of encouragement for his new position. Billy Farrow offered his hand. Dan shook it solemnly, and then, to Billy's delight, gave him a matey hug and ruffled his ginger curls playfully. He did the same to young Tim Taylor under the watchful gaze of his grandfather. Bill Taylor acknowledged Dan respectfully and the two fell to talking. Council business no doubt.

Tom smiled to himself. 'We accept Saddling with all its unknowns,' he said.

'Aye, and I can see you thrive on them, Tom Carey.'

Irene was at his side, he hadn't noticed her arrive. 'Mistus Cole…'

'Now then,' she interrupted keen to avoid sympathy. 'I been thinking 'bout your bedding arrangements. Seems a me the pair a you could do with a new lid for your bed.' She took his hand. 'Walk me to the inn, Tom, and tell me what colour you'd be wanting fur it. I got a madder wool and plenty a green. Prehaps the two a'gether…'

Above them, watching and satisfied, the harrier ascended until it became one with the sun-washed sky.

The wake was held on the green. Susan served ale, assisted by Irene as on any other busy day, and Rebecca Rolfe, in an unusually charitable mood, cooked enough lamb stew for everyone.

Tom and Barry sat on the grass leaning against their house. Tom's head had settled though it still ached, and he was tired from the hour spent standing in the churchyard. He was distracted by what Jack had said about Aaron. His suspicion that Aaron had been acting under someone else's guidance had been confirmed, but the question remained, who?

Trying to fathom the answer did nothing for his headache, and he let the matter go for now. Barry had just buried his father; Tom should be attending to him.

'How are you doing?' he asked before sipping ale from his tankard.

'Be the same as any other day fur me,' Barry replied. 'You'll get used to this sort a thing, Tom Carey. And one day we'll be the ones they throw earth on.'

'Not fur a long while yet I 'ope,' Tom said, slipping into his Saddling accent. It was becoming harder not to use it.

'You means you be in 'opes,' Barry corrected with a tut. 'Lore's sake, Carey, you still can't get the 'ang a speaking, and you be the cooting clerk.'

'I gives you me apologies, Mr Cole,' Tom returned the friendly jibe with gentle sarcasm. 'I be in 'opes we ain't ready fur burying come many years yet.'

'Better.' Barry took a slug of ale.

Across the green, Aaron Fetcher sat alone as Jenny Rolfe approached with a pan, offering stew to anyone willing to take it from her. Few did.

'Oi,' Barry said nudging Tom. 'I got a gossip fur ye.'

'What's that?'

'Well…' Barry inched closer and whispered. 'And I got this of off Steven Rolfe, so I trust it, but the thing be, Mistus Rolfe's gone and made Aaron swear a-wed Jenny. You know, 'cos a what they did. Be the only way they'll be forgiven. They be 'eading for marriage.'

'I took that as read.'

'Well, it certainly won't be white.' Barry roared at his own joke, but it took Tom a moment to catch up.

'You're right jokesy, Farmer Cole. But why be that gossip?'

'It be worthy of note, Carey, 'cos the last thing Aaron bloody Fetcher wants in this world right now is a-be shacked up wi' a Rolfe, especially that one. Steven told me 'e was afeared.'

'And so 'e should be,' Tom said. 'I'm grateful that Dan didn't marry the girl. Aye, it's put 'im in this weird downer about not marrying no-one, but that'll pass. I'll find a way a-reverse that oath 'e took. You watch, your marker'll be wed and childed afore the time 'e's thirty.'

'What I meant,' Barry said after another slug, 'is that *Steven* be afeared.'

'Fur what?'

'Fur what Aaron might do next.'

'Such as?'

'Such as… Well, Steven said, go out marsh.'

'Aaron's shown enough disrespect for our Lore, it wouldn't surprise me.' Behind Tom's words was his concern that Aaron had been plotting with an out-marsher and behind that, was the even deeper fear that it could somehow be William Blacklocks. How else would Aaron have known about the missing Lore?

'But,' Barry said, interrupting Tom's thoughts. 'If 'is way a getting out a what 'e's done be a-run away, well, that's up to 'im. We couldn't let 'im back, and none would want 'im. So, I'd be 'appy 'bout it. He pushed himself to his feet, sliding up the wall for balance. 'Now, I says we go and join Minister Vye and…' He froze. 'Well, that be a sight.'

'What?' Tom leant on the cane and groaned to his feet with Barry's help. He wasn't sure if his unsteadiness was caused by the ale, his thumping head or his apprehension. His balance returned once he was upright and resting against the wall.

An argument was in full swing on the far side of the green. Jenny stood cradling her pan while Aaron faced her, and Billy tried to pull him away. Tom couldn't hear the words but he could see from those close by and the way they turned away, that Aaron was being less than polite. He shoved Billy to one side and grabbed hold of Jenny's collar.

'Hey!' Her brother, Steven, had seen and was running to her defence. Dan caught him and held him back.

There was no need for Steven to intervene. Jenny threw the pot of stew at Aaron's feet, splashing him and he leapt in the air with a yelp. She turned and fled to the shop.

'That drama's going graze a long while,' Barry laughed. 'Meantime, what you say we stagger back a the inn and get these jugs filled?'

As he limped across the grass with Barry swaying beside him, Tom noticed Jason at the bench. He had turned his back on Aaron's antics and was deep in conversation with Lucy Cole. If Tom wasn't mistaken, he was gradually inching his arm across the back of the bench and leaning more and more towards her. She appeared not to mind.

'Going fur a pint?' Billy Farrow caught up with them outside the inn.

'Aye, we be doing just that,' Barry said.

'Come wi' us.' Tom drew the scrawny lad closer. 'I owe you a drink fur your 'elp wi' Eliza's riddle.'

'No, you don't owe me nothing, but I'll come wi' ye just the same.'

'Shouldn't you be rounding up your marker?' Barry asked, pointing to where Aaron was stomping from the green in a sulk.

'There's none can shepherd that…' Billy stopped himself. 'Begging your pardon, Mr Clerk. I were going to use a misword but there don't seem a-be one rough enough fur Fetcher.'

'Get in there.' Barry held the door open. 'I'll learn you a few good'uns.'

Tom hung back, resting on the cane and taking in the green. It was as if with the eastling dead, its presence had never been felt. People carried on as before, tidying up after the wake or happy to sit with neighbours talking, celebrating the end of the harvest. The sky was changing from blue to white as the sun began to set, and shadows grew longer across the grass. The first chill of autumn blew in on the breeze, and Samuel Rolfe wheeled a handcart of logs towards his shop.

Set against the background chatter of evening birdsong and the wafting smell of harvest pies, it was an idyllic scene, and yet Tom felt simmering unease. The east window of the church-house was darkening as the light faded, its colours dimmed, dampened by the approaching night.

Tom shivered and ducked into the inn.

Aaron Fetcher walked with purpose, his heart seething and his mind churning. He took the lope-way towards the southern bridge coming close as the sun disappeared beneath the marsh. He veered off at an angle to reach Eliza Seeming's plot of land and stood on the dead earth. Scanning the line of far trees, he waited patiently. When his legs tired, he sat on the dried mud feeling no connection to the wise woman who had once lived there. He was unwanted and unfulfilled. He had failed in what he had promised to do, and they had ridiculed him. He had no connection to the village nor to anyone who lived in it and yet it was his home.

What mattered now was what he did next.

Owls swooped close by as he plotted and wondered until night completed day and there was nothing to be seen but the darkness mirroring his soul.

He wrapped his jerkin tighter, buttoning it when cloud swamped the sky and the breeze became a chilling wind. Trees hissed unseen as they shed their leaves, and the rushes on the deek bank shivered, as unsettled as he was.

He was unaware of the time, but it was late when he saw what he was waiting for. Between and beyond the poplars at a distance he couldn't judge, a light approached. Someone was walking in from the south swinging a lantern.

Aaron unwound his legs and brushed dried mud from the palm of his hands as he hurried to the deek, eyes straining. He saw nothing but the light growing nearer in the blackout. He reached the bridge, only visible when the cloud temporarily uncovered the rising moon, and stood on the planks. He could hear breathing now, and the crunch of dry grass under foot. The lamp lit the path as the stranger neared the deek, and Aaron took a step forward.

The moonlight died as they met in the middle of the bridge, neither on Saddling land nor off it. The water of the border-deek lay still and stagnant beneath them.

Aaron knew he had to speak first. 'I tried,' he said, unable to see who he was talking to but recognising the man's presence. 'I did what you told me, but it were that bloody Carey.'

'It's okay, lad.' The voice in the night was deep and kind. 'I've had my fill of Careys the same as you.'

'You didn't tell me afore.'

'There's a great deal I haven't told you, and I have done so on purpose, but my association with Tom Carey goes back a while now. We failed this time, but we will try again.'

'Cole died,' Aaron said. 'But they found the missing page and he made Daniel Vye the minister.'

The stranger lifted his lantern to the level of his eyes, allowing Aaron to see his face. Not an old man, but not young either, his features were mainly shadows, and his hair was short and greying.

'We must wait,' he said. 'The time will be right before long. Meanwhile, Aaron, you live your life as if we had never met.'

'But…'

'It won't be easy, but it is what you must do. Your time will come, I will see to that. Everything will be mended, and what you desire, you shall have.'

'Aye, Sir, as you say.'

'I will be in touch.'

The stranger turned to leave, but Aaron stopped him. 'Sir,' he said. 'As I've done all that you asked, might I be allowed to make an ask of you?'

'It seems only fair.' The man turned back, lowering the lamp which lit his legs.

He wore strange trousers, grey in colour that matched his jacket. It was a costume Aaron had not seen before, a suit from off-marsh.

'You says you've 'ad your fill a Careys, but what do you mean?'

The man sighed patiently. 'It's a story that goes back a long way,' he said. 'But as Tom Carey has robbed you of your dream to lead your village, so his family robbed me, and did worse to my cousin.'

'But, Sir…' Aaron feared what he stood to lose if he upset this man, but curiosity ate at his gut just as anger devoured his heart. 'May I know what he did? And might I know your name?'

The stranger thought before answering, and Aaron imagined him looking to where the village lay sleeping.

'It was the old woman,' he said at length. 'Carey's great aunt, the one who brought him here. I did everything for her. I kept her alive until Tom Carey was man enough to stand up to his responsibility. I interrupted my life to ensure he gave his, and on the understanding that her inheritance became mine when he did. But Carey failed. She failed, and I have vowed that I never will. Maud Carey made a promise to me which, being as dishonourable as her nephew, she refused to keep.' His voice had soured, and his tone sharpened. He pulled himself back from anger and spoke softly. 'I shall say no more, Aaron, but as to my name…' The out-marsher lifted the light to his face, closer this time, and Aaron gasped when he saw his eyes, black and oddly familiar. 'You shan't even whisper my name in the village for fear that Carey will know my lineage, understood?'

Aaron nodded.

'Then know me as Philip,' he whispered. 'Philip Nigel Blacklocks.'

Printed in Great Britain
by Amazon